Our Strange New Land

Elizabeth's Jamestown Colony Diary

· Book One ·

by Patricia Hermes

Scholastic Inc. New York

Jamestown, Virginia
1609

August 11, 1609

Today, we came to land at last! It seems there are no bones in my legs. I hugged my friend Jessie. We held each other up. Still, the land seemed to bob around beneath us. Seventy-one days. That is how long we were on the ocean.

Nine ships sailed from Plymouth, England. But at sea, a hurricane struck. Oh, how it struck! It became blacker than night. The waves brought us up into the dark sky, and then slammed us down. Men were washed off deck and into the sea. Some men tied themselves to the mast. But then — the mast broke off. Our ship rolled and rats came out. I tried to hold back tears, but could not. Jessie cried, too. Mama said we should not show fear or dismay. But soon, she cried, too. Prayers flew up to heaven like little birds. After the storm, when it became quiet, we looked about. Then, even Papa had tears in his eyes. For five of our ships were gone. One missing ship is the *Sea Venture*. It held our food! Were the ships blown off course? Or are they at the bottom of the ocean? We do not know.

Still, we are safely in Jamestown. I am here with my mama and papa. Soon, our new baby will be born. But it will be a home without Caleb, my twin. He stayed behind with Mama's cousin because his lungs are weak. He will join us come spring. I pray that spring comes soon, because without Caleb it will be a sad home.

August 11, later

It is *hot* inside this fort where we shall live for a while. Nothing stirs but nasty mosquitoes. They bite and sting. They get in my ears. Jessie and I compete for who can swat the most. I have killed twenty-seven. Jessie is winning, for she has slain thirty. Mama rubs fennel into the bites. Already, though, my neck is as fat as a melon.

Papa says that tomorrow we shall begin to build our house. He says there will be no bugs inside our house. Captain Gabriel Archer was one of those in charge of our expedition. He has lived here before. He says, "You wait and see. There are always bugs."

Gabriel Archer is a dreadful, unpleasant man.

August 11, again

I close this book. I open this book. I fear I shall use it up in one day! But there is much to write about here. Like this: To cool off, Jessie and I splashed in the river. I fell down in the water. A fat, silver fish swam right into my lap! It was as big around as a newborn pig. I squealed and laughed. Mama did not stop our play though our skirts poured water. I think she is happy that we run free. For now. But soon we shall begin to work.

Also today, I met Captain John Smith, the leader here. He is jolly and has wild ginger hair. It flies about his head as he races around camp. He shouted a greeting to me. He called me "Lizzy." I believe I shall like Captain Smith.

August 11, yet again!

I know I am going to use up this book and all my ink in just one day. But I must write this. Today, oh joy! I met an Indian, two Indians, three, and even more! We have heard much about them. And now I have seen them with my very own two eyes.

This is what happened: An Indian came to me. He bent close and looked right into my face. He smelled like fish and smoky fires. And oh, guess what? He was almost naked! I could not help it. I covered my eyes and turned away. But Papa said, "Elizabeth! Daughter!"

I quick took my hands away. Then, the Indian put his two golden hands on my head. He touched my cap. And he smiled at me. He spoke some words, but what, I cannot say.

I believe that what he said was gentle. For his face was kind.

Oh, to think that I have truly met an Indian! To think that I am in Jamestown. I am not on a ship! To think that we are here at last!

August 11, darkness falls

I talk too much. I talk too fast. I even walk too fast. Mama scolds. She tells me, Elizabeth Barker, do not babble. Be proper.

Papa does not scold. He just smiles and calls me by his pet name. He says, Sweet Beth, try to go slowly.

I do try. But it is hard to be proper. It is also no fun at all. This evening, I raced Jessie to the well.

She pushed a little.

I pushed a little.

She pushed more.

I pushed more.

And I tumbled and fell headlong into a

pricker bush. Mama spent much time pulling prickers out of me. I spent much time trying not to cry. Jessie held my hand. Mama again told me to go slow! Be proper, Elizabeth! I think I hear those words in my sleep.

I promise to go slow. I shall try to be proper. And I shall try not to babble. I shall write clearly. But tonight, I am tired. And sore from prickers! I shall write more tomorrow.

August 12, 1609, morning

Last night, we returned to the ship to sleep. This morning, we are back on land. This is what I see from where I sit. Before me is a clearing, shaped like a triangle. Around it is a palisade, a tall wooden fence. Inside the fence is a church and a well. There is a large storehouse for food. There are thatched houses, with pine trees all around. But there is no schoolhouse —

not yet. Papa says perhaps someday there will be. And in this New World, he says, perhaps girls may attend school! In England, only boys go to school, which I think unfair.

The fence has two gates. One faces the James River. The other opens to the woods. The woods are dark and thick with pine trees. The wind sighs in the treetops. It makes a rushing sound. It makes me think of the ocean. Small bugs and creatures hum in the grass. I hear birds calling and twittering. Last night, I heard an owl. It seemed to ask my name. Who, who, it called, who, who?

It is a strange land. But it is very, very beautiful.

August 12, later

I must tell why we are in the New World. We came to seek gold and rich things. Those will be sent back to the Virginia Company in England.

Papa and Mama do not want rich things for themselves. They want only land. In England, Papa paid much to rent land. Here, he can own land. He can *be* a landowner. That is what we will work for in Jamestown.

I do not mind working for land with Mama and Papa here.

But secretly, I would like to have gold and some fine, rich things, too.

August 13, 1609

I am writing in this book for Caleb. I will tell him all we see and do.

And now I must tell of a troublesome thing. This journal where I write is Caleb's drawing book. The night before we sailed, I hid it in my trunk. I meant to ask Caleb if I might take it. But I forgot. No, that is not true. I did not forget. If I write here, I will be truthful. I learned to read and write at home. I wished to write about our journey. Yet, I knew 'twas wrong, and went to give it back. But in the morning — the trunk was gone! It had been moved onto the ship.

I pray that Caleb will get a new drawing book.

August 13, later

I must tell about Jessie Bolton, my new friend. I did not know her in England. We met on board our ship. We are much the same. She is nine years old, like me. She has yellow hair and blue eyes. Like me. She was born in October. Like me. She has freckles. Like me. We are the exact same height.

But Jessie is fair to look on. I believe I am

rather plain. And we are different inside. Jessie is thoughtful. She does not babble. And she has a prayerful mind.

I am sometimes careless. And though I mean to pray, I do forget at times.

But I do not talk back to any elders. And Jessie does. She even talks back to Gabriel Archer. And oh, how she can mimic him! He puffs out his cheeks when he talks. He looks like a big fish. Jessie goes behind his back and makes faces. I think I will burst when she does that.

Jessie and I have made a plan. When there is no one looking, we shall shed our hot English clothes. Already, today, we shed shoes and stockings.

I told Jessie that we must also shed our petticoats and shifts. She laughed and said that then we might look like the Indians!

Imagine wearing so little! But we did not

shed our shifts or linen skirts. It would be too improper.

Sometimes Jessie is sad, though. Her mother is very ill. We are afraid. For crossing the ocean, we saw many die.

August 14, 1609

Good news! Today, we shall begin to build our house. Jessie's papa will build a house beside ours! And this I do not like — the mean Bridger boys will have their house on the other side. The Bridger boys make it their life's work to torment Jessie and me. John Bridger is the worst, worse than James and even little Thomas.

Today, John saw me writing. He snatched my journal and held it behind his back. And believe this — I did kick John Bridger to get back my book. How dare he try to read my secret thoughts!

I snatched it and hid it in my skirts.

When I heard about the Bridgers' house, I ran to Papa. I said I did not want the mean Bridger boys next to us. Must they be our neighbors?

Papa laid a hand on my head. He smiled at me. He said I must remember this: We are all neighbors here.

August 15, 1609

The men who were here before us make a fuss over us children. Those men came here two years past, but they brought no children. Our ships brought seventeen boys and seven girls. Jessie and I are the youngest girls. I wish Caleb were among the boys!

Mr. Foster, a thin, ragged man, has been here two years. His eyes were sad when he saw Jessie and me. He said he has children in England. He misses them sorely.

I felt dreadful sad. We brought mail on our ship. But there was no letter for him. Still, in the storm, many things and people were tossed into the sea. Perhaps his letter was among the lost.

I shall try to be a friend to Mr. Foster.

August 16, 1609

I have a puzzle, and it is this: I know now why there is a fence. It is to keep out the Indian warriors. Mr. Archer says that at night they creep silently to scale the walls. He calls them treacherous, thieving rascals.

Yet, I have met these Indian men. They were kind. And now, in this morning light, they are all around. They are helping with corn. They taught the English men to plant. They taught the men to fish and hunt.

And the Indian patted my head and smiled at me.

So here is more of the puzzle: Captain Smith says the Indians are good, but they do attack. Only, he says, because the men here treat them badly.

So how do I understand this puzzle? I cannot. If Caleb were here, he would talk about this. Together, we would understand.

August 17, 1609

I must tell about Gabriel Archer, though it pains me just to say his name. He is rude and thinks he should rule all! Still, he is an important man. He says he had a letter from the Virginia Company. That letter told that

Captain Smith was no longer the leader here. It said others should be leaders. The letter though was on the *Sea Venture*, lost in the hurricane along with some of the newly appointed leaders. So we do not know if he tells the truth.

Most of the men want Captain Smith as their leader. But some choose one of the men named George Percy. And some choose Mr. Archer. I asked Jessie, "Why choose a big fish for a leader?"

Mama heard and scolded me. But I only spoke the truth.

Sometimes I have this thought. I pretend that Gabriel Archer was swept away in the hurricane. But then I tell God that I do not really *wish* that. It is just a thought. And thoughts sometimes come unbidden. They just run around like little mice inside my head.

August 18, 1609

Today, Papa sent Jessie and me to the woods to gather reeds. We shall use them to thatch our roofs. Mama told us to look for herbs, too, especially what is called snakeroot here in Virginia. Many here are ill with fever.

Many are healthy, though. Yet some refuse to work. They say they are gentlemen and need servants.

Papa thinks they are very foolish. He smiled at Jessie and me when we brought home the reeds. He said he is proud that we work so hard to build our homes.

I smiled back at him. One cannot help but smile when Papa smiles. But today I am sad. This does not feel like home. Home is England. Home is where Caleb is. What is he doing now? I wonder. Has he found a checkers partner? We played together and, mostly, I won! Does he know I took his book?

Does he still cough?

I wonder if he misses me.

August 18, night

When it is night, I miss my twin brother most. When Mama and Papa were planning our journey, Caleb and I lay awake, listening. We heard that Caleb might stay behind because of his lungs! I told Caleb: If a cough is coming, run outside. Even if it is cold, run so no one will hear. He did. But then in his sleep, he coughed and gasped even more. Mama and Papa would hurry in. I was afraid. Did he cough more because he ran outside?

August 19, 1609

Some things are good here. And some are very bad.

This is today's list:

Good: Jessie's mama took some broth.

Bad: I had porridge for breakfast. And dinner. And supper.

Good: Our house is rising.

Bad: The Bridgers' house has posts raised too.

I shall end with a good thing: Mama is happy. She says Jamestown begins to feel like home.

August 20, 1609

I despise John Bridger! Jessie and I go to hidden places so I can write in this book. But John Bridger does sneak and follow us. Tonight, he says he will tell Mama that I write secretly.

I do not want Mama to know, for what shall I say? Shall I say that Caleb *gave* me this book? I do not want to lie to Mama. But I lied to John. I said I was writing a poem for Mama. I do not think he believed me. He waddled off, laughing. He sways when he walks, just like a hog.

He is certainly not handsome!

August 20, later

A secret to tell. Though it was crowded on our ship, room was found for eight horses. Here, the horses stay within a fenced pasture. Jessie and I sit on the fence and talk to them. Charlie is our favorite. He frolics like a child. I think it is because he has been cooped up for so long. A ship is as hard on a horse, says Papa, as it is on a child.

Today, as we sat on the fence, I saw that no

one was about. I smiled at Jessie. Then I leapt
from the fence onto Charlie's back.

And then do you know? Jessie leapt up
behind me. For a moment, Charlie galloped
like the wind. I hung on to his mane. Jessie
hung on to me. It was a wonderful moment. Till
we both fell off.

Tonight, I cannot tell Mama why it is that I
cannot sit on my bottom.

August 21, 1609

Today, Jessie and I again went outside the
palisade gates. We searched for herbs and
berries, for food is scarce here.

The day was hot, and after a bit, we waded
in the river. I made up a water song. I sang:
Plash! My feet have a bath.

Jessie made up a food song: We eat our
porridge. It tastes so horrid!

We laughed as we gathered up the reeds.

After a time, though, we became quiet. Birds flitted by, singing their songs. These birds are not gray like English sparrows. Some are brilliant blue and some are yellow. Some are red with crests on their heads. Even the black birds are not dull black. We saw a black bird with red and yellow stripes on its wing. It sang sweetly, clinging to the side of a reed. Jessie and I listened and maybe forgot our task. But just for a little while. For it is strange here. It is not home like England.

But it is a sweet and beautiful land.

August 22, 1609

Today, Jessie and I were gathering reeds. We had shed our shoes and stockings. Suddenly, at the river, Jessie grabbed my hand. A funny brown-and-black monkey ran past us! It had a sweet face and a small black mask. It stopped and watched us, not at all afraid. It dipped its paws in the water. Then it ate something from its paws. I do believe the monkey had caught a fish.

Who ever heard of a fish-eating monkey?

I could not wait to tell my papa.

August 22, later

I am in disgrace. I lost my shoes in the forest. I was so excited to see the monkey — and it was *not* even a monkey! It was a raccoon, I have learned. In my hurry to tell Papa, I forgot my shoes. For hours I searched for them. Jessie came with me, for she forgot her shoes, too.

Mama scolded me. She asked where I thought I might get another pair!

I will be content with Indian moccasins all winter! That is what I said inside my head. For

I was feeling rebellious. And ashamed of myself. But I did not speak those words.

I have never seen Mama more angry.

Papa was not angry. He was just quiet. Still, I know that he was disappointed.

I am disappointed in myself.

August 22, night

My shoes are still missing. And Mama is still cross. She scolded me again at supper. She said I was foolish and careless.

I know I deserved the scolding. I *was* foolish and I *was* careless. But I think there is another reason Mama is angry. There is much disease and illness here. I think she worries for the baby. She worries for Jessie's mama, too. She still lies on her pallet, pale and silent.

I wonder if Mama knows about this book. She frowns at me when I open my chest where

I keep my things. Does she know I took Caleb's drawing book? Perhaps she knows I am not only a foolish child, but a thieving child besides.

August 23, 1609, such news!

This afternoon, two more ships from our fleet arrived! They were *not* at the bottom of the ocean. They were blown far off course in the hurricane. And here they came upriver! Oh, it was such a sight. We watched them come, their white sails billowing in the wind. Jessie and I raced to the riverbank to greet them. The people who came off ship looked ill. Some were pale and ghostly-looking. For they are very hungry. And they have no news of the ship, the *Sea Venture*. We have great need of that ship, for it holds so many men and much-needed supplies.

We helped them to unload. And oh, Jessie and I rejoiced. Because new children have arrived! There are no boys, but there are little twin girls, Sarah and Abigail. There is also another girl of nine years named Claire. She ducks her head as though she is shy. But she smiles sweetly and her eyes twinkle. I think that I will like her.

The church bells toll, and we thank God for their deliverance.

Secretly, I thank God there are no more boys like the Bridger boys.

August 24, 1609

Mistress Bolton becomes more ill. Today, Jessie stayed by her side.

And I have again spent the day searching for our shoes. And promising myself that I will no longer be a foolish child.

August 24, late

I have found our shoes! And our stockings. They were on the rock where we left them. But they were hidden by vines, which seem to grow a yard a minute! They smell dreadful, for things rot quickly here. But I rubbed them with salt. Then I laid them in the sun to dry. I think they will be fine to wear again. Mama smiled at me this morning. When she brushed my hair, her hand was gentle. I think she has forgiven me. This time.

I wish I could forgive myself so easily. This book feels heavy in my hand at times.

August 25, 1609

Something good! Today, our papas raised the forks to support our roofs. Now they are adding upright timbers for the walls. But they need someone to scamper up the roof to do the thatch.

I have become strong and agile. So I quickly offered to do it.

Papa agreed.

But Mama said no.

I begged.

Mama refused.

I begged more.

Mama refused more. She said it was work for a boy.

She turned her back then, but I saw a tear. I thought I knew why she cried.

I took her hand. I told her that Caleb will be here, come spring. I told her that I want to help. I promised to tie my skirt so to appear like breeches. For I know Mama wants me to be proper.

She said then that I might do it. But her eyes were still sad.

Poor Mama, she acts so brave. But I believe she misses England and English ways. I know she misses Caleb. We all do.

August 25, later

Our house is rising fast! The sides are up, and now I start to thatch the roof.

Captain Smith came by and called up to me. He told me that I put many men to shame with my hard work.

And then, do you know? He climbed right on the beams to work beside me. He spoke to me as though I were a grown person. He said many men here do not want to work. They think that they are gentlemen. They want everyone to be their servants and slaves. I have seen that myself. The men stand by the well, fanning themselves. Some lie on the riverbank. Some sleep all through the hot afternoons. They order the Indians to do their work.

Well. I told him what I thought. I said that if these men do not work, they should not eat! Food is hard to come by here.

Captain Smith laughed. He says I should help him govern. Imagine that! I believe I would enjoy that. I would tell people what to do. I would send John Bridger to work in the hottest field. And in the hottest part of the day. And I would make Gabriel Archer work with him. And I would allow my papa to rest. He looks tired now.

Captain Smith looked worried, though. Papa is worried, too, I know. I think Papa is also disappointed. We came for land. But this land is filled with sickness and hunger and danger. It is a vastly different land from what we had been told.

August 25, later

Papa sent me to lie under a tree to rest. He said I look flushed and ill. I know he fears the summer sickness. But I am not ill. I am only hot!

It *is* hot work thatching the roof. Yet although I would not say it to Mama, I like it better than mending stockings!

Still, Papa said I must lie in the shade.

And so I lay and watched the boys working. I thought about Caleb. If he were here, he would work hard. And maybe with the sun and heat, he would not cough. Oh, and if he were here, he would make pictures. He would draw portraits of Jessie and the Indians. He would sketch this whole entire town. I believe he would put in all the details — birds, and even mice and voles. He might even draw the cricks and cracks in the wooden fence. And oh, I cannot wait till he sees the raccoons! What a portrait he will make of them.

But I have his drawing book.

That still troubles my heart.

August 25, nighttime

Tonight, I think about girls and boys and other strange things. Today, as I lay resting, I saw Mary Dobson and John Bridger talking together. John came and sat by Mary's side. They sat very close. Very close!

John Bridger is not a bit handsome. And still, Mary blinked her eyes at him and smiled.

They thought I did not see. But I did. For a moment, John Bridger lay his hand over Mary's hand. For fifteen seconds it lay there. I counted each second.

Imagine holding the hand of John Bridger. It makes chills go up and down my spine.

August 26, 1609

Today, we had a picnic. We brought food and drink to share. That was Captain John Smith's idea. He worries about the strife here. He wants us all to be one big family. But that is hard with so many who will not work.

Before our picnic, Papa took me, Jessie, and my new friend, Claire, to gather food. We dug in the river for clams. Suddenly, an Indian came silently from the woods. He stood right by me in the river. At first, I was afraid. My heart did knock and thump. But Papa nodded that it was all right. And then the Indian man took my hand. He gave me a forked stick. He showed me how to dig a crab. It takes patience and a slow motion. I was very patient and very slow. And I caught one! It was large with fierce claws. I dangled it in Jessie's face. She squealed. Then, the Indian scooped up a fish with his bare hands. He handed it to Claire. She jumped back and waved him away. The fish flopped itself into the waters.

Then, the Indian jumped backward. He wiggled his hands before his face. He pretended to be Claire and to be afraid. We all laughed. Even the Indian laughed. Only Claire did not laugh. She ducked her head and twisted her hands beneath her apron.

I told her we did not mean to tease.

August 27, 1609, night

It was so hot today, even my teeth felt hot. Tonight, a small breeze blows and cools us some. I wonder if it is hot where Caleb is this night.

Papa misses Caleb dearly. When he speaks of Caleb, his eyes get sad like Mama's do. Yet I wonder if either Mama or Papa miss him as I do. I think it is because we are twins. We twins know each other's hearts. And thoughts.

Now, I have a new fear. I fear that in this long year apart Caleb will forget me. So this is what I do — at night, I send him thoughts. I picture them as tiny birds. They fly to Caleb and make him think of me.

If those bird-thoughts flew to Mama tonight, I know just what she would say. She would say again — you are a foolish child.

August 28, 1609

Mistress Bolton has eaten nothing for three whole days. Each day, we fear that she will die. Jessie has become most quiet.

Mr. Bolton has taken to talking loudly to his

poor, sick wife. He tells her all he's seen and done each day. But she can no longer hear him. So he talks louder until Papa leads him away to rest.

One of the women who came last week has died. Her name was Mistress Pickett. She died in childbirth. Her baby boy lived for just a few hours.

I feel sad inside. I am sad for Mistress Pickett. But I am more sad for her tiny baby. It seems dreadful to be newly born, and then to die so quickly.

Tonight, I remembered to pray. I prayed for Jessie and her mama and her papa. I prayed for Mistress Pickett and for her poor dead baby.

I prayed for Mama and our baby.

August 29, 1609

An Indian girl came to our town! She is perhaps thirteen years old. They call her Pocahontas. Her father is the chief called Powhatan. She has smooth skin and black eyes and thick black hair. She is lively and ever so funny!

When she came to the clearing, she stared at Jessie and me. Then she ran to me and tipped back my cap. She touched my hair. She said, "Look! 'Tis gold!"

I could not have been more surprised had a blackbird spoken to me. She spoke in English!

I laughed. I said, "Not gold, yellow."

And then, oh this is hard to believe, but it is true. She climbed a tree. She clapped her hands. "Come!" she said. "Climb up with me."

I looked at Jessie. She looked at me.

Oh, I wanted to climb that tree. But I wore a skirt and petticoats. I thought of what I had said — that we should dress as Indians do. Perhaps someday. But today, we had to shake our heads. We told Pocahontas, no. We could not climb that tree.

August 29, later

I must tell more about Pocahontas. She is sweet and kind. She is also very, very good. She is a dear friend of Captain Smith.

Her father, Chief Powhatan, once captured Captain Smith. The chief believed Captain Smith meant to harm his people. And so, it is said, the chief meant to kill Captain Smith. Captain Smith was held down, his head against a rock. The warriors were about to club him to death. Imagine that! The thought of it makes me weak and shivery. But Pocahontas, her father's favorite daughter, sought to spare Captain Smith's life. Since then, she goes between us and her people, keeping peace. Captain Smith learns the Indians' language from her. And this is how she learned our language. Each time she comes, she brings gifts.

Today, she came with a gift bearer. His name is Rawhunt, and he is a small, twisted man. He carried gifts for us, things we need so badly. There was corn and two large fish in a beautiful woven basket.

It was a gift, a sign, said Captain Smith, that the Indians wish us well.

Gabriel Archer said not to trust such signs.

Sometimes, I become weary of Gabriel Archer.

August 30, 1609

Here is the newest mean thing John Bridger did. I was on the rooftop, working with thatch.

It cuts your hands and makes them raw. A reed slipped from my sore hands. It fairly flew into the space between the Bridgers' house and ours.

John Bridger stood there looking up. Of course, he was not working — just looking. And he shouted at me to come down. He said I was a foolish girl and had no business on the roof.

I told him he should come up then and work. But then I said no. If he did, the roof would break, for he is as big around as a hog. I said that right out loud.

Just as Mama passed below.

And now I am in disgrace. Again.

August 30, later

Mama has not stayed angry for long this time. I think she, too, is not fond of the

Bridger family. Mr. Bridger does little work. After weeks here, their house has just a few posts raised. And when he does work, he begs! He begs nails from Papa, things he should have brought himself. And Papa is too kind to refuse. Then, Mama becomes angry. They are all lazy, and do not work for the common good, even the mother. Today, we women and girls went to the river to wash clothing. Mrs. Bridger came, too. Like her son, she waddles. She was breathless and sweating. At the riverbank, she did no work! She sat on a rock, her smelly feet in the river. She fanned herself with a leaf. She sighed about the heat and bugs. And then — believe this! — she ordered Jessie to wet a cloth and bathe her neck.

Jessie did it, but her face was set with anger. If it were me, I'd wish for the courage to put a viper inside that wet cloth.

I turned to Mama. I whispered that in

England, the Bridger family would not be our friends.

Mama tightened her mouth. She looked away. After a moment, she said this: We are not in England now.

August 31, 1609

There are others here as ill as Mistress Bolton. Some call it the summer sickness. It comes on quickly. The body burns with fever. There are deliriums. Many times death comes in just two days.

The medicine kit that Mama brought is near empty. There is only aqua vitae. That must be used sparingly. It can make a person wild in the head. Also, herbs that Mama brought to plant are not flowering in this dry heat. We look in the forest and field for feverwort and Virginia snakeroot and everlasting. We work and we pray. And when we can, we play. It is hard now for Jessie to laugh and play.

September 1, 1609, a new month

Papa says this month will be better than last. He counted our blessings at prayer time last evening. He said, "Six ships have made the crossing safely. We have food to eat and work to do. Mrs. Bolton is no worse. Soon, our house will be built. Let us be thankful."

It is odd, perhaps, to count Jessie's mama as a blessing. But we have seen the sickness kill quickly. Many more of the new people have died. We have a burial most every night now. But our hopes are raised, for Mistress Bolton clings to life.

And when Papa came to tell me sweet dreams last night, he called me Sweet Beth.

He also told me a secret. He brought a card of pins from England and a pincushion. He has hidden it from Mama. And now, if I will make a design of pins, we will give this gift to Mama when our baby is born. I might spell out a welcome with pins. What shall I write? *Welcome, little stranger?* I am so happy at the thought.

September 1, later

Today, Captain Smith declared a holiday for the children. We went outside the fence to play. Jessie and I swung from the vines that hang from the trees. The bigger girls watched us play. They did not join us. They pretend to be too old. But they did play with the hoop toy that Claire brought from England. Mary Dobson sat on a rock with her skirts spread about her. She squealed if anyone stirred up dust. I am afraid that I did deliberately cast a bit of mud onto her feet. It seemed almost like an England summer day.

Until John Bridger spoiled it all. He flung a fat yellow frog at me. It landed with a dull thump on my bare feet.

Jessie and I fled.

We did not scream, though. And we did not tell our papas. Instead, I plan revenge.

September 1, nighttime

In the forest, I found a fat dead snake. It was horrid and smelled bad. I picked it up, though I felt squeamish. I hid it beneath my skirts. I called Jessie to me and showed her. We went behind the well where the weeds are tall. It was almost dark, and no one was about. Jessie acted as lookout. I hid the snake in the weeds.

That is how we plot our revenge.

September 2, 1609

We always know when the Bridger family is asleep. That is because Mr. Bridger makes horrible, whistling snores. Tonight, when they are asleep, I will do it.

By moonlight, September 3, 1609, about midnight

The fat black snake is there. I left it curled beside John Bridger's face.

September 3, morning

We woke to shouts and yelps. Big, brave John Bridger was howling.

I laughed and buried my face in the pillow.

Later, I told him sweetly that black snakes are poisonous.

He squinted up his eyes at me. He asked how came it there.

I smiled.

September 3, night

Some things I do not understand. Like this: The men here learned many things from the Indians. They learned to plant corn. They learned to fish. They learned to lay traps for deer. They learned to make canoes from hollowed-out logs. But the Indians frighten us, too. They carry bows and arrows. There are tales told of how they attack at night. Some nights, I wake shaking with bad dreams.

And we know that they *do* attack at times. Captain Smith says they attack sometimes only to free their brothers. For some of our own men have taken Indians as prisoners. Right here, within the palisade, they force the

Indians to be their slaves. I would attack, too, if Caleb were held prisoner. And he would attack if I were held prisoner.

Tonight, clouds race across the moon. I hear an Indian drum like the beat of a huge heart. I hear whoops, as dismal as an owl calling.

Tonight, I feel afraid.

September 4, 1609

Oh, I can hardly contain myself. Oh, joy! This is what has happened. Captain Smith wishes to soothe things with the Indians. So in the morning, he will sail to the mouth of the river to their village. And I — Elizabeth Mary Barker — I shall go with him! He and Papa and Mama talked a long while yesterday afternoon. They think that the chief will find it pleasant to see another girl as young as his daughter Pocahontas. And since she has befriended us, I will go to befriend them. But this is sad — Jessie shall not go. She must stay and tend her mother. But I have promised to tell her every single thing. I cannot bring my journal, but I can remember every little thing. And I shall. I am so happy, I think I will not sleep at all tonight. To think that I shall go to a real Indian village. Who would have thought of such a thing?

September 5, 1609

This morning, when it was barely light, we sailed. Captain Smith, ten men — and me! We sailed the river through darkness, the trees hanging thick about us. My heart pounded wildly. I sat in the center of the canoe. I held tightly to the gift basket that Mama and the women had prepared. In it were beads and pins and shells. Captain Smith also brought gifts.

The sun was high when we arrived at the village. Never did I see such a scene! The village was alive with people and dogs. There were mat-covered houses, some round, some long. Fires burned in pits and children played — and oh, yes, there were dogs and creatures everywhere.

The elders and warriors welcomed the men. And the children and women swarmed about me. Some were brave and touched me. Some were shy and hid themselves. Some wanted to touch my skin, my hair, my skirts. I stood very still while they explored me. For I did not wish to frighten them.

One woman — no, she was little more than a girl — she had a baby strapped to her back. It was a tiny boy baby. And oh, looking at him, my heart did swell! He was just a few days old, his small head crowned with fine black hair. I wondered — is this what our baby will look like? I was so happy, I felt tears come to my eyes. A baby, a tiny, healthy baby.

And then, when the children had their fill, Pocahontas came to me. She led me to a roundhouse. I had to duck my head to fit inside. It was dusky like a cave, and cool, and smelled like the earth. I thought of our hot lean-tos. Could we learn to build such houses? And there, I sat on the ground. And Pocahontas gave me cool water to drink and corn cakes and venison. And oh, never have I had such a day of surprises and fun.

When it was time to leave, Captain Smith made promises to the Indians. And they made promises. Each promised to live with the other in peace.

Returning in the canoe, I carried gifts, too — a soft pair of deerskin moccasins, a beaded necklace, and a small woven basket. As we sailed home, I hugged the memories to me. I reminded myself of what I must tell Jessie. It seemed that all the way home my heart and mind sang happily.

September 6, 1609

Mistress Bolton has visions now. She is confused. She knows not where she is.

Jessie stayed by her side today.

September 7, 1609

Mistress Bolton died today. I cannot write more.

September 8, 1609

Mr. Bolton rubbed his dead wife's hands. It was as though he thought to bring her back to life. He has not stopped talking to her. But his voice is just a whisper now. I think he pleads with her to come back to life.

Jessie looked on.

I turned away. I did not know what to do.

September 8, later

I am filled up with sadness. Jessie does not cry. She does not speak. I asked Mama if she could have been struck dumb?

Mama says she will speak when she is able.

My heart hurts inside me.

September 9, 1609, midnight

We buried Mrs. Bolton tonight in the graveyard by the river. All of our burials are at night now. We do not wish the Indians to know how much sickness is here. They must believe that we are many. Reverend Harper said some prayers. We hurried back inside the palisade.

During these whole two days, Jessie has not spoken. She acts as though we are not here. After Jessie's mama was buried, Mr. Bolton did not speak. He just held Jessie tightly by her hand. My heart aches for them.

I am frightened for us all.

September 11, 1609

My hand shakes so I can barely hold my pen. My friend Claire is ill. She is delirious and hot with fever. Also, Jessie's papa fell ill.

And Mr. Foster, that dear man who cried to us about his children — he has died. Who will make the journey across the ocean? Who will bring the news to his children?

Two of the Bridger boys are also sick. I despise the Bridger boys, but I do not wish them ill. We have two or three deaths every day now.

Much of this day, I sat by Claire. I sang to her. I whispered tricks that Jessie and I will teach her when she is well.

I whispered to her, "Please do not die."

Today, even Papa grows silent and grim.

September 12, 1609

More bad news today. The men went to the storehouse where the supplies are kept for winter. They found little. The huge supplies are almost gone. Even the things we brought on ship — cheese, onions, biscuits, bacon, cloves, nutmeg, prunes, dates — most are gone.

At first, we thought our own men had been the thieves. But we found that the thieves were not men. The thieves were rats. They came aboard our ships. They disembarked with us.

Even Captain Smith looks tight and fearful this night. Gabriel Archer says this proves he should be in charge. As if he himself could stop those rats! But then, perhaps he could. He sneaks about like a rat himself.

September 13, 1609

Things do not stay grim for long with Papa here. He and Captain Smith have made this plan: Each day, each man must hunt for food. And each person must bring back as much food as Captain Smith brings back. If not, says Captain Smith, that person shall be locked outside the palisade gates. It sounds cruel. But it makes sense. For many do not pull their weight, like the Bridger boys. The ill ones are better. Still, not one of them works.

The rest of us begin to forage. We look for nuts and acorns, and herbs and fish. There are also deer and turkey. There are even those strange raccoons to eat. Also, Mr. Ratcliffe went up along the river and claims to have seen a bear. One large bear will see many people through the winter.

Papa tells me not to fear. Hard work and God will see us through.

I do believe in God. And in my papa. But in spite of that I am afraid.

September 14, 1609

Jessie's father is better. And Jessie smiled at me today. She spoke to me. Her eyes are sad, but Mama cares for her. Sometimes, I feel envy. It seems Mama is more tender with Jessie than with me. But I know Mama tries to ease Jessie's loss. I wonder what it is like to have no mother.

I will not think of it.

September 15, 1609

Jessie came with me today to search for food. Close in, the forest has been scavenged clear. So we go farther on. I do not mind. The Indians are not about, or perhaps they are. But they hide themselves well. They bother us not at all. We are too worried about food to worry about Indians right now.

Captain Smith is worried, though. The Indians are becoming more hostile. This is why: Rather than find food in the forest, some men have stolen the Indians' food. They have stolen the Indians' corn and robbed their gardens!

Captain Smith says his sympathy is with the Indians in this matter. He says they are badly treated by the wicked men here who want to spoil our good relations with the Indians.

It worries me much. Is it to be that neither

we of the settlement, nor the Indians, shall have food come winter?

September 16, 1609

I have made a new friend, Francis Collier. Who would have thought that a boy could be a friend? He has a funny mind and he is a wondrous story teller. All his stories are about food. He says he can taste food in his dreams.

I do not believe him. But he makes me laugh.

I think Francis and Caleb will be friends. When Caleb joins us here in the spring.

September 17, 1609

The men have built an open shed, a sick house. Each day, we women and children help there. Jessie and I give water to the sick ones. We lay wet cloths on their heads. Sometimes, we just hold their hands. Claire is no better. Her body is still hot with fever. And one of the twin girls, Sarah, lies ill. I sang to her today. She did not speak. She did not even open her eyes. But she knew I was there. I could tell because she squeezed my hand.

After a while, Francis Collier came and sat with me. He told Sarah a story — about food, of course. I listened closely so I could write it down. This is the story he told:

Once there was a strong young boy who met a girl in the forest. The little girl was sick. But the strong boy — his name was Francis — brought her cakes and scones. He brought a vat of butter as big around as a fat raccoon. He spread it on the scones. And the little girl, named Sarah, sat up and ate it. She got all well again. And on the morrow, she will get up from her bed.

That is how he told the story. Jessie and

I laughed. We thought perhaps Sarah smiled, too.

Abigail, her twin, laughed. She wanted her name put into the story. She will not leave her sister's side, though we tried to make her go. We fear the sickness will spread to her.

September 18, 1609

The whole fort is taken with madness. And I will tell you why. One of the new men has decided to go up the river to the falls. He will take many men to start a settlement there. He says that was part of the new charter with the Virginia Company. That charter was lost, though, on the *Sea Venture*!

Captain Smith sends them with his blessing. But I know he fears for their safety.

And then, more confusion! John Martin, another of the captains who thinks ill of

Captain Smith, said he, too, will take one hundred men. He means to go to the Nansemond territory. He wants to trade for food. Yet these men have stolen from the Indians and robbed their corn! They have continued to rob the Indians, even after our visit to the Indian village. I know that Captain Smith thinks them thieves and fools.

The men sailed away from our sight.

We wonder what will happen. We wonder how the Indians will greet them. We pray they come to no harm.

September 19, 1609

Such fun! Last night, Jessie slept in my lean-to, her bedroll beside my own. This is why: Yesterday, just as Mr. Martin was leaving, Jessie's father joined him. Papa tried to dissuade him. But Mr. Bolton was set on going. He said better to die at the hands of the Indians than to starve to death. He thinks lack of food caused his poor wife's death. He says he can bring back food for us. He promised to stay safe — as if anyone could promise that in this forest! Still, we count on his return.

So now, Jessie and I are really like sisters. Last night, we lay on our backs, holding hands. We looked up at millions of stars. It is almost as dark here as it was on board ship. But there was no creaking and swaying beneath us. And we did not bob up and down. We are a bit fearful, but not unhappy. We are together. A mockingbird sang in the new-fallen dark. And we whispered about the morrow.

September 20, 1609

Papa works furiously on our house. Jessie and I work alongside him. Mama still frowns, though, when I climb to the roof. And in the lean-to beside us, John Bridger lounges with his lazy brothers. They will be sorry when winter comes! But we will have our home ready. And we will be ready for our new baby. Mama's time will be soon, I know.

I pray to God to watch over her when that time comes.

September 21, 1609

Jessie and I have learned to walk as quietly as Indians. We practice on our tiptoes. Today, we tiptoed to spy on John Bridger. He sat on a rock, picking lice out of his head. From behind a tree, we sang out, Lousy head, lousy head! And then we ran like anything.

September 22, 1609

Something so bad. So terrible. I cannot write. Yet, write I must. Claire died last night. Little Sarah died today. Her twin, Abigail, lies near death herself. They are only four years old! They are babies. And Claire is nine years old like me.

Mama found me in the sick shed. I sat by the twins, holding their hands. I did not cry. I did not think I cried. Yet water ran out of my eyes and down my face. Mama took my hand and lifted me up. She held me close. She whispered, hush, hush.

But I cannot hush. And I cannot stop the crying.

September 22, almost dark

Tonight, I went to the river to think. It seemed as though God followed me there. So I talked to Him. I said, I am *furious* with You. Perhaps it is evil to speak so. But it is true what I did say. And I know He would not want me to lie. I said, I do not understand. Why do You let children die? And mothers and babies?

I said that I was scared.

I do not want to be motherless, like Jessie.

And then I began to cry. My tears have wet this page.

I am longing for Caleb and longing for spring. Yet spring is far away. For winter is not even upon us yet.

September 23, 1609

A little better today. Again, Pocahontas came to our settlement. She came at dawn, alone. She touched her left hand to her heart and raised her right hand to wave to Jessie and me. Then she went to Captain Smith.

For a long time they talked. Then Captain Smith called Papa to him. Pocahontas came to Jessie and me.

She beckoned to us and said, "See!" And she turned herself upside down, over and over like a tumbler. With her thin, deerskin leggings, her movements were free. Her legs flew into the air.

But Jessie and I wore skirts and shifts and petticoats.

Pocahontas tumbled again.

I looked at Jessie.

She looked at me.

We signaled to one another with our eyes. Then we signed to Pocahontas to follow us.

We ran to our secret place behind the well. We took off our skirts. We tied our petticoats to make breeches. And then, we turned ourselves upside down. We tumbled and tumbled. We tumbled until we were dizzy and fell on the ground.

I have not been so happy in a long time.

September 24, 1609

Such news! Captain Smith has called Papa to him. Papa is to be in charge while Captain Smith goes away. Captain Smith goes to see how the men have fared who sailed upriver to the falls. He is very worried about the Indians now. So now we will see if the men will obey Papa. We will see if Mr. Archer will stir up more trouble.

I feel sure that Papa will handle whatever might come.

September 25, 1609

I am weary of eating fish. And stewed vegetables. And fish. And stewed vegetables. Mama cooks it all in the big iron pot over the fire. Fish. And stewed vegetables. I think I would not mind if it tasted like fish. Or vegetables. But it tastes mostly like smoky fires and iron pots.

But at least it is food. So I am thankful. I think.

September 25, again

With Captain Smith gone, all is mostly well here. Mr. Archer has not been able to stir up trouble. But not because he does not try. Last night, he told Papa that perhaps we should feast on the food from the storehouse.

Papa just shook his head mildly. For I know Papa thinks about the coming winter.

Mr. Archer gave him an evil look and turned his back. He likely went to think up more mischief with his friend, George Percy. Most men, however, do not care just now about who is leader. They are more worried about food. And Indian attacks.

Last night, we heard hooting like owls. Yet most here say they are not owls, but warriors. We heard rumbles of drums upriver. Some here think that the Indians make ready to attack.

Jessie held my hand tightly tonight. I know she fears for her father. It would be too awful to have neither mother nor father in this world. I pray to God to keep Mr. Bolton safe.

September 26, 1609

We are less fearful today. Pocahontas again came to our town. She has taken Jessie and me as her special friends. We walk around, arm in arm. It is as though we are at home in England. With her bit of English, we can talk. She tells us names of plants. She helps us find the herbs that Mama needs. She tells us tales of the stars and moon. She gives a name to each wind that blows.

We play for hours. Even Mama does not tell me it is time for tasks. That is because many fear the nearby Indians might attack now. They surely know that Captain Smith is gone. But with Pocahontas here, we believe no harm will come to us.

Sometimes, I think I would like to be an Indian girl. How free and fearless she seems to be. Her voice is sweet and her laughter is merry.

Could it be that someday, we too will live free of want and fear?

September 26, nighttime

Mama was troubled today. Her eyes had a far-off look, and I saw her lip tremble.

I went to her and held her hand. She said it was Caleb. She misses him so. She said there is a hole in her heart. And oh, I know, I do. For there is a hole in my heart, too. But then Mama said, And to think we know nothing of how Caleb is. And he knows nothing of what happens here.

I knew I had to tell her. My heart pounded hard inside me, but I did, I told her. I said that I have been writing in a book for Caleb.

Mama smiled and nodded. She was not surprised. She already knew!

I waited for her to ask how I came to have

the book. But she did not ask. After a time, she touched my hair. Softly, she told me she was sure Caleb would not mind.

Oh, Mama, I cried. And I hugged her tight.

A big burden seems to have lifted from me tonight.

September 27, 1609

Such dreadful news! Captain Smith has returned. But he is injured! There was an explosion of gunpowder on his boat. He was badly burned. His pain was so severe, he leapt into the river. He almost drowned.

When he returned today, he called Papa to him. He told Papa even more bad news: It is true, what we feared. The Indians have been at war. They have killed many of our men who went to the falls.

So, even after Captain Smith was burned,

he went back. He did all he could to make peace with the Indians. For now, all is quiet. Our men are on their way back. But only some will return. Will Jessie's father return? We do not know. Tonight, Jessie was most silent. Inside my head, I said many, many prayers.

September 27, later

I must write two times in the same hour even though Mama calls me to my tasks. Jessie's papa has returned! He is silent though, and has been injured. One arm hangs limp by his side. He is in pain. But he has returned! He tells us to pray for the many who do not.

Also, Captain Smith suffers greatly. Mama treats him with aloe from the storehouse. She says she believes that he will live.

Captain Smith, too, says that he will live. I brought him fresh-dug clams today. He smiled at me. He told me that it would take more than gunpowder to kill John Smith!

And do you know what? I do believe that is the truth.

September 28, 1609

Something wonderful! Tonight will be our last night to lie out-of-doors. Our house is finished! The walls are up. There is a fireplace and a wondrous large chimney. Papa has daubed the chinks with mud. He even found enough glass at an abandoned glass house to make one window.

And I have helped to build this house!

We have not let Mama come inside to look. Not yet. First, Papa has hung a blanket in the middle. That is for Mama to be alone. It is the only thing I have heard Mama wish for — a private place. We brought in our bedding. We carried in the table we brought aboard our ship. We have three chairs that Papa has made here. We moved in the dishes and the iron cooking pot and Papa's tools. I brought in my chest with my clothes and my journal. Then, I gathered flowers. I put them in a jug. It is on the table inside the door. When Mama comes in, she will see a curtain for her private place. And flowers in our new house. I cannot wait.

September 29, 1609

Tonight, we moved into our house. Jessie came with us, for she is my sister now.

Mama stepped inside. She saw her curtain and her jug of flowers. Our house, our *home*, she said over and over. And then she began to cry!

At first, I was worried. But then I saw. She was not crying sad tears. She cried happy tears. She laughed, and hugged Papa. She hugged me and she hugged Jessie. They were strange hugs, for she could not get us close. Her belly is large now.

Papa smiled. And he, too, whispered, *Home.*

Home, I thought. But I could not say that word. For inside of me, I know it is not home. Not yet. It will not be home till Caleb comes. But it is *almost* a home.

September 30, 1609, early morning

A breeze blows in our open window and door. Outside, the birds are singing a morning song.

Inside, Mama and Papa sleep behind their curtain. Jessie sleeps beside me, her head pillowed on her arm. She looks peaceful in her sleep. She seems not so sad.

And I lie here and write. Now that Mama knows about my journal, I need not hide it.

This house is a good place. For now, almost-a-home is good indeed.

October 1, 1609

It is a worrisome time. Captain Smith must leave. He will return to England on one of the ships that arrived last month. His burns are severe. He cannot see to the work. He cannot calm the arguing. Captain Archer, with George Percy, is already taking control. And the men who have returned are terribly ill. Captain Smith is too sick to even go and see the Indians. And so, he must leave us.

My heart grieves. We shall miss him. We wonder what will happen without him here.

October 1, later

Jessie's papa has become grim and silent. He stares off into the woods. He has not added a single stick to his house. He is as idle as the Bridger boys. He looks about, shaking his head. It is as though his thoughts fly this way and that way. Jessie and I watch and worry.

We wonder if it is his injured arm that ails him.

October 2, 1609

I have a plan. I shall ask Captain Smith to visit Caleb when he returns to England. I believe he will do that. But Captain Smith has many important people around him. Somehow, I must find him alone. I want him to tell Caleb that all is well. And that I cannot wait to see him, come spring.

October 2, later

Captain Smith's ship is being prepared with what supplies can be spared. It has also been loaded with goods to take back to the Virginia Company. And here is something funny: Some men wanted to load the ship with gold. But there *is* no gold here. There is just earth with glints of yellow. Oh, how Captain Smith thundered, in spite of his weakness. He shouted that it was dirt! And he would not haul dirt to England!

Some men say it is pure gold. But we know it is pyrite — fool's gold.

So as usual — maybe for the last time — Captain Smith has had his way. His ship will sail on next Thursday. It will not haul dirt. It will sail with cedar wood and sassafras roots and furs. Wood takes up much room on board, but is needed in England.

We wish him Godspeed. But many of us feel sad. And frightened. Captain Smith will be sorely missed.

October 3, 1609

The days grow short. Winter, we know, will soon be here. Jessie's papa said it will be dreadful here come winter. But Jessie and I like the cool nights. Last evening, we dug deep into a pile of fallen leaves. We hid and spied on John Bridger. He was again scratching himself and picking at lice. But then I sneezed and blew leaves all over. John yelled and called us nasty, spying imps.

I thought that a nice compliment from John Bridger.

Later, when Jessie and I went to bed, I realized I miss sleeping out-of-doors. I miss the sky and the blanket of stars. I miss the breeze in the trees.

How odd, to miss such a thing. For in England, who would have thought to sleep outside?

I do believe one can become accustomed to most anything.

October 3, afternoon

Mama is restless. I think her time is almost here. She has been up since dawn. She walks back and forth. She goes out of our house to the village. She comes back in.

What kind of baby will Mama have? Jessie and I hope for a girl child.

I have the pincushion that we will give to Mama when the baby is born. I am spelling out a greeting with the pins. It says: *To Baby. Welcome to the world, the New World.* I do think that is a nice sentiment.

I believe Papa wishes for a son. I know that

in this land, a boy's strength is needed. Yet girls are just as strong as boys. I do know now that is the truth.

October 3, later

Today, Captain Smith called us to the Fort's open square. He was too weak to stand. But he sat on a tree stump to address us. Many men were knotted around him — those who wished to return to England with him. Captain Smith asked us to work with our new leader. He turned to Gabriel Archer who stood at his side. He turned to George Percy.

All of the men shook hands. For once, Mr. Archer's big fish mouth was quiet.

Watching, I thought: I do not like these men. But if they are to be our leaders, we will do as Captain Smith asks.

Then there was much to-do as men vied to

be chosen as crew. The Bridger family wishes to go. But Papa says that Captain Smith has already refused them. I know why — they would not work on board ship.

Captain Smith will choose his crew in the days left. I saw Mr. Collier at Captain Smith's side. I pray that Francis does not leave us!

October 5, 1609

I have just four days before Captain Smith leaves. I see him often, speaking quietly with Jessie's father and the other men. But I have not seen him alone.

When I asked Papa, he said, "What is your message, Elizabeth, my dear? I will take it for you."

I just shook my head. How could I say, I want him to visit Caleb? One must not ask important men to spend time on small matters.

Yet, inside of me, I know it is not a small matter.

It is a very large matter indeed, to me.

October 6, 1609

Mama's time has come. All night last night she paced. She picked up a flower. She put it down. She walked about. She lay on her pallet. She is pale and tired. Sometimes, she cries out with pain. She told me not to fear. This is the way of birthing, she said. When it is over we shall have a lovely baby. She smiled at me.

I tried to smile and tell her I know. But I do not know. Or could it be I know too much? So many babies and mamas have died in childbirth. But I have tucked the pincushion inside my apron. It is ready for Mama. And our baby, too.

October 6, later

It is taking a long time for this baby to be born. Two women are with Mama now, Mistress Collier and her sister, Mistress Whistler. Mistress Whistler is a silent old woman whom no one likes much. But they say she has experience with birthing. I worry and hope she indeed knows what she is doing.

Jessie and I have another worry — her papa. Tonight, in the dark, we saw him working silently. He was in his lean-to. He seemed to be taking things down — not raising them up! It is as if he has a great, dark secret.

October 6, night or is it morning, October 7?

It is taking too long! Mama cries and moans and cries out again. There are whispers from the women on the other side of the curtain.

Will Mama birth a dead baby? Or worse, will Mama die? Jessie knows my fear. She takes my hand and we sit outside. It is comforting to feel her hand. And to see the stars above our heads.

October 7, morning

The baby has still not been born. It is almost two days now. Papa said that it *will* happen. He said that Mama is being brave. Then he said, "You must be brave, too, Elizabeth. Babies can take a long, sweet time getting born."

He said it with a smile. But his face was grave. And he stayed beside our cabin this morning.

Jessie went with me to the riverbank. We sat together and stared into the water.

I think this makes her think of her own mama.

I think we are both tired of being brave.

October 7, later

Glory! A baby is born! Our baby, our brand-new baby. Mama is fine and well. Our baby is fine and well. And oh, Mama did not die. I was so afraid. A baby. A new beautiful baby. Mama laid her in my arms. . . . Oh, yes! I am so excited that she is here that I forgot to say — it is a girl. Her name will be Abigail.

I wanted to name her Americus. But Papa smiled and said we must save that name for a boy baby.

Abigail is beautiful. She is perfect. Her first cry was great and loud. And oh, I think that is the most beautiful sound I have heard in this land.

Papa keeps on smiling. Jessie and I laugh much. We gave Mama her gift. And when she read, *Welcome to the world, the New World* —

she cried! But I knew they were happy tears. She said it was the best gift ever.

Oh, to think — we have a tiny baby girl. She is already well-loved.

October 8, 1609

Baby Abigail continues to clamor loudly. She has a red, red face and a fierce little temper. When she wants to nurse, she howls. Sometimes, she howls even when she does not want to nurse. Last night, I took her outside. I showed her the stars. I told her of the things we would do together. For I am a big sister now. I turned her face up to see the moon. I told her the names of the winds as Pocahontas has told me. I told her about trees and raccoons and deer in the forest. I told her about Jessie. I told her about Francis Collier.

I especially told her about her brother, Caleb. She listened quietly a while. Then she began to howl again.

I touched her tiny mouth. She is a fierce little girl. I think she will do well in this new land.

October 8, later

Such news! I saw Captain Smith alone in the open place near the church. He called me to him. He said he wished to say good-bye.

And so I dared. I asked. I said, Oh, please, go see my brother.

And oh, my! Captain Smith put his hand on my shoulder. He told me that if God would bring him safely to England — then he would go see Caleb! That was his promise. He said it was his solemn promise.

October 8, night

I cannot bear it. I cannot bear this news. Mr. Bolton will return to England with Captain Smith. And Jessie, my friend, will go with him! She will go with him! How can I bear to have her leave?

But men are needed to man the ship. And with his skills and the way he works hard, Mr. Bolton will be useful. Their lean-to is already emptied out. He tells us we are fools to stay. He said those words to Papa. Oh, my heart is breaking this day.

Jessie and I sat at the river and held hands. We did not even talk. We wept.

October 8, later

Papa says there are many kinds of courage. Our courage will keep us here, he said. Mr. Bolton's courage will send them back to sea.

I do not have any courage.

Francis Collier came by to see baby Abigail. He says his family has chosen to stay and that makes me glad. But still, I cry. I do.

I cry.

October 9, 1609, morning

Just one more day Jessie and I will have together.

I think my heart will break. Almost time to sail and neither one of us can find a word to say. And me, I am the one who rushes on. I babble! Today, I have no words.

October 9, later

But oh, then more news! Life is up, and life is down. It is like the ocean in a hurricane. Mr. Bolton came to say good-bye. He promised Papa that he would go with Captain Smith to Caleb. He would tell him how we fare here. Then, just like that, my breath caught in my throat. I gasped and I blurted out words! I asked him to please take my journal to Caleb.

Mr. Bolton just stared at me. But Mama smiled and Papa, too. I do not know where that thought came from. It just flew into my head.

I asked again. I said that Caleb would then know how we fare here.

Mr. Bolton nodded. And he agreed. He did!

And then I thanked him again and again. I told him it was wonderful. Oh, it is. It is so wonderful!

I was so pleased, I babbled. Just as Mama tells me not to do. But I could be forgiven this time. So now, they will all go to Caleb — Captain Smith and Mr. Bolton — and Jessie! Jessie will go and meet my brother. I am so happy. I think my heart will fly right out of me.

Now, I hurry to finish writing here. So Caleb, my brother, my twin — so he shall know what has happened here.

October 9, as the sails are being unfurled

I sit at the dock, writing frantically. I have just these few moments.

Oh, Caleb, do you read now what is written here? I did not even tell about the ink. I ran out of English ink long ago. This ink is made of the juice of berries. I pray it holds and does not fade.

First, forgive me for taking your book. It was

wrong of me. But now you can know all that has happened to us. If the ink holds, then you know about baby Abigail. Just know that in spite of my worries and complaining here, all *is* well.

Mama and Papa and I — we are well. We are lonely. I am very lonely, for my dear friend Jessie is leaving me. Next to you, Caleb, she is my best friend in the whole world. But if you have this book, then you have met her. Oh, do you like her as well as I do? I believe you do, you must!

And Caleb, with each month's passing, you come closer to being with us. You will meet my friend, Francis Collier. You will meet the Indian men. You will like it here. Caleb, sometimes we are hungry. Ofttimes we are frightened. But we have a home here. Papa and I built it ourselves! And yes, I climbed the roof. I have done many things we did not think of doing in England. It is a small house. And I must admit, it smells a bit damp. It is different from England. But it is a house, Caleb, a home. It is our home. And it is beautiful to us.

Oh, Caleb, it is a lovely land. When you join us here come spring — we will rejoice.

For then it will be a real home indeed.

Home in America.

Historical Note

In 1607, the London Company in England sent an expedition to the Americas under the leadership of Captain Christopher Newport. The purpose was to settle there, in the hopes of finding goods and materials, and maybe even gold, to send back to England. On a warm spring day, the settlers landed on the Virginia coast, then sailed about thirty miles up the James River to the site of their new settlement, the first permanent one in the New World. Here they hung the flag of England. They hoped that by being far enough inland, they might be safe from the marauders and pirates who had been attacking other colonies.

Arrival at Jamestown.

This plan might have been a good one, but several things went very wrong. First, the land that they chose was poor for settling. It was in a wet marsh, full of mosquitoes that spread disease. Second, the land was inhabited by Indians who were wary of such strange visitors. But there were other problems, too, problems that the settlers brought with them from England. Some of the men who came on board the ships were lazy, and expected others to do their work. They did not know how to work hard. In addition, they had brought the wrong things — clothing that was too hot for this climate, foods that spoiled.

Some of the advertisements in England told how exciting life in America would be. Settlers came thinking they were headed for great adventure. Instead, they found hard times, hunger, disease, and trouble.

Relations with the Indians were unstable at times. And matters amongst the settlers also became tense. Eventually, a young colonist named John Smith took control of the colony and brought

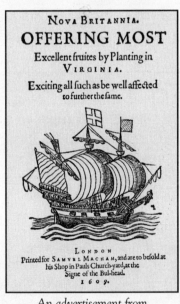

An advertisement from England urging people to travel to Virginia.

some order to it. First, he made rules for the men there. One was "If you do not work, you do not eat!" Then, he worked at creating friendly, working relations with the Indians.

Captain John Smith.

Building a house at Jamestown.

He befriended Pocahontas, the daughter of the Indian chief Powhatan. The men traded with the Indians for food and necessary supplies. The Indians taught

Pocahontas leading John Smith through the woods.

the colonists how to plant corn, how to fish, and how to make canoes out of hollowed-out logs. All these things helped the colonists to survive, and even thrive, for a while.

When women and children came with more settlers in 1609, things were quiet at first. But soon there were more problems, mainly brought on by overcrowding and hunger, as the fort swelled with the newcomers. Also, the

Trading with Indians.

colonists and the Indians had become reckless in their relations with one another. Many people were killed in hostile, angry scuffles.

Then, in the fall of 1609, when Captain Smith was injured and had to return to England, things in the colony became much worse very quickly. Disease, discontent, and rivalry spread among the colonists. It was known as "The Starving Time," as hunger was their constant companion. The very survival of the colony was in doubt. When the next supply ship returned the following spring, only a few colonists were there to greet them. The rest had died of starvation or disease.

However, the arrival of those ships brought much needed food and supplies and many new people. The colony again began to thrive and soon, Jamestown was named the first capital of Virginia.

Women and children arriving at Jamestown.

About the Author

Writing about Jamestown, Virginia, enabled Patricia Hermes to work with some familiar material in a familiar setting. She says, "At one time, I lived in Tidewater, Virginia, just a few miles from the original Jamestown settlement. I remember how hot and humid the summers were there. I know about the bugs. I know about the winter cold. I know about the swaying pines and the whisper of the rivers and the sandy soil and the rich marshland alive with birds.

"I also remember how lonely I first felt when I moved there. So, when I created Elizabeth and her twin brother, Caleb, I think I knew something of how she felt. I knew how hard it is to leave family and friends. I knew how scary it was to be in a strange place with strange people and new foods, and different customs. I knew how lonesome it could be."

Patricia Hermes is the author of over thirty books for children and young adults, including *Mama, Let's Dance*; *You Shouldn't Have to Say Goodbye*; *Cheat the Moon*; and *Kevin Corbett Eats Flies*. Many of her award-winning books were named ALA Best Books or received the IRA-CBC Children's Choice Award.

Acknowledgments

Grateful acknowledgment is made for permission to reprint the following:

Cover portrait and frontispiece by Glenn Harrington.

Page 100: The arrival of the first English colonists at Jamestown, Virginia, wood engraving, American, nineteenth century, The Granger Collection, New York, New York.

Page 101: Advertisement, Charlotte Engraving Co., Charlotte, North Carolina.

Page 102 (top): Captain John Smith, line engraving, detail from Smith's map of Virginia, 1616, The Granger Collection, New York, New York.

Page 102 (bottom): Building a house at Jamestown, wood engraving, nineteenth century, ibid.

Page 103: Pocahontas brings corn to the colonists at Jamestown, wood engraving, American, nineteenth century, ibid.

Page 104: Trading with Indians, North Wind Picture Archives, Alfred, Maine.

Page 105: Wives of the settlers at Jamestown, Library of Congress.

For Jessica Camille Hermes

While the events described and some of the characters in this
book may be based on actual historical events and real people,
Elizabeth Barker is a fictional character, created by the author,
and her diary is a work of fiction.

Copyright © 2000 by Patricia Hermes

Library of Congress Cataloging-in-Publication Data
Hermes, Patricia.
Our strange new land: Elizabeth's diary, Jamestown, Virginia, 1609 by Patricia Hermes.
p. cm. — (My America)
Includes bibliographical references
Summary: Nine-year-old Elizabeth keeps a journal of her experiences in the New World
as she encounters Indians, suffers hunger and the death of friends, and helps her father
build their first home.
ISBN 0-439-11208-7; 0-439-36898-7 (pbk.)
1. Jamestown (Va.). — History — Juvenile fiction.
2. Virginia — History — Colonial period, ca. 1600–1775 — Juvenile fiction.
[1. Jamestown (Va.) — History — Fiction.
2. Virginia — History — Colonial period, ca. 1600–1775 — Fiction. 3. Diaries — Fiction.]
I. Title. II. Series.
PZ7.H4317Ou 2000
[Fic] — dc21   99-056356
CIP AC

10 9   6 7 8 9/0

The display type was set in Caslon Antique.
The text type was set in Goudy.
Photo research by Zoe Moffitt
Book design by Elizabeth B. Parisi

Printed in the U.S.A.
First paperback edition, May 2002

SEEDS OF HOPE

THE GOLD RUSH DIARY OF SUSANNA FAIRCHILD

BY KRISTIANA GREGORY

Scholastic Inc. New York

THE *CALIFORNIA*
1849

Monday, the 1st of January, 1849
aboard the *California*,
somewhere in the Pacific

We've been at sea now for eighty-seven days. The rolling gray waves spread in every direction as far as I can see. We're still south of the equator, sailing toward the country of Peru. The sun is so warm I carry my parasol when strolling on deck; the thermometer reads 73 degrees.

At this moment I'm sitting in the shade of the mainsail, my dress a hot nuisance around my legs. The barrel next to me is sloshing with only two inches of drinking water. Because of the storms we are two weeks behind schedule and are desperate for fresh meat, water, and vegetables. Many of us are bleeding in our mouths. The voyage around the Horn was rough . . . there was so much loss . . .

Just this morning I finally had the courage to open Mother's trunk. It was in her stateroom, strapped to the wall to keep it from sliding across the floor in heavy seas. When I lifted the lid, a familiar scent of lavender filled me with such longing for her I found myself in tears again.

Still, I wanted to look. On top of her folded night-gown was her journal, the one in which I now write. I flipped through the blank pages. The only thing she had written, in her beautiful script, was the date of our departure from New York Harbor and our names: Dr. and Mrs. Fairchild; Clara, age sixteen; Susanna, age fourteen.

I am Susanna.

LATE AFTERNOON

Some weeks from now we will land at Fort Vancouver, then travel by wagon to Oregon City where Papa will carry on his medical practice. We have family and dear friends who settled there last year. We are all from Missoura — they traveled over-land by wagon and we're going by ship. Papa had long dreamed of an ocean voyage, but we didn't de-cide on emigrating until after the others were already on the Oregon Trail. Since mail takes so long they won't even know we're coming until they see us walking up their lane.

To finally be with old friends will be a great comfort. But who will tell them what happened to Mother? Must I? Or will Papa? He is so distraught he cannot speak of her without turning away. Clara, too.

The sun seems to be lingering over the western horizon, spreading a pink glow. In moments it will slip out of sight, and darkness will be upon us. Already some of the lanterns on deck are being lit. This ends the first day of the New Year and my first entry in this journal. I plan to record the dreams of our family and my own thoughts as well. It is what Mother had intended. These empty pages testify to her sickness the first weeks of our voyage, when she was unable to eat or even hold up her head. Now, so many weeks later, the empty pages speak of our tragedy at sea. I will write of it another time.

SATURDAY, THE 6TH OF JANUARY

We are still anchored in the sheltered harbor of Callao, Peru. The breeze is as warm as summer. Oh, the pleasure of hearing crickets again, and the croaking of frogs. Other familiar sounds brought me comfort: A dog barked from somewhere in town and there was a church bell at midnight.

On this day three months ago — October 6, 1848 — our family sailed out of New York. Such excitement. Bystanders stood on the pier waving handkerchiefs, shouting "Godspeed!" It was a crisp autumn day; I remember it well. Mother wrapped her shawl around me against the wind as our ship passed the breakwater and hit open sea. The Atlantic Ocean that day was green and calm. Clara and Papa explored the deck arm in arm. Our grand adventure was beginning.

Our vessel, the *California,* is a side-wheeler steamship, heading for what is to be her home port of Panama City. From there she will sail up and down the Pacific coast delivering and picking up mail. That is why most of her cabins are empty at this time. Not counting the crew there are only a few of us aboard, though there is room for about 200 passengers.

Captain Forbes says we are making history because we will be the first American steamer to sail from the east coast to the west coast.

A curious sight aboard ship is the Tar Heads. This is my name for the sailors who paint their hair with tar to keep it from blowing in their faces. Last night I watched one of them dance to the music of a squeezebox . . . his pigtail bounced on his shoulders like a black stick.

TUESDAY, THE 9TH OF JANUARY

Once again we're at sea.

About seventy new passengers, mostly men, came aboard at Callao and are unpacking their bags in the empty cabins. For some reason these Peruvians — every one of them — are in a rush for California. Their language is Spanish but some know a little English, though it is hard to understand their accents. When Papa heard the word "gold," he looked at Captain Forbes.

What is this about gold? they said to each other.

For supper Cook is serving fresh chicken, potatoes, and one whole onion per person, to eat like an apple. Papa says the vitamins will help our scurvy and keep us from losing teeth. This scurvy is a horrible disease. It has made our gums swell and bleed because we've been so long without vegetables or fruit. We eat at the captain's table, under the skylight. That is why Clara is handing me a clean apron to tie around my soiled dress . . . I confess that one of the things I most look forward to about Oregon is being able to do a proper laundry and to soak in a proper bath.

Most of all, Clara and I yearn to be reunited with friends who knew Mother — Aunt Augusta and Uncle Charles especially, and our cousins.

WEDNESDAY, THE 10TH OF JANUARY

Sunshine lit our porthole early this morning. It is now 6:30; breakfast will be at seven bells. I am dressed, my face washed, and my braid is tied with a blue ribbon. I am ready to face the day but Clara is still barefooted and struggling into her corset! With so many men on board she wants to look like a lady. I told her it is enough that she combs her hair atop her head and wears her tiny pearl earrings. Clara doesn't realize that she is as pretty as our mother and does not need to pinch her waist.

While I wait for her, a breeze comes in through our window. Looking out I can see seagulls diving into the waves after potato peels the cook has thrown overboard. We are not far from land, but Captain

Forbes says it may be another week before we reach Panama City.

Clara and I have been reading *Poems of Ralph Waldo Emerson,* one of the many books and pamphlets Mother packed in her trunk. She knew there would be no school on our long voyage, so she wanted to make sure we could keep our minds active.

I ate only half my onion for it is foul. The fumes made my eyes cry, and its juice stung the sores in my mouth. The rest I will try to eat tomorrow.

Saturday, the 13th of January

I have made the acquaintance of Rosita Sepúlveda. She is traveling to California with her husband and seven brothers. Her blouse has more bright colors than I have ever seen on one person. It is made from a square of woven cloth with a hole in the center for her head. The rest of the cloth drapes down to her knees. I admire her thick dark braids tied with red string. They hang down her back. She is perhaps twenty years old.

Rosita smiles every time she sees me and speaks in her rapid Spanish mixed with some words of English. Yesterday she invited me into her cabin. From her satchel she unfolded a beautiful length of cloth, the same vivid colors of her blouse. She tenderly arranged it over my shoulders.

Her generosity so touched me there was a lump in my throat as I climbed up to the deck.

WEDNESDAY, THE 17TH OF JANUARY

Four days since I've written — I must make a better effort. Today was a thrill because once again we are near land.

From the railing of the deck I could see the rounded, lush hills of Panama. Captain Forbes let me raise his spyglass to my eye. I squinted. Shacks and ruined buildings came into view. Chickens and hogs were running through streets with patches of over-grown grass. I had never seen such a shabby town.

As I looked toward the harbor, the view that came into focus startled me. It appeared as if I were inches from a man's face. I twisted the lens to pull back. Several men were looking toward us, dozens of men. I pulled back even more and scanned the length of the beach.

Now I could see hundreds of men, hundreds.

Arms raised. Their mouths were open as if shouting at us, but of course I could not hear them. It seemed they wanted to board our ship.

THURSDAY, THE 25TH OF JANUARY, PANAMA CITY

At anchor for eight days now. The weather is hot and it has rained nearly every afternoon. Repairs are being made to our vessel, supplies loaded, animal pens restocked. More bunks are being built in the steerage compartment. The mystery why so many men greeted our ship has been solved.

It seems that after we sailed from New York and had been at sea for sixty days the President of the United States, James Polk, announced that gold had been discovered near San Francisco. Word traveled like fire. Soon boats were leaving New Orleans bound for the Caribbean side of the isthmus. By donkey and canoe they traveled across this narrow neck of land to Panama City. Hundreds and hundreds of men did this. They knew our ship was coming 'round the Horn so they waited for us.

These same men are now shouting at Captain

Forbes. Fifteen hundred of them want to buy passage! When told there is room for only two hundred, and when these men saw the dark skin of the Peruvians, bedlam broken out.

"No foreigners!" came the cry. "Americans only!"

Clara and I are huddled in our cabin, afraid to hear the full wrath of the "legal miners," as these men call themselves. Papa keeps coming below to make sure we are all right and to talk to us.

He says the Americans want to drag the Peruvians off the ship! Complaints are that the foreigners are taking up space and if allowed to step on Californian soil, they will be trespassing. Since the gold belongs to the United States they will be thieves, plundering what is not theirs.

I thought of Rosita and her husband and brothers, but I could not think of them as thieves.

WEDNESDAY, THE 31ST OF JANUARY, PANAMA CITY, STILL

Tomorrow some 250 passengers will be allowed to board . . . all Americans. As there are no piers in this harbor, everyone must get wet wading from the beach to the little boats that will row them out to us. Papa said many will pay one thousand dollars for the privilege.

Before dinner I went through Mother's trunk again — oh, everything I touched brought the memory of her to me. A brooch she had worn our first day at sea was in a small box with her other jewelry. Clara agreed I could give the pin to Rosita.

Our new friend was overjoyed. She fastened it to her blouse by her shoulder, and said to us in English, "Thank you, lady friends."

Thursday, 1st of February, 1849
At sea

At 8:45 this morning we weighed anchor and steamed away from Panama. Captain Forbes decided he would not force the Peruvians to get off the ship, but they must haul all their gear topside. They are to sleep on deck, in hammocks or beds of their own making. Foul weather or fair. I told Rosita she may sleep with us, but the captain overheard us talking. He said no.

"Cabins and steerage are for Americans only."

The *California* now has approximately 400 people on board, weighing our decks down a little lower in the water. If Captain Forbes is worried about her sinking, he is keeping it to himself.

Clara and I brought supper down to our cabin. She is now reading by the swinging lamplight. In these hours alone in our cabin I find myself missing Mother so much it hurts to breathe. To hold her diary in my hands and fill these blank pages with my thoughts is strangely comforting. It is as if she and I are sharing these words. . . .

NEXT DAY

At dinner Papa was quiet. He folded his napkin under his plate, put his cap on his head, then climbed the companionway without saying anything to us. Clara and I followed him up to the deck. Steam was puffing out of the smokestacks and Tar Heads were coiling ropes after trimming the sails.

"Papa?" I said. "When we get to Oregon, can we plant a garden first thing?"

For so many weeks since Mother's accident, we

hadn't dared breathe any of our hopes or dreams. I don't know why we stopped talking of these things, but now it seemed all right to do so. We were just a couple of weeks away from once again being with loved ones.

Clara and I are now in bed. We have whispered for an hour and still don't understand why Papa is suddenly so quiet.

WEDNESDAY, THE 28TH OF FEBRUARY, SAN FRANCISCO BAY

Things have not turned out the way my sister and I had planned.

This morning, just when the sun rose behind San Francisco's hills, our ship sailed through the Golden Gate. This narrow channel is perhaps one mile across, with steep cliffs on either side. It opens up to a huge protected bay, the most sensible harbor I've seen in my five-month voyage.

Wood houses and buildings are along the shore, but otherwise the town seems empty. I counted thirty ships of various sizes already at anchor, but oddly most of them had no sailors on board swabbing decks or up in the rigging, as I'm used to seeing in port.

A band welcomed us by playing "Yankee Doodle" and some boys waved at us with American flags. In just 146 days our beautiful little ship sailed from the east coast to the west, the first mail steamer to do so. Captain Forbes stood proudly in the bow, wearing a clean blue coat and cap. He saluted the Stars and Stripes that were snapping in the wind.

Though I'm unhappy to write what happened next, I will, because Mother would have done so. Clara is on her bunk and has started to cry again. I am coming down with a terrible headache.

Here it is: Papa has changed his mind about settling in Oregon! We will get off here, San Francisco, with all our bags and trunks.

"We can't pass up this opportunity," he told us at noon while we were eating our soup. When he explained that he was going to become a miner, Clara and I set down our spoons.

"*What?*" we both said at once.

We are just sick over this. Our own father has gold fever, and Mother isn't here to talk him out of it.

It is ten o'clock in the evening, but there is no one to ring the ship's bell. Besides my family there are just two crew members remaining on board. Two. Captain Forbes and one of the boys from the engine room. That is all.

In the mad rush for shore our captain quickly realized that in addition to the American passengers and the Peruvians, his mates themselves were going ashore. Every single one jumped ship. His navigator, helmsman, first mate, second mate, every Tar Head and cabin boy, even Cook, the firemen, and chief engineer. Everyone.

Our Captain is beyond fury. He held up his hands, pleading with his crew as they hurried away.

"Who will sail my ship?" he cried. I watched him stand there in his crisp uniform, so proud moments earlier. To see a fine captain deserted, mutinied on his own vessel, made me extremely sad. No sheriff or jailer came to help him, for they too have fled to the gold fields. The other ships in harbor have been abandoned as well.

The reason *we* are still on board is that Clara and I told Papa we refuse to leave. Oregon is to be our home, not a mining camp. We want to sail north on the next tide.

"That is what Mama wanted for us," Clara said, "and for us to be close to Aunt Augusta." My sister then broke down crying and would not be consoled. Papa put his hand on her shoulder, but she shrugged it off. When he reached for me, I shook my head and walked away.

FRIDAY, THE 2ND OF MARCH,
STILL ABOARD THE *CALIFORNIA*,
SAN FRANCISCO BAY

A cold wind is blowing across the bay, but we are cozy below. I am writing by lamplight at the navigator's table. Last evening was spent without Papa because he went to shore for mining supplies.

Clara and I find ourselves struggling not to cry out of fear and worry. Are we to follow our father or should we go on to Oregon without him? I wish someone could tell us what to do.

Captain Forbes is stricken. He stands on the deck looking out to sea, smoking his pipe. This morning we watched with him as a beautiful three-masted schooner sailed into the bay. As soon as her anchors had splashed into the water, we counted some forty crew members abandoning ship.

"My God," our captain said. "Everyone has the fever."

SATURDAY, THE 3RD OF MARCH

Papa was in the galley making coffee this morning — we were so happy to see him!

During breakfast our plates nearly slid off the table because heavy swells were rolling the ship. As we ate our salted potatoes, he spoke of everything he'd learned while in the streets and shops of San Francisco.

Gold is easy to find as apples on a tree, he said, trying to convince us to come to the mining camps with him. Just for a few months, he says; a year at most, until he makes enough to buy land in Oregon and build a house. Papa said that as a doctor sometimes he earns just thirty dollars a month, but the men mining gold are pulling in nearly three hundred dollars a *day*.

He lowered his voice and stared into his coffee. "I want to try to recover what was lost."

Papa did not mean Mother, of course, I knew that. Nothing would bring her back to us. He was talking about our life's savings, nearly two thousand dollars.

The memory of how it all happened fills me with such heartache I have put off writing about it . . . but I shall try now to get it out of my mind and onto paper.

Several days after leaving New York we finally recovered from seasickness, except for Mother. She was quite ill. Papa examined her and said it was because she was expecting a baby! We were overjoyed. Gradually she gained strength and by the time we were south of Argentina she was able to walk around her stateroom.

The captain and his navigator decided that instead of sailing around treacherous Cape Horn, they would take a shortcut through the Strait of Magellan. This channel is some 350 miles long and the quickest route from the Atlantic Ocean to the Pacific. We were to learn later that it is also rough with currents and unpredictable winds.

But Mother didn't care. She finally had her sea legs and was feeling so wonderful she wanted fresh air. She took Papa's arm and they strolled on deck,

Clara and I behind them. What happened next came so fast that when I recall it I still can't believe it.

Mother bent over to adjust the hem of her skirt, letting go of Papa's arm as she did. In that instant a wave broke over the bow, sending such a flood of water on deck that we were all swept off our feet. Clara and I grabbed a lifeline that was strung around some barrels; we knew to do this because we'd been at sea many weeks. But Mother had been ill for so long below deck, she didn't know. She threw up her arms in surprise and passed us swiftly in green water that was waist-deep. I reached for her, our hands touched, but she was swept away. The ship rose on a swell and tilted to the side, the gunwale dipping under a wave.

Before our eyes Mother floated overboard. The look on her face was of bewilderment; she called my father's name, then we saw her no more. Papa screamed such a scream I'll never forget. He ripped off his coat to jump in after her, but a sailor caught his arms and wouldn't let him.

The longboat was lowered and two mates began rowing. Our helmsman turned the ship so we could circle, and another mate climbed the mast for a better look. All hands were on deck, trying to help.

Meanwhile, Clara and I clung to each other, clung to the rope. Our dresses were wet and so heavy we couldn't move our legs to stand up. With a growing horror I realized that the weight of Mother's dress would have pulled her under the waves in seconds. The search for her was useless.

I don't remember anything more of that day.

BEFORE SUPPER

To continue . . . Papa had sewn all our money into the folds and seams of his jacket. He thought that by doing so, no one could steal his life's savings. But it was washed into the sea that day as well. I'm beginning to understand why he wants to dig for gold. It could be the quickest way to earn what was lost, the money part at least.

I feel desolate.

One minute Mother was there, laughing, the next she wasn't. There was no warning, no chance for good-byes, and her watery tomb means we'll never be able to gaze on where she rests. I try to shed this cloak of loneliness, but I cannot. To think about that terrible day brings such heartache.

This is what has brought me to my decision about Oregon. I will talk it over with Clara first, then Papa.

WEDNESDAY, THE 7TH OF MARCH, STILL ABOARD THE *CALIFORNIA*

In these past days much has happened.

When I told Clara I thought we should go with Papa, her face brightened. She agrees that Mother would want us to stay together. By some miracle we feel hopeful about this adventure. Not until we imagined life without our father did we realize how much we want to be with him.

And so it is. We remain on board, through the kindness of Captain Forbes. He is still trying to muster a crew, and we are saving on a hotel bill. To earn our keep, Clara and I have been cooking the noon and the evening meals. Papa has been rowing to shore with some of the furniture we brought from New York, to barter for the supplies we'll need. Our dining-room chairs, tables, and bureaus brought a few dollars — we don't need those things now.

Papa purchased an assortment of miner's gear: a pan and pick, flannel shirts, a slouch hat, and tall boots; then for our comfort, a canvas tent and a sturdy Dutch oven. We agreed not to sell anything from Mother's trunk. It is small, about knee-high and three feet long, so we'll take it with us. Our tickets for the riverboat cost thirty-two dollars each.

After the breakfast dishes were cleared, Papa spread out one of his maps on the captain's table. Sunshine from the skylight made it easy to read the small print. With his thumb he traced our current position aboard the ship, across the bay, and to a point where a small boat will take us up the winding Sacramento River, some seventy-five miles. At its junction with another river is the town of Sacramento and, nearby, Sutter's Fort. We'll stay there a few days so Papa can hire a wagon to take us up into the hills.

We have been at sea for precisely five months and tomorrow will say farewell. I will miss the fresh, salty air, but not the terrors of the deep.

MONDAY, THE 12TH OF MARCH, SUTTER'S FORT

In this, our second day at the fort, we've seen nearly two hundred men on their way to mining camps. We recognized Cook and our navigator from the *California*, along with some of the Peruvians. I counted forty-eight Tar Heads who must have jumped ship. One of them told Papa that there are at least fifty abandoned vessels in San Francisco Bay.

I have seen all types of cities in the East, but I've never seen anything like Sutter's Fort. Clara described the people here as "motley," meaning there is every sort of man from every sort of background. Crowds of them are in all stages of departure. Some are camped along the riverbank while waiting for a blacksmith to mend harnesses or wheels. Some are piling their gear onto the backs of mules and are just hurrying away.

Others are bartering their belongings. Clara and I watched one fellow try to sell five thousand ladies' hats he brought with him from New Orleans, which he had hoped to sell at a profit. We laughed because we are the only ladies in sight and we do not need a fancy hat. Another man is trying to unload a case of razors, but there are no buyers because men don't shave their faces around here.

The thick walls of the fort are some fifteen feet high, made of adobe. Within the fort are barracks for soldiers, but we saw no one in uniform. Word is they, too, have abandoned their posts and fled to the hills. There is a bakery, two jails, a carpenter's shop, a grocery, and Captain Sutter's house. His sawmill up the river is where his partner, John Marshall, discovered gold more than a year ago.

Cows and livestock have trampled the surrounding wheat fields and vegetable gardens. There is a bare look to everything. Papa said even the Indians who worked for Captain Sutter have left. Everyone has gold fever.

We've been staying in a room with dirt floors and a pile of straw for our bed. The corners are muddy because we are so close to the water. I should mention that we are now on the American River, not far from Captain Sutter's sawmill. While I'm writing, this page is spotted with fleas! As soon as I brush them off, more hop on — they are terribly irritating. Clara and I are bitten raw about our hands and ankles.

TUESDAY, THE 13TH OF MARCH

It rained all afternoon. The mud within the walls of the fort was so sticky it pulled off my shoe as I stepped around the campfire. Never mind, for at supper there was great excitement.

A group of men came down from the hills to get provisions — they are originally from Oregon Territory! After talking to them Papa learned that in the past few months some *three thousand* men have journeyed here from that northern territory. In fact, his dearest old friend, Jesse Blue, is nearby at Miner's Creek.

I watched Papa's face when he heard this report. He ran his fingers through his beard and smiled in a way we have not seen him smile since Mother died. It seemed he stood taller, such was his relief that a loyal friend was so near. I admit feeling hopeful myself, but perhaps not for the same reason.

Mother and Mrs. Blue were next-door neighbors all their growing-up years and were dear friends. Our families shared Christmas and birthdays for as long as I can remember. Mr. Blue is like an uncle to me. To look at him will be to look at someone who has heard the voice and seen the smile of my beloved mother.

Maybe the mining camp won't be so lonely after all.

NEXT DAY

When the Oregon men finish getting their supplies together, they will guide us along the North Fork to their camp where Mr. Blue and possibly more of our friends are mining. When they unrolled a map by the light of our campfire, I was equally relieved that we wouldn't be traveling alone.

There are at least six places called Miner's Creek!

And to confuse things further, four places are named Angel's Camp, several are Dead Man's Gulch, same for Whiskey Town, Gouge Eye, Rough and Ready, Murderer's Bar, Poverty Bay, Old Dry Diggings, Hang Town, and so on. Papa marveled at so many duplicate names, wondering aloud how folks would ever find one another. But my eyes grew wide at the words themselves: poverty, murderer, dead man, hang town. . . . Clara and I looked at each other, and I could see that the deep breath she drew was as shaky as mine.

What is Papa getting us into? In my quiet moments I wonder if he worries, as I do, about his new profession. How will a man trained in medicine know what to do with a pick and shovel?

Because my sister and I are the only females at the fort, Papa watches us carefully, making sure that men who stare at us keep their distance. He is ner-vous for our safety because many of these miners are ne'er-do-wells, that is, thieves, murderers, and pick-pockets who are hiding from the law.

P.S. At the store I found a little book called *A Christmas Carol* by Charles Dickens. Before bed Clara and I take turns reading aloud, then Papa reads to us. Even though it is long past Christmas, we are still enjoying the story. So far it's about Mr. Scrooge, a greedy man with money but no friends.

A lantern set on the floor casts long shadows up the wall. Clara wants me to hurry this so we can blow out the light and crawl into our bed of hay. She and I have returned to a childhood habit that com-forts us. Before we fall asleep, we pull the blanket over our heads and whisper our prayers.

FRIDAY, THE 23RD OF MARCH, MINER'S CREEK

Well, here we are.

From Sutter's Fort we followed the American River to its North Fork. For one solid day our trail took us past many rivulets of white water that poured down from the hills, most of which our mules and wagon crossed without getting too wet. At last our guides led us along a wide shallow river with sandbars curving out from the beach.

White canvas tents are planted along the shore and hillsides, dotted everywhere like wild mushrooms. Men stand knee-deep in the river, bending over their pans. Others dig with shovels, some are swinging picks to break apart rocks. Papa said this is called placer mining, when dirt is washed with water to find gold.

As we drove into the settlement, someone looked up and shouted, "Wimmin!"

Every head turned our way and stared as if they had never seen two girls in sunbonnets before. Some fellows lay down their tools and approached us, removing their hats respectfully. When they wouldn't stop looking at us, Papa tipped his own hat to them.

"Gentlemen," he said, "get about your business." Then he snapped his reins until our mules pulled the wagon forward.

The town of Miner's Creek sits in a clearing at the lower end of a meadow. It does not look like a town. It is just rows of shacks and dirty tents facing one another with planks of wood sticking out the front doors like tongues. These walkways are so people don't lose their shoes in the deep, sticky mud. There are several saloons and stores, a blacksmith, and a hotel. A lady in front of the dance hall was watching men go by. Her dress was satin, her cheeks and lips were painted red. Papa wouldn't look at her, and he told us to never go near that place.

Our new "home" is on the sunny side of the creek, on a wide flat ledge of dirt. If the river rises we will stay dry. And when the sun moves across the sky, our tent will be bathed in warm light instead of the shadow of a mountain. Because the elevation here is nearly one mile above sea level, the air is cold and the shade even colder.

When Papa drove in the last stakes, he brushed his hands against his pants and said he was going to look for his old friend, Jesse Blue.

NEXT DAY

Early this morning I woke to a new sound: hammers and picks striking rock, rhythmically, like the ticking of a tin clock. Miners are everywhere along the river.

For breakfast I fried thick slices of ham in our skillet. Our campfire sits in front of our tent, then beyond us about twenty feet is the river. Clara fetched water in our pail so we could boil potatoes. Apparently we are camped on what used to be a grove of little pine trees. They were chopped down, leaving stumps of various heights, some tall enough to use as a table, others low enough for stools. This is where we were sitting when a great commotion broke out, an hour after sunrise.

"Gold!" someone yelled above the noise of the river. "Mile north of Old Dry Crik!"

Suddenly the noise of picks and shovels stopped. Before our eyes a swarm of men hurried out of camp to where their horses were grazing. They mounted, then disappeared into the woods. Others packed tools and bedrolls onto their mules; some just started walking.

I was amazed at the power of that one word, *gold*.

"Where'd everyone go?" Papa asked as he emerged from the tent. He was rolling up his sleeves and squinting across the brightness of the river.

One of our neighbors is an elderly sea captain. I have never seen such a curious sight as his long, white beard. It has small colorful beads and bells braided into the strands, which make clicking sounds when he moves. He called over from his campfire, "Mister, those boys have gone for better diggings, that's where." Then he waved his hand as if to say good riddance. "There's always something better somewhere. That's gold fever for you."

Papa sat down on one of the stumps. When Clara handed him his coffee, he lifted his cup toward the old sailor. "Say, my friend, have you had breakfast yet? Come on over." And that is how our friendship began with Captain Clinkingbeard. That is his honest-to-God name; I am not making this up.

Meanwhile, there is no sign of Jesse Blue.

Tuesday, the 27th of March

Am writing in the tent by lantern light. There is a sweet fragrance of balsam coming from our beds. Papa cut branches from pine trees and spread layers on our cold, dirt floor. With our blankets on top, we have soft beds protected from the frost. Clara is reading; Papa and the Captain are outside in front of the fire trading stories.

About today . . . We learned that to find Jesse

Blue is not as simple as knocking on someone's door. The hills around here are spotted with caves and men hauling rocks out of them. When their luck fails or they hear of a better strike somewhere else, they move on. That's why a fellow's tent might be here one day, gone the next. Also, there are creeks, streams, rivulets, and waterfalls — so many places a man can pan for gold.

Papa walked around for a few hours that first afternoon looking for our friend, but soon realized the search could take longer. When he said he wanted to post a message in town, I tore out a blank page from this journal and gave him my pencil.

We went with him to the Mad Mule Saloon. Letters and advertisements were tacked up outside all over the front wall. Papa pushed his note onto a nail and said if Jesse sees this he'll know where to find us.

WEDNESDAY, THE 28TH OF MARCH

This afternoon Papa started his new occupation, mining for gold. I do not think he knows what he is doing.

First, he and the Captain had a long conversation

around our campfire, enjoying each other's company while Clara poured them cup after cup of hot coffee. I fried flapjacks. They burned around the edges because I am not used to cooking out in the open — the wind makes the fire too hot. Anyway, when the sun was nearly overhead, Papa turned his pipe upside down and tapped the ashes out against a rock; the Captain did the same.

"Well!" they said, then off they went with shovels and picks over their shoulders. They didn't work near our cabin because the shore is already crowded with miners.

Meanwhile, Clara and I broke off a pine branch to sweep the dirt from our tent. Then we pulled the blankets off our beds and shook them outside. We took our dishes down to the river to rinse, then left them to dry on one of the larger tree stumps. Tomorrow we will figure a way to wash clothes, but for now we wanted to explore the little town, maybe see if the store had any fresh eggs.

Something we noticed the first day we arrived is that everyone walks with his head down! I wondered, *Why are folks so sad?* But we learned they are not sad; they are on the lookout for gold, all the time, every day, hoping to stumble on a nugget that has washed down from the hills. Last week a man found one the size of a yellow apple, right behind the Bliss Hotel. A rainstorm had loosened the earth, and people were finding gold everywhere, in the street and in wagon ruts, even under the plank sidewalks.

This is how it happened that Clara and I bumped into the dance-hall lady — our heads were down. We were courteous to her but hurried past the saloon where she was standing. I noticed that her shoes were blue satin.

BEFORE BED

It is late, almost nine o'clock. Clara and I are outside warming up by the fire. As we look across the river, we can see campfires scattered along the banks and tents glowing with lantern light. Every few minutes we hear the music of guitars rise above the sound of the rushing river. I am sleepy, but before closing these pages will tell about Papa. . . .

He and Captain Clinkingbeard returned at sundown, soaking wet up to their hips. Papa shivered with cold, but he was so excited to show us his day's earnings. He opened up his leather pouch and poured the contents into his palm.

"It's a start," he said. "Maybe a dollar's worth." Clara and I leaned closer. Cantaloupe seeds, that's what the gold looked like, tiny yellow seeds of hope.

Papa was exhausted so we made him sit in front of the fire while I fixed him a plate of stew, and one for the Captain. Clara brought out two dry shirts for them to change into. We spread Papa's wet socks over the stones and propped his boots there, too. As he ate and warmed up, I noticed his pale white feet. He did not complain about standing in icy water all day, nor that his hands were blistered raw.

Suddenly I realized that without our mother here to encourage him, Clara and I must do so. We hurried into the tent and opened her trunk. We found a small brown bottle containing lanolin, scented with cinnamon. After tearing strips of cloth from one of my petticoats, we sat by Papa in front of the fire and soothed this oil into his bleeding palms, then bandaged them. Clara rubbed his shoulders.

When he smiled up at us, my heart melted. I am worried about him. He is not used to such hard work.

The thin leather strap on Papa's money pouch broke, so I made a new one. I braided together some string with one of my old red hair ribbons, then threaded this new strap through the pouch opening. It is sturdy without being too fancy.

FRIDAY, THE 30TH OF MARCH

Hooray! Clara has given up her corset and packed it away with Mother's things. It hurts her ribs, she said. And she didn't like so many men staring at her womanly figure.

We spent yesterday and today sewing the blue calico Papa bought in San Francisco. Now we each have a loose-fitting dress that hangs from our shoulders. We do not want to look exactly alike, so we made ourselves collars from the torn petticoat; hers is plain white, mine has a laced edge. Clara's sleeves button at the wrist, mine are rolled up to the elbows. She wears a long white apron tied at her waist with a big bow, I wear none. Aprons get in the way. If I need to wipe my hands or my nose, I'll just bend over and use my hem.

In my opinion we look rather plain, but Papa doesn't think so.

When he came into camp after his day of standing in the river, he set his shovel down and opened his arms to hug us. "My beautiful girls," he said.

MORNING, BEFORE BREAKFAST

Last night the Captain told stories around the fire. My eyes grew wide when we learned he is descended from the English pirate, Old Clinkingbeard, who wove pieces of broken glass into his beard to scare his enemies. The name carried down through six generations of honest sea captains, the seventh being our new friend. But some months ago, when he sailed into San Francisco Bay, his sailors jumped ship, every single one of them. With no money to hire a new crew, he hung a white flag of surrender from the bow of his schooner. Then he himself headed for the hills.

I like Captain Clinkingbeard. When he laughs or rubs his chin, the bells in his beard make a sort of gentle music. I wish Mother could have met him. She admired people who weren't like everyone else.

Monday, the 2nd of April

Wash day. If Mother were here, we would boil water in a kettle with soap, then scrub, then boil again for a clean rinse. It would take all day, which means we would have to start before sunrise in order to hang the clothes out long enough to dry. It would be supper-time by the time we folded and put away everything.

Well, since we have no kettle or soap, we just use a shallow eddy of the river. There is a large, wide rock offshore that we can leap onto. From here we bend over the water with Papa's shirts and whatever else is dirty. A few dips and we're done. To dry, we shake things out, then spread them over bushes in the sun. And all this is done before noon, before the sun is overhead.

I forgot to mention that three men were killed last week when the mine they were digging caved in on top of them. Their friends auctioned off their tools and clothes. That is how Papa got his second pair of trousers and blue suspenders; now with his boots and slouch hat he looks quite like a miner.

Friday, the 6th of April

Yesterday several wagons pulled by mule teams came into town. The rattle of their harnesses and wheels brought most of us out to look. There was great excitement as goods were unloaded, mainly premade buildings that had been shipped in flat bundles from around the Horn. I am now sitting on our rock in the water, writing to the noise of hammers echoing off the hills. Men are putting up new stores and painting signs with bright yellow and red letters. I can see a bakery, a smithy, two hotels, and a grocery that sells fancy goods. There are more tents, too, as every day new gold-seekers arrive. A hoosegow was also built, that is, a jail.

Someone even set up a chicken coop, so soon there will be fresh eggs. The rooster struts through town as if he's the marshal.

Sunday, the 8th of April

A quiet day.

Sunshine warmed our camp early, making it pleasant to be outside without our shawls. After breakfast the Captain leaned against a tree stump to read. Papa sat nearby, smoking his pipe. Despite all the new buildings there still are no churches in Miner's Creek, so we took turns reading from the Bible and sang a few hymns from memory. Even on Sundays we see a lot of men digging or swirling their pans in the river or driving their mules. Many work every day all day long, not stopping until sundown; there's the constant sound of picks striking rock.

Papa says a man should rest his animals and himself one day a week so that they can do well the other six. He doesn't care if these men find more gold than he does or if they will end up richer.

"I don't need a mansion," he said to us at supper. "Just a place where you girls and I can plant a garden."

"Doc, I'm with you," said Captain Clinkingbeard. "No matter how much we have, there's always gonna be some fellow with more. That's the truth."

The four of us have decided to share meals. It is no extra work for Clara and me, just one more spoon and plate to wash, that's all. As Papa sopped up his gravy with a chunk of bread, I noticed his hands are no longer the graceful hands of a surgeon. They are red from the sun and cold water; his blisters have turned to hard scabs. I think he has more courage than I ever will.

Yesterday afternoon we all walked into town to visit the assayer. This is the man who weighs, tests, then buys the gold that men find. His office is a narrow shack between two saloons. He took Papa's pouch and poured the little yellow specks onto his scale. What Papa dug up last week came to five dollars' worth, much less than what he could have earned doctoring. I watched his face for disappointment, but there was none. He smiled enough that his mustache lifted, then he looked at us. "Let's go see about those eggs you wanted."

The store had a basket of straw out front with fresh hen eggs, ten dollars a dozen. Papa looked at the coins in his hand, then went inside. He pointed to a crate sitting on the floor. It was filled with what looked like oranges, but they were blue! A sign said FRESH CORMORANT EGGS, $6 A DOZEN. The man behind the counter said the cormorant is a large sea bird that dives into the waves for fish.

With his earnings Papa bought four of these big blue eggs, some dried figs, and a sack of flour. These things arrived yesterday by stagecoach from San Francisco. This same coach then left this morning with sacks of gold to be minted or deposited into banks.

When we were ready to leave, the storekeeper gave Clara and me each a square of chocolate candy wrapped in waxed paper. Its aroma was so delicious that I ate mine right away, before I was one foot out the door. Not Clara. She tucked hers into her sleeve to save for later. When we were outside, she whispered that ladies are not supposed to gobble up sweets.

I was furious at her all day for saying that.

WEDNESDAY, THE 11TH OF APRIL

A horrible thing . . .

Early this morning Clara and I went to the river to wash our faces. As we were scooping up the water with our hands something big floated by, just inches from us. It was a man! But he was on his back with dead staring eyes. We were so startled that not until he drifted beyond our reach did we see the knife in his chest. We screamed for Papa.

Now it is evening. Nothing is known about the miner except that he was murdered and his killer hasn't been caught. One of his friends has been showing around the knife, but no one has seen it before.

MONDAY, THE 16TH OF APRIL

I have been too busy to write. Papa and the Captain are building us a cabin! It has taken three days for them to chop the trees and cut grooves for corners, but now the walls are going up. The door faces the river. Soon we will be warmer at night and safer. Papa wants us to have a door to lock in case he and the Captain must be away overnight. The murderer is still on the loose.

When Clara and I began carrying rocks from the river up to the cabin, we were surprised by some men who wanted to help. I say surprised because they were Peruvians we met aboard the *California.* Their camp is downstream. I asked about Rosita but they didn't understand until I brought out the colorful shawl she had given me. *Oh, yes,* they said, smiling, and pointed toward their camp. I don't know why it makes me so happy to think she is nearby, but it does. I can't wait to visit her.

They helped Papa build our stone chimney and fireplace in just two days. The rocks are stuck together with mud.

This will be our first night to sleep under our own roof, a real roof, since last October.

WEDNESDAY, THE 18TH OF APRIL

Rain for two solid days. No sooner did Papa and the Captain wedge in the final log overhead and tack down a tarp than the skies opened up. The river is running high and from our open door we see no one standing in the shallows panning. Miners are taking cover in their shacks or in town, going from one saloon to the next. The street is a swamp of mud.

Our cabin is plain, but cozy. A low fire keeps the room warm. We are using Mother's trunk as a table and sitting on the floor when we eat. In the corner by our bed we hung a curtain of canvas made from our tent; this protects us from drafts while we sleep and also allows Clara and me to dress in privacy. Papa has a bunk on the other side of the room. Right now he is playing checkers with the Captain.

Everywhere I look there is something useful.

Shelves near the fireplace hold our flour and eggs, some tins of fruit, and our drinking cups. We are keeping our pans and Dutch oven on the stone hearth, ready for cooking. Papa made hooks for our clothes from deer antlers he found in the woods. His shotgun hangs over the top of the door. For light we have candles and two oil lamps. We have arranged all of Mother's books along the top of the crate.

This morning when I was at the hearth frying bacon I noticed that Papa was looking through Mother's trunk, touching the fabric of her clothes. After some moments he took out his black bag and ran his hands over the leather. I turned toward him, wanting to say something — I don't know what — but he shut the lid and hurried out the door.

He misses Mother, I know it without words. And I think he misses being a doctor.

NEXT DAY

Happy news! Our old friend Jesse Blue saw Papa's note at the saloon and ran to find us. He was out of breath when he knocked on our door last evening. I almost didn't recognize him because of his full beard and sunburned cheeks. He picked me up by the waist and swung me in a half circle. But when he saw Clara he removed his hat and held it over his heart.

"Such a lady now," he said to her. "Two years since I've seen you last and aren't you the picture of your mother. . . . Where is she?" He looked around, then nodded toward the curtain. "Sleeping?"

There was a moment of pained silence. The whole image of what had happened to Mother played through my memory but I could find no way to explain. Finally Papa cleared his throat.

"Julia went to be with our Lord," he said. Our cabin was so quiet that when a log in the fireplace rolled into the coals, its thump startled us.

Jesse took a deep breath. "Oh, Doc, I'm sorry." Then looking at Clara and me, he swallowed hard as if words were stuck in his throat, but he said nothing.

After he left we went to bed. I stared up at the log ceiling and listened to the crackle of the fire. Somehow, by Papa saying aloud that Mother was gone, it became more real. The loneliness I now felt for her was so sharp. Clara and I lay there for some time, quietly holding hands.

Also, I was thinking about Jesse's trip from

Missoura, across the prairie and deserts. He had loss as well. Clara and I fell silent when he told about his nephews. One died from a rattlesnake bite and two were poisoned after mistaking hemlock for wild carrots. Agonizing deaths, all of them, he said. Soon after this, Jesse and his wife were forced to abandon their wagon with all their belongings when their oxen died. By the time they arrived in Oregon, they had nothing but the clothes on their backs.

"Every treasure we owned is rotting in the middle of some desert," he said. So when he heard that gold was discovered, he headed for California along with hundreds of other men from Oregon.

Friday, the 27th of April

Nearly one week since I've written.

The placer Papa and the Captain were mining near our cabin has no more gold, so they hiked upstream to find better diggings. They packed a mule with their tools, bedrolls, the Captain's tent, and our shotgun so they'll be able to hunt for food. Papa gave us his money pouch, wrapped tight with the red strap; inside was eighty dollars in silver coins.

"I'll be back as soon as I can." He reminded us to latch the door at night and said he had arranged for some of the shopkeepers to check on us.

The day after they left we woke to a thundering rainstorm and a crack of lightning that was so loud Clara and I bolted up in bed. The walls of our cabin shook as if something had struck it; our tin plates rattled off the shelf down to the floor. Clara threw her shawl over her shoulders and ran to the door; I followed. Rain hit our faces as we peeked outside. A huge pine tree had fallen so close to our cabin, branches were touching it. We tried to push our way outside, but the limbs were heavy and prickly. We were trapped.

"Papa!" we cried. I began to feel panic. Our father was too far away, we knew that, but still we called for him. Would anyone else hear us through the noise of this storm? We left the door open for light and stirred up the fire in our hearth because cold air and rain were coming in.

To console ourselves we baked a little pot of beans with pork and ate them with biscuits saved from the night before. We stared out at the wet tree. It might be hours before anyone would notice what had happened to us. It would take many men with mules to drag the tree away from our door. We had enough food to last a couple of days, but only a small jug of water. It would be empty by evening.

Suddenly I remembered Papa's black bag. I hurried to open Mother's trunk and pulled it out. When I held up the saw, Clara caught her breath. It was a tool Papa used in surgery, to amputate legs, arms, or fingers. Once I watched him cut off a man's broken foot that had turned black with gangrene. The operation was successful, that is, the man lived, but it was horrible to see.

And with this same saw we made a narrow little path from our cabin to the river.

All day long we took turns sawing and peeling away tiny branches. We also took turns drying off in front of the warm fire because the rain chilled us. Finally there was enough space for us to step over the larger limbs and through, like a tunnel. Our arms hurt they were so tired, our hands were scratched and sticky. I don't think we'll ever get the sap out of our dresses. By sunset the storm had softened and men were stumbling out of the saloons. Some of them noticed the fallen tree and came by for a closer look.

"Hello!" we shouted. "We're in here!"

"Well, boys," one of them said, "at least they ain't dead." Then they turned back toward town.

Clara and I looked at each other in disbelief. *How could they just walk away?* Those men made me so mad I leaned out through the tree and yelled at them. Clara pulled me inside and slammed the door.

"Susanna!" she cried. "Don't. It's foolish to make stupid men angry. We must be wise. Papa isn't here to protect us."

I think it's true that mining camps are full of ne'er-do-wells. It seems that as soon these fellows have gold in their pockets they spend it on drink.

NEXT DAY

We are alone in our little cabin, missing Papa more than ever. This morning we realized this is the first time we've been without both our parents. No friends or family either. Sometimes I feel so lonesome my forehead aches from trying not to cry. I wish we had gone to Oregon after all. Truth be told, I now wish we had never sailed from New York in the first place.

This morning we looked through Mother's trunk

until we found her butterfly net. We took turns holding it in the stream from our washing rock and after an hour caught two speckled trout. Fried up with bacon grease and pepper, they were a delicious breakfast.

MONDAY, THE 30TH OF APRIL

Last evening after Clara and I were in our night-dresses we heard a man outside, calling our names. We listened hard, trying to recognize the voice, but were afraid to open the door.

We wrapped ourselves in our shawls, blew out the lamp, and waited. When he called again, then he said he was Jesse Blue, we still didn't answer.

Finally Clara lay her cheek against the door and called out, "If you are who you say you are, tell us the childhood name of our mother and where she was born."

The man laughed, then answered correctly: Julia Campbell from Boonesville, Missoura. And he remembered our pet rooster named Caesar.

We flung open the door and waved Jesse in through the path.

AFTER BREAKFAST

Jesse stayed until ten o'clock last night, helping us with chores and telling us about Papa. He fetched two pails of water for us and with his axe he chopped wood for our fire. He did not use the branches we'd sawed off because that wood is too green; it wouldn't burn and its sap would make terrible smoke. While he is in town for supplies, he will find some fellows to haul away our tree.

What cheered us up was his news about Papa's claim and his. They are several miles up in the hills and are so close together they can holler to each other back and forth. Our father is well, Jesse said, and working hard. Come nightfall everyone gathers around their campfire to hear Captain Clinkingbeard's stories about pirates.

Clara and I tore paper from this journal and wrote a quick letter to Papa. We folded it, then dripped wax from our candle over the edge. To seal it we pressed a little stone into the wax before it hardened, then handed the letter to Jesse. In exchange he took out a small cloth pouch and gave it to Clara. When we realized he was giving us some of his own gold, we handed it back.

"We'll make do until Papa returns, but thank you kindly."

BEFORE BED

There has been another murder.

The day Jesse left we walked to town for eggs and dried fruit. Wildflowers are blooming along the sunny parts of the river so we picked a bouquet and put it into an empty bottle we found in the grass. A crowd of men was gathered in front of the hotel. Voices were loud. I started to ask them what they were saying, but Clara held my arm.

She said it is not polite for ladies to approach men without a proper introduction.

I don't know how my sister knows everything, or she thinks she does; she's only sixteen. I am sick of her bossing me around. So when we were in the store I asked the grocer what the fuss was all about. He told us a young blacksmith had been murdered last night behind one of the saloons.

Presently it is eight o'clock and Clara and I are ready for bed. We're glad no one has come to chop away our tree. For all we care, it can block our door until Papa comes home, however long it takes him. It makes us feel safe.

Our bouquet of white, violet, and yellow flowers looks lovely in its "vase." There are so many empty bottles and jars strewn around camp we've begun gathering them. They're all colors: green, red, brown, blue, clear. We've arranged them outside along the western wall of our cabin, poking them upside down into the soft earth. With the afternoon sunlight playing through the glass they are a pretty sight. Other things we found and brought home are an empty cracker tin, a ladder-back chair, and a shovel with most of its handle broken off.

From our leftover calico Clara sewed me a sunbonnet to match my dress. I'm not so mad at her now.

Clara and I are sharing *The Last Days of Pompeii.* She reads at night while I write in my diary; I read in the morning after chores. It's a historical novel set around A.D. 79, very interesting. We discuss it in depth and wish Mother were here to give her opinion as well.

TUESDAY, THE 1ST OF MAY

After buying groceries we now have sixty-three dollars. We have hidden Papa's money pouch in the tin we found. The tin is wide enough for this journal to fit inside, but flat so it can slip under my pillow.

Caught five trout this afternoon. We fried up two, then hung the others on a string and gave them to our favorite storekeeper. He gave us a nice red onion in exchange.

BEFORE BED

After breakfast we did our chores quickly, then packed a picnic of buttered bread and figs. As we were leaving, we swept the dirt in front of our cabin so we'd know if anyone tried to get in while we were gone.

For nearly an hour we walked downstream, toward the Peruvian camp. Along the shallows men were squatting in the water, swirling their wide pans with gravel as they searched for gold.

As soon as we came around a bend in the stream, we saw a clearing with several tents and a large fire for cooking. Rosita was standing in the sunshine, hanging shirts on a rope strung between two trees. When we called her name, she set down her basket and ran toward us. Such a happy reunion. We had parted two months ago thinking we would never see one another again.

We were surprised she has learned more English, and also surprised to see that she is going to have a baby!

Her brothers are placer-mining along this fork of the river and up some nearby creeks. Rosita's husband, Tomás, called hello and waved us over to where he stood ankle-deep in the stream. He and another man have built a wooden box about three feet long with ridges in the bottom, like a washboard. One of them shoveled dirt into it, and the other poured water from a pail. All this washed over a smaller box inside that looked like a sieve. They then rocked it back and forth like a cradle to strain out the gold flakes. It is much more complicated than with just a pan, so I asked why they do it this way.

Tomás said that to sit all day in a cold river was to bring an early death.

With sudden alarm I thought of Papa, remembering

how chilled he was after a day in the water. I worry about him getting sick because he's not used to such rough work. The next time Jesse Blue comes into town he must tell us how to find our father so we can hike up to visit him.

Clara and I helped Rosita hang the rest of her wash, then sat with her by the fire where she had buried twenty potatoes in the coals. When we noticed she was using a miner's pan to fry onions, we asked where all her cooking things were, for we'd seen her using pots and a skillet aboard the ship.

"Yankee come and take everything," she said, "and told us go back to Peru." There was no anger in Rosita's brown eyes, just weariness.

There are other foreigners, she said, who have been beaten and robbed of their tools. Chinese especially. She pointed to two of them with shovels, digging into the side of a hill. They wore wide straw hats but did not have the usual braid hanging down their backs.

"Yankee cut their hair off," Rosita said. "To shame those poor boys."

I was upset to hear these things.

At noon we rested by a stream. We shared our figs

with Rosita; she gave us each a roasted potato. When we were thirsty, we leaned over the grassy bank to drink from our cupped hands. Such good, cold water.

We returned home before dark; the dirt in front of our cabin was smooth except for tiny paw prints of rabbits and squirrels. No humans. Clara and I have rekindled our fire, and there's a nice pot of soup simmering on the coals. All the way home we talked of wanting to help Rosita, but we're not sure how.

NEXT DAY

Pork and beans for breakfast with dried apples. We are out of coffee.

A little burro that lost its mother was wandering through town. This morning when Clara and I saw some boys kicking it, we lifted the hems of our skirts and raced over. This time my sister did not stop me. I picked up some stones and threw them at the boys' feet, not to hurt, but to let them know we meant business. Clara peeled a thin branch from a tree and began whipping their legs until they finally ran from us.

We wrapped our arms around the burro's neck

and spoke softly. It was shaking and it felt bony, as if it hadn't been eating. While Clara stroked behind its ears, I pulled the long blue ribbon out of my braid and tied it around its fuzzy neck. Its head reaches only to my waist; it is that young.

So that is how we came to have a pet. After we led her to the stream to drink, we took her to our campsite and fed her some oats and a scrambled egg. Then we carved out a thicket from the fallen tree and made a bed of pine boughs. The little thing fell right asleep, her legs curled underneath her small body. During supper we decided to name her Lilly.

SATURDAY, THE 5TH OF MAY

I am writing by our small oil lamp. Clara is already asleep. Our faces are sunburned because we forgot to wear our bonnets and we were outside all day.

After breakfast we scrubbed the plates in the stream then packed another picnic. We had made a harness and little saddle for Lilly from one of Mother's aprons and some straps of leather. To this saddle we tied on our Dutch oven, our frying pan, and a sack filled with spoons and plates we wanted to give Rosita, and some flour we bought yesterday. We did not bring eggs because we were afraid they would break.

Rosita was thrilled with our gifts but worried we were doing without.

Our family is small, we told her. Rosita has all those brothers and needs more cooking things than we do.

We helped her sweep out the tents and fill her water buckets. Her baby will come at the end of July. She said if only her dear mother had journeyed with her to California, there would be no troubles with the birth.

I told her not to worry, that Papa has delivered hundreds of babies. Clara looked at me as if to say, *But we don't know where he is.*

Will blow out the lamp now. The nights seem so much darker and longer without Papa. He's been gone for just a week, but we wish he would come down from the hills soon.

MONDAY, THE 7TH OF MAY

This morning Clara and I hurried through our washing chores. With just two of us we have only a few things: aprons, handkerchiefs, and such.

The days are getting warm, though it is still cold

in the shade. Our garden of colored glass grows with each new bottle we find. Now we've made a pretty path down to the river. Lilly grazes nearby and follows us at a trot when we walk into the woods or into town. Those boys don't bother her anymore because Clara carries a switch and I keep pebbles in my pocket. They see us coming and quickly turn around. Some of them work in stores with their fathers, others were cabin boys who jumped ship in San Francisco. I don't know if they are miners or just loafers.

I am writing this outside, on what has become our favorite rock, the one offshore where we fish and wash clothes. Clara is reading a pamphlet of Shakespeare's poems, but I think really she is dozing because her head keeps dropping to her chest. The sunshine makes me sleepy, too, and the splash of the river reminds me of being at sea. Water flows past our rock as if we were on a ship going fast.

LATER

We saw Jesse Blue this afternoon at the assayer's office, selling his nuggets. Papa loved our letter, he told us, and is still working hard. He and Captain

Clinkingbeard built a Long Tom, which is bigger than the cradle and works even better for sifting gold. Just as I was asking him where exactly Papa's camp was, a fight broke out with gunshots in front of a saloon. There was so much dust and shouting Clara and I hurried away with Lilly.

Now it's time for bed. We still don't know how to reach Papa's camp. Another thing bothers me: The tree blocking our door is beginning to dry out; the pine needles are brown and dropping fast. Clara thinks we need to move it away from the cabin because a spark from our chimney could turn it into a torch.

It is not easy to sleep with worries. I wish Papa were here. We comforted ourselves with sponge baths this evening. The hot water felt wonderful on my face, but we long to have a real soak in a real tub. Before I blow out the lamp, I'm going to start reading one of Mother's favorite books, *Jane Eyre*, by Charlotte Brontë. Clara just finished it.

TUESDAY, THE 8TH OF MAY

Last night Clara and I awoke to noises that horrified us. We sat up in bed, straining to see through the dark cabin. I was afraid to breathe. It sounded as if someone was outside, pushing his way through the tree to our door.

We crept across the cold floor to look out through a crack between logs. Darkness was all we saw. I wished we had Papa's gun or the frying pan we had just given to Rosita.

We could hear the snap of small branches being stepped on and the rustling of larger ones being pushed aside. My heart raced with fear. There was a sound of someone or something breathing heavily, and there was a terrible stink. Not like whiskey, but an odor like rotting cheese.

I felt so alone standing there in my nightdress and bare feet, too afraid to even whisper. My sister and I clung to each other, waiting. We listened to the footsteps slowly circle our cabin, then pace along the wall of our chimney. At long last, the noise faded away into the woods. When we thought it was safe, Clara lit a candle so we could look outside for our little burro. Lilly was in her nest, awake but shivering, protected by the tree's thick branches.

After breakfast we went together to fill our bucket and to wash dishes. That's when we saw the prints in the soft dirt. They were from some animal, huge ones, bigger than my own hand spread out. A miner standing in the river answered our call to please come look.

"Grizzly," he said.

It is windy tonight and the air smells like rain. Clara and I are ready for bed. We have latched the door and rolled heavy stones in front of it. A low fire is burning in the hearth in case we need to make a torch. The miner told us that flames are about the only thing that will scare away a grizzly.

SUNDAY, THE 13TH OF MAY

We are worried about the bear, but more worried about our dry tree catching fire. So on Tuesday we asked one of the storekeepers if he could find some men willing to help us drag the tree away. He came to our cabin that evening with two hatchets and a ball of twine, then apologized that no one else was willing to help.

Never mind. Clara and I have been chopping branches all week. We gathered bundles, tied them with string, then hooked them onto Lilly's harness. Every couple of hours we rested from our wood-cutting by walking with our pet a short distance from camp to dump the wood. If there's a forest fire everything will burn, but at least we won't be trapped in our cabin.

The long tree trunk is still there, but with the branches gone we were able to roll it a few yards away. It is quite heavy. Every day we listen and look out for the bear.

Papa's been gone two weeks.

MONDAY, THE 14TH OF MAY

It took longer to do wash this morning because our calicoes were so dirty. But while things were drying in the sun, Clara and I put on our traveling dresses from our sea voyage and walked with our burro to visit Rosita. When she heard about our tree, she called to her husband in Spanish. Within an hour he and four of her brothers had axes over their shoulders and were escorting us back to our camp.

From the tree trunk the men cut four pieces and brought them inside for us to use as stools. Then from the thickest part of the trunk they cut a piece that stands about two and a half feet high. They rolled it into the middle of our room and settled it with its flat side up — so now we have a round table.

Clara found a pretty white cloth among Mother's things, which we have spread over our new table. In the center is a tin can filled with wild red roses we picked from along the river. The room is most homey. We wish Papa were here to enjoy it with us. Clara and I find ourselves talking more and more about our mother, and without tears. *She would love these flowers. . . . Mother would be pleased with the way we keep house. . . .*

I almost forgot — Rosita gave us a straw hat she found floating down the river. With her help we cut two holes in the top and fit it over Lilly's tall ears. Then we tucked some wild daisies into the crown. Just looking at our dressed-up donkey we laugh and feel hopeful.

NEXT DAY

Our flour and sugar are low so after chores we will go into town. First, to tell how we cooked our eggs this morning.

The shovel we found is made of stiff metal. We

washed it in the river, scraping away the dirt with our penknives — our fingers were numb from the cold water after this! Clara set the shovel in our fireplace to heat over the coals; its broken handle is just long enough for us to grab without burning ourselves. I rubbed bacon grease over the surface, which curves up like a skillet, and then when the grease sizzled, Clara cracked in seven eggs. They fried up nice and golden. We ate them with biscuits and dried apricots.

Just fifty-six dollars in Papa's money pouch. We hope he returns soon.

THURSDAY, THE 17TH OF MAY

This was the worst day in Miner's Creek.

After breakfast Clara and I were down by the stream cleaning the shovel and our plates. We could see into town. When we noticed that Jesse Blue was walking out of the new bakery, my sister and I looked at each other.

Why does he come into town so much, but Papa doesn't?

We quickly put away our utensils and tied on our

bonnets and clean aprons. As we marched toward town our little burro followed us, braying with concern. In front of the assayer's we adjusted her hat and told her everything was going to be all right. I don't know if she understood us, but she is as loyal as a dog — we don't have to tie her up.

Jesse Blue was inside. He smiled when he saw us and held out a small pouch. "Take it, it's from your father. One solid ounce."

Clara opened it and poured the golden flakes into her palm, about a teaspoon's worth.

An ounce is worth sixteen dollars. I thought to myself that Papa has been gone for three weeks and he is working awfully hard to make so little money. I didn't thank Jesse because there was only one thing on my mind.

"Draw us a map so we can find Papa's camp." I expected Clara to scold me with her eyes for not saying "please," but her gaze was also on Jesse.

He promised he would come by this afternoon with a map, but it is presently 8:30 in the evening and Jesse Blue is nowhere in sight. One minute we are furious at him for breaking a promise, the next we are worried that something may have happened to Papa's old friend.

There's something worse, though.

After supper, when I reached under my pillow to pull out our tin, I noticed the lid was on crooked. Carefully I opened it to take out my diary. My breath caught in my throat.

Papa's pouch was gone.

Clara and I are distraught that a thief came into our cabin while we were away. Nothing else seems to be missing, but we are still upset. What I didn't tell her is how angry I am that a stranger may have read these pages, my intimate thoughts and feelings.

Mother would not approve of this, but we now bring Lilly into the cabin every night. I don't know why the grizzly didn't eat her that night, but we're not taking any chances. We've made a soft bed for her from the hay the storekeeper brought us, and hung up her hat. She sleeps in front of the door. If anyone tries to get in, he will bump into Lilly and she will not be happy. When our burro is mad or worried, she brays so loud she sounds like a goose. Her cry will wake us and, we *hope*, scare away the intruder.

On the subject of thieves, the murderer has not been caught.

Friday, the 18th of May

We spent today sweeping out the cabin and doing wash. The weather is so pleasantly warm we prefer to be out in the fresh air. Unless our door is propped open, it is gloomy to be inside the cabin. Clara and I want to put in a window, but there is no glass in town for sale and even if there were, we have only Papa's sixteen dollars that Jesse gave to us.

As for reporting the thief, we don't know whom to go to, so have said nothing to anyone.

Before bed

Lilly is asleep by the door. Clara is kneading bread that will rise overnight on the hearth. We have been talking all evening about what happened earlier. I will write quickly so we can get to bed and talk more.

This afternoon we were in the store buying ginger to bake a spice cake. A man leaned against the counter talking to the owner as if they were good friends. This man glanced at me, then feasted his eyes on Clara, with a slow grin. His teeth were brown with tobacco juice that ran down into his beard.

Horse manure coated the man's boots and his pants were soiled with grease.

Clara turned to me and whispered, "Susanna, let's go."

I placed a nickel on the counter for our little sack of ginger, then met her by the door. As I nodded good-bye to our grocer friend, I noticed something that put chills up my spine.

The man was paying for a plug of tobacco with coins he pulled from a leather pouch. There was no mistaking the braided red strap that I had made for Papa.

Clara had seen it, too, because she squeezed my arm. How I wanted to kick that thief and grab away Papa's pouch, but remembered Clara's words: *We must be wise.* So we quickly left.

Once home we brought Lilly in and rolled more rocks against the door. There was something other than the man's filth that scared us. His eyes were cold. We worry because he knows our cabin and probably knows we're alone. But we don't think he knows that *we* know who he is. He seemed too stupid and dirty to realize that the pouch he stole is unique and could easily be claimed by its owner, our father.

Meanwhile, we will keep this to ourselves. We are more anxious than ever for Papa to return.

Clara has finished with the dough and placed a damp cloth over the bowl. By morning it should be a tall, soft loaf ready to bake. Off to bed now and more talk . . . we are too nervous to sleep. Our poor little burro has no idea how much we are counting on her.

MONDAY, THE 21ST OF MAY

A new development. It is late, nearly midnight. I am writing quickly while Clara wraps some food and blankets for Lilly's pack. We'll leave tomorrow at first light.

While we were sitting by the stream this morning, a miner rushed into our campsite. He was covered with black soot and was crying out for Dr. Fairchild.

Before we could explain about Papa, two men carrying a stretcher came into view. On it was a boy about Clara's age, moaning with pain. His face was bloodied and he was breathing hard. When the men pulled back the blanket and I saw a broken bone sticking out above his ankle, my thought was only of myself: *I will die before I use Papa's saw to do surgery.*

I soaked my handkerchief in the river and gave it

to my sister. As she kneeled over the boy to wash his face, she asked the men what had happened.

They said there was an explosion in a mine up-river. The fuse was short so the black powder exploded too soon. Three boys were killed right away, but Sam was rescued from underneath some rocks. The men demanded to see the doctor.

"He's not here," I said. Clara and I were examining the boy's neck and face, his shoulders and arms, touching gently. We'd seen Papa do this, work his way down the body, searching for injuries. When we came to his ribs, he screamed.

Clara pointed to his chest, where she had felt a broken rib. "If he moves, it will puncture his lung," she said. "We have to wrap him so he'll stay still."

I hurried into the cabin to find cloth to use as bandages, but as I opened Mother's trunk something better came to mind.

Clara's corset.

We cut away Sam's shirt, then gently slipped the corset underneath and around him. As Clara laced up the front, our burro came over and stood beside me. Her nose moved as she sniffed the air. The men watched without saying anything.

When we examined the damaged leg, Clara and I glanced at each other.

"We have to get Papa," she whispered.

I nodded.

So that is what we are doing tomorrow. We will follow the river upstream and ask anyone we see about our father. We are praying that God will guide us to him.

Sam is asleep by the fireplace, on a pallet we made. One of the men who carried him is in Papa's bunk and will stay while we're gone. The reason my sister and I are going instead of the men is we want to urge our father to come home for good. No more mining. We need him, and this boy needs him. Rather than one of us staying behind while the other looks for Papa, we're going to be together. Two are braver than one. And safer.

Because the broken bone is exposed to air, Sam is in so much pain he keeps slipping in and out of consciousness. The whiskey his friends poured down his throat numbed him for only a few hours. Clara hunted through Papa's bag and found a bottle of laudanum. We gave the boy a few teaspoons, and he soon fell into a deep sleep . . . no wonder, it's opium mixed with alcohol.

At long last, to bed. I will take this diary with us because I do not want that man to snoop around and find it.

ON THE TRAIL SOMEWHERE

It is dark except for our fire. Clara and I made camp under a rocky overhang, protected from the wind and wild animals. We are nervous knowing this is grizzly country. I do not like being out here away from our cabin and so far from Papa, wherever he is. At this moment I'm angry with him for leaving us behind. We don't care if he earns back the money he lost at sea. It doesn't matter anymore.

This opening in the rocks is like a wide cave, large enough for us and Lilly to bed down and stay dry if it rains. The only sign that anyone ever camped here is blackened rock overhead, from an old fire perhaps. We are away from the trail, up in a ravine, so we don't think anyone will bother us tonight.

I worry about Sam's broken leg. The wound was

terrible, though we did clean it as best we could with hot water and peppermint leaves. The poor boy begged us to stop, it hurt him so. The bottle of laudanum should last four days.

In a few minutes I'm going to carve Clara's name and mine on the wall, farther in. Then to sleep.

Oh, for supper we boiled potatoes and drank water from the stream. Earlier today some miners told us they didn't know Papa personally, but that there was a fellow everyone calls "Doc" about five miles upstream — we'll head out at first light.

NEXT DAY

I've lost track of the date, but there are two wonderful things to report.

Sometime after noon we were resting by a quiet little creek and letting Lilly graze when we heard a familiar sound. It was the clinking of tiny bells.

Clara and I jumped up and yelled, "Papa . . . Captain!"

They came through the trees, Papa first. He was so thin, I thought we would crush him when we embraced. We all talked at once. To our delight he agreed immediately to return with us, for the boy's sake, and for ours.

This brings me to our second good thing. I saved it until supper when we were around the fire. Captain Clinkingbeard cooked flapjacks and we ate them rolled up with bacon inside. Good hot coffee, too.

"Papa," I said, "Clara and I found something last night." Reaching into my pocket I pulled out a rock and held it in my palm. It was yellowish, the size of a walnut.

He leaned forward in the light to see better. He put it in his mouth and tapped his teeth against it to make sure it was smooth, not gritty. Even through his beard I could see that his cheeks were hollow and there were dark circles under his eyes. My heart skipped with alarm. He was worn out. When he asked where we had found the rock, I held up my penknife.

"Last night, when I was carving our names." Then I told him about the yellow stripe running through the length of our rocky shelter.

"There's more, Papa." Clara opened up our tin, where I'd been keeping my journal. When Papa saw the gold dust and pebbles, and when he felt how heavy they were, he started to speak, but instead a single tear slipped down his cheek into his beard.

More later.

NOON, NEXT DAY

Will write this quickly — we have stopped by a stream for a short rest. Papa and the Captain broke camp before sunrise. Their mule has made friends with our little Lilly. They were nuzzling each other as we loaded their packs.

When we reached our shelter from the night before, Clara and I were flabbergasted to see six men with shovels and picks. We started to march up and tell them to go away, but Papa held us back. He asked if we had staked a claim.

No. Since we were in such a hurry to find Papa we didn't take time to think through everything. We thought if we swept away our tracks and put brush in front of the opening, it would be as we left it when we returned.

The Captain shook his head in sympathy. The ornaments in his long white beard clicked as he rubbed his chin. He called those men "opportunists," said they must have been watching us from afar then moved in after we left.

Clara's face was red as she struggled not to cry. "It's not fair," she said.

"No, it's not," said Papa. "But life's not fair."

As we walked he explained how easy it is to make a claim. All we needed to have done was write our names on a piece of paper, tack it up in front of our spot, then hammer some stakes into the ground marking it off. Or sometimes a person just leaves his tools there to say the place is his. That's it.

I burst into tears, embarrassed by our costly mistake. My misery reminded me of the filthy man who had broken into our cabin so I told Papa about that as well.

He put his hand on my shoulder. "It's my fault for not teaching you girls to file a claim and I never should have left you alone for so long, I'm sorry. As for the thief, a dangerous man is best left alone, especially with no sheriff to enforce the law." Papa said that some injustices we must leave up to God to make right.

HOME AGAIN

Finally, after a month of being apart, our family is under one roof again. Clara and I are so relieved. Papa may not be able to fight off a grizzly, but we know he will keep us safe from terrible men.

Captain Clinkingbeard put up his tent outside next to our wall so he'll be more protected from the weather.

The splint Clara and I made for Sam's leg held together, though the skin around the wound is bright red, spreading in green streaks up toward his knee. It smells bad. The man watching over him for four days kept Sam bathed, but still the room stinks of urine and rotting meat.

Sam was hot with fever. His lips were dry and bled a little as he tried to talk to Papa. "Please . . ." was the only word we heard.

I heated a pot of water so we could all wash our hands. When Papa opened his bag, he looked at his saw through squinted eyes, then looked at us. In whispers we explained about the fallen tree. Sam's friend has hurried the saw to a blacksmith's to have it sharpened. Now we wait.

Sam is sleeping again. Meanwhile, there is enough hot water for Papa to take a sponge bath behind our

curtain. Clara has laid out a clean shirt and dunga-
rees for him.

I am cooking potato soup in a small kettle we found
off the trail, but I don't feel like eating. The thought
of what awaits poor Sam makes me feel sick inside.

WEDNESDAY, THE 30TH OF MAY

Days are hot now. The ground outside our cabin is
carpeted with pine needles that smell wonderful from
the sun. We keep the door open all day for fresh air,
though doing so lets in flies that swarm in the center
of the room.

About Sam. The night we returned, Papa readied
him for surgery, near 11:30. His pallet was raised
onto the log stools to make it easier for Papa to work.
We lit all the candles and lamps, putting them high
on shelves and hanging from beams to cast the
brightest light. Clara and I prayed with the boy and
gave him a good swig of laudanum. He was panicky.

"Don't take my leg, Doc," he pleaded. Papa didn't
answer. The infection was deep, and there was no
way to repair the bone, not in a mining camp anyway.

Clara knelt on the floor and held Sam's head with

her cheek against his, to comfort him. Because of his broken ribs I could not drape myself over his chest to hold him down. Instead, we strapped his hips to the cot; his friend held one arm, I held the other. I watched Papa's face. There was kindness in his eyes and a calm determination to save Sam's life. I felt such love for my father and relief that he was home again.

But suddenly my courage failed and I turned away. As the boy struggled under Papa's saw, I began to cry.

Then it was over.

Later . . . Papa's clean shirt was spattered with blood. So were the bed and floor. We all worked quickly through the night, first caring for Sam, then spreading buckets of clean dirt on the floor. Clara and I took the soiled blankets and clothes to our washing rock, and under the light of a half moon we rinsed everything out. The friend dug a hole beyond the cabin to bury the damaged leg, then piled rocks on top to keep animals away. We took turns watching Sam until dawn.

Presently Papa and Clara are at the assayer's, having our gold tested and weighed. I have been so tired I forgot to ask about Jesse Blue, if he's all right.

We have a smoky fire in the cabin to keep flies and mosquitoes off Sam. His stump is bandaged with strips of my old petticoat that are changed every few hours. To clean the rags, we dip them in boiling water, then hang them in the sun to dry.

Must go. Sam is whispering my name . . . I think he needs a sip of water.

Friday, the 1st of June

We have good news. And bad.

First, the good. The gold Clara and I dug out of that cave with our penknives weighed seven pounds, three ounces. Papa made me do the arithmetic. At sixteen dollars an ounce . . . we now have $1,840.

"That's more than you found, Papa," I said when he returned from town, "in all those weeks of standing in the river." I immediately put my hand over my lips, realizing too late that I should not boast, especially when Papa worked so hard. He looked at me, puzzled.

"What do you mean, you found more than I did?"

My mouth went dry as I thought about this question. We were sitting at our table, sunlight coming in through our open door. The only sounds were outside, the squawk of a blue jay and a squirrel chittering.

Now the bad news.

Papa explained how he sent Jesse Blue to town several times, to give us the gold he had mined. He didn't know exactly how much each sack weighed, but he figured each was as heavy as a frying pan. A few pounds, he knew, probably worth four thousand dollars total. Since Jesse's own claim had run dry and he was penniless, Papa told him he could have five ounces of dust for himself, each time he went to the assayer. Clara and I were speechless. For all of our father's hard work she and I were given just one ounce.

Papa stared out the door, shaking his head.

Clara burst into tears. "It's not fair. . . . I hate gold! It makes people greedy and do bad things."

I was too furious to cry and was full of questions. Did they have a fight? Did Clara and I do something wrong?

Nothing like that, he said. They were friends. Jesse Blue loved us as daughters.

"Then why did he steal from us?" Clara cried.

Papa put his head in his hands. Some moments later he said, "I guess the temptation was too much."

It is late now, almost ten o'clock. Everyone has turned in. I am tired, but too upset to sleep. I must write everything down, but first will give Sam some water and a cool cloth for his head. He is tossing on his cot. He will stay with us so Papa can watch over him until his wound begins to heal. Besides, the cabin he shared with those boys who were killed is no longer his. Several miners moved in and took over. They auctioned off Sam's things because they didn't think he would live.

MIDNIGHT

Back to Papa. He does not want to speak harsh words against his old friend, but the truth is in front of us. We spent the afternoon in town, asking if anyone had seen Jesse Blue. Maybe there's been a terrible misunderstanding, Papa kept saying to us.

Then all hope was lost. The assayer told us Jesse weighed in with dust worth $4,750 and left on the morning stage for San Francisco.

We are heartbroken.

As Papa lay down in his bunk tonight, he stared up at the ceiling. "Daughters," he said, "I would rather be a poor man with honest friends than a rich man with none." He never dreamed Jesse would think otherwise.

The quiet of this late night helps my mind rest. In a moment I'll blow out the candle.

As for that filthy thief who came into our cabin and stole our coins, I was surely mad. But with Jesse Blue, it's different. He was our friend for so many years, Clara and I looked up to him. He knew our mother; she loved him. I am just sick with disappointment . . . his betrayal has shamed all of us.

I remember when Papa, Clara, and I read *A Christmas Carol*, about Mr. Scrooge, the rich man with no friends. We loved the story because Scrooge ended up a changed man with a generous heart. I know anything is possible with God, but I don't know if Jesse Blue cares.

MONDAY, THE 4TH OF JUNE

Wash day. There is more work now, but we don't mind, we're so happy to have Papa home. We also wash clothes for Sam and Captain Clinkingbeard.

News from back East finally reached us here at Miner's Creek: We have a new president of the United States, Zachary Taylor. He was sworn into office three months ago, March 4. This came to us by way of a newspaper printed at Sutter's Fort. Several issues of *Placer Times* were sold at our grocery store for one dollar, that's how we got a copy. Also bought fresh carrots and tomatoes.

At supper I read one of the stories out loud to everyone, but it is a dreadful story.

It seems that a few weeks ago dozens of Yankees made a rule that foreigners are forbidden at Sand Creek Bar, which is not too far from here. They also ran off the Mexican, Peruvian, and Chinese men who were working around Sutter's Mill and Sutter's Fort, told them to go back to their own countries. When some of them put up a fight, vigilantes found a tree and hanged five of them! Then they jumped their claims and stole their gold. Vigilantes are men who take the law into their own hands. Sometimes they are honorable, but often they're just thugs who want everything to go their way.

Clara and I worry about Rosita and her family, but don't know how to protect them from vigilantes. At least Papa is home now and can help with the birth of her baby.

A wagon arrived this morning full of cats! They are strays that a ship captain collected in San Francisco. He is visiting mining camps, selling them for ten dollars each to help with rats that live in the garbage heaps. Papa bought us a kitten, a little gray thing with white paws. We named him Sergeant Boots.

This reminds me . . . before sundown I walked along the river to stretch my legs. It seemed that someone was following me, but every time I turned around nobody was there. Then a noise in the brush startled me. I saw what looked like a deer, but quickly realized it was too low to the ground and too swift, for as quickly as it appeared it ran off.

When I told Papa, he and the Captain returned with me to the spot. They studied the dirt for prints, following tracks up the hillside. Papa's face was pale when he announced that it was a mountain lion. He said from now on Clara and I must never walk alone. We must always keep careful watch of our surroundings for this big cat had been stalking me, he said.

WEDNESDAY, THE 6TH OF JUNE

Well, first it was cats, today it was a bull with horns. It came into camp tied to the back of a wagon and is now corralled by itself, away from the other animals.

Clara and I didn't now why such a creature would be brought to Miner's Creek until we saw posters in town.

Bull and Bear Fight, Come One, Come All No Bets Refused

We asked the storekeeper. He said it's a big event, only they have to catch a bear first. That's what some of the boys are doing now, out hunting a grizzly to bring back alive.

As we walked home we passed a blacksmith. He was hammering iron into a large cage on wheels. Several men with nothing to do stood watching, their thumbs hooked in their suspenders. They were making bets about the bear, whether or not it would fit inside the cage.

When we arrived back at the cabin Papa was out front, sitting by the stream with one of his friends. After introductions the friend explained he has quit panning for dust and now drives a mail wagon between mining camps and San Francisco. He charges four dollars a letter! If the letter then goes onto a ship for other parts of the United States, there are more costs. A thousand dollars a day is what he makes.

The man continued, "There's more money to be made off the miners themselves than by turning the earth inside out. Lord, that's hard work."

I glanced at Clara, but for once I kept my mouth shut. One thousand dollars was a fortune.

At supper I ladled fresh tomato soup into our bowls while Clara sliced johnnycake. Sam sat in the chair, as it is more comfortable for him than a stool. As soon as the Captain prayed over our food, my sister cleared her throat. She told Papa we thought he should hang out his shingle because the town needs a good doctor.

She and I had rehearsed a speech to convince him, so when he nodded, we didn't know what to say. He wiped his mouth with his napkin.

"Daughters, I miss helping people. I don't care if we're poor, my God, I miss it."

BEFORE BED

With our money Clara and I purchased a hipbath from Dell's Fancy Store. It looks more like a feeding trough, but this evening we each took a long hot soak, behind our curtain. It was wonderful.

Papa bought a barrel of flour for forty dollars, but when Clara and I removed the lid we almost fainted. It was full of worms and stank like an outhouse! We rolled the barrel to the river, then dumped it, hoping the fish would eat the worms.

He also bought a pound of butter for six dollars and half a pound of cheese for three dollars. Captain Clinkingbeard paid sixteen dollars for a tin of sardines, two dollars for a tin of tea. Groceries are so expensive, it's no wonder most miners are poor.

Yesterday a grizzly mauled two men while they slept in their tent. Papa was called to help, but it was too late for one of them. The other lost his right ear and right eye and most of his scalp. Papa was able to stitch up his cheek where the bear had clawed him. When Clara and I saw the dead man being carried into town, we couldn't help staring. His face was completely gone and one shoulder had been eaten.

Then as we were walking back to the cabin, we caught a glimpse of the mountain lion in a distant tree. Actually, all we saw was its yellow tail hanging over a branch — the rest of it was hidden. Papa said these giant cats like high places so they can watch their prey. One pounce can kill a girl my size.

My sister and I can't decide what we're most afraid of: wild animals or a murderer who hasn't been caught.

TUESDAY, THE 12TH OF JUNE

We have another pet.

This morning I dipped a cup into our pail that Clara had just filled from the river. When I drank I felt something bump my upper lip. I held the cup up to the light and saw in the water a tiny speckled trout. So Clara washed out one of the bottles from our garden, a clear one, and filled it up in the stream. We made a funnel with a piece of paper to pour the fish down through the neck of the bottle. It is now swimming around in its new home in the center of our table. Sergeant Boots is also on the table, watching the fish closely. I wonder if this is how that mountain lion was watching me.

On the subject of pets, our burro sleeps outside now that Papa has returned home. We made a lean-to in the space between our cabin and the tent. With fresh hay on the ground it is quite cozy for her.

During the day we put Lilly in the corral with the mules and donkeys so she won't feel lonesome. She wears her hat only when we take her someplace, because the other animals try to nibble it.

SATURDAY, THE 16TH OF JUNE

Today is Papa's birthday. Clara and I made a cake in our shovel, by setting a miner's pan over it like a lid. Since it was three layers it took three baking times, most of the day, in our outdoor fire. Truth be told, I burned the first two attempts because I took a walk and forgot we were cooking. Anyway, icing was powdered sugar and chopped walnuts.

Rosita and Tomás came for supper and to spend the evening with us. We all fancied up . . . Clara and I wore fresh aprons. Papa, Sam, and the Captain wore clean red shirts with blue suspenders. They looked like members of a fire brigade. We put fresh daisies in Lilly's hat and dressed Sergeant Boots in a little vest that we made out of an old sock. He didn't much like it; he kept trying to push it off with his front paw.

It appears that Rosita's baby will be born sooner than later, for she is quite round in the middle. She is relieved that our father is nearby.

Papa has some new patients. One is the dance-hall lady, but he won't say what the matter is. The others are three fellows up Waterfall Creek. They fell ill from eating mushrooms so Papa tended them until they were back in their right minds. He was paid with a plump hen, which he gave to Clara. She flung it over a tree stump and swiftly chopped off its head with her hatchet. After we plucked it, we roasted it on a spit outside, with plenty of salt and pepper. Cooking indoors makes the cabin too hot.

Back to Papa. Good color has returned to his cheeks and he is looking more robust. Yesterday the storekeeper asked him about Jesse Blue. Papa just shook his head and walked out of the store. Clara and I haven't brought up his name, we all get too upset.

WEDNESDAY, THE 20TH OF JUNE

A grizzly was brought into town, hanging upside down from a pole between its legs, its paws tied together and its jaw muzzled. That's how the men carried it down from the hills. After they shoved it into the cage, someone cut the ropes so it could stand. Its claws were long and curved like daggers. When I saw it tossing its head with an angry noise in its throat, I felt sad. Even if this is the bear that bothered us or mauled those miners, I wish they would let it go free. I wish they wouldn't force it to fight a bull.

The men with nothing to do are now out beyond camp, building an arena. I saw it. It's a large circle of dirt, about forty feet across, with a rail fence surrounding it. An iron stake in the center is where the bear will be chained on the day of the fight. One of the men told me the bear will then attack from a sitting position and try to drag the bull down to the ground. But if the bull is stronger it will hook its horns into the bear. Either way, one of them will be killed.

Distressed by this news, I rushed back to the cabin.

FRIDAY, THE 22ND OF JUNE

Bought groceries today. Bacon is fifty cents a pound, fresh eggs are still ten dollars a dozen, and a pound of brown sugar is sixty-two cents. The man with the chickens now has a milk cow so he makes butter and cream to sell.

There was another killing last night. This time, upstairs in the Blue Sky Hotel. The dance-hall lady found the body and ran out screaming; we could hear her from across the river. This fellow was shot. He bled all over the stairs.

Clara and I worry about a murderer still being on the loose.

I forgot to mention the man who cut his foot on broken glass. Papa gave him twelve stitches and is trying to keep him from walking in the dirt. If the wound gets infected, it could turn into gangrene. The man paid Papa with three ounces of gold dust, equal to forty-eight dollars.

SUNDAY, THE 24TH OF JUNE

We wake every morning to the rooster crowing. We can hear him even above the noise of the rushing river.

Miner's Creek is suddenly deserted, except for most of the shopkeepers. Men have swarmed up to the North Fork of the American River because of a bonanza, that is, a strike, where two huge nuggets were found yesterday. One weighed forty ounces; the other was a bit over *twenty-five pounds*! Clara and I did the arithmetic. At sixteen dollars an ounce the small nugget is worth six hundred forty dollars; the big one nearly seven thousand dollars.

I don't know why one man has a lucky strike but others work hard to find only small bits of dust. Or why Papa wasn't the one to carve his name on that wall instead of Clara and me. He would have known to stake a claim, we did not. I don't understand why some things happen the way they do, such as why Mother was taken from us, but thieves and vigilantes run free. When I get to heaven, I'm going to ask God about all this. It makes my head hurt trying to figure out everything.

LATER

I found a place to hide our money.

Clara and I dug a hole outside in the dirt under Lilly's bed. If anyone were to see us go into her little house, it will appear that we are just saying good night to our pet. During the day when she's in the corral, we rake her bed with clean straw and check to make sure our tin is still buried. It's been nearly a month, and no one has bothered us.

To keep any prowlers from reading this diary, I've hidden it in my satchel, wrapped inside my traveling dress. It's a bother to take it out when I want to write, but I feel more secure.

The days are hot, so we keep the door open. Flies and mosquitoes are a constant irritation, but no different than in Missoura. I'm surprised that I enjoy this heat! Papa explained that California is a drier climate than back home, and being high in the mountains makes the air feel lighter.

Sam is doing better, though his stump pains him greatly. His leg being amputated stopped the infection. Captain Clinkingbeard made him a nice crutch from oak. The handle is polished and smooth so it won't cut into Sam's arm when he leans on it. As soon as he is able to hobble around better, he will find his own place to live. He is a quiet boy, very polite, but I don't feel I can be myself when we're all under the same roof. Sometimes I feel like crying for no particular reason or because I am missing Mother. Sam always looks over at me as if he wants to help, but I do not need help.

Clara is the only one who understands about being a girl. When we get to feeling this way or that, we say, "Excuse us," to Sam as we pull our curtain closed. Then we whisper together or pray or cry in privacy. It seems we miss Mother more, not less. Some days thinking of her makes us smile, other days bring tears. I don't know why.

Finally I figured how we can make a window without buying one. With our hatchets Clara and I chopped a rectangular hole in our eastern wall, about eye level. Into this hole we've placed two dozen colored bottles from our garden, the necks facing outside. We filled the gaps with mud to keep the bottles in place. As we ate breakfast this morning such beautiful light was coming into the room, it reminded me of the stained-glass window in Mother's parlor in Missoura. This memory brings us joy.

MONDAY, THE 25TH OF JUNE

The bull and bear fight will be next Sunday afternoon at two o'clock; cost is three dollars a person. I am curious to see what will happen, but Papa forbids us to watch.

I keep forgetting to write that Miner's Creek grows week by week with more stores and saloons, more miners. Some families with women and small children are up in the hills, but we've not met them yet. There's a gypsy woman in town who set up her tent on the main street. A big sign says PALM READER. Miners flock there because for ten dollars she tells fortunes. They all ask the same thing: *Where will I find the big strike?* Word is that she makes more money than her customers do.

Yesterday we saw a group of Tar Heads fresh from jumping their ship. One of them told Papa that San Francisco Bay now has two hundred abandoned vessels. Goods from all over the world are rotting in the hulls of these ships or are being looted. Some captains have had to put their crews in chains to keep them from leaving.

Papa said that gold fever is turning reasonable men into fools.

SUNDAY, THE 1ST OF JULY

Clara and I discovered a crate of empty bottles behind one of the saloons. We weren't supposed to be walking there, but another gunfight had broken out on the street and we had to run for safety. We took the bottles home and with our axe cut off their lower halves. Then we stuck candles in the dirt by our cabin, lit them, and placed a bottle over each. The colored glass makes such festive light and the necks act as chimneys. We snuff out these lanterns before going to bed.

Sergeant Boots sleeps between Clara and me, on top of our blanket. He purrs quite a lot. I think he's happy with us, but his mouse-hunting job is not going well. Clara said it's my fault because I keep feeding him fish heads.

On the subject of fish, tonight I boiled a large trout in our kettle, one we caught with Mother's butterfly net. When it was cooked enough that meat was sliding nicely off the bones, I noticed something sparkly in the bottom of the pot. Captain Clinking-beard was sitting next to me in front of the fire. He leaned over to look, then smiled. It was gold, he said, sure enough.

Papa showed us how to brush the flakes into a cup where they can dry, then we'll have them weighed. It looks to be about half a teaspoon, maybe eight dollars' worth. From now on we will cook our fish in a pot instead of roasting them on sticks over the fire.

This "bonanza" reminded Captain Clinkingbeard of a story. Before we arrived in Miner's Creek, there was a funeral for a man killed in a gunfight. As his friends were lowering his casket into the hole, they noticed some glitter in the dirt. Immediately the coffin was pulled back up, set aside, and the friends started digging feverishly. After some days the hole had branched off into trenches, and the men were finding nuggets and flakes worth thousands of dollars.

At last they remembered their poor dear friend, but only because the body had begun to stink. So they laid him out under a pine tree and covered him with rocks.

Captain Clinkingbeard said he knows that story is true because he was one of those men. He felt so bad about disgracing his mate his gold fever cooled off. He just hardly cared anymore, about getting rich that is.

After hearing the Captain's tale, I understand why he and Papa get along so well. They just want enough to put bread on their table and sleep under a dry roof. At supper tonight when Papa prayed, he thanked God for providing the fish with gold in its belly.

"Lord," he said, "please grant us enough money so

we won't have to steal to eat, but not so much that we'll forget You. Thank you, amen."

MONDAY, THE 2ND OF JULY

Days are blazing hot. Mosquitoes swarm around our faces every time we step out of the cabin. Near the river they swarm over every inch of us. There is nothing to do but spit them out of our mouths and stand in the smoke of our fire. Winter is the only cure for bugs.

The bull and bear fight for yesterday was postponed due to rain and thunder. The fight will be today in about an hour, so we are leaving town. Papa and Captain Clinkingbeard will be hiking around to check on patients. One miner needs some teeth pulled; another is suffering from chest pains. They live up Foxtail Creek.

Sam will stay here at the cabin. He's up and about now, but will never be able to get out into the hills unless it's on the back of a mule. His ribs have healed enough that Papa said he could take off Clara's corset. We washed it, dried it in the sun, then packed it away in Mother's trunk.

Just the other day I noticed Sam's eyes are beautiful. They are green. He has a pleasant smile and soft brown hair that falls to his shoulders. When he says my name, "Susanna," he says it gently, as if it's part of a song. I enjoy his company. When it's my turn to change his bandages, I ask him lots of questions. He is eighteen years old and has an identical twin brother who is mining down at Mokelumne Hill. They and the rest of their family emigrated to Oregon City last year, coming all the way from Missoura, my home state.

Anyway, about today . . . Clara and I are packing a picnic with some small gifts for Rosita. Even though we'll be gone just a few hours, I'll take this journal so Sam won't be tempted to read my thoughts. We've dressed Lilly in her hat, fresh fern leaves adorning the brim. I wanted to carry Sergeant Boots with us, but Clara said that was nonsense. Cats are supposed to stay home, not go on picnics.

EVENING

Things are not going the way we planned. I'm writing by lantern light, in Rosita's tent, which is where we'll be tonight.

This afternoon when the sun was still two hours high, we began packing to go home. Rosita was lifting a pan of cornbread for us to take when she gave a little gasp. I thought a pail had tipped over because the ground around her feet was suddenly wet. The three of us looked at one another. After a moment Clara's mouth dropped open.

We need to get Papa right away, she said. Rosita's waters have come; that means the baby is coming, too.

Night is also coming. The sky is pink from the sunset, but in the east it is already deep blue with one bright star rising. Tomás insisted that Clara and I stay with his wife, while he and a brother search on horseback for Papa. We told them Foxtail Creek, but we didn't know where it was exactly. And what if there's more than one place by that name? It is growing darker by the minute. Even carrying torches they will find it difficult to see where they're going.

Clara just stepped into the tent with a bowl of hot water, in case we need it. But we've never delivered a baby, we don't know what to do.

Mosquitoes are driving us mad! They buzz in our ears no matter how much we wave them away.

Near Midnight, I Think

I am never going to have a baby! Rosita twists in pain every few minutes. Her face is red and she cries out in Spanish. I don't know what she's saying, but I know she's not happy.

Later

Just took a walk. The air is cool. I stood for a few minutes listening to the river and staring up at the canopy of stars. Across the valley is the dark shape of a mountain, outlined on both sides by speckled sky. It is a beautiful night. But I hurried back to the blazing campfire in case that mountain lion is nearby.

Clara is washing Rosita's face and neck, trying to make her comfortable. We are staying calm for her sake, even though we don't feel calm. I myself am terribly anxious. We've never done this before! I'm angry that Papa's not here, but it's not his fault he's so far away or that the baby decided to come early.

Where is he?

Before dawn, maybe an hour

We have kept the lantern going all night. I am grumpy from no sleep. Rosita was so silent after her last pain that we became frantic, thinking she was dead. At last we realized she was in a deep sleep, that's all, because one minute later she was wide awake and breathless with another pain.

Clara and I have other worries that we keep to ourselves. Throughout these long hours we have heard rustlings in the woods, as if something is watching us. Every so often I carry the lantern outside, hoping its small flame will protect me from animals as I watch the trail for Papa. Just a prick of light in the distance could mean a torch coming our way. But it is dark.

Morning

I am writing this in between sips of strong hot coffee. The campfire smells wonderful from the sausage and hotcakes some of Rosita's brothers are cooking, and the billowy smoke has chased away the mosquitoes.

One of the men just took out his pocket watch, clicked it open, then showed me it is 9:20.

Poor Rosita! She has been laboring for eighteen hours, her voice is hoarse. How I wish her mother or mine were here — even one of the new women from camp could help us, but they are too far away.

Oh — Clara's calling. . . .

NOON

Finally, a moment to rest and write a few words . . .

After Clara called for me, I set my coffee in the dirt and hurried into the tent. She was at that moment lifting a tiny wet baby into her arms.

"It's a girl," she cried. There were tears in her eyes as she wrapped the little thing in a clean apron, then lay her in the crook of Rosita's arm. She has dark black hair, lots of it, and a wrinkled, scowling face. To me, she looked like a gargoyle, but I didn't say so. I'm learning not to speak my every thought.

At the Cabin

By the time Papa arrived, we had cleaned up the bedding, washed the baby in a tub of warm water, and helped Rosita bathe, too.

Papa was astonished that everything went so well and said he might have to hire us as his assistants.

After examining mother and child, he declared both healthy and said Clara may stay with Rosita a few days to help. Papa and I will return then to see how they are and to escort my sister back home.

Tonight Sam and Captain Clinkingbeard are fixing supper, a chicken stew with dumplings. I see a ginger cake cooling on the shelf. Sam is whipping up some cream in a bowl to dribble over the cake. He gets around on his crutch quite well; in fact our dirt floor is dotted with "crutch prints." Sam now bunks with the Captain in his tent.

Before I forget, the baby's name is Esperanza. It means "hope."

There was another grizzly attack up Landlubber Creek. No one was killed, but it carried off a poor howling dog. I should have known the caged bear has a friend or two.

WEDNESDAY, THE 4TH OF JULY

Late, about ten o'clock. I'm on my bed, the curtain closed around me. My candle sits on a little shelf Papa built into the wall above my pillow. It's as if I'm in my own cozy room because Clara is still with Rosita, our first time away from each other. I miss her! I wish I could whisper my secret to her, but for now will write it down. About today . . .

Papa loves the Fourth of July because his grandfather was one of the men who signed the Declaration of Independence. It's an important holiday to our family, so everyone took baths. Papa, Sam, and Captain Clinkingbeard went downstream to clean up. Where the river turns out of sight, there's a waterfall that pours into a pool deep enough for swimming. It is a pretty place, surrounded by boulders and baby pine trees. If my sister and I could be sure of privacy, we would go there daily. But since miners are working nearly every inch of the river, I bathed in the cabin.

After breakfast and chores we all went to town, even Sam on his crutch. The Captain carried a burlap sack over his shoulder with our picnic inside. The day was hot; a thermometer at Dell's Fancy

Store read 93 degrees in the shade. I wore the bonnet Clara made for me, to keep the sun off my face.

Papa wanted to listen to the men giving patriotic speeches. They took turns standing on a platform, built just this morning under the shade of a tall oak tree. Many were long-winded fellows who waved their arms and shouted. Some were miners complaining that foreigners take all the gold.

Finally about two o'clock in the afternoon an elderly white-haired man climbed the steps to the stage. He had fought in our war against England and he described the battlefields and bravery of General George Washington. He became choked up with the memories. When he read the Declaration of Independence, the audience was silent with respect.

After the old gentleman stepped down, the parade began. A band marched in front, which was really just three boys: One played a trumpet, another a fife, and one beat a drum. Then came a wagon with some miners sitting in back, proudly holding up their bags of gold. Six mules pulled the iron cage on wheels with the poor grizzly inside. His fur stuck out between the bars, he was squeezed in so tight. Following the bear came an assortment of men with no particular purpose, dressed in their best shirts and suspenders. It seemed they just wanted to be in the parade.

At last the crowd wandered through the streets, then out to the arena. The aroma of roasting meat came on the breeze. Papa asked what was cooking in the large fire pit.

A man standing next to us said it was the bull that was killed Sunday. The bear will be taken to Gouge Eye mining camp to fight another bull.

Must light a new candle . . .

Back to the picnic. My tenderhearted father did not want us to be around men guzzling whiskey or eating the spoils of a bear fight. So he led us to a meadow where a creek twisted its way among stones and wildflowers. It sparkled in the sunlight and looked so refreshing I quickly took off my shoes and stockings. The ice-cold water felt so good, and the little pebbles under my feet were soft as sand. Had I been alone with Clara I think we might have dunked ourselves, dresses and all.

Meanwhile Captain Clinkingbeard spread the burlap sack onto the grass, then laid out our dinner. Early this morning I had baked biscuits and stuffed them with crispy fried ham, tomato, lettuce, and red onion. We each had a plump juicy orange and a square of chocolate. I washed my sticky hands in the creek and had a drink at the same time. After eating, Papa and the Captain stretched out in the shade of a pine tree to nap. Sam and I were alone. We put our feet in the water (my two, his one) and talked through the afternoon. His eyes welled up when he spoke of his mother at their new home in Oregon.

"She is one of the kindest women on earth," he said. "Like you, Susanna. You are very kind."

I gulped in surprise. As I tried to think of what to say, Sam reached under my chin to untie my bonnet. He let it fall to the grass. I looked at him. His green eyes were gentle, and a breeze was lifting his hair off his shoulders. It struck me that Sam is handsome. He is not a boy at all. Something in me stirred, I don't know what it was, but suddenly I felt so hot I leaned forward to splash water on my face.

"I'm sorry, Susanna, I shouldn't have done that. . . . It's just that your face is so pretty, I wanted to see you better."

This is why I wish Clara were here, she could help me understand.

MONDAY, THE 9TH OF JULY

Today I am fifteen years old. The rooster crowed right on time, but I didn't want to get out of bed, remembering with sorrow that Mother wasn't here to wake me as she always had done. But Clara was up early, cooking breakfast for me. Sunshine was glowing through our colored-glass window and a bouquet of fresh daisies was on the table.

"You're not lifting a finger today," she told me. "I'll do everything, all the chores, everything. Happy birthday!"

Papa presented me with a stool he had secretly made in the cabin of one of his patients. He had painted it a cheerful blue with yellow trim, and it is perfect for sitting outside. This is where I am now, writing with my journal on my lap. I was surprised to receive a gift from Captain Clinkingbeard: a piece of ivory, as white and flat as this page and on it, etched in black ink, is a beautiful drawing. It shows a clipper ship in full sail with a man in the bow and two young girls standing next to him. He called this art "scrimshaw" and said it is how he and other sailors passed their time on long sea voyages.

Clara is kneeling by the stream washing our supper dishes. Sam is sitting by the fire talking to Papa. Since our picnic a few days ago I feel shy when he smiles at me.

LATER, ABOUT 10:00 P.M.

Everyone has turned in for the night so the cabin is quiet. Sergeant Boots is purring in my lap. To continue about today . . .

Clara baked brownies — she knows how I love them — so after supper the five of us sat around our table with a pot of tea. I am missing Mother, but otherwise this was the happiest birthday ever. Sam's gift to me . . . was the best. It all started this morning at sunrise. After breakfast I dressed Lilly in her hat and harness, which Sam loaded with some of his gear. We then walked upriver. He is nearly a foot taller than I am, but he bends over to lean on his crutch. It slows him down a bit, but he moves right along. I often forget he is missing a leg. With the sleeves of his shirt rolled above his elbows I can see that his arms are strong.

When the river branched off to a creek with a wide sandbar, we stopped. Sam pointed with his crutch.

Before us was a claim, neatly marked by four stakes. It blended across the bar into a rocky hillside.

This was his place before the explosion, he told me. Some rough fellows jumped it while he was sick, but the Captain and his shotgun helped him reclaim it. Just this week he has found nearly two hundred dollars.

Sam untied Lilly's pack and pulled out two wide pans. He gave one to me and demonstrated how to dip it in the stream, then swirl gravel. It was cold standing in the water! My dress was soaked up to my knees, but the sunshine beating down on my back kept the rest of me warm. Ten feet away, Sam kneeled on his one knee to work his own pan.

"Susanna," he said after some minutes. "You can come here anytime. Whatever gold you find, it's yours. See?" He nodded toward a piece of paper nailed to a board. I walked over to read it.

NOTICE!

I, THE UNDERSIGNED, CLAIM THIS
PIECE OF GROUND, 900 SQUARE FEET,
FOR MINING PURPOSES AND FOR THE
BENEFIT OF MISS SUSANNA FAIRCHILD.
NO TRESPASSERS ALLOWED.

Signed, Samuel James
June 27, 1849

When I saw my name, I looked at him with questions.

He said Captain Clinkingbeard told him about the mine Clara and I had found, but lost. "You were in a hurry on account of me. Your family saved my life."

I didn't know what to say. I was stunned by his generosity, but wondered why my name and not my sister's. As if reading my silence, he said, "I spoke to Clara and she wants nothing to do with a placer. Maybe you and I can help your father earn back what Jesse Blue stole."

Sam got up, balancing on his leg as water flowed around his boot. He hopped to the beach, then leaned down for his crutch. He came over to me.

"Susanna," he said, "please forgive me if I'm being forward . . . but I love it when you and I are together. . . ." At this, he looked away. His face was red.

I picked up my pan and scooped it along the bottom of the creek, keeping my head down so he wouldn't see my sudden tears. I was overcome with how good he made me feel and wanted to tell Sam that *I* liked being with *him,* but didn't know how. When at last I looked at him, he smiled. Then, as if nothing had happened, we went back to our pans and talked about regular things. We worked for a couple hours, until the sun was overhead.

Must close . . . Clara just asked me to blow out the candle.

TUESDAY, THE 10TH OF JULY

The mail wagon arrived to the usual excitement. Men line up outside the post office, which is really just a cubicle in one of the hotel lobbies. They wait for hours until someone has sorted all the packages and letters.

Sam is the only one we know who's received mail — two notes he read aloud to us after supper. One was from his mother in Oregon City. She had not yet heard about his leg. The other was from his brother, Virgil, who was himself recovering from an injury: Some children playing with a gun accidentally shot off three fingers of his left hand. I think if this dear mother ever sees her sons again, she will faint.

LATER

Clara and I saw the man who stole Papa's money pouch. We immediately looked away so he wouldn't notice us watching him. He was leading a mule across the river into town. Draped over its pack-saddle was a dead bear cub. The sight of this poor little animal made me sad. At supper Papa told us the man tried to sell the bear's fur, but no one in Miner's Creek would buy it.

Papa keeps his gun by the door, loaded. He said he will trust God to deal with this thief, but he must still be ready to protect us from him.

WEDNESDAY, THE 11TH OF JULY

A most terrifying event . . . my hand is shaking as I try to write. It is midnight, Clara and I are alone.

It started when Papa was called away after supper to tend some men wounded in a gunfight. All day the heat had been unbearable. Clara and I wanted to sleep outside under the stars, where the air was cool, but we knew it wouldn't be safe. It was still sweltering inside the cabin, so we decided to leave the door open. We pushed the solid log table to the threshold so it would block anyone from walking in. It left enough space for a breeze, and if Papa returned he could call to us. It seemed a good idea at the time.

It was so hot we slept on top of our blanket in our thin cotton petticoats. I woke to Clara's foot nudging mine. My eyes flew open. There was something in the doorway on the table. I could see its silhouette against the pale moonlight.

Mountain lion.

It was the size of a large, thin dog. Its face was in shadow, but I knew it was looking at us. I could hear Clara breathing fast; my own heart raced with terror. We were trapped. There was no way to reach Papa's gun without moving toward the cat. Because of the heat we had not built a fire in the hearth, so there was no way to make a torch.

I know Mother would forgive us for what we did next. Two of her books were on the floor by my side. Quietly I reached down for them and slipped one to Clara, all the while watching the animal that was staring at us.

Without a word my wonderful sister understood the plan. In one, swift moment she launched her book, then I did the same. Clara hit the mountain lion squarely on its nose, mine struck its cheek as it turned away. When it leapt off the table out into the night, I thought it was the most beautiful horrible thing I'd ever seen.

Papa has not returned, but we've latched the door, of course. Finally I'm calm enough to blow out the candle. We shall lie in the heat, thankful for these four good walls our father built.

THURSDAY, THE 19TH OF JULY

The palm reader studied tea leaves to help the vigilantes catch the killer of those men. She said he would be a foreigner who lives alone. Well, they found him after someone pointed him out. He's in the hoosegow, to be hanged at sunset.

This morning, when Clara and I were at the store, we saw men sawing a hole in the platform where the Fourth of July speeches had been given. The oak tree had a rope draped over one of its branches. As we walked by, we overheard someone say that the murderer was a "no-good Mexican."

We told Papa.

"Why, those men should be ashamed of themselves," he said. "Less than a year ago this whole territory of California belonged to Mexico."

BEFORE BED

Clara and I didn't watch the hanging. Papa had asked us to stay at the cabin; he didn't want us to see such a gruesome sight.

So, at sunset we sat by the river, on our rock. We could hear a rumble of voices, then the crowd burst into cheers. Papa was asked to be there because he's the only doctor around. Someone had to declare the man dead or they'd have to "string him up" again.

When Papa came home, his face was white. Clara and I sat with him by the fire — she rubbed his shoulders and I unlaced his boots. We didn't know how to comfort him.

Some minutes later he sighed. "This fellow was just a lad of seventeen," Papa said. His English was rough, but he kept pleading for people to believe that he had nothing to do with any killing. The one witness who accused him couldn't be found for questioning, yet those thugs went ahead with the hanging.

We are feeling wretched about this.

NEXT DAY

Morning. Just finished breakfast, the dishes are drying outside.

Miner's Creek is astir with unpleasant news. Someone confessed to the murders last night, apparently sorry that an innocent boy was hung.

I am writing this quickly because Papa said we may attend the trial, today at noon.

LATER

So much has happened. Good and bad. First, the good . . .

When we were around the fire last night, Sam asked Papa for permission to court me! Papa was so surprised he took his pipe out of his mouth and said, "What?"

"When I'm around Susanna," he said, "I feel like a

whole man, not a cripple." Sam glanced over at me, then shyly looked down. I wanted to faint, his words were so beautiful. Most of all I admired his courage saying them to my father.

So . . . Papa is going to think about Sam's request. I wish Mother were here to explain certain things such as courting — what is it anyway? I will ask Clara to teach me about hair. Maybe if I wear mine up off my neck, instead of braided, I'll appear more ladylike. When we were in bed, I asked if she was upset with me or if she felt left out.

Not at all, she said. Then she whispered a secret of her own. I'll write of it later.

This morning, before putting on my dress, I tried on Clara's corset. She cinched the ribbons so tight I was miserable. One minute later it was back in Mother's trunk. What a nuisance those things are.

Meanwhile, this pencil has worn itself down to a stub . . . will walk to town for another.

Monday, the 23rd of July

For several days I have put off writing the awful news. The trial was held in front of the hotel, on the platform. When I saw the prisoner brought out from the hoosegow, I couldn't believe it.

It was the dance-hall lady.

Her hands were tied in front of her. She wore a blue satin dress with red trim along the sleeves and hem. A vigilante named the three victims. When he asked the lady if she had killed them, she spoke in a voice that surprised me.

"Gentlemen," she began. "I am guilty of one death, not three. He was a thief, a man without integrity." Then she said that no one listened to her when she asked for help. She admitted she shouldn't have taken the law into her own hands, but did.

"My silence yesterday cost the life of that poor boy — for that I am deeply sorry." Her voice was cultured and reminded me of Mother's. How did she end up alone in a mining camp?

Suddenly the thick rope was put around her neck, like a brown collar that came up to her chin. She was calm but asked the hangman for one favor. "Please allow me some modesty," she said.

He nodded, then tied a smaller rope around her knees so her dress wouldn't fly up when she dropped. That's when Clara and I turned away. We walked back to the cabin.

Papa came home later and wanted no supper. The woman died instantly, he said. And the crowd was so quiet you could hear the creak of the rope as she swung.

Friday, the 27th of July

During the day the heat is fierce, but by sundown it cools off. I love living in the mountains.

My favorite time is supper, when the five of us sit around the campfire. The smoke blows this way and that, it stings our eyes and makes us cough, but it is a refuge from mosquitoes and, we hope, wild animals. This is when Captain Clinkingbeard tells stories. Tonight I learned my father has tales of his own.

After the hanging we remembered that the dance-hall lady had been one of his patients.

Was she sick? we asked.

No, he said. He stitched up some cuts in her hands. Someone had stolen her money, then tried to stab her. When she held up her hands to stop the blows, the knife made deep wounds.

"I never dreamed she had anything to do with a fella being killed." Papa said she was very well mannered and wanted to talk. She told Papa that some months ago she had come to Miner's Creek with her husband, but he had gotten pneumonia from standing in the cold rivers. When he died she was forced to earn her own living. Didn't know what else to do except dance in the saloons. She was trying to save money for a voyage back east, where the rest of her family lived.

Now she lies in an unmarked grave outside town. No one knew her name or even her husband's name. He had been buried somewhere along the North Fork.

SUNDAY, THE 5TH OF AUGUST

Our day of rest wasn't at all restful, but wonderfully busy. Tomás and Rosita brought baby Esperanza and five of Rosita's handsome brothers.

They were here to help Sam build his very own cabin, just downstream, where the beach opens up into a glade. Papa and the Captain cut logs last week, so the walls were up in no time. By afternoon the roof was slanting skyward and wedged around a stone chimney. Sam himself cut out two windows and filled them with glass he'd bought in town. All this he did by hopping around, sometimes without his crutch.

Clara and I made sure there would be a good dinner. We set a kettle over the fire, simmering with three plump chickens, potatoes and tomatoes, onions and turnips. As the meat cooked, we scooped out the bones so by supper the stew was easy to eat. Rosita brought the Dutch oven. First we baked cornbread, then a sugary white cake, then some biscuits to eat with fresh butter.

Now everyone has gone home; Clara and I are both in bed. Though the cabin is stifling, we are keeping the door closed. Just when I think my sister is asleep, she starts whispering again. "*Antonio . . . Antonio . . .*" She can't stop talking about Rosita's brother, Antonio. He is about twenty years old and quite a gentleman. I remember him from our voyage and from all our visits to the Peruvian camp.

Anyway, Antonio has learned English well enough so that he and Clara conversed today as if they are old friends. At sunset he took out his guitar, and along with his brothers, serenaded us with beautiful melodies, first in Spanish, then English. When he sang "Dear Lady with the Soft Blue Eyes," we all turned toward my sister, but she was too charmed to notice our stares.

So that is Clara's secret. Her three days helping Rosita must have been filled with starlight and music.

Friday, the 10th of August

This morning Sergeant Boots was on the table watching our pet trout. He pushed the bottle with his paw until it wobbled enough to fall over. Before I could rescue the fish, it poured out with the water down to the floor in a muddy splash. With one quick leap our cat scooped the flopping fish into his mouth. So that is the end of *that* pet.

Tuesday, the 14th of August

Yesterday after doing all the wash, Clara and I picked flowers from the meadow. We made a bouquet, tying the stems together with a yellow ribbon. We walked out beyond town, past the arena to the little hill with crosses and wooden markers. Fresh dirt showed where the dance-hall lady had been buried.

We kneeled in the grass and placed the flowers on the mound. I recited a psalm, then Clara said, "We're sorry there was no one here to love you."

This morning we went with Papa to the lady's hotel room. The owner was there putting cosmetics and petticoats into a trunk to be auctioned off. Clara noticed a satchel under the narrow bed and rushed to retrieve it. When we saw a parcel of letters tied with string, Papa reached in his pocket for his money pouch.

"Sir," he said to the man, "I'll give you two ounces for the lady's bag, thirty-eight dollars."

"Doc, you got yourself a deal."

"Back at our cabin we read the letters, carefully unfolding the thin tissue paper. I felt embarrassed, as if we were peeking through a keyhole into someone's private room. But Clara and I wanted only to find her relatives, to let them know where she was buried. Maybe it was because we would never be able to visit our own mother's grave that we couldn't bear the thought of this lady being lost to her family.

So that is how we learned her name, Jenny Winslow of Deer Isle, Maine. From the letters we learned that her brother and nephews were eagerly waiting for her to return . . . her sister gave birth to twin daughters at Christmas . . . her parents sold part of their farm to a neighbor. . . .

This evening after supper Clara and I will sit down to write them. The next mail wagon going to San Francisco should be here tomorrow.

Sam cut two pieces of wood for us and notched them together in the shape of a cross. Next Captain Clinkingbeard did scrimshaw with his black ink, a beautiful drawing of a lady looking out at the mountains. Along the top he carved her name and the date she died — July 20, 1849. Now if Jenny's loved ones visit Miner's Creek, they'll be able to find her.

Friday, the 17th of August

This afternoon Sam and I were sitting in front of the cabin, peeling potatoes for Clara's soup. Papa walked into camp and set his black bag in the dirt. He had been on the other side of the river, doctoring a man who broke his arm in a fight. Sitting down on one of the tree stumps, Papa unrolled his tobacco pouch and filled his pipe. He struck a match against a stone, held the flame over the bowl, and puffed until it was lit.

He squinted at Sam through his smoke. "I've done a lot of thinking," he said. "You're a hard-working fellow, and I've observed that you are honorable. I trust you to protect Susanna's virtue."

"Why, yes, sir, of course. Absolutely."

And that is how Papa gave permission for us to court. It only took him twenty-eight days to think about it.

LATER

Summer is nearing its end. I can feel coolness in the early mornings and there's a sharp, cold smell at night when the campfire dies down. I asked Papa if we're going to live in Miner's Creek through the winter or push on to Oregon as we had first planned.

"I'm not sure what we should do," he said. He is concerned that Miner's Creek is too rough a town for Clara and me. Also, winters in these mountains are harsh. Last month Papa wrote friends as well as Aunt Augusta and Uncle Charles in Oregon, just to say what happened to Mother and to tell them where we are. They will be distraught to hear about her death, yet also surprised that we're in California. We never told them about our voyage because we knew we'd arrive on the West Coast before our mail. What we didn't figure on was our detour for gold.

No one knows this but I wrote a letter to "Mr. and Mrs. Jesse Blue, c/o Oregon City." I asked him to return Papa's gold, and maybe his wife will make him do so. She was one of Mother's dearest friends, after all. There was so much else I wanted to say, everything I've written in these pages, but I kept it simple, then signed my name. I pray that his heart will change like Mr. Scrooge's did.

What will we do if we see him again?

Next day

This morning started out pleasant enough until I forgot my manners.

After breakfast Clara and I dressed up Lilly in her flowered hat and tied a picnic sack to her harness. It was a beautiful day to visit Rosita and her baby. I brought the colorful shawl she had given me on the ship, because it is becoming cool along the river and in the shady groves. We are ever looking about us for mountain lions, knowing they are quiet and hide themselves well.

It was so good to see little Esperanza. She is six weeks old and has much dark hair, more than Papa has! We took turns holding and rocking her while Rosita busied herself around the campfire. Clara's eyes were dreamy as she kissed the tiny nose and fingers.

"Oh, I love babies," she said. "I want one of my own."

"Well," said I, "you must have a husband first, everyone knows *that*." It felt good to boss my sister for once, but when I saw her face I wanted to take back my words. Her lip trembled as she tried to keep from crying.

"That's a mean thing to say, Susanna." She called me sassy. Then, because I wanted to have the last word, I said she was a terrible cook.

Poor Rosita didn't know what to do with two quarreling sisters. She just sang to her baby until she fell asleep, then tried to make cheerful conversation in her broken English.

On the trail back to the cabin I apologized twice, but Clara was too mad to listen. She kept her head high and marched with long strides ahead of me. Her dress made a snapping sound, like a sail in the wind.

Now we are back at the cabin. I'm writing at the table in a small pool of candlelight. Clara is in bed, turned toward the wall. She hasn't spoken to me since this morning.

Antonio must have been working up at one of the creeks because we didn't see him all day.

Sunday, the 19th of August

I woke early this morning and began cooking breakfast before Clara was out of bed. I fried bacon and onions, then stirred them into a skillet of eggs. Made one dozen corn muffins from a muffin tin I found last week by the river. Boiled a pot of good, strong coffee. Sunlight cast colors on the floor from our glass window and when I opened the door the whole room turned bright. Clara stepped out from behind our curtain in her nightgown and mussed hair. She looked at me.

"I shouldn't have let the sun go down on my anger," she said. "That's what Mother always told us, remember?"

At the mention of our sweet mother we both burst into tears and fell into each other's arms. After some moments we noticed three men standing in the doorway: Papa, Captain Clinkingbeard, and Sam. They looked bewildered and ready to help us. But we didn't need help.

Clara and I are the only ones who understand girl things.

LATER

The *Placer Times* reports that our former President James Polk died of cholera. That was two months ago, on June 15. Mrs. Polk is especially sad because no children were born to their marriage.

WEDNESDAY, THE 22ND OF AUGUST

Spent the day with Sam up at his claim. Captain Clinkingbeard came as well. We sifted out nuggets and dust that weighed one pound, nine ounces on the Captain's little scale, nearly four hundred dollars worth. Sam split it three ways, even though they did most of the work. I just scooped up gravel.

In my heart I worry about Sam. It has been difficult for him to kneel in the cold water for hours on end. He told us that after a day in the river his leg aches so bad he lies awake at night. I worry because placer mining is the hardest work on earth, and it is wearing him down and out, like it did Papa.

Right now Clara and I are in bed. Papa is outside by the fire with Sam; they've been talking for at least two hours.

SUNDAY, THE 26TH OF AUGUST

In the middle of the night I woke suddenly and sat up in bed. I finally figured out that since Jenny Winslow killed one man and not three, a murderer is still on the loose.

Rosita and Tomás came for supper with Esperanza and Antonio. Our evening was not as jovial as our last Sunday together because Papa brought up the subject of Oregon. When asked why not just winter in San Francisco, he explained that we have family up north. Since he has taken Clara and me so far away from home, he wants us at least to be near relations. We have aunts, uncles, friends, and my favorite cousin, Hattie, who is the same age as I am.

My heart is heavy on two accounts. Clara and Antonio looked miserable during this conversation. If we leave Miner's Creek they probably will never see each other again, and I know this would upset my sister a great deal. My other heartache is because of Sam. We have grown quite fond of each other, and I would be distressed if we had to say farewell.

Antonio took out his guitar after supper. He sang only in Spanish this time. Clara and I went to bed without our usual late-night chatter. We weren't angry with each other, just sad.

We don't know what Papa will decide.

NEXT DAY

I love to sit outside after chores. For some reason the stool Papa made is a comfort to me. Often I just listen to the river and watch animals. A flash of blue up in a tree means a blue jay has landed. Squirrels leap from branch to branch, chasing one another in circles down the trunk then back up again. They make me laugh. And there's our gray kitty with the white paws. Sergeant Boots is always on the lookout for birds and has caught several — I don't know what kind, but I often see little brown feathers lying scattered among the pine needles.

The sun is pleasantly warm, not too hot. It is lower in the sky now, so the trees along the river cast lacy shadows over our camp. I think autumn will come sooner than what we're used to.

Tonight Papa wants to talk with Clara and me about Oregon. He wants us to tell him what we think, but I think so many things! It's just that I don't know what is best.

TUESDAY, THE 28TH OF AUGUST

Made hotcakes for breakfast, the dishes are washed and put away. Clara and Captain Clinkingbeard are walking to town for flour and coffee beans. At last I have a moment to sit at the table and write.

Last night we agreed with Papa that it is best for the three of us to continue on to Oregon, though there was a lump in my throat as we talked. It will be as we had planned. As Mother had dreamed. We sat in the cabin by the fireplace, where a low blaze warmed us against the evening chill. Papa smoked his pipe and looked around at our cozy furnishings.

When he asked Clara about Antonio, I expected her to dissolve into tears. But she didn't. She gazed into the fire and turned her palms upward, as if asking a question. After a moment she said, "I will miss him very much."

Papa then looked at me. I wish I could say I was as brave as my sister, but I struggled against tears. "Papa, I love Sam."

He drew on his pipe, nodding.

So that is how our evening ended, quietly.

WEDNESDAY, THE 29TH OF AUGUST

Didn't sleep well last night.

We will be buying a wagon and mules this week for our journey. Lilly is still too little to bear any great load, so my favorite pet will have to stay behind in Miner's Creek.

I suppose I'm elated about finally settling in

Oregon and once again being with family. I will miss the mountains and the wild beauty of its rivers. I will miss the excitement of gold, at least the possibility that one of us might stumble upon the next big strike. I will miss Captain Clinkingbeard and his stories, as well as Rosita and her large family.

Last night when I was getting undressed for bed I heard Papa and Sam outside. I quickly leaned against the door with my ear pressed to a crack, straining to listen. Sam was talking about how he loves his new cabin and about his brother over in Mokelumne Hill, but that's all I really heard. I want him to come to Oregon with us! Can I tell him this? In a courtship is it proper for a girl to say such things or must everything be *his* idea?

I'm confused and upset. How I wish Mother were here.

TUESDAY, THE 4TH OF SEPTEMBER

These past days have gone by quickly and much has happened, so I'll be brief.

When we awoke this morning the ground was dusted with snow. It was frosty outside, but by noon the snow had melted. Trees high up in the hills are turning golden and red, and their leaves are falling with the breeze.

Tomorrow we leave Miner's Creek (TOMORROW!).

Rosita and Tomás will live in our cabin with baby Esperanza because they are staying through the winter. Sergeant Boots will be their good cat, and they will watch over Lilly.

A shootout last night at the Mad Mule Saloon landed four men in the hoosegow and four full of bullet holes. Their bodies were displayed on Main Street, propped up inside their open coffins. Clara and I happened by, not realizing why the crowd was there until we saw for ourselves. It was gruesome, but I couldn't stop staring. Their faces were purple and bloated. Flies swarmed over the wounds. At sunset some men nailed the coffin lids shut, loaded them on wagons, then hauled them out to the cemetery. A trial will be held tomorrow. If there are to be any hangings, fortunately we will be gone.

Well, I haven't been as brief as I planned. Clara is calling for me to help with supper so I will finish later. . . .

Most everything is packed. We have two crates by the door full of food and cooking things. I hope I can sleep.

Earlier I didn't have time to write why I am so cheerful.

Sam is coming, too! He and Captain Clinkingbeard have their own little wagon and mule team, so they will take the trail with us to Sacramento. Sam's brother, Virgil, wrote that he won't be returning to Oregon yet. He will stay in Mokelumne Hill until next summer because his claim still brings him a few hundred dollars a week. Despite his missing fingers he wants to "work 'er till she's dry." That's what his last letter said.

I forgot to mention why the Captain is coming with us. When he learned of our plans to leave, he told us a story that brought Clara and me to tears. . . .

Three years ago he was sailing a schooner around the Sandwich Islands, with his wife and two young daughters aboard. When they anchored in a cove, friendly natives paddled out to the ship with fresh fruit and other gifts. They climbed aboard and were welcomed by the passengers and crew. After some minutes, however, Captain Clinkingbeard noticed the natives were feverish and had blisters on their chests and faces. By the time he recognized the signs of smallpox, it was too late. Everyone on deck had been exposed. Within days many of his Tar Heads and passengers were dying, including his beloved wife and daughters; the girls were just eight and twelve years of age. Because the Captain had been vaccinated as a child, he didn't fall ill.

Burying them at sea, he told us, broke his heart. He no longer loved the ocean. That's why abandoning his ship in San Francisco and heading for the hills was so easy to do.

At that Clara and I burst out, "Oh, do come with us, Captain, please. We want you to."

His eyes were moist. When he ran his hand over his beard, the bells made the tiniest bit of music.

ON THE TRAIL

I am sitting in the back of our wagon; Papa and Clara are sharing the reins in front. It is rather bumpy to be writing, but I will try.

About a mile behind us are Sam and the Captain.

They are keeping that distance because of the dust our wheels stir up. Last night we camped outside Sutter's Fort. It looks much as it did when we passed through six months ago. All sorts of men are busy hurrying for gold country. I don't mention this to Papa, but I am always looking at faces, wondering if we'll see Jesse Blue. It's still hard to believe our old friend no longer cares for us.

As we were saying our good-byes to Rosita and Tomás, her brothers began building bunks into Sam's cabin. All seven of them will stay warm this winter in front of that little fireplace. I'm pleased knowing friends will enjoy our cozy log homes, and that our hipbath will get good use.

Antonio and Clara shook hands as a gentleman and a lady. He bent forward to kiss her cheek, but she turned away and climbed up into our wagon. Her back was to me so I couldn't tell if she was crying. She sat stiffly for some miles. Finally she looked over her shoulder at me and said, "Oh, Susanna, we're on our way!"

It has started raining. Papa just turned around from his seat to say he wants to keep going. Well, then, I shall pull a tarpaulin over my head and watch the scenery. More later.

*　　*　　*

Sacramento is a boomtown! While waiting for a boat to take us downriver, we walked around the wharves, or what they call the *embarcadero.*

When we were last here, lots were priced at five hundred dollars each. Now they are selling for five thousand dollars! "Ready Cut" houses are being hammered together throughout town, along with stores and a magnificent new hotel fit for Queen Victoria. Clara and I were delighted to see women in beautiful satin dresses walking here and there (most were wearing corsets, we were certain). Oh, the charms of a bustling city.

We are not rich, but we have enough gold to stay the night in a hotel and buy passage for the riverboat. We'll sell our wagons and mules, sail downstream to San Francisco, then wait for the next ship sailing north to Oregon.

By the way, it is warmer here than Miner's Creek. A large thermometer in front of a café reads 87 degrees. Once again it feels like summer.

Aboard the *Lady Luck*

We're on the Sacramento River, heading west toward the sea. It is, of course, much faster than when we sailed up against the current. I am sitting on the floor of the deck, leaning against the soft fabric of my satchel. A breeze off the water makes it pleasant to be in the sun. My bonnet is packed away for now, and my hair is braided as usual. I lost interest in combing it up fancy like Clara's because my arms grew tired — it is such a chore. Perhaps in Oregon I will work harder at being a lady.

Sam is sitting in the bow with Papa and Captain Clinkingbeard. Clara is lying next to me, her head pillowed on her shawl. She's watching the clouds — I think she'll soon be dozing.

It is beautiful along this river. Wild grapevines hang from tree limbs over the water, making shady arbors as we drift by. Here and there our boat steers around little islands that are forested with oaks and manzanita. Smoke from a campfire rises above the trees, bringing a delicious aroma of roasted meat. Papa said Indians live here. A trail on the south bank is lined with sunflowers, like bright yellow faces saying hello. I will miss California.

At this moment we are passing an adobe ranch house. I can see a señora hanging up her wash and her dark-haired children playing. Now they are hidden by a curve in the river.

Oh, Papa is asking if we might have some dinner. It's noon, so I'll write later.

We ate boiled eggs, crackers, cheese, and crisp red apples we bought in Sacramento. We sat together on deck, I next to Sam, quietly enjoying this last bit of gold country. I am happy Captain Clinkingbeard is with us. Without saying so, we have become his family. Now *he* is like our uncle, a pleasant dear man who tells stories and listens to ours.

After the Captain said he would come to Oregon with us that day, I walked over to Sam. He was sitting by the river, cleaning some fish he had just caught. When I asked if he had decided about Oregon, he set his knife down and smiled up at me.

"Susanna," he said, "I can't wait to see the looks on my parents' faces when they meet you. Does that answer your question?"

I felt myself blush. Yes, I said. My voice was flat, but inside, my heart was leaping.

And here we are.

SUNDAY, THE 9TH OF SEPTEMBER, SAN FRANCISCO

Our hotel is so noisy none of us slept last night. The walls are just thin strips of canvas hanging from the ceiling. Clara and I could hear two ladies arguing in the next room. And against the other wall we could see silhouettes of men taking off their shirts and trousers. We were so embarrassed we blew out our candle early and covered our heads with pillows.

Now we are dressed and waiting in the lobby for Papa to pay our bill — seven dollars for two filthy rooms. We are covered with fleabites all over our arms and legs and in places where it's not polite for ladies to scratch.

I wonder if the hotel next door is as dirty. I laughed when I first saw it because it is a *ship*. Somehow men were able to haul an abandoned vessel from the bay onto shore. They wedged it between two buildings, built a ramp leading up to its deck, and turned it into a rooming house. We saw others like it along the street facing the ocean. Captain Clinkingbeard noticed his own ship propped up on a wharf, now a loud saloon. We saw dancing ladies on deck. They leaned over the rail and called down to men passing in the street.

Papa is here; it's time to go. A carriage is waiting for us out front to take us to Pier Eight where our next voyage begins. I bought a newspaper to read later so I will tuck it into this journal.

WAITING ON THE DECK

While men load our ship with supplies and luggage, Clara and I are sitting on a trunk. A nearby seagull is perched on a piling; he is watching Clara eat a biscuit. The cries of gulls fill the bay as they circle little fishing boats that come and go. I love the smell of the ocean.

ABOARD THE *SANTA CATALINA*

We've just sailed through the Golden Gate and once again are at sea, this time aboard a three-masted schooner. There are approximately sixty passengers, mostly rough-looking men, but we did count five women and two children. Clara and I are relieved to have the clutter and babble of San Francisco behind us, and I think our beds tonight will give us good rest. We have a cozy cabin with a porthole facing east, which means we'll have a view of the coast the whole trip. Depending on weather it should take four or five days.

It is cold as winter! I'm wearing Rosita's colorful shawl and we are warming our room with an oil lamp. Clara is resting on her bunk. We have nearly an hour before supper so I'll try to get a few thoughts down.

Being at sea reminds me of Mother, but I am not in despair. Somehow our six months in Miner's Creek was a good place for me to reflect. There were just three of us, now there are five. Papa is ready to be the good doctor he'd wanted to be in the first place. We have enough gold to buy land and build the little house of Mother's dreams. I feel closer to her because of this.

Supper bell . . . must go!

Before bed

Clara and I are in our nightgowns. She is reading an adventure story called *The Three Musketeers*, so we are sharing lamplight. We are a bit queasy from the rolling of the ship, but not nearly as ill as on our first voyage. I haven't yet told her about this evening.

At sunset Sam and I strolled on deck under the full, white sails. The glowing sky made the water look pink, and there were dolphins leaping above the swells alongside the bow. The wind made our voices seem small, and the deck was wet from sea spray. This was how I slipped and fell against Sam. But before I could gather myself, he enfolded me in his arms and bent down to kiss me. For the rest of my life I will feel silly for what happened next: I burst out laughing. I don't know why.

Sam had the grace and good humor to laugh as well.

Surely he is now lying on his bunk, wondering what sort of girl he is courting. Clara just looked at me over the top of her book and asked why I am smiling.

I'll tell her after we blow out the light. I am glad I have a sister to talk to.

NEXT DAY, AT SEA

The forests of Oregon Territory are now off our starboard side as we sail north. It is so green and pretty. I wish the captain of this ship would anchor and let us row to shore, but he says the best place to stop will be up the Columbia River in a harbor called Fort Vancouver. From there it'll take another day or two by wagon to reach our new home.

The breeze is cold, but the fresh salt smell is wonderful. There are places to sit out of the wind, such as among water barrels and the thick coils of rope. Most of the passengers stay below where it is warmer. This morning a longboat that is usually stored upside down on deck was rolled upright so that it could air out. Clara and I climbed inside and settled low between the benches, wrapped in our shawls. We were as snug as if in a little sunroom. It was here that I remembered the newspaper.

I took it from between these pages and unfolded it carefully so the breeze wouldn't take it. It's just one sheet, printed on brown paper. My eyes fell on a story that I immediately read aloud to Clara.

Sometime last week a fire destroyed one of San Francisco's rooming houses, burning nearby buildings before the flames were put out. Fortunately no one was killed. The article reported that one of the miners who fled for his life was now suing the landlord. It seems that this fellow had kept a safe in his room to protect his money. But when he returned to the ruins the following day and combed through the ashes, he found only a chunk of melted iron. His cash — some four thousand dollars — had turned to cinder. The man filing the lawsuit? Jesse Blue of Oregon City.

My sister and I gathered our skirts to climb out of the longboat. We found Papa belowdecks, playing cards with the others. After I read the story, he looked sad.

"I'm sorry for Jesse," he said, shaking his head. "He chose money over friendship, but now he has neither."

LATER

Back in the longboat . . . it's nearly noon judging by the short shadows on deck. The navigator is glancing at the sun to take measurements from his sextant. Next to him stands our captain, scanning the horizon with his spyglass. Overhead, high in the masts, sailors are flung over the yardarms to adjust sails, their feet balanced on a thin walking rope. I feel nervous watching. If one of them falls, there is nothing to catch him. They're all working hard, but I wonder, were they put in chains so they wouldn't jump ship in San Francisco?

I also wonder about gold fever, why it makes some men crazy and others wise. Such as Sam, my father, and Captain Clinkingbeard. They suffered heartbreak and loss, just as Jesse Blue had, but they didn't become thieves or liars. *Why?* I asked Papa. *What makes the difference?*

His eyes were gentle when he looked at me. "Susanna, it seems that true character often isn't revealed until a person is faced with temptation."

And so, as I gaze out at the rolling sea, I ponder my father's words.

FORT VANCOUVER

I am writing from a small log cabin inside the walls of this fort, where Clara and I have been welcomed by one of the soldier's wives. We will be here another day or two until Papa can arrange for a wagon and horses. Meanwhile he, Captain Clinkingbeard, and Sam are camped outside the walls, along a stream that flows into the great Columbia River. Mountain men and fur traders are camped there as well, many living out of tepees. I have seen my first Indian, a woman with long black hair, carrying a baby on her back.

It is hard to believe we are nearly home. I think I will love Oregon Territory for it is beautiful. Lush pine forests come right down to the sea and are thick along the rivers and streams.

I am to the end of Mother's diary. It seems she has been with me on this long journey after all, through these pages and my thoughts. I miss her, Clara and Papa miss her, but we will start our new life with her dream.

There's a small window looking out to the fort's busy courtyard. I can see Sam! He is walking this way, leaning on his crutch. My heart feels light at the sight of his clean shirt and freshly barbered face. He is carrying a bouquet of wild fern tied with a white ribbon. I will close Mother's journal now.

Sam has come a'courting.

EPILOGUE

When the Fairchilds arrived in Oregon City, their relatives and friends were overjoyed to see them. Three weeks later a new wave of emigrants also arrived, after six grueling months along the Oregon Trail, many of them from Missouri. Among them was one of Susanna's childhood friends, Betsy, now a bride with an infant son.

Until he was able to build his own house, Papa and the girls stayed with Aunt Augusta, Uncle Charles, and their young cousins, Bennie and Jake. Over the years Dr. Fairchild's medical practice flourished due to his skill and his kindness.

The day after Sam put glass windows in his new cottage he and Susanna were married in a field of wildflowers, surrounded by their families and friends. They had five daughters in five years, then a set of triplet boys who died at birth. Susanna lived out her days next door to her cousin Hattie and across the road from their friend Betsy.

Sam's twin brother, Virgil, returned to Oregon

with enough money to build a luxurious hotel, and they went into business together. Brothers Inn was host to three United States presidents and scores of other dignitaries.

Clara never married. Because of her love for children she started an orphanage and became known throughout the area as the adored "Aunt Clara." She lived to the age of 101.

Captain Clinkingbeard married a young widow from Missouri whose husband had drowned when crossing the Snake River. The Captain adopted her two children, then they had seven of their own. After his voyage from San Francisco he never returned to the sea. He earned his living as a wood-carver.

When Susanna and Clara visited Mrs. Blue, they learned she hadn't received Susanna's letter. She didn't know her husband had stolen Papa's money, so the girls decided to keep the matter to themselves. Jesse Blue was never heard from again.

LIFE IN AMERICA
IN 1849

HISTORICAL NOTE

When President James Polk addressed Congress on December 5, 1848, he made statements that electrified Americans. He confirmed that there was indeed gold in their new territory of California, bought just a few months earlier from Mexico. In fact the mines were "more extensive and valuable than was anticipated." Four days later Horace Greeley's *New York Daily Tribune* proclaimed, "We are on the brink of the Age of Gold."

Yes, gold! The rumors were true after all. The rumors had persisted for many years, but here was confirmation from the President himself. The United States had just acquired the California territory ten months earlier in the Treaty of Guadalupe Hidalgo, which ended the war with Mexico. The United States paid fifteen million dollars in return for the territories of California, New Mexico, and the Rio Grande region.

Mexico had failed to act on the rumors of gold in California. It already had productive copper, silver, and gold mines in its districts of Guanajuato and

Sonora. Why bother with California, just a remote and sparsely populated province? This indifference made it easier for Mexico to sell California to the United States.

The timing couldn't have been better for America.

On January 24, 1848, nine days before the treaty was signed, there had been a momentous discovery in California. While working at Sutter's Sawmill on the American River, a man named James Marshall found gold in the tailrace, which is the part of a mill where the river flows after spilling over the water-wheel. Marshall, a former farmer and wheelmaker from New Jersey, shared the discovery with his partner, John Augustus Sutter, a gregarious and highly ambitious German-born Swiss merchant.

Sutter had wandered the New World, suffered more than one bankruptcy after fleeing creditors, and eventually found himself in California in 1839. He persuaded the Mexican governor of California to grant him fifty thousand acres of land, located east of San Francisco Bay, at the confluence of the Sacramento and American rivers. Here Sutter began anew his dreams of a business empire, building a fort. He called it New Helvetia, although everyone else called it Sutter's Fort. He also bestowed upon himself the title of captain, for supposed service in the Swiss Guard of Charles X of France. New Helvetia was eventually renamed Sacramento in 1848.

In 1847, Sutter took Marshall into a partnership. It was while Marshall and some workers were establishing the sawmill that the discovery was made. A worker's diary briefly noted: "Monday 24th this day some kind of mettle was found in the tail race that looks like goald first discovered by James Martial the Boss of the Mill."

Within weeks of Marshall's discovery of "goald," Captain Sutter complained that all his able-bodied employees had deserted his sawmill, his fort, ranches, and stores and had become miners themselves. By mid-May of 1848, the streets of San Francisco were empty, as nearly every citizen — some eight hundred people — had headed for the gold fields.

They were just a small advance party compared to the deluge of humanity to follow the next year. The vision of striking it rich captured the imagination of Americans — and foreigners — everywhere. Overnight people quit jobs, abandoned their farms and families, and sought the quickest way to California to find their fortune in the creeks, rivers, and the western slopes of the Sierra Nevada. They were eventually called the Forty-niners, for the year the stampede began. Because so many of these prospective miners came by sea from distant shores, another name for them was Argonauts, after the men in Greek mythology who sailed with Jason in search of the Golden Fleece. Natives and foreign-born residents of the Hawaiian Islands sought passage on every ship bound for San Francisco; South American miners sought ships bound for North America; Mexicans sailed from Mazatlán.

In May 1848, only a few hundred gold seekers were mining. By the end of the year there were between six thousand and ten thousand as the news traveled fast.

Ultimately hundreds of thousands of people participated in one of the largest voluntary migrations in history. They were not just miners, but also part of the huge supporting cast. Merchants, blacksmiths, saloon keepers, carpenters, washerwomen, and entertainers often made more money than the Forty-niners themselves. Though the actual rush lasted less than a decade, $465 million worth of gold was uncovered and dozens of mining towns sprouted up throughout California. It was on its way to becoming one of the most populous states in the Union.

*   *   *

There were several ways for Easterners to travel west. At the time overland routes took six months and cut through vast deserts, prairies that were inhabited by many Indian nations, and then over rugged mountain passes. Another route, which took between five and twelve months, was by sea, around Cape Horn, the southern tip of South America. This in itself was harrowing because of the unpredictability of the weather. If a ship floundered in violent storms, her crew and passengers might vanish without a trace. Unlike a wagon breaking down on the trail, there was no way for other travelers to help.

The quickest route was across the Isthmus of Panama, which took just weeks instead of months. This narrow neck of land was about seventy-five miles across, but it was a swampy jungle, infested with mosquitoes. Poor sanitary conditions often led to diseases such as malaria and cholera. Alligators, poisonous insects, and snakes added to the dangers. Unfortunately many fortune seekers died before ever reaching California.

This route was taken by the scores of Forty-niners who swarmed the docks of New Orleans after President Polk's speech. Within two months eight thousand

Americans had boarded vessels headed for Chagres, on the Caribbean side of the isthmus. From here they trekked west to Panama City, a shabby town that overlooked the Pacific Ocean. Here they waited. They knew that whalers and merchant ships would eventually arrive and could transport them north to San Francisco.

One such vessel was the *California,* a side-wheeler steamship on her way from New York to provide mail service along the Pacific Coast. Her journey around Cape Horn, actually through the Strait of Magellan, had been slowed because of storms. Captain Cleveland Forbes had no idea that fifteen hundred men were waiting for him in Panama City, for he had been far out to sea when the rest of the country learned the tantalizing news. One glitch in Captain Forbes's arrival was that he had anchored earlier in Callao, Peru, for supplies and allowed seventy Peruvians on board.

The sight of foreigners on a United States vessel bound for United States goldfields enraged the waiting Americans. These Peruvians were considered trespassers, thieves who would be taking what didn't belong to them. Sadly this was just the beginning of xenophobia, the hatred or fear of foreigners that would become rampant in coming years. By the end of 1849, some ninety thousand people had headed for California, and nearly twenty-three thousand were not U.S. citizens.

Gold fever also spread to the Oregon Territory, where much of its population had recently emigrated from the East. Without a glance backward hundreds of men left their work and families for a chance at a fortune. By October 1848, about three thousand Oregonians had arrived in California, some of the first Americans to reach the goldfields. This was two months before President Polk gave his unforgettable message to Congress.

Marshall and Sutter never profited from the California Gold Rush. Both died bitter and penniless. Marshall's mining claims were swept aside, and he eventually became a blacksmith in a little town near Coloma, site of the first discovery. His last years were spent in abject poverty. He died in 1885 and was buried on a hill overlooking the site where he had bent down thirty-seven years earlier for the discovery that changed the course of United States history.

Sutter's decline was more spectacular, as he was prone to grandiose plans and gestures. For a brief period he was one of the most important men in the American West and ran unsuccessfully for governor of California. Ultimately his lack of business savvy led to his downfall. Once again, his willingness to incur vast debt led to severe problems with his creditors. He was forced to sell Sutter's Fort. Later, he lost his last remaining property, a ranch, to a flood and suspected arson. He then moved to Washington, D.C., to persuade Congress to grant him $125,000 for what he claimed was owed him as reimbursement for aid furnished to California emigrants. After fifteen years, and seemingly on the brink of successfully realizing his claim in 1880, Sutter died in his sleep.

Note:

**The drowning of Mrs. Fairchild in *Seeds of Hope* is fiction. There is no record of a woman being swept overboard from the decks of the *California*, although the voyage around the Horn or through the Strait of Magellan was one of the most treacherous ordeals for the Argonauts. Dozens of ships did meet tragic ends during the Gold Rush, with all aboard perishing.

**The bull and bear fights that took place in early California provided jargon for Wall Street that is still used today. When the animals were brought into the ring, the bear was tethered to a chain. It would dig a hole several inches deep and lie down. From this hole it would fight, either in a prone or sitting position. The bull would stand. Thus, in America's financial centers a bull market means stocks are going up; a bear market means stocks are going down.

**Hoosegow* is slang for a guardhouse or jail. It comes from the Spanish word, *juzgado*, meaning court of justice.

When President James Polk confirmed that gold had been discovered in California, the newly acquired territory became a magnet for those seeking the riches gold would provide. From all over the country and all over the world, people found their way to California. Some traveled over land, but others who could afford it got there quicker by crossing the Isthmus of Panama, which cut the trip from the east to west coast down to weeks instead of months.

When ships arrived in San Francisco Bay, the possibilities were so enchanting that along with the passengers, the crew often abandoned the ship. The result was a "town" of ships on the bay. This ship, Euphemia, became San Francisco's first jail.

The year 1849 brought so many people to California that a guide was created to help the settlers find their way in this golden land. It helped them figure out the terrain and routes around the area, but most importantly, it instructed them how to find gold.

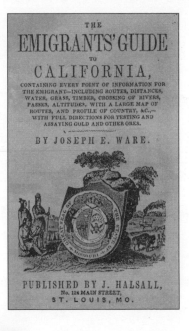

THE
EMIGRANTS' GUIDE
TO
CALIFORNIA,
CONTAINING EVERY POINT OF INFORMATION FOR
THE EMIGRANT—INCLUDING ROUTES, DISTANCES,
WATER, GRASS, TIMBER, CROSSING OF RIVERS,
PASSES, ALTITUDES, WITH A LARGE MAP OF
ROUTES, AND PROFILE OF COUNTRY, &C.,—
WITH FULL DIRECTIONS FOR TESTING AND
ASSAYING GOLD AND OTHER ORES.

BY JOSEPH E. WARE.

PUBLISHED BY J. HALSALL,
No. 124 MAIN STREET,
ST. LOUIS, MO.

Mostly, the miners were inexperienced. Indeed, some had dropped successful careers as doctors and lawyers to take a chance at striking it rich in the gold fields.

174

As women were few and far between in the region, the arrival of a single woman in a mining town was quite an event. The miners were so deprived of female companionship that they often proposed marriage at first sight.

Even though the corset was an important part of a young woman's life in the city, it was difficult to function in the rough conditions of the gold-mining communities while wearing these constricting and cumbersome pieces. Women's new lives in the wilderness gave them all the reason they needed to free themselves of this garment.

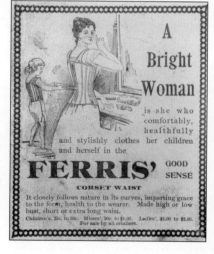

A Bright Woman

is she who comfortably, healthfully and stylishly clothes her children and herself in the

FERRIS' GOOD SENSE

CORSET WAIST

It closely follows nature in its curves, imparting grace to the form, health to the wearer. Made high or low bust, short or extra long waist.

Children's, 25c. to 50c.   Misses', 50c. to $1.00.   Ladies', $1.00 to $2.00.
For sale by all retailers.

Gold mining was a tough business. There were many methods employed by the miners, including filtering sand through a rocker that shakes out everything but the gold. However, after spending long days in the cold, mountain streams searching for gold, miners often came up empty-handed.

Aside from food, medical tools and medicines were the most vital, but least available supplies. This amputation kit was used to saw the limbs of the unfortunate miners who suffered accidents in the treacherous mining process.

Miner's Griddle Cakes

Ingredients:

1 cup yellow cornmeal
1 cup all-purpose flour
1 teaspoon baking soda
1 teaspoon salt
1 teaspoon sugar
2 cups buttermilk
2 tablespoons vegetable oil
1 slightly beaten egg yolk
1 stiffly beaten egg white

1. Mix dry ingredients.
2. Blend in buttermilk, oil, and egg yolk.
3. Fold in egg white.
4. Let stand for ten minutes.
5. Spoon batter carefully onto hot griddle (frying pan) and cook.

Makes 16 four-inch pancakes.

As ingredients and supplies were scarce, recipes were simple but hearty.

Clementine

In a cavern, in a canyon,

Excavating for a mine,

Dwelt a miner, Forty-niner,

And his daughter, Clementine.

CHORUS:

Oh, my darlin', oh my darlin',

Oh my darlin' Clementine,

You were lost and gone forever,

Dreadful sorry, Clementine.

Light she was, and like a fairy,

And her shoes were number nine,

Herring boxes, without topses,

Sandals were for Clementine.

CHORUS

Drove the ducklings, to the water,

Every morning just at nine,

Hit her foot against a splinter,

Fell into the foaming brine.

CHORUS

Ruby lips above the water,

Blowing bubbles soft and fine,

Alas for me, I was no swimmer,

So I lost my Clementine.

CHORUS

A folk song about the Gold Rush, Clementine is still popular today.

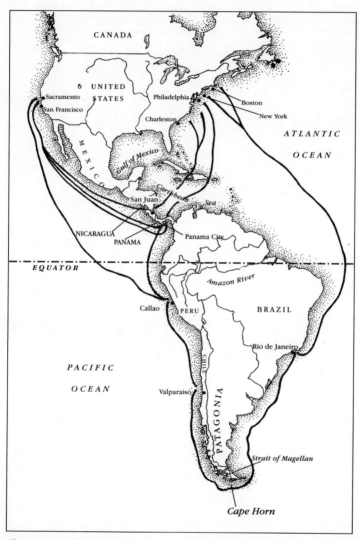

This is a map of the approximate routes to the gold-mining region of California from the east coast of the United States.

ABOUT THE AUTHOR

Seeds of Hope is Kristiana Gregory's fourth title in the Dear America series. She loves to write about the historic West, especially about the people who moved there to start new lives.

When her editor asked her to write about the Gold Rush, Ms. Gregory was thrilled because California is her native state and she grew up with the lore of the Forty-niners. She decided to tell this story through the eyes of a family who just happened to be aboard the steamship *California* when it encountered the first miners heading for gold country.

"I wanted to show the pandemonium and the hopes that people had. Most everyone wanted to become rich and believed that it was possible. I also wanted to show how sometimes the dreams we have are interrupted or changed because of circumstances beyond our control.

"The Fairchilds found themselves in the midst of one of the most exciting times in American history. Despite their personal tragedy and despite Papa's gold fever, the family managed to pull together. It was strength of character that saw them through, not the money they made."

Kristiana Gregory has written two other Dear America books about the great western migration: *Across the Wide and Lonesome Prairie: The Oregon Trail Diary of Hattie Campbell*, and *The Great Railroad Race: The Diary of Libby West*. Her most recent title is *Cleopatra VII: Daughter of the Nile*, for the Royal Diaries series. This and *The Winter of Red Snow: The Revolutionary War Diary of Abigail Jane Stewart* have been made into movies for HBO.

She lives with her husband and sons in Boise, Idaho. They have two golden retrievers who do nothing but nap and wait by their bowls for dinner. In her spare time Ms. Gregory likes to read, swim, daydream, and walk those lazy dogs.

SEEDS OF HOPE
IS DEDICATED TO MY EDITOR,
ANN REIT, IN CELEBRATION
OF OUR MANY BOOKS TOGETHER
AND A GOLDEN FRIENDSHIP.
THANKS, ANN.

ACKNOWLEDGMENTS

Grateful acknowledgment is made for permission to reprint the following:

Cover portrait: Detail of the painting *Jeune berger debout* by William Adolphe Bouguereau, Christie's Images, New York.

Cover background: Detail of the painting *Miners in the Sierras* by Charles Christian Nahl, Smithsonian American Art Museum, Washington, D.C./Art Resource.

Page 173 (top): Crowded steamer to California by Panama. Courtesy of Corbis-Bettman.

Page 173 (bottom): The brig *Euphemia*. Courtesy of The Society of California pioneers.

Page 174 (top): *Emigrant's Guide to California*, 1849. Courtesy of The Granger Collection, New York.

Page 174 (bottom): Portrait of Forty-niner. Courtesy of The Society of California Pioneers.

Page 175 (top): Men surrounding woman. Courtesy of Hulton Getty/Archive Photos.

Page 175 (bottom): Corset ad from Ferris Corset Co. Courtesy of National Museum of American History, Archives Center, Warshaw Collection.

Page 176 (top): Detail of the painting *Miners in the Sierras* by Charles Christian Nahl, Smithsonian American Art Museum, Washington, D.C./Art Resource.

Page 176 (bottom): Amputation kit. Courtesy of Henry Groskinsky.

Page 177: Griddle cakes recipe, public domain.

Page 178: *Clementine*, public domain.

Page 179: Map by Heather Saunders.

OTHER BOOKS IN THE DEAR AMERICA SERIES

A Journey to the New World
The Diary of Remember Patience Whipple
by Kathryn Lasky

The Winter of Red Snow
The Revolutionary War Diary of Abigail Jane Stewart
by Kristiana Gregory

When Will This Cruel War Be Over?
The Civil War Diary of Emma Simpson
by Barry Denenberg

A Picture of Freedom
The Diary of Clotee, a Slave Girl
by Patricia C. McKissack

Across the Wide and Lonesome Prairie
The Oregon Trail Diary of Hattie Campbell
by Kristiana Gregory

So Far from Home
The Diary of Mary Driscoll, an Irish Mill Girl
by Barry Denenberg

I Thought My Soul Would Rise and Fly
The Diary of Patsy, a Freed Girl
by Joyce Hansen

A Light in the Storm
The Civil War Diary of Amelia Martin
by Karen Hesse

A Coal Miner's Bride
The Diary of Anetka Kaminska
by Susan Campbell Bartoletti

Color Me Dark
The Diary of Nellie Lee Love
by Patricia C. McKissack

One Eye Laughing, the Other Weeping
The Diary of Julie Weiss
by Barry Denenberg

My Secret War
The World War II Diary of Madeline Beck
by Mary Pope Osborne

Valley of the Moon
The Diary of María Rosalia de Milagros
by Sherry Garland

While the events described and some of the characters
in this book may be based on actual historic events
and real people, Susanna Fairchild is a fictional character,
created by the author, and her journal and its epilogue
are works of fiction.

Library of Congress Cataloging-in-Publication Data available.

ISBN 0-590-51157-2;
ISBN 0-439-44566-3 (pbk.)

10 9 8 7 6 5 4 3 2 1   02 03 04 05 06

The display type was set in Golden Cockerel.
The text type was set in Bookman.
Book design by Elizabeth B. Parisi
Photo research by Zoe Moffitt

Printed in the U.S.A. 23
First paperback printing, October 2002

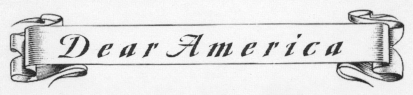

Dear America

ACROSS THE WIDE
AND LONESOME PRAIRIE

The Oregon Trail Diary
of Hattie Campbell

BY KRISTIANA GREGORY

Scholastic Inc. New York

Booneville, Missoura

1847

Booneville, Missoura
January 15, 1847, Friday

Sleet and rain.

Ma said that because today is my birthday I may have two slices of chocolate cake. So I did! After supper she gave me a blue satin ribbon for my braid, then when Pa went to bed she let me unwrap another gift. It was a camisole with a matching lace petticoat. Since I'm now thirteen years of age, Ma said it's proper for me to have pretty underthings.

Aunt June agreed, then she gave me this journal. She said every young lady must have a place to record her private thoughts. I will try to do so.

January 20, 1847, Wednesday

Still raining. Our roof is leaking upstairs over the hallway and in my room by the foot of my bed. I've moved the pot there to catch the drips.

I hide this diary under my pillow, but take it out often to look at. I love the smell of its coarse paper and have decided to use my new hair ribbon as a bookmark. The blue looks pretty lying across the page.

February 2, 1847, Tuesday

Three nights ago my poor uncle Milton fell off our roof while he was helping Pa fix a leak. He died right there in the barnyard, there was nothing we could do.

His funeral was today, one of the most interesting days in a very long time. It all started when his coffin fell out the side of our hay wagon and slid down the bank into the river.

Ma held the horses while Pa went after the coffin through the mud and weeds. I hurried after Pa, but my skirt caught in the brush. He grabbed the coffin and had his arms around it to haul it up, but just then a St. Louis steamboat rounded the bend with its big paddles churning up the water and making waves higher than Pa's head. He held on tight, but all of a sudden he floated out into those waves like a cork, me and Ma screaming for help.

Some folks on the top deck yelled until the captain pulled the whistle long and loud. Pa was being sucked into those tall white paddles when someone threw him a rope and pulled him aboard just in time.

We watched the coffin go under. Some moments later it popped free, its lid gone and Uncle Milton, too. Where he went, we don't know, but this is how we came to be acquainted with the riverboat captain who felt so sorry for us that he said he'd take us anywhere we pleased, no charge.

"Anywheres?" Pa asked, as he stomped the water out of his boots.

"Yes, sir," he said. "Anywhere."

This very evening Pa made a shocking announcement: He said that because of the captain's kindness we can now afford to take a riverboat up to Independence, where the Oregon Trail begins. We will take on board our old wagon and our belongings. We will buy some mules in that town, then we will head west.

Just like that.

Ma's mouth dropped open, but no words came out. She was so mad I suspect the next funeral will be my pa's.

February 3, 1847, Wednesday

Wind blowing through this creaky old house kept me awake most of the night, so here I am in my shawl, looking out the little window by my bed, trying to stay warm. Since my room is in the attic it stays cold until Ma opens the stair door. My fingers are numb, so I will write quick.

I can hear Ma downstairs frying up bacon and putting coffee on. She did not speak to Pa the rest of yesterday, nor has she this morning, for all I hear is silence after Pa's questions.

When Ma gets mad, she stays mad a long time.

February 5, 1847, Friday

Three days have gone by with Ma only speaking to me, my little brothers, and Aunt June. Finally at supper tonight she looked at Pa and said, "Charles Campbell, Oregon is two thousand miles away."

Pa nodded. He seemed so relieved to have Ma talking again. She said, "Tell me why, Charles, and I will tell you yes or no."

My, it was a long evening. I took up the plates and set to washing them with Jake. He is six and likes to splash the water, but still he is a help. Bennie's two so he stayed on Ma's knee while she listened to Pa.

Pa said he'd been unhappy about so many people settling here in Missoura. It's crowded. Taxes are high. And there's swamp fever that kills folks every summer.

At the mention of swamp fever Pa grew quiet. He swallowed hard, then looked at Ma with tears in his eyes. In a soft voice he said her name: "Augusta," he said, "we'll be able to start a new life, where there ain't no sad memories. There's space out West, all the land we want. Free for the taking. Winters are mild, that's what these pamphlets say."

6

He held up a booklet called *The Emigrant's Guide to Oregon and California* by Lanford W. Hastings, and another by the explorers John C. Frémont and Kit Carson.

I took my candle upstairs. I'm not sure if Ma said yes or no, but I'm happy to once again hear them whispering together in their room.

February 7, 1847, Sunday

We have given up hope of finding Uncle Milton's body. So today in church folks took turns walking up to the pulpit to say a few kind words. My friend Becky, she's exactly my age, she sang a hymn so sweet all the ladies dabbed hankies to their cheeks.

Afterward my Aunt June and Uncle Tim came in a freezing rain and we sat together in front of the fire. I served up coffee and two peach pies made from last summer's preserves. My, it was delicious. When they said they wanted to come to Oregon, too, well, Mama smiled for the first time in days for Aunt June is her dear younger sister. (It was their brother Milton that died.)

February 9, 1847, Tuesday

Word spreads fast in a small town. Everyone's talking about Oregon and California.

Becky says she would positively perish from loneliness if I left Booneville, which is where we were born and have lived our whole lives. "Please don't go, Hattie," she said. "If you leave Missoura, we may never see each other again." I feel sad when Becky talks so.

It's pretty much divided down the middle who thinks which is the best place to go to.

Pa said that since California is like a foreign country and we don't speak Spanish we best head for Oregon. It's occupied by the British, but at least those folks speak English.

Our new president is James Polk. Pa says the only reason he won the election is because he promised to make Oregon and California territories of the United States. So if enough of us get up and go, it'll help push the foreigners aside for good.

It's our "Manifest Destiny," according to President Polk. It's our responsibility to spread democracy all the way to the Pacific coast.

Ma was at her mending this morning, in the window seat where the light is good. I sat on the little stool with the embroidered cushion. When I looked up I saw she was crying.

"What is it, Mama?"

She lifted the hem of her apron to dry her cheeks. "Hattie, I don't care about 'Manifest Destiny.' The West is wilderness. It'll be a frightfully long journey with no turning back. All our dear friends live in Booneville, and besides, I don't think I can bear to leave behind your sisters."

I lay my face on Ma's lap. She was talking about my four sweet sisters, three older, one younger. Last summer — the most horrible summer of our lives — they died one right after the other, from swamp fever, and they are buried next to my grandparents under the big walnut tree out back.

I am now the eldest of the Campbell children. I am thirteen years of age and am afraid of only four things in the whole world:

1. Indians
2. copperhead snakes
3. a toothache
4. losing my little brothers Ben and Jake, they're all I got now.

February 18, 1847, Thursday

Yesterday Aunt June received another letter from her friend, Narcissa Whitman, who went to Oregon ten years ago. Her husband is Dr. Marcus Whitman and they have founded a mission near Fort Walla Walla to help the Cayuse Indians. Aunt June had us to tea; Becky, too. She let us girls pour and pass around the scones and butter so that she could read the letter aloud. This much I remember:

There is tall timber and soil so rich a farm can grow over night it seems. June, you'll see how fair is the climate. If I can cross the Rockies, any lady can.

Aunt June folded the letter into her sleeve. She said Narcissa and Eliza Spaulding were the first white women to travel all the way to Oregon. There've been hundreds since, hundreds. We could visit her, maybe even stay a while since Narcissa's been begging us to come for years.

Aunt June is not at all sad to leave Booneville. She thinks everything is an adventure and (I'm writing this in tiny letters so no one can read over my shoulder) she confided to me that the way their brother Milton's coffin went sailing down the Missoura was "Splendid! The best amusement in months."

Aunt June and I think alike.

March 4, 1847, Thursday

Two weeks of packing and sewing and cooking and repacking. We leave aboard the riverboat *Eliza May*, in just ten days.

TEN DAYS!

Pa sold our house and our chickens, our three horses and our cow to a neighbor for $65 — this plus $800 is what we'll take to Oregon. (Having free tickets is what finally gave Pa the courage to say we're going.)

Every evening we visit with friends or relations for supper and tearful good-byes. Suddenly I realize how much I shall miss Becky — we have known each other since we were babies and when we walk together down the lane I get a terrible lump in my throat knowing we'll soon be parted. She is my very best friend ever.

Pa is ready to get going, but Ma is gathering keepsakes from each friend and packets of seeds saved from their gardens. One whole trunk is filled with my sisters' things — a favorite doll and dress each, baby knits and such — Ma's wedding dress and my grandparents' Bible and washbasin.

Pa said, "Are you sure we need all this?" Ma, tight-lipped and teary, said nothing. She just kept on folding quilts and tucking a china dish or bowl or picture frame between the folds.

I am allowed a small satchel. There is space for a folded dress, leggings, my hairbrush, two petticoats, and this-and-that. My journal will fit in the side pocket with three pencils. Aunt June says I must record things daily — the good and the bad — because this will be the adventure of my lifetime.

"Hattie, whether you realize it or not, we will be part of history."

March 15, 1847, Monday
Aboard the Steamboat *Eliza May*

We are fifteen miles west of Booneville, finally. Our first day out we got stuck on a sandbar until the tide floated us off.

I am sitting on a bench on the top deck and can see all around for miles. There are trees everywhere and tiny houses along dirt roads.

There is such a breeze up here that I've had to tie my bonnet tight under my chin. I am writing quick because I must get back to help Ma with Bennie and Jake. If I lean over the rail I can see them on the lower deck among our baggage. Pa and the other men are tightening ropes around the wagons, for they were taken apart before loading. Nearby our wagon wheels are stacked like hotcakes.

Already I'm lonesome for Becky.

March 16, Tuesday

The *Eliza May* is packed with travelers, some from clear down in Kentucky and Tennessee, who've been aboard for days and days. A lady in the cabin next to us was sick all night, but it turns out she was just having a baby. It was born at sunrise, a tiny little girl they named Eliza May.

I ain't never heard of a baby being named after a riverboat. The mother and father already have five young daughters and they are all named after trees! I wonder if the family will fit in one wagon all the way to Oregon.

I write this from my berth. An oil lamp gives light as Ma changes Bennie for bed. Jake is tucked in with Pa, and even though Pa is snoring, Jake keeps asking questions about Indians and scalpings, buffalo, and other things he wants to see out West. He's as ready for our adventure as I am.

There . . . I've just covered him up and whispered a prayer to him. He fell fast asleep before I finished. Ma is so tired.

March 25, Thursday
Independence, Missoura

Pa said there must be 500 folks living here, and that don't count all the emigrants like us roaming the streets, buying last-minute supplies, repairing wagons, and just plain getting ready. There are blacksmiths, harness makers, and wheelwrights busy morning and night.

After we docked it took one full day and evening for men to unload the *Eliza May*. First thing Pa and Uncle Tim did was put the wheels back on our wagons, load our trunks, furniture, and tools, then find a boy who could help us buy some mules.

I am writing this on my lap by the campfires as I keep an eye on Ma's roasting chicken. It is on a low spit over the coals we're sharing with another family. Behind me are the houses and barns and stores and streets of Independence.

But in front of me, it's open prairie, miles and miles of grass spread out like Ma's old yellow quilt. There are dozens of families with tents and wagons also camped here, looking westward.

Pa says we are waiting for the grass to green-up. When there is green grass, why then we'll be able to feed the horses and other animals pulling us west.

Pa is patient, but I ain't. The stench from there being no outhouses gets worse every day. Oh, I wish we could just get on with things.

March 30, Tuesday

Rain. Roads are so muddy most of the emigrants are staying around their fires in camp. We have made friends with three families who are also bound for Oregon. We hung tarps between the wagon tops and now have a dry space in between where Ma and the other ladies sit with babies and needlework.

It is no fun just sitting, sitting, sitting. How I wish Becky was here so we could roam together.

There are many boys my age and older. They have made a sport of shoving each other into puddles and wrestling in the mud. Four boys jumped on the back of a poor old milk cow and tried to ride her through camp. When her calf came bawling after her there was near a stampede.

I don't like the way these boys yell and wave their rifles around. One of them accidentally shot a nine-year-old in the neck. He died quick, right where he fell. His family is so brokenhearted they have packed up and headed home to St. Louis. I'm sad for them.

Now I keep a closer eye on Jake and Ben. If they got shot I think I'd take a whip and make those rough boys sorry they was ever born.

Aunt June made the acquaintance of a family going to San Francisco. The have twins, a boy and a girl about six years old. It seems we'll all start out together and somewhere in the Cheyenne country when the trail splits, some of us will head north and the others south to California.

April 5, Monday

Bad news swept through camp this morning like a fever, news brung by mountain men back from the West. Ma looked so upset I feared she was ill.

"Maybe we should go home, back to Booneville," she said to Pa. "There's just too much danger . . . I cannot lose another one of my children, Charles."

Even the men are talking among themselves. This is what I heard:

An emigrant train that left Independence last spring got trapped in a blizzard high in the Sierra Nevada Mountains near California. Forty-some people froze or starved to death. To stay alive, folks ate their livestock, their pets, and then — this is the worst part — they ate parts of their dead friends! These were the Reed and Donner families and some were rescued just this February. A whole winter in the mountains without food or shelter or warm clothes — how they must have suffered!

Word is that they took the Hastings Cutoff, but something went wrong somehow. Ma is worried because the written guide we are following is also Hastings'. What if his maps are wrong for us too? She is by the fire with Pa, pleading for him to turn back.

I must be brave for Bennie and Jake, and I must be

brave for Ma. But what if something happens to us and we can't get over the mountains in time?

April 6, Tuesday

Pa went into town to trade our mules for oxen. A mountain man in furs named Tall Joe told us the grain that mules eat is expensive and takes up room in the wagons. Oxen are better because they eat grass along the trail and are so slow Indians won't steal them.

Tall Joe said, "Whatever y'folks do, hurry along as fast as y'can and don't take shortcuts like them Donners did." People crowd around asking advice: "What about Indians?" or "What about crossing the desert?"

On Tall Joe's belt he has what looks like two short brushes hanging with a string of beads. Ma was admiring the beadwork and reached out to touch them when Tall Joe said proudly, "Them is scalps, ma'am . . . Pawnee."

Ma's hand flew up to her throat. Before she could gather herself, the little twins and my brother Jake leaned forward for a better look. Jake said, just as calm as if he was asking for lunch, "Did the Injuns yell when you scalped 'em, mister?"

"No, sonny, jest when I shot 'em."

Then Tall Joe lay down by his fire with three of his friends. They fell asleep so quick, they looked like old rugs rolled up.

I stared at the scalps.

Indians?

April 7, Wednesday

The Anderson family is camped near us — the one with baby Eliza May and her five tree sisters. I get them mixed up, but here's the names anyhow: Hazel, Holly, Laurel, Olive, and Cassia. Cassia is about two years old and has hair the color of cinnamon. She has taken a liking to me, I think, because she comes and sits on my lap whenever I'm holding Bennie.

The baby Eliza May cries night and day with a high-pitched wail that reminds me of a steamboat whistle. When Mrs. Anderson greeted me yesterday morning after a long and loud night, I said (in a nice way, I thought) that it's a good thing she named her baby after a steamboat because she sure did sound like one.

Well, Mama overheard and said I must apologize for being rude. It's not nice to make fun of people, she said, especially their habits or names.

There's a dance most every evening on account of there are plenty of fiddlers and foot-stompers. Ma said it's so pleasant and folks're so friendly, she'd be content to camp here all summer then go home. Home to Booneville.

April 12, Monday

Pa says any day now the grass'll start greening and we must be ready to go. Some of the men are trying to pick leaders, but there are so many arguments about who will be boss and what the rules will be, Pa says we'll just move on out with Tall Joe as he seems to be the most experienced.

Our wagon is so handsome you wouldn't guess it used to be our old farm rig. Pa and Uncle Tim added six tall hoops to hold the canvas on top. It looks as plump and white as a fresh-raised loaf of bread.

Inside it's neatly packed, but crowded. Our boxes of food, dishes, and pots are in back to make cooking quicker, tools and furniture are in front with our barrel of water. In the middle, between sacks of flour and beans, is a small nest where I can sit with the boys. Two lanterns hang from the hoops, along with extra coils of rope, our canteens, tin pans, and tin cups. It is noisy as a tinker's cart.

There's not one spare inch for anyone to stretch out inside, so every night we must pitch tents . . . one for

Ma and Pa, the other I'm to share with Bennie and Jake. Ours fits like a lean-to alongside the wagon and is cozy and out of the wind. Still, I'm bothered to sleep outside for the next six months. What about snakes? What if Indians come in the middle of the night?

April 14, Wednesday

I have made a friend! She is fourteen, one year older than I am, with freckles over her nose and cheeks, and beautiful green eyes. She is not as bossy as Becky, matter-of-fact she seems real shy, but I think I shall like her very much anyhow.

When I told her I am scared of Indians she said, "Don't worry, Hattie, there are probably plenty more good Indians than bad." We have been walking to the edge of town together, to watch the blacksmith repair tools and such. My friend's name is Pepper Lewis and she has a twin brother named Wade.

Camped near us is a lady who is so fat she can barely walk; she must weigh 300 pounds. Her arms are as thick as my waist. It is hard not to stare, especially on account of that her husband has no legs. Either she carries him around or he rides in a little cart she pulls. I hope they don't come over to visit with Ma because I won't know what to say.

April 22, Thursday
Alcove Spring

We are three days west of Independence, camped at Alcove Spring. Water gushes from a ledge, down ten feet into a pool where there are ferns and deep shade. How delicious the water tastes! Ma and I waited our turn with other women in the wagon train to fill our canteens and jugs. A tiny frog swam into my palm, then out again — all the while we were serenaded by crickets.

My feet are sore and blistered, so much that it hurts to walk. It felt good to soak them in the cool pond. I want to go barefoot, but Mama says there are too many stickers and thorns. Soon enough the blisters will turn to calluses, she said.

When we finally pulled out of Independence, leaving behind the Missoura River, the sun wasn't up yet. Two dozen wagons were already ahead of us. Behind were hundreds of cows, horses, and sheep. I was so excited I yelled, "Hooray, hooray!" At long last we were on our way to Oregon.

But, oh, the dust! So much dust, we could barely see the rumps of our own oxen. My eyes stung and we all were coughing.

Pa steered to one side of the trail, but other families pulled alongside, making four abreast. I soon tired of the bumping and jolting and rattling, and sitting in a cramped space, so I gathered my skirt about my knees and jumped to the ground.

I ran between the wagons until I saw Pepper sitting up with her pa. I hollered to her. When she leapt down her skirt flew up, showing off her leggings, white as cattails. We hurried away from the trail where it wasn't as noisy.

We walked for six hours and talked the whole time! She said, "Hattie, when we get to Oregon let's ask our fathers to build houses right next door to each other." And I said, "Then we can share a garden. I'll plant the lettuce and corn, you plant tomatoes." So as we walked along, Pepper and I planned out our whole future, down to the matching lace curtains we'd make for our bedrooms, the pet kittens we'd raise, and so on.

My, how the dust leaves a gritty taste in our mouths. It is awful. With every step our hems pick up burrs from the tall grass, dried brush scratches our ankles. Finally that first day, when the sun was directly overhead, everyone stopped. Pepper and I were so wore out, we fell back into the shade of our wagon, laughing.

"Do we have to keep going?" we asked Pa. He just smiled at us as he carried water to the animals.

The first night camping was a late one with singing and dancing. Pepper and I swung in a circle with Jake and the little twins, 'round and 'round.

We are on our way! was the cry heard over and over. Even Ma joined in when folks started singing "Buffalo Gals," but when Pa asked her to do-si-do she lifted Bennie onto her hip and turned for the wagon.

"Time for bed," she said. Maybe when Mama sees Oregon, she will dance.

April 25, Sunday

At 4 o'clock in the morning, when it is still pitch-dark, the bugle sounds. This is when breakfast fires are started and men ride out to herd in the animals, but today there was a loud discussion. Some families want to rest because of the Sabbath, for prayer and worship. But some, including Pa, say we must press on with no delays. Winter could come early and we need to be over the mountains by then. We must not make the same mistake as the Donners.

No one says much about them, but I often think about the terrible, terrible business of eating dead friends. I'm brave, but not near brave enough to do that.

So we must hurry along. October is six months away. Will it really take half a year to reach Oregon? I wonder.

Finally, just before sunrise, the men agreed to travel

on Sundays, but families will take turns reading Scripture and giving a prayer at each meal.

The prairie is wide and lonesome without a house or barn in sight. We caught up to several heavy freight wagons drawn by mules. Pa said we are on the Santa Fe Trail. In a few miles the trail will split: The freighters will head southwest toward the Territory of Mexico and we shall continue northwest.

With every mile it feels like the sky and trail are moving with us, as if we're walking in place. Everything looks the same no matter how far we've come. Only when I look down at my dusty shoes and see that, yes, I am walking forward and the footprints behind are mine, can I believe that we are actually moving.

Girls are gathering dandelions in their aprons to make a salad, also young leaves from tumbleweed plants. Aunt June said to look for wild carrots and onions from seeds dropped by last summer's travelers. The little twins found sunflower stalks and pretended to ride them like ponies. They are such dear children, I shared some taffy with them at supper.

April 27, Tuesday

A few days ago we crossed the Kansas River. At first I was scared watching the horses wade in because water splashed their heads, and I worried they wouldn't be able to breathe. But somehow they managed to swim, paddling like dogs, their necks stretched high and strong.

Now we are at the Big Blue River, which is much wider and faster than the Kansas. The men are discussing how we should cross it, and whether we should do so now before dark. Everyone is dead tired. Most families want to spend the night on this side because there's plenty of dry firewood and they want to rest.

One lady yelled out, "We are wore out, mister. Can't you see that?"

But Tall Joe just stood high on a wagon seat and held up his arms for quiet. "We gotta cross now," he shouted back. He said the river's low, but it could rise overnight, no tellin'. Another thing he said, come tomorrow morning the animals will be so frisky they'll be harder to force into the water.

I must help Ma wrap up the cheese and figs we ate at noon, and change Bennie's wet pants. Already two men are riding to the other side. Water is up to their saddles and the horses' tails are floating. Several boys on horseback are whooping and yelling as they ride across. Their rifles were taken away from them so they wouldn't shoot anybody by mistake. Hooray.

April 2?, Wednesday, I think

While crossing the Big Blue, Jake, Bennie, and I sat in our little spot in the wagon, As we floated I could feel the pull and jerk as the animals struggled to swim. We could see forward through a small space between boxes. There were many wagons ahead of us, their white tops swaying from the current.

Suddenly Pa jumped into the river to turn our oxen because they were trying to swim downstream. Ma grabbed the reins and wrapped them around her hands.

When we began tipping over on our right side I screamed, terrified we'd sink. Water poured in through the canvas. I could see that Ma's bonnet had fallen back over her shoulders and she was pulling the reins hard, trying to turn the animals. Everything in the wagon not tied down slid toward us. Two sacks of beans rolled onto my legs and a bag of flour burst open when it fell against the rocker.

While looking straight ahead, Ma yelled for us to lean with all our weight against the high wall. As we clung to an overhead hoop one of the lanterns swung and hit my head so hard I wanted to let go, but I knew I must keep my arm around little Ben so he wouldn't get washed away.

Pa kept swimming with the oxen and with Ma's

help, we somehow tipped back up. It seemed forever, but was probably just a minute.

Bennie was crying because he was scared and his clothes were wet. The three of us were covered with a gooey white paste from the spilled flour. It felt awful. My sleeves were sticky and my braid was stiff as a broom.

Finally there was a thump as our wheels touched bottom, then there was splashing as our team pulled us through the mud and onto the beach. More water rushed in, soaking our blankets, but we've hung them over brush to dry while we wait on shore for the others. It might take two days to get everyone across.

I hope we don't have to cross any more rivers!

This afternoon my little friends the twins wandered off to pick berries, but now it is near sunset and they've not returned. Their parents are frantic and I'm worried sick. Tall Joe and Pa are leading a search party. I wanted to help, too, but Ma said she needs me to watch Jake and Bennie so she can go sit with the twins' mother, to comfort her.

Oh, those poor children — they're much too small to be lost.

Next day

When the bugle sounded at 4 o'clock, I awoke with a sick feeling, remembering I'd fallen asleep to the voices of worried adults. Some had taken torches beyond the corral of wagons to search the grass and riverbanks, late into the night.

When I crawled out from the quilt, Bennie and Jake rolled sleepily into my warm space.

"Mama?" I called.

"I'm here, Hattie." Her voice came from her tent.

"Have the little twins been found?" I whispered.

Ma stepped out of the doorway. Dark circles were under her eyes, and her braid was over her shoulder, not combed out since yesterday.

"No dear, they ain't been found."

Ma hurried us through breakfast of cold biscuits and jam. When Pa brought in the oxen and began harnessing them, I cried out, "We can't be leaving!"

He and Ma looked at each other. "Two other families will stay behind to help the parents search, Hattie. We must keep going."

"But why? Why can't we stay and help, too?"

Pa came over and put his strong arms around me. "I'm sorry the children are lost, Hattie. But their ma and pa have insisted that everyone keep going. They understand we can't all stay. I'm sorry."

As we pulled out I watched the campsite. The mother was just a small shape until we rounded a bluff, then I saw her no more.

I pulled my brothers into my lap and started to sing

them a song, but my heart was so heavy I burst out crying.

Later

I taught Jake how to shake out his blanket then roll it up with string. I must do Bennie's because he just drags his in the dust. Ma is too tired to notice their dirty faces so I wash them myself.

Another day

Today we came to the Little Blue, but thank God we didn't have to cross it. Our wagons are so heavy, the oxen strain to pull us up the trail. We'll follow the river into Nebraska.

Every time we stop and the dust has settled, I look back to see if the little twins and their family have caught up. No one speaks of them and I don't know why.

This morning I made batter for pancakes. I went to the stream to fill my pitcher, but when I returned to camp the batter was black with mosquitoes. I started to dump it into the dirt, but Aunt June put her hand on my arm.

"Hattie," she said, "don't waste — just stir them up

good. The griddle's hot enough to cook 'em through and no one ever died from such."

So we had mosquitoes for breakfast. Jake called them "skeeter cakes" and he said they tasted just fine soaked in molasses, but to me they were like sand in my teeth.

When we opened one of our sacks we found the bacon to be green and crawling with maggots, fifty pounds of it. Ma was so furious she shouted at my father.

"That butcher in Independence said it would last months and look here," she said to Pa, wiping her finger along the meat. "There ain't a lick of salt anywhere." Every day it seems there is a new disappointment for my poor mother.

Jake thought it was all right by him if we cooked up some maggots, but Pa dragged the sack outside of camp and buried it.

At least three other families were sold rotten meat also.

Three days later

I have lost track of days and dates so from now on shall not worry about them. Aunt June has also lost track because she's been sick with dizziness. Uncle Tim drives while she lies in the wagon, the canvas sides rolled up from the bottom to let air in. Ma herself is tired and grouchy. She says the dust gives her a headache something fierce.

There's no sign of the little twins' family.

A lady by the name of Mrs. Kenker brought over a cup of soup last night, but Aunt June was too vomitty to even taste it. Mrs. Kenker has gray hair wrapped on top her head and she has all her teeth. She smiled real pretty and asked "how y'be" to everyone; she reminds me of my sweet old grandma.

She and her husband are well-liked, it seems. At night when the fiddler starts up, they lead out with a waltz or polka, depending on how slow or fast the music. Soon the married couples join in, then the younger men with sweethearts.

"How lovely they are together," folks whisper about Mr. and Mrs. Kenker.

But I know something folks don't.

This morning before sunrise, as we were taking down our tent, Mrs. Kenker came to check on Aunt June, so sweet and gentle-like. She lay her hand on my aunt's forehead then kissed her cheek. Then just as smooth and quiet as you please, Mrs. Kenker reached into our cooking box and slipped one of Ma's silver spoons into her apron pocket!

I thought my eyes was playing tricks on me. My mouth dropped open, but no words came out.

What will Mama do if I tell her?

Evening

When we reached the high grassland of Indian country we saw wide open prairie filled with wildflowers, yellow, blue, and red, like patches on a quilt. Tall Joe says that some days ahead we'll meet up with emigrants coming down from Iowa and Wisconsin Territory. There could be twice as many of us then, all heading west.

Pa wonders if there will be enough grass for all our animals or enough firewood for our camps.

I've decided to walk to Oregon on account of there is no comfortable way to ride. Our rocking chair broke when it fell out the back and Ma insists on keeping it even though Pa says it takes up more room broke. She is so cross with him, she will not listen to reason. And I don't want to upset her even more by telling about her stolen spoon.

All day our wagon drove alongside the Anderson family with baby Eliza May and her tree sisters (Mama says I must stop calling them that). How their mother cleans Eliza May's and Cassia's diapers is an amazing sight:

After breakfast she pins them with thorns to the canvas sides of their wagon. As they flap in the breeze they dry and the sun bleaches them whiter than they were hours before. By noon, there are more tacked to each side, and just before we turn into a circle at sundown, the Anderson wagon looks like a creature with many tiny wings.

Pepper and I and some other girls hunted for food near old campsites. She has such a pleasant way of giving orders that several younger girls tagged along, eager to look here or there, and dig in the dirt with their fingers.

"Like this, Pepper?" they asked, and she would pat them on their shoulders and say, "Why, yes, that's perfect. Good work." After a couple of hours we had found small red potatoes, some pearl onions, and rosemary.

Next day

Our train has about 135 wagons, so at night we divide into groups, spread out over a couple miles. For the past week we've had the same 23 wagons in our circle. The littlest children can play safe inside while mothers gather around the fire to cook or visit. We are all becoming well-acquainted.

This is how we pull into a circle: The tongue of our wagon rests near the inside rear wheel of Uncle Tim's and his does the same with the wagon in front of him and so forth. All the wagons together form a horseshoe with an opening about 20 feet wide so folks can come and go.

After the animals are unhitched they are let out to pasture with the rest of the stock. Men take turns guarding so in case of an Indian attack they are ready to herd them into our corral and pull chains across for a gate. Thus far we ain't seen any Indians and I'm glad for that.

(Folks say they are dirty and vicious, but I don't know.)

Ma is more cheerful today, but Pa still avoids arguing with her. She's been caring for Aunt June and this morning said the illness was on account of Aunt June going to have a baby! Before we get to Oregon!

Two large kettles are on the fire tonight — one with beans and the other with vegetables and beef bones left-over from last night's meal. Some families spread a cloth in the dirt to make it look nice, but us — Ma and Aunt June —are already sick of washing dishes so sometimes we just take turns dipping cups in and sharing spoons, then it's not so much to clean.

Mrs. Kenker uses white linen with china plates and two crystal wine goblets, for she and the mister tip back a few each night. I am keeping an eye on her.

Two days later

Now that Aunt June's feeling better she took her calendar around until she found someone who'd been making notches in the side of a wagon. We think it is May 8, Saturday, 1847.

In the distance there's a light green ribbon stretched through the middle of a wide valley. Pa said this is the Platte River and it will guide us into the mountains. The days are warming up so Pepper and I take our shoes off to walk — this is after we're out of our mothers' sight. The tops of our feet are brown from the sun, the bottoms are tough as leather.

She is more talkative now and not at all shy about lifting her skirt to cool off when no one's looking. I'm fond of her, for she knows how to laugh, and she also has a soft heart. Like me, she's worried about the lost children and their poor mother, more so maybe because she and Wade themselves are twins. We still look behind us, hoping to see dust from their family's wagon trying to catch up.

Wade joined us today with one of his new friends, a tall boy with curly brown hair and a gentle manner. His name is Gideon. He's seventeen years old, but so shy he took one look at Pepper's beautiful green eyes and blushed. He stared down at his feet almost the whole three hours we walked together.

Wade, now, he's not shy. He told a joke when he figured I was the only one listening to him. It went like this:
XXXXXXXXXXXXXXXXXXXXXXXXXXXXXXXXXXXXXXXX
XXXXXXXXXXXXXXXXXXXXXXXXXXXXXXXXXXXXXXXX
XXXXXXXXXXXXXXXXXXXXXXXXXXXXXXXXXXXXXXXX
XXXXXXXXXXXXXXXXXXXXXXXXXXXXXXXXXXXXXXXX
XXXXXXXXXXXXXXXXXXXXXXXXXXXXXXXXXXXXXXXX
XXXXXX

(Aunt June saw over my shoulder while I was sitting after supper and said I must not repeat such naughty jokes, and that I best cross it out before Ma sees.)

But I still think it was funny.

May 10, Monday

As we headed down a bluff toward the Platte River there was already many campfires, tents, and wagons. It felt the same as when our steamboat arrived in Independence —so many people!

Most are from Wisconsin Territory — they have "northern" accents, a speech that is not near as slow as folks' from Kentucky. Some brothers from Iowa have brung with them 800 young fruit trees to plant in Oregon. The seedlings are just a few inches tall.

"Well," said Pa, "seems these here are our new traveling companions."

The trail is broad and sandy here on the south side of the Platte, and it feels like we're pulling uphill. Pa says we'll go over one hundred miles before we have to cross, and it'll take maybe ten days.

(I do dread having to cross another river.)

Mosquitoes are fierce! There are itchy bites on my arms, neck, and cheeks, even on my head where my hair is parted. It is near impossible not to scratch vigorously.

Every morning we fry up "skeeter cakes." I've tried and tried to stir quick and even if the batter is clean when I pour, somehow bugs see it as a place to land, and land they do, like specks of pepper. I can see no way around it.

At night there are campfires way across the river, on the north side. Our men are talking low among themselves, wondering if Indians are following us. (If they *are* following us, what are we to do?) Come sunup, all we can see is dust and horses and what looks like wagons, but Pa says if they ain't Indians what are they and why do they travel alone?

Evening

Tall Joe and three of his friends crossed over by way of sandbars and shallows to see who these strangers are.

"They're Mormons, from Illinois," Tall Joe reported

back to us. "Their leader is a big fella named Brigham Young. There is only three women and two children and the rest is men, about one hundred forty we counted, and three nigras, servants looks like."

Tall Joe said they're heading West, maybe to the valley of the Great Salt Lake to start a colony. "Thousands more will come next year, don't ask me why, it's just a desert full of dead things."

Pa asked Tall Joe, "But why do they stay on the other side of the river? There ain't no trail."

"I dunno," the old trapper said between mouthfuls of beans. "Maybe they's worried there won't be enough grass, I dunno."

A wagon train is like a small town the way talk spreads. Soon everyone, it seems, had a story about the Mormons, mainly that Mormon men each have several wives and the reason they left Illinois is because they want to find a place to live where folks won't keep telling them they're committing adultery.

Mrs. Lewis said, "Frankly I prefer they stay on the other side of the river on account of I don't want any pole-igamist getting friendly with our daughters and sisters. Leave ol' Brigham Young be. Let them go their way."

Myself, personally I think something's wrong with a religion that says men get to have as many wives as they please all at once. Pepper says so, too.

Before bed

Forgot to say that today Bennie took off his shirt and threw it in the river. I don't know why he did this except that he's two years old and doesn't know better. Now he has one shirt to last all the way to Oregon. I must watch carefully to make sure he don't also throw away his shoes!

Next day

At noon Mama was looking through our kitchen box, taking things out then putting them back.

"Hattie?" she said. "Have you seen Grandma's china plate, the little one with roses? I thought I put it in after breakfast."

I helped Ma look. We tried to think together where we last set it. Suddenly I caught my breath, remembering:

Pepper and I had carried our families' dishes to the stream where we dipped them in cold water and rubbed them with sand. To dry, we lay them on the grassy bank and sat for a while talking. There were other women doing the same. One of them was Mrs. Kenker.

I'm worried Mrs. Kenker has stole something else from us, but if I tell Ma, there might be arguments and Ma is already wore out and nervous as it is. I don't want to bother her with something new to worry about.

(How can someone who looks like my dear old grandmother be a thief?)

After supper when the fiddlers were getting warmed up, I walked over to the Kenkers' wagon, just to see what I could see. Mister and Missus were sitting on stools by their wheel, talking sweet to the Anderson family. The five little girls were on a blanket that was laid out in the dirt, playing with a tea set they made from acorn caps. Cassia was singing a song to her baby sister, Eliza May.

"Hello, Hattie, dear," Mrs. Kenker said. "We're having cocoa in a moment, would you like to join us?"

"No, ma'am, I would not." I kept walking.

"My, my," she said.

I know it wasn't polite to answer her so sharp, but I don't care.

Later

We are camped by the Platte. Smoke from the Mormon campfires drifts toward us with a good smell of beef roasting. I would like to meet the two Mormon children and see what they're like, what kind of clothes they're wearing, and so forth. How lonesome it must be for them not to have friends to play with on such a long journey.

Mosquitoes are still a terrible nuisance. Every bit of my skin itches! Ma says the only way to keep them off is to smear mud on our bites, but I tried this three nights in a row. By sunup my face was so tight I couldn't smile and when it was all washed off my skin was dry as a stone, which itched almost as bad as the bites.

Pepper and I followed a tiny stream out of camp to a marshy area. Growing nearby was a small crop of wild carrots and parsnips. We pulled their bushy tops until we had enough to fill our aprons. I dislike vegetables, they make me feel vomitty, but Aunt June says to gather any food we see because we don't know what tomorrow will bring. Along the path we also found a tree with tiny green apples, but left them as they weren't ripe.

Another day

Something horrible has happened and I fear I'm to blame.

Just before supper last night little Cassia came to where Pepper and I was cutting up potatoes and onions for soup. While Cassia watched, I sliced all the parsnips and gave her a couple bites when she held out her palm.

The kettle was hanging over a fire near the center of camp, so Pepper and I brung the vegetables along with three salted ox tongues, preserved from those that died the other day. We dumped the meat and onions into the boiling water, but saved the rest to add later.

We returned to help Mrs. Lewis — Pepper's mother — make pies. I rolled out dough on the wagon seat, enough for six pie crusts. This took near an hour. While I was pressing them into pans, we heard screams.

Lying in the dirt by the kettle was three boys. They were shaking and twisting and foaming at the mouth and gasping for breath. When we saw that one of the boys was Wade, Pepper and her mother ran with their hands in the air crying out his name.

Such was my hurry that when I jumped down from the seat my skirt swept the pie crusts off, down into the dirt.

"What is it? What's happened?" Wade's mother cried, pulling him into her arms. Pa noticed the basket of vegetables had been knocked over.

He scooped up a handful and yelled, "No one eat anything! No one!" He leapt onto a crate so folks could see him, and kept hollering. "Who made this soup? What's in it?"

I was so frightened my insides were shivering, but I stepped forward. Pepper did, too.

"Pa," I said, trying not to cry, "it was our turn to cook tonight, we made it."

"Hattie, show me what you put in, quick." To the gathering men he shouted, "Bury all this, bury it now." Meanwhile some of the women were scooping charcoal from the fire and crushing it into powder. They tried to force it down the boys' throats with water, but their jaws was clenched too tight.

Pepper and I showed Pa where we cut the meat and vegetables. He picked up the potato peelings, smelled them, put a piece on his tongue and waited a moment. He did the same with an onion skin. He tasted a sliver of beef.

"These here are all right," he said. "What else, Hattie?"

I showed him the parsnip tops we'd broke off and set aside for salad.

Pa's face fell. He looked up at Mr. Lewis then back at me. He sniffed the greens, then placed a tiny bit of the root on the tip of his tongue.

In an instant he spit it out. "God help us," he said. "This is water hemlock . . . poison. Hattie, wash your hands right quick."

Next day

It's midmorning and we are still camped.

There is so much upset and noise that I am alone in our wagon for a few moments. No one can see me because I'm hidden among the flour sacks; wish I could disappear for good.

When Pa said the word "hemlock," panic broke out. Folks who hadn't eaten yet suddenly thought they had. Mothers cried for their children. Suddenly I remembered Cassia.

We called her name. Gideon found her curled up inside his family's wagon. When I saw him carrying her limp body in his arms, and when I realized she was dead, I broke down.

"Only two bites," I sobbed. "It was only two bites."

Three graves are being dug by the side of the trail. The two younger boys died thirty minutes after becoming sick. Wade hasn't woke up yet. His eyes just stare, and his body stiffens and shakes so wildly they've had to tie him down so he won't hurt himself. Pepper is too upset to speak.

It crushed me to look at Wade. He is breathing hard and fast through clenched jaws so it sounds like he's hissing. Blood is at the corners of his mouth. I have never seen such a violent sickness.

What happened was the boys were so hungry they sampled the vegetables while waiting for supper.

We don't know how much hemlock Wade ate, but we're praying it ain't as much as the others. He was the only one whose jaws they were able to pry open long enough for him to swallow. Maybe charcoal in his stomach is absorbing the poison.

There is much weeping.

Pepper and I showed the men where we found the plants. We are showing them to everyone, walking from wagon to wagon, telling children to be careful, to stay away and not even touch them if they find any while out playing.

Pa said at first there is a sweet taste when you take a bite, but then there is a bitter, burning taste. Carrots and parsnips, he showed us by drawing in the dirt, have one root, that's what they are, a root. Hemlock has a few roots joined together, like a hand with plump fingers. The color is white, just like parsnips and wild carrots.

Even the tops are deadly. Sheep and cattle die from grazing on them. Uncle Tim said that one small root can kill a horse, one bite can kill a man.

He showed us that when you cut hemlock it drips with an oily yellow goo. The other thing is the roots are hollow with rungs. Like rungs in a ladder. I'm sick to think I didn't know these things.

Later

We have pulled out and left behind that terrible camp along the Platte. Gideon and Mr. Lewis — Wade's father — carved the children's names onto a plank of wood, along with a warning, and placed it by the graves.

The funeral was unbearable . . . oh, the tears. We stood with Cassia's parents and sisters. The boys' families also had many aunts, uncles, brothers, and cousins. A lone fiddler played "Amazing Grace" as men shoveled dirt onto the common grave. Moments later the sun set, spreading gold and purple across the wide flowing river. I ached something fierce.

Mrs. Anderson looked at me with eyes full of sorrow, then gently brushed my cheek before turning away.

Later, when the stars were out and no one could see me, I ran into the brush and fell down weeping. My heart was broken. Everyone says I'm not to blame, but still I feel dead inside. It's a miracle no one else ate the vegetables.

Wade seems to sleep, but his eyes are open and he mumbles words we don't understand. They gave him a sip of rum this morning which has made his arms and jaw relax. Pepper lifts a spoonful of water to his lips every half hour and rubs her finger along his throat so he'll swallow. He must have bitten his cheek because there is still blood in his mouth.

Our mothers pray. They are asking God, that if it be His will, to please heal Wade.

I look over at the Anderson wagon and start crying again. There are half as many diapers pinned to their canvas top. Ma said there's nothing worse than losing a child. And to leave behind the grave, never to see it again, is an unspeakable pain.

Lord, please don't let Wade die.

I don't know what day this is

We crossed the South Platte. I've not felt like writing until now.

This river is near a mile wide and so shallow lots of folks walk across. This was a very great relief to me.

Pepper and I challenged Gideon and some other boys to a race, but we were soon slowed down by our wet skirts. When Gideon saw us struggling to run in the waist-high water, he stepped between us, took our hands, and helped pull us across.

It was the first time any of us had laughed for two days.

Once ashore we flopped down in the warm sand and

stared up at the sky. It was such a lovely blue I felt, for that moment, happy again.

While Pepper and I wrung out our hems, Gideon turned away, embarrassed to see our bare legs. He is the nicest of all the boys we've met except for Wade. I feel sad Wade's been sleeping these two days. His mama keeps a damp cloth over his eyes so he won't go blind.

Later

Now that we're in the North Platte River Valley the air feels dry and thin. My lips are so chapped they bleed when I talk. The only thing to do is dip our fingers into the bucket of axle grease and rub our lips every hour or so. It smells bad, it tastes bad, and the blowing dust sticks.

It feels like we must be halfway to Oregon, but Tall Joe says, no, we've only gone five hundred miles. He also said the worst part of the trail is to come.

Does he mean more rivers to cross? Will there be Indians? I'm afraid to ask what he's talking about.

The Andersons' wagon had an accident when we climbed up Windlass Hill and were heading down the other side. It was so steep that at the top of the hill we unhitched the teams and led them down separately. Then we chained the wheels to keep them from turning.

Also we cut small trees and tied them behind each wagon for drag, to slow it down as men lowered them with ropes and pulleys. (That's why this place is named Windlass Hill.)

It took hours and hours. I was nervous watching the men strain so hard, their heels dug into sand, their palms bleeding from the ropes. Ma and some other ladies tore their petticoats into rags to wrap around the men's hands.

What happened with the Anderson wagon is that their front axle hit a stump which caused the smaller rope to snap. Before anyone could help, the wagon flipped over and over and over, landing in splinters at the bottom. Folks screamed, but it was just the shock of seeing such an accident. No one was hurt. Thank God Mrs. Anderson and her daughters were watching from the top of the hill, for they had climbed out earlier to lighten the load.

The only belongings they could rescue were clothes and blankets that were strewn over the rocks when their trunks split open, and a few tools. Aunt June and Uncle Tim right away invited the family to share their own wagon and supplies for the rest of the journey.

We also will share. Hazel, Holly, Laurel, and Olive will take turns riding with us. I don't mind giving up my very small spot inside as it's hot from the sun beating down on the canvas top. I am tired of the bumping and rattling, besides something always tips over, yesterday it was Ma's bureau. Things are packed in so tight that the bouncing makes the ropes fray. (My opinion is it ain't safe in there.)

Two other wagons got "stumped" today, so those families will double up with others. There's enough wreckage to completely build a new rig, but no time to do it. We must keep moving. The mules and oxen will go to others who need them.

After supper Gideon came over to where Pepper and I were sitting. He nodded to me then looked shyly at Pepper. "Woncha please dance with me?" he asked.

Pepper leaned over to whisper in my ear. "Do you mind, Hattie?"

I turned to whisper in her ear, "He's handsome!"

She smiled, then squeezed my hand. So there they are, circling the fire with other dancers, shuffling, stepping, turning — his left hand on his hip, his right hand around her waist. Folks watch them and smile.

I wish Wade was well enough to ask me to dance.

Ash Hollow

The Platte split into two, so now our trail is along the North Platte River. Our reward for making it down

Windlass Hill is the most beautiful campsite yet. It's called Ash Hollow because of so many thick, shady ash trees.

There's a spring with fresh icy water so we can fill up our barrels and such. Everywhere we look there's firewood and good pasture for the animals. It is so peaceful Ma said, "Oh, Charles, can't we stay here forever?"

A few years ago some emigrants did exactly that. A family built themselves a cabin and plowed a field. They are friendly to us and have offered to post our letters with the next travelers heading back to Missoura. Many of us quick wrote to friends. I tore out a sheet of paper from this journal and sent Becky a drawing of hemlock, telling her all.

The moon is full so I'm writing by its light as I sit near the wagon. There are hundreds of campfires tonight, and singing. Ma is walking along a creek with Mrs. Anderson, who has been silent for days. Ma says she's grieving, that she finally realizes little Cassia is gone and that her grave is far away, in a lonely place along a river she'll never see again.

I'm so very sad for her. This makes me watch Bennie and Jake more close for I don't know how Ma and Pa and me could go on if they became lost or died somehow.

There are Indians, about twenty, camped nearby. The sight of them makes me so nervous I feel vomitty.

Some women came near, holding their hands out, talking in their language. Their deerskin dresses have tiny beads sewn along their sleeves. Their hair is braided over their shoulders. One of them wore a basket on her back with a baby inside, a dark-haired baby with dark quiet eyes. They accepted Ma's corncakes without a smile.

I asked Tall Joe why they was begging. "They ain't begging," he said. "Indians are hospitable people and if they was passing through our land they'd give us a gift. They're just asking for ours."

They look like beggars to me, but they are not making trouble. Matter of fact one of the women did something real nice. She saw Mrs. Anderson off by herself, crying, and walked over to her with a square of deerskin, the size of a plate. On it was several chunks of cooked meat.

She picked up a piece and put it to Mrs. Anderson's lips, nodding for her to eat. The woman then pointed to the little Anderson girls playing in the stream, then motioned with her hands and mouth, like she was eating.

Finally Mrs. Anderson accepted the gift. I think she understood that the Indian woman wanted her to take nourishment for the sake of her little daughters.

Later

Aunt June wears a smock dress now on account she's getting bigger. I helped her and Ma do laundry. The stream was busy with ladies talking and working. By afternoon the bushes were covered with petticoats, shirts, calicoes, blankets — all drying in the hot sun.

The youngest children ran naked into the water. Pepper and I loosened our braids and stripped down to our camisoles then jumped in, too. How good the cold water felt pouring over my face and through my hair, and how good it felt to wash away the dust.

We swam downstream along the bank where willows made a canopy of shade. It was shallow enough to sit on the sandy bottom, the water up to our shoulders. Ma don't know this, but we then took off our drawers and camisoles until we was bare as the day we were born. Reckless with joy, we dove below the surface to stare at each other through the bubbles.

It was several minutes before we realized our clothes was floating downstream far beyond our reach, down in the direction of the men and boys.

Pepper and I soon learned it ain't easy to walk upstream crouched down so only your head is above water. Also, it is near impossible to swim without your bare backside showing.

We was rescued by two grandmothers holding blankets for us.

There is dancing again tonight (Ma still refuses to join in). Pepper was fetched by Gideon and this time he held her hand all the way through camp.

Oh, yes, a little baby girl was born this morning at Ash Hollow.

Another thing, that fat lady came over and brung Ma a fresh pie, mince it turns out. I hurried off to watch from the trees. She must eat ten pies a day, I reckon; she's that huge.

Next day

In the far distance the prairie and low hills are black. I thought there must have been a fire, but Tall Joe said, "Nope, it's just buffalo, thousands and thousands of 'em."

After supper I sat by the fire to mend Bennie's blanket. He lay next to me in the dirt, talking about this and that, then suddenly he was fast asleep. I like the way he folds into my arms when I carry him to bed.

Later

We are starting to find buffalo droppings, and Tall Joe says, "Where there's buffs, there's Injuns."

Hunters leave the wagons every morning to look for game. They brung down two buffalo near enough to the trail so folks can see them being skinned and butchered. Jake went with some older boys to watch but I stayed behind.

Aunt June was resting in her wagon with Olive and Laurel, who are three and four years old. To make room inside, Uncle Tim pulled out several sacks of bacon and flour.

(It is so much work to pack and unpack that at noon Pa just lies flat in the dirt to rest and he's sound asleep before his eyes even close.)

We're camped next door to Aunt June with a tarp stretched between the tops for shade. I saw Mrs. Kenker wave howdee.

"Hattie dear," she said, "may I borrow one of your mother's tablecloths please? Mine is soiled and Mr. Kenker is ready for his lunch."

I felt stiff toward her. "I'm afraid not, Mrs. Kenker."

My aunt's voice came from her wagon. "Hattie Campbell, we are not a family to refuse hospitality. Help Mrs. Kenker take what she needs."

Well. By the time Mrs. Kenker had snooped around,

we were quite a bit lighter. She took our lovely lace tablecloth that Grandmother made, five doilies, a tea cozy, and one English teacup. She also grabbed one of Ma's brown calico skirts and draped it over her arm, but I snatched it back.

Our eyes locked, then finally she turned away. "Thank you, dear," she called over her shoulder, her arms too full to wave.

Jake was so excited to tell about the buffalo skinning and he pulled my hand to go see, but I was bothered about Mrs. Kenker and wouldn't.

When Ma came back I told her, but she said the same thing as Aunt June: "We must share."

This makes me mad. I like to share with nice folks, not those that takes advantage. I'm afraid if I say anything more about Mrs. Kenker I'll sound wretched, so that's all for now.

Later again

There are more and more buffalo. They are so many, the herds look like a dark stain moving over the hills. The droppings are flat, full of dried grass and make good coals, but it takes near a bushel to make a decent cooking fire.

I would rather pick up twigs and logs than buffalo

dung, but this is what we must do. As long as they're not fresh and gooey, it ain't so bad.

The boys, including my naughty brother Jake, spend much of their chore time throwing these buffalo chips at each other, like a snowball fight, instead of helping. They also think it's fun to ambush us girls, but I think it's nasty.

Pepper and I feel nervous when we go out to gather the chips. The other day two horsemen were watching from a distance, so we told our fathers who told the rest of the men. Now they all ride with loaded guns. It scares me to think Indians are following us.

Maybe Indian women are nice, but the men carry weapons. I do not trust them.

I walk alongside Wade's wagon with Pepper. She and I sing to him "Yankee Doodle" and other songs. We feel silly, but maybe he'll wake up. He's swallowing the broth she spoons into his mouth and his arms no longer shake or stiffen. Mrs. Lewis and her friends look in on him constantly and I will say he's the most prayed-over boy I ever met.

Evening

The sun is scorching hot. Ma insists I wear my bonnet to protect my face, but the cloth itches my scalp. When

Pepper and I are out walking we carry them like baskets to gather flowers. It feels cooler to let the wind blow my hair back and besides, I think boys like looking at us better without them.

The Mormons are still on the north side of the Platte. Sometimes all we see is their dust because they move faster. Ma says it's because they're traveling with just two children instead of 200, like we have in our train; babies slow things up — that's just the way it is, she says.

I told Pa that Brigham Young must be very religious because he makes his people rest on the Sabbath — no traveling.

Pa laughed. He said, "I still ain't in agreement with Brigham Young's theology but if he wants to rest on the Sabbath good for him. But, Hattie, don't judge a man only by how strict he keeps rules."

Tall Joe said that up here soon the routes will meet at Fort Laramie and, like it or not, we'll be traveling alongside the Mormons and their 73 wagons. Pepper and I plan to meet the two children.

Later

There is much celebration today and tears of joy.

After three days of sleeping, Wade sat up, looked

around and said, "Mother, I am hungry as a bear." Just like that.

Pepper and I joined hands with Gideon and the little Anderson girls and Jake and Bennie. We danced around Wade's wagon and sang. Mrs. Lewis cries and cries she is so thankful to God for healing her son.

He is too weak to walk, but his father carried him down to the river's edge, to a sandy beach. He bathed him then helped him dress into clean clothes. Now Wade's sitting in the shade, wearing a blue shirt and pants.

I am so glad to see his beautiful green eyes again. Pepper can't stop giggling she's so happy. She sits by her brother just talking and talking to him.

Another day

Clouds build up like white towers, then in the afternoon they turn black. Near every day we hear the low rumblings of thunder, and we feel heavy drops of rain — enough to settle the dust and coat the wheels with mud, but no downpour.

We see mighty herds of buffalo in the distance, to either side of the trail. Often there are men on horseback moving along a ridge. If Indians are following us, they're keeping their distance.

Maybe they are just curious and don't plan to murder us.

This morning I read back through this journal and laughed when I saw what I'd written about Booneville: ". . . I am afraid of only four things . . ."

Ma says that people who are thinkers often change their opinions. It means you're growing. So here's what I think.

Some things I was afraid of I'm not afraid of now and the other way around. I am not so scared about snakes anymore, I have not had a toothache, and the Indians haven't hurt us. Even Bennie and Jake don't worry me so much, they are much stronger on their legs and stay close to the wagon. So here is my new list.

1. I'm afraid of hemlock
2. fast rivers

That's all!

Later

Wade walked today, for about fifteen minutes. He steps slow and gets tired easy. When we ask if he remembers what happened he squints and looks up at the sky.

"Nope," he says after a while. He knows we're on our way to Oregon and he does remember being on a

riverboat some time ago. He knows his family and today he said my name.

He said, "Hattie, your cheeks are sunburned." Then
he smiled at me.

At noon we sat by a stream where it was shady. Aunt
June and Mrs. Anderson have become close friends and
the four girls are like having my very own sisters again.
Ma helps care for baby Eliza May. We were cooling our
feet in the water when we heard loud voices arguing.

Two men were yelling words I can't repeat. I ran
through the grass and saw Mr. Kenker with a pistol
pointed at Tall Joe and there was Mrs. Kenker, her
hands on her hips, also yelling.

Tall Joe yanked off his beaver hat and threw it to the
dirt. "Fifteen miles a day is what we'll do like it or not,"
he said, his face two inches away from Mr. Kenker's.
Spit came out he was so mad. "And the next time you
point a gun at me, mister, I'll slice your ears off — don't
you forget."

Mrs. Kenker piped in. "How dare you speak to my
husband that way, we're just poor old people looking
to start a new life and you're nothing but a liar who
stinks to high heaven. I don't know why we ever let you
be the leader."

Tall Joe's eyes narrowed. "And you," he said, pointing his finger at her, "you bother me worse than a

corpse on a hot day." He grabbed Mr. Kenker's pistol and aimed it at their wagon seat where a pie was cooling. The first shot made the pan spin, the second splattered it.

Mrs. Kenker's hands flew up in shock and what she screamed at Tall Joe, I ain't repeating that either.

Pa later told us that the Kenkers have been pestering Tall Joe to slow down because they are plumb wore out. The mister has something wrong with his backside so it hurts him to sit so many hours driving their team and she don't like the bugle at 4 o'clock every morning and there's too many crying children and so on, one complaint after another.

I was upset to see old people yelled at, they must be 50 years of age. Even though I don't trust Mrs. Kenker she sometimes still reminds me of my grandmother, the way she looks I mean.

Last week in May, thereabouts

In the far distance we can see something poking up from the horizon like a thumb pointing at the clouds. Tall Joe says this is Chimney Rock. It is the closest thing to a mountain that I have ever seen.

The woman who had a baby back in Ash Hollow

died of fever this morning. She was buried on a bluff overlooking the valley. Her newborn daughter is being cared for by another mother, and friends are helping the father with his three little boys.

Chimney Rock

For two long days we approached Chimney Rock . . . it seemed to take forever. Two evenings we watched the sun set behind it as we ate supper.

Now that we're here it's a curious sight, a huge pile of rocks with what looks like a stone chimney rising up from its center. Jake and several boys hiked around its base and counted ten thousand steps. I don't know how they kept track of so many numbers, but they did. Tall Joe said some other folks counted years past and they also said ten thousand.

Boys with rifles are shooting at the top of Chimney Rock to see what will happen. They like the fuss and noise. Now some families have souvenir chips tucked in their wagons.

The plains are dry with no trees. We are slowly moving toward the Pacific Ocean, but it's near impossible for me to picture a sea other than this sea of grass. All around is open space with colors of gold, green, and brown. I feel we are specks, like bugs crawling across a kitchen floor.

It is very pretty, but I miss the sight and smell of trees and I do miss my Missoura River. To think I might never again hear the long, high whistle of a steamboat makes me feel lonesome.

Scott's Bluff

I have never seen a real castle, but today we passed what Pa says looks like one. On the side of the trail, high above us, rose a sharp wall of stone called Scott's Bluff. Jake wanted to climb it when he saw some older boys trying, but Ma held his shirt and said, "No."

The bluff hugs the river so close we had to steer the wagons aside and pull around it, up a rocky ridge. Tall Joe said this place was named after the fur trader Hiram Scott who got sick and was abandoned by his companions. He crawled sixty miles trying to find them. When the trappers came this way again they found his skeleton and what was left of his boots right here.

This morning after we were on the trail for an hour, a boy playing with his father's gun accidentally shot our front ox in the head. It dropped dead so quick the ones behind stumbled onto it and what a tangle of hooves and harnesses. Pa was so mad he stormed over to the boy, grabbed the gun, and threw it into the river.

"You coulda killed one of my children, young man."

I have never seen Pa so red in the face.

I ran to Jake and Bennie, even though I knew they was safe, and gathered them to me like I was an old hen. That boy made me so mad that after supper I marched over and kicked him hard in the leg. Twice.

Sixty miles until we reach Fort Laramie, four days if we push.

Later

Thunder and lightning with heavy winds. Rain turned to sleet then hail. I scolded Jake for throwing hailstones at another boy who ran to his mama crying.

Fort Laramie

When Fort Laramie drew into sight I felt shaky. Indians were camped everywhere! But I looked at them careful and did not see any trouble brewing. They was mostly families, seemed like.

Tall Joe said we're now in the middle of Sioux country and this is the biggest trading post around. It's built from logs and is owned by the American Fur Company. There are dozens of trappers and mountain men dressed in beaded leather and skins and living in tipis. Many seem to be married to Indian women for there are half-breed children playing among the tents.

We're staying for two nights and one full day so folks can make repairs on wagons and buy supplies. A Frenchman runs this place.

Way on the other side of the river we can see Brigham Young's camp. The trail, such as it is, ends so they must cross to our side. The Frenchman has a flatboat. For fifteen dollars he'll ferry their wagons across. Fifteen dollars is a fortune, but Pa says the river is deeper here so it's probably worth it for them to pay.

We were already on the trail again before the Mormons had crossed over, so I reckon they'll be traveling in our dust.

There are signposts every few miles. These are messages written on pieces of board stuck in the sand, also there are buffalo skulls with writing on them. Some notes are impossible to read because the sun has bleached out the ink, or rain has smeared it. There are warnings of bad water, rattlesnakes, and danger, like this one: "Willie Henderson and two others died here June 1846, buffalo stampede . . ."

Early June

Aunt June feels poorly. Ma says it is just weariness. She needs to rest and to drink more water. I asked when her baby will be born because she walks slower and her middle is bigger by the day it seems.

"Soon, Hattie, in a few weeks."

Mr. Lewis's mules are gone. Sometime in the night they were stolen from their pickets, their ropes cut.

"Injuns," he said, shaking his head with worry. We gave him one of our oxen, now we have four. Uncle Tim did also, so now Mr. Lewis has a team of two.

The Mormons passed us today while we were nooning. Tall Joe pointed out Brigham Young on horseback. He was wearing a black hat and he lifted his arm to wave, then galloped ahead. Pepper and I stood on our wagon seat and shaded our eyes, hoping to see the Mormon children, but we saw only dust.

Someone said that just one wife is with him, all the others are back in Illinois.

Register Cliff

The trail goes through limestone which is soft when wet. Pepper and I carved our names into a boulder by the side of the road using a sharp stone. Our hands grew tired, so we didn't spell out our full names or hometowns.

During the long, hot hours of the day, many of the men driving wagons doze, their reins in hand. It's a wonder none have fallen off the seats. Pa looks wore out. Yesterday a wasp stung him on his neck and it has swollen up. Ma keeps dabbing mud on, but it is still sore and red.

We are so tired by nightfall, we roll into our blankets and stretch out on the hard ground, lately not using tents. It means one less thing to unpack and repack every day.

The breeze is cool on my face. How I wish I could keep my eyes open long enough to study the stars, but suddenly it is morning. The bugle has sounded and campfires smell of fresh coffee.

Afternoon

Pepper told me a secret last night.

We were setting up a tent to share with little Holly and Laurel, for there was thunder and the smell of rain. It was pitch-black, no moon or stars. Every minute or so a sheet of lightning flashed in the west, so bright we could see the whole prairie, the way it is when someone holds up a lantern in a barn. For two full seconds we could see each other, then it was dark again.

After we tucked ourselves into blankets, Holly and Laurel already asleep between us, Pepper whispered.

"Gideon has asked me to marry him . . . and I said, yes. Tell me what you think, Hattie."

"Well, Pepper, I'm real happy for you."

But what I didn't tell her was that I was filled with envy. How I wanted to have someone love me, too. If she is fourteen and old enough to marry, then I at thirteen am old enough to fall in love.

We whispered until the rain began hitting our tent and we could no longer hear one another.

It rained all night. Pepper and I moved closer and held the little girls against us so they wouldn't be cold. Thunder rocked the ground as if horses were running by.

Water seeped under our tent and up into our blankets. I did not sleep a wink on account of being wet and chilled.

Next day

Wet blankets were hung to dry inside the wagons and outside, pinned to the canvas. They soon were so full of trail dust that it was a chore to shake the mud loose. Tall Joe says last night was just a dribble, nothing compared to the heavy rains he's seen in years past, so we should shut up and count ourselves lucky.

When word spread that Gideon and Pepper planned to marry, the women began putting together a wedding chest for them. Aunt June emptied one of her trunks and began folding and packing gifts that folks brought.

A beautiful down quilt came from one family. There was bed sheets and linens, a tarp, lantern, and dutch oven, an axe and a kettle. I gave her my tin of Babbitt's powdered soap. One lady brought over her own lace nightgown and petticoat, never worn that she'd been saving to wear once she got to Oregon.

"May as well have a bride enjoy them now," she said. "Oregon is a long way off and who knows what'll happen between now and then."

Pepper and Gideon take long walks in the evening, then appear in time for the last dance. They hold hands until the fire is low. She's late crawling into our bed and I wake up to her whispering in my ear, "Hattie?"

For a while we watch the stars and talk and wonder about the mysteries of marriage. But I worry, will she still be my friend? Will we live next door to each other like we planned?

Later

I am ashamed of myself.

Today the fat lady came over to visit, but Ma was down by the creek. I was figuring on how to act busy when the lady said, "Hello, honey. I've made some taffy for you to share with your brothers. Here you go."

She handed me the candy wrapped in oilcloth and smiled at me so kindly I felt ashamed that I had avoided her so. Right quick I invited her to tea, recollecting Aunt June having told me to be hospitable.

While the kettle was set over the fire to boil the lady went to her wagon and came back with her husband riding on her wide shoulders. They introduced themselves as Mr. and Mrs. Bigg. (Cross my heart I did not laugh at their name.)

Mrs. Bigg said she has to drive the wagon on account of her husband being crippled. He sits next to her to keep her company and now I recall seeing them talk and laugh together hour after hour, like old friends. Because he has no legs and the trail is so rough, he ties himself to the bench so he won't bounce off.

They said that a few years ago he was trampled by horses from a runaway wagon and his crushed legs had to be amputated. Poor man. I've decided they are two of the nicest folks I ever did meet and I will strike anyone who makes fun of them or the fact that her name describes her.

(I am so glad I kept my first opinions to myself! If Pepper knew how unkind I can be, I would melt from shame.)

Later

When Mrs. Bigg heard that Pepper is to be married, she dug in her trunk and pulled out one of her lace tablecloths. She marched over to our camp pulling a cart where Mr. Bigg sits like he's riding in a little train. She held the lace up to Pepper and said, "Honey, I'm gonna make you the prettiest wedding dress you'll ever set eyes on."

And she did.

For five evenings Mrs. Bigg sewed and cut and measured until she had a creamy white dress with long sleeves and a bow that ties at the waist. Mr. Bigg sat beside her in his cart, sewing, too. He made a lacy overskirt from curtains that had hung in their parlor back in Missoura.

Finally we gathered by her wagon and held up blankets to make a private room. Pepper carefully stepped into the dress. As her mother buttoned up the back, the ladies caught their breaths she looked so beautiful.

The wedding is planned for when we arrive at Independence Rock, a few days away.

A hot afternoon

Mrs. Anderson came over this morning as we were packing up our breakfast plates. She looks very thin, but there's more color to her cheeks. I can hardly look at her without wanting to cry for little Cassia.

She said to Ma, "It was so warm last night I think I left my shawl by your fire. Have you seen it, Augusta?"

Together they looked under the wagon, by the crates and stools, then in Aunt June's wagon. I remember it was a pretty blue shawl with fringe. We looked and looked.

Wade is feeling good enough to dance, but when the fiddlers started up he asked another girl! I was so upset I ran outside the circle where it was dark. For a long time I sat in the dirt where no one could see me, watching the dancers. I felt so alone.

I want someone to love me the way Gideon loves Pepper.

Mid-June

The North Platte River runs west, but now we've come to where it makes a sharp turn to the south. We must cross it in order to continue toward Oregon.

Imagine our surprise to see that the Mormons not only had come and gone, but left behind nine men to build a ferry. Two ferries. And they would be glad to help us get across for just a dollar fifty per wagon.

My, the arguments that broke out because of this. Tall Joe said that over his dead body would he pay one penny to cross a river that he saw years before Brigham Young even knew it existed.

But Pa said, "I think it's mighty enterprising of the Mormons to start a business in such a faraway place."

Mr. and Mrs. Kenker cursed something fierce thinking they might need to part with some of their money. Several families said this: "Those Mormons are so high and mighty they stayed on the other side of the river and wouldn't associate with us. But now that they can make a dollar off us they're friendly as can be."

"Come on, folks," Pa said. "Brigham Young's people are trying to start a new life, just like us. And I'll tell you something else . . . we ain't their judge, God Almighty is, so let's get going and not be so mad about everything."

He and Uncle Tim bargained with the Mormons.

Two sacks of cornmeal paid our passage across, on rafts made from thin logs and strips of leather. Each raft, they said, could hold up to 1,800 pounds, but I don't know.

It felt unsteady, and water washed over my feet as I helped Ma hold the wagon. I was so scared we'd sink, my knees ached from standing stiff. The littlest children sat safe inside, real still so the wagon wouldn't rock.

Pa and Uncle Tim swam with the animals, my little brother Jake on the back of a mule. The water came up to his waist, but his fingers were hooked tight into the harness. I kept an eye on him, ready to dive in if he should slip off.

Once our family and the Andersons were all safe across that deep river, I was not so nervous.

It took six days to get everyone over. Many refused to pay the Mormons and instead forded the river without help. Except for wet belongings and scared children everything was all right until the last day, when we heard screams.

I looked out and there in the middle of the current was two wagons side by side, their mules swimming hard, their big brown heads straining for breath. Somehow one of the mules drifted downstream into the other team and got its hooves tangled in the harnesses.

That poor mule panicked, then right before our eyes

the animals began to drown. They sank so fast they pulled the wagons underwater before anyone had a chance to jump out. Two families disappeared just like that. I am sick at heart. The screams of their friends on shore I will never ever forget as long as I live.

For one day the men searched for bodies while the last of the families came over. Meanwhile everyone stayed busy doing regular things, almost like nothing bad had happened.

Pa said the nine Mormons will take apart their wagons to build a cabin, then stay till more pioneers come out next summer.

This gave Pa and Mr. Lewis an idea.

Soon enough they had bartered wood to make a small wagon with three hoops. They bought a tent, and with the help of Mr. and Mrs. Bigg's sewing, turned the canvas into a top. They traded beans for two mules with harnesses and neck collars.

"What on earth?" asked Ma. There stood a miniature prairie schooner, about five feet long and three feet wide, with one set of wheels.

Mr. Lewis grinned when he answered, "It's a wedding gift for my daughter and Gideon."

Pa made friends with one of the Mormons, a man named Appleton M. Harmon and they got to talking about something Brigham Young and his men invented on the trail to measure miles. It's called a "road-o-meter." He drew Pa a picture in the sand and it looks like four or five wooden cogs attached to a wagon wheel. Somehow it works.

The Mormons also have something like a thermometer that measures "barometric pressure." This is how they know the altitude.

Later

We are camped at the Sweetwater River. I watched from shore while my brothers played in the shallows with some other children. The current is slow but still I worry they'll be swept away.

Independence Rock

From a distance this sloped rock looks like a bear sleeping on its side. Up close, it's huge and easy to climb. Folks have been going up to the top to see the view and carve their names. Some boys raced each other up, then fired pistols in the air to celebrate. Jake asked Pa if he could have a few sticks of dynamite to throw off the top, just to see what would happen.

Pa thought a moment. When he said yes, Jake let out a happy yell.

Pepper and I were at the river when we heard the explosion. We turned in time to see a puff of smoke floating down from the top. Some cattle took off running in fright, but were rounded up quick by men on horseback.

I don't understand why boys like such things or why Pa thinks dynamite is safer than rifles.

The wedding was late afternoon, in the cool shadow of Independence Rock. Pepper was beautiful. She was barefoot with a wreath of wildflowers in her hair, and her dress seemed to float with the breeze. Gideon was so shy that when someone yelled, "Kiss the bride!" he blushed redder than a sunburn and just kept holding her hand.

Soon enough there was music and dancing and food, plenty of it. Wade came up to me smiling, but instead of asking me to dance, he said, "Hattie, wanna play a trick on my sister?"

He led me to their new wagon. Mrs. Lewis and the ladies had made up a cozy bed with curtains for privacy, and there was a lantern hanging from one of the hoops inside. Wade opened a sack that he had brung over earlier, and began pulling out pots, pans, and other trinkets, which he tied with string under the wagon.

I brushed at my apron, nervous. Darkness had

fallen. Soon we saw Gideon holding Pepper's hand and leading her away from the campfire. Wade and I ran into the shadows.

When the newlyweds climbed into their wagon, Wade whispered, "Get ready, Hattie." He gave a little whistle and, to my surprise, out of the darkness appeared dozens of men and women, some children, too. All waited for about five minutes, real quiet.

Finally Wade whistled softly. Two men hurried to the front of the wagon, lifted the tongue and began running as if they was mules. Noise erupted from the pans clanging underneath. The crowd that had gathered ran alongside, whooping and yelling and banging spoons, making the wildest noise I'd ever heard.

We followed the wagon until the men halted at the edge of the prairie, about a mile from camp. The noise stopped. For a moment we heard the perfect quiet of night: crickets and wind sighing through the grass. Then Wade began singing a hymn, in a beautiful slow voice: ". . . May our good Lord watch over you always . . ." After the first verse, everyone joined in, then slowly began walking back to camp where there was still music.

Wade caught up to me. In the firelight I could see his green eyes and he was smiling. "That shivaree was some fun, wasn't it, Hattie?"

Now I was the one to feel shy. Before I could think of

something to say, he took my hand and led me past the fiddler to join the other dancers.

Another day

About the Sweetwater River: Tall Joe says it got its name from some trappers who tried to get their mules across during a storm. One of the packs was full of sugar and when its saddle broke, in went 300 pounds of sugar.

Rocks on either side rise up about 400 feet, forming a narrow river canyon called Devil's Gate. The trail drops into nothing so the wagons had to drive on the outside, about half a mile away. It took all day.

Some of us climbed to the top of the cliff for a view. It was spectacular, but it made my stomach turn to look over the ledge, the river was so far down. Tall Joe told us that a few years ago a young bride fell to her death doing what we'd just done.

Another day

My little brother Ben fell off the wagon seat just before noon as we were pulling to a stop. The wheels rolled over his left arm so that it hung like a broken stick. He cried and cried, while Pa set it in a splint.

I ran among the families to look for brandy or rum or something to help his pain. I knocked at the Kenkers' wagon and leaned in. Mrs. Kenker sat on a quilt knitting, her husband asleep beside her

When I told her about Bennie she said, "Oh my word, how terribly dreadful," and set down her needles. She uncorked a jug and poured whiskey into a tin cup, about two inches deep. "Give this to your brother, dear, and he'll not feel a thing."

I thanked her and hurried back to Ma, trying not to spill the whiskey. Soon Bennie was quiet and as Pa rocked him to sleep I remembered Mrs. Kenker's knitting. Her yarn was the same color blue as Mrs. Anderson's shawl that disappeared.

I'm sure we have a thief among us and worried that I'm the only one who knows. I don't want to bother Pepper about it, and Aunt June is so tired. Ma probably won't believe me on account she says we must always respect our elders no matter what. Grandmothers don't steal, is probably what she'd say.

My cheeks and the back of my hands are peeling from sunburn. I rub in axle grease, but dust sticks to my skin. It is tiresome to feel dirty all the time.

Later

Six oxen died yesterday and one mule. After butchering them where they fell, we kept going. They're too heavy to move and there ain't time to bury them.

Tall Joe made an announcement at supper: We must lighten our loads to make it easier on the tired animals.

Ma said to me, "The dresser and rocker can go, but I will never part with your sisters' things."

When we pulled out this morning there was an odd assortment left in camp: a washtub, an oval mirror, two trunks filled with brand-new shoes, a piano, and a birdcage.

Someone had put several dozen books onto the shelves of a china hutch, neat and tidy as a library. Maybe folks coming behind will get to enjoy them, but who has time to read?

Tall Joe caught Mrs. Kenker picking through the items and said, "Madam, if your oxen drop dead from all the junk you're making them pull, why, I ain't waiting for you or that husband of yours to find a new team."

The trail seems to be uphill. Today it was our turn to be in front and I thought, at last, we'll have no dust. But the wind was at our backs, so we walked in blowing dirt all day long. My skirt pressed behind my legs, often tripping me.

Jake and I take turns riding in the wagon to help Ma.

I don't like it one bit because it is so hot inside — stuffy and cramped — but we must keep Ben still so his arm will heal. Pa said it was a blessing the bone didn't poke through his skin, else they might have had to amputate on account of infection.

Poor Bennie. He wants to play and run alongside the oxen, but Ma is too scared. A boy in one of the other wagons — we don't know the family — was riding on their sideboard. No one knows what happened, but somehow he fell and was trampled by the mules behind. There was so much dust that it wasn't until three wagons passed did they find him.

We all stopped for an hour. They buried him in the middle of the road so wolves won't dig him up. We can hear the boy's mother and sisters wailing, even above the noise of our moving wagons.

Along the Sweetwater

Today when I saw Pepper and Gideon's little wagon she waved me over. "Please walk with me, Hattie," she called.

I was so happy to be with her again. As Gideon drives and she walks alongside, they keep smiling at each other. She is more talkative than ever, which makes me feel good. I think she is glad we are friends.

The next miles of trail twisted through ravines and sandy slopes. We were nervous to see rattlesnakes everywhere, draped over rocks and coiled in the hot sun. Pa said the West is home to these snakes so we must just learn to be careful, is all.

Way ahead in the distance we can see dust from the Mormons. They're at least one day away.

Mosquitoes are terrible and now there're also biting flies. My arms are covered with welts that bleed because I can't help scratching. My sleeves have bloodstains such that I want to rip away the cloth they look so soiled. I wish I had many, many clean dresses instead of this old ragged thing. I yearn to feel pretty again.

Funny, but now I do wear my bonnet and Pepper wears hers. I tease her about being an old married lady but the truth is our faces hurt from sunburn and the skin keeps peeling. The ridge of my nose is so raw it stings. Every night I rub axle grease on it and my lips, too, not hardly minding the stink of it anymore.

There was another wedding last evening. The bride is also fourteen and her new husband about thirty years old. He is a carpenter, the one whose wife died a few weeks ago, before we reached Chimney Rock. So now this girl is a mother of three young sons and a newborn daughter. Some older women are helping her care for the baby and one is nursing it every few hours.

I feel sorry for the girl, all at once having to learn how to be a wife and a mother of four children.

But Ma says things will probably turn out all right because the bride and groom need each other. He was a widower and she was an orphan traveling with an elderly cousin. "They'll grow to love one another, Hattie."

South Pass

Tall Joe says we've come near 900 miles — that means we're almost halfway to Oregon! There are cheers and singing and gunshots.

Pa thought crossing the Continental Divide would be treacherous, but the gap here is twelve miles wide and gentle as a cornfield. The slope is so gradual we hardly knew where we were. To the north are the Wind River Mountains covered with snow. There is a carpet of yellow and blue wildflowers spread between boulders and pine trees, so beautiful. It's sunny, but the air is thin and cold because of the elevation, about 8,000 feet.

Women and girls are picking bouquets to hang upside down in our wagons, so they'll keep their color while drying — this way we'll have flowers during our winter in Oregon.

Tall Joe says the nights are so cold at South Pass we must keep going, down the western slope to a campground called Pacific Creek.

End of June
Pacific Creek

We're camped here for two days to rest and celebrate. It's a wondrous feeling to think we are finally in the West. Now the rivers and streams flow to the Pacific Ocean instead of eastward toward the Atlantic.

Everyone who was able, dipped a cup in the water and held it up for a cheer. The fiddlers got busy and soon everyone was ready to dance. Everyone except Mama. She said not until her feet are in Oregon City will she celebrate. (Some moments Mama is so grouchy I know for certain I mustn't upset her with news about our thief.)

For part of the day we shared a campsite with the Mormons. Pepper, Gideon, Wade, and I walked over to their wagons, curious. There was a fire where a spit held a roasting side of beef.

We saw three women busy carrying plates back and forth, but didn't see any children. (I wondered which one was Brigham Young's wife.) A colored man came over and introduced himself by the odd name of Green Flake, then asked us to please leave on a account of his people resting.

Someone said he once was a slave, but now is Brigham Young's personal servant.

Sandy Creek

Here the trail splits. Tall Joe said there's a shortcut heading north that'll save seven days. But it's 50 miles of desert, no trees, no water or grass for the animals. The days are blistering hot. The only time to travel is after sundown, when it's cooler.

Or, he said, the safest is to swing southwest down to Fort Bridger. It'll take longer, but it skirts the Wyoming desert.

Our family had a discussion. Pa agreed we'd go with Tall Joe, the safest way, on account of Aunt June might have her baby any day now. Both Ma and Mrs. Anderson begged for the safe route — they're afraid of being stranded in the middle of nowhere, and of watching the children die from thirst.

After supper eight families pulled out, heading north across the desert, along the Sublette Cutoff, maybe to reach Oregon a week earlier than the rest of us.

We no longer see buffalo or their droppings. Tall Joe says the herds have gone north and with them, the Indians.

I am somewhat pleased we may not run into them again, though it's true they haven't bothered us.

Later

Jake hit Bennie with a stick because (he says) Bennie threw sand at him. I scolded them both and made them walk the rest of the afternoon with me. Sometimes I wish they were grown-up.

Early July

After dark I walked beyond camp, around the circle to the Kenkers' wagon. A lantern lit the inside, so I stood back in the shadows to see what I could see. The mister was sound asleep, matter of fact he was snoring loud, but Mrs. Kenker was busy with something in her lap.

I stepped closer.

She had Bennie's blue sweater! She was as quick-as-you-please unraveling the sleeve and rolling the yarn into a ball. I wanted to grab her by the throat. When did she steal Bennie's sweater and why?

I must tell Ma, even if she won't believe me. I hurried away to find her.

At the edge of the camp I saw Pepper's little wagon. The curtains were closed and lamplight from inside made it glow like a small cozy lantern. (I feel jealous that she has a husband and I have no one yet.) How I wished she and I could watch the stars together and talk, like we did at the first of our journey. I missed her and felt more lonely than ever.

"Evening, Hattie," a voice said from the darkness.

"Who's there?" I asked.

"Come sit with us, honey." There on a blanket was Mr. and Mrs. Bigg, leaning against their wagon wheel. "We was just enjoying the sky. Why're you out here by yourself, Hattie?"

I sat with them, pulling my knees up inside my skirt for warmth as there was a cold breeze.

We were facing west. A smear of pink just above the horizon was all that was left of the sunset. Behind us, inside the circle, was campfires and singing. Folks were warming up for a dance.

After some moments I spilled out the story about Mrs. Kenker, starting with Ma's silver spoon.

They listened.

Finally Mr. Bigg said, "That poor woman." With his strong arms he pushed himself a few inches off the ground and scooted closer to his wife. She spread her shawl over their laps.

"Hattie," she said, "the Kenkers were our neighbors back in Elmcreek, Missoura. There's something you need to know about them."

Mrs. Bigg then told me that a few days before the families from Elmcreek planned to set out for Oregon, the Kenkers' house caught fire and burned to the ground. Everything was lost, all their supplies and belongings, everything. But worst of all their two grown sons died. These sons were going to drive their wagon west and help them start a new life.

"It ain't right for her to steal, Hattie, but maybe she does because she's so full of grief and empty inside."

For several minutes there was silence. The sound of crickets seemed so loud I was relieved when Mrs. Bigg spoke again. "Hattie dear, we need to think very careful how to handle this. Let's give it a few days before deciding what to do."

When I walked past the campfire back to my wagon I began to feel better for having told my story to a grown-up, so I'll not upset Ma about it. But now I feel mixed-up about the Kenkers.

July 7, Wednesday
Fort Bridger

This is as busy as Fort Laramie, but not as many Indians. Tall Joe pointed out two mountain men who were stretching beaver pelts onto circular frames.

"That one fella with the knife is Kit Carson, the scout who helped find a trail to Oregon. And that fella, that's Jim Bridger himself." Tall Joe lifted his hat in greeting when the two saw him.

"Bridger started this trading post to help emigrants, that's why it's outfitted with a blacksmith, horses, plenty of provisions, you name it. He's the first white man to see that godforsaken salt lake where Brigham Young is headed, the scoundrel."

Tall Joe blew his nose into his hand then wiped his fingers on his pants. He said, "Jim Bridger has got a map of the entire western continent stored in his brain, every river, mountain, and tree stump practically."

We camped two days here, outside the log walls. There are tears now among the women because here is where the trail splits for good. About 30 families are heading south to California, while the rest of us are going northwest for Oregon. Many friendships were made over the past three months, close friendships.

I am relieved that Pepper and I don't have to say good-bye to each other. Also, Mrs. Bigg, for I've grown very fond of her. Aside from Aunt June, she is my favorite lady friend.

Fort Bridger is also where we part ways with the Mormons. Hooray good riddance, said Tall Joe. I watched the colored fellow named Green Flake climb into his wagon and take the reins. He waved at me and smiled. Then they were gone. Pa says that next year many of the wives and children will follow.

Jim Bridger has an Indian wife. I saw her with some other squaws on the sunny side of the fort, staking down deer hides to skin. She was pretty and very young, about my age I think. I wanted to talk to her, but didn't know what to say, so instead I waved howdee. She looked down at her lap. Maybe she is shy.

Mrs. Anderson and Ma was by a creek washing our blankets. To wring them out they stood three feet apart, each holding an end and twisting until all the water dripped out. Aunt June spread them in the grass to dry. When they saw me they stopped talking, but I had already heard them.

They were saying they'd be quite content settling at Fort Bridger, never to travel again. There was water, good earth to plow, plenty of people, and all our families were safe. "Maybe Narcissa Whitman is braver than we are," Aunt June said about her friend. "I don't know how she did it."

Ma said, "And who knows what's in Oregon? Who knows what will happen between now and then? There are Indians farther north. I'm sure there's more danger that Tall Joe ain't telling us about."

Next day

Bennie's arm is healing. Pa made a new splint so it's easier for Ben to move. The other good news is that Wade is back to telling jokes. The only problems left over from the hemlock is that his tongue is numb on the right side, and his jaws ache. Tall Joe says he probably didn't eat very much of it, but Ma says it's a miracle from God, that's all there is to it, a miracle.

Mrs. Bigg called me over this morning before we pulled out from Fort Bridger. As she folded their blankets into a crate she said, "Hattie, Mr. Bigg's cart is missing. Someone took it in the night."

At noon I helped Mrs. Bigg make a search of camp. She is so large that her steps are slow. The first wagon we went to was the Kenkers'.

"I don't know what you're talking about," Mrs. Kenker said, "and how dare you accuse us; we're just poor old people, besides I'm not feeling well, neither is my husband, maybe everyone would like it if we just plumb keeled over and died before we get to Oregon, maybe y'd be happy then . . ."

Mrs. Bigg held up her hand. "That's enough," she said. "Go back to your nap, Mrs. Kenker, sorry to bother you."

When we were out of hearing distance I said, "If Mrs. Kenker's so innocent why did she make excuses for herself and why ain't she upset to hear someone stole Mr. Bigg's cart?"

"Hattie, if she is a thief, then soon enough she'll make a mistake and folks'll find her out. It's not like she can leave town or hide." Mrs. Bigg rested a heavy hand on my shoulder.

"Be patient, honey."

Afternoon

After a long pull up a creek called the Muddy we've come to the Bear River. There's a beautiful campsite with a trail coming in from the right. A piece of paper was nailed to a tree. Tall Joe read it first, then passed it around.

"They made it, folks," he shouted. "The other wagons made it 'cross the desert and just a few days ahead of us seems like." Cheers went up.

Our horses, mules, oxen, and cattle are grazing along the broad river bottom. It is the most peaceful sight. Groups of men are fishing or sitting in the sun or exploring the meadows.

There is the sound of children splashing and playing along the river. The women are spreading washed clothes on the bushes, also sitting in the sun, talking, resting. Some are busy over cooking fires.

Now it's not just Ma and Aunt June and Mrs. Anderson talking about going no farther, but several other families are discussing the very same thing: Why not settle here in the Bear River valley?

At supper five families made an announcement. This place suits them so well they've decided to homestead, said they'd not seen finer farmland ever. But Pa wants to keep going. He is so set on Oregon and living by the Pacific Ocean, he can't think of anything else.

Pa said he's had too many dreams that were lost or forgotten or that he just gave up on.

"This is our last chance, Augusta, to fulfill a dream as big as Oregon. Please stand by me. I need you."

Ma says all she dreams of is keeping her family safe. As for me, my dream is that Pepper and I will always be friends, and that I will someday be adored by a husband I love. And maybe Pepper and I can still live next door to each other!

So, we're on the trail again, ten days from Fort Hall.

Sheep Rock

One side of Sheep Rock rises up like a stone wall. Pine trees surround it on all sides and among the cliffs are mountain sheep. Tall Joe said that back in '42, John C. Frémont explored this place and named it Sheep Rock.

We're still on the Bear River. It's the same beautiful green as Pepper's eyes, and Wade's. When we saw how deep it is we were relieved to learn it makes a sharp turn south and we don't have to cross it. Tall Joe says it empties into the Great Salt Lake; he followed it once.

An amazing sight has made us all want to camp for several days. There are pools bubbling up with hot water! There's even one with a geyser called "Steamboat" because somehow it makes a high-pitched whistle that sounds just like a boat on the Missoura. Hearing it made me so happy-homesick I almost started bawling.

Folks are swimming and floating in the warm water, and drinking it. To me it smells like eggs on the rotten side, but the taste ain't bad at all.

Wade and Gideon dared each other to sit on the geyser. They took turns and, oh, what an event. While Pepper and I watched from the banks, Gideon swam out to the center and waited.

Soon enough heavy bubbles began lifting him up and up and up. His arms and legs waved like a turtle's on its back as the geyser bounced him up and down. By the time it stopped, Gideon had lost his shirt. Wade rode the geyser next and lost his pants which caused folks to erupt in hilarious laughter and so the day went.

I was so pleased to have Pepper to myself all afternoon. We lay in the grass and stared up at the clouds. I asked her what it was like to have a husband.

After a long while she turned her face toward me. How pretty she looked, her green eyes, and cheeks high with color.

"Oh, Hattie, you are such a dear. Marriage is, well, it's the most wonderful of wonderfuls. Someday you'll understand."

I wish Pepper would tell me exactly what she means, what it's really truly like to be loved by a man.

Later

At supper Ma stirred several cups of sugar and a pint of raspberries into a pail of the mineral water. Mrs. Bigg did the same with citrus syrup to make lemonade, and they was the most delicious bubbly drinks any of us had ever tasted. Pepper and I drank so much though, we were not hungry for supper, and I had a stomachache all night long. She told me the next day she did, too.

Tall Joe said one of the pools was named Beer Spring because mountain men swear they get drunk after a few sips, but Pa says that's likely just another tall tale.

Before bed

Jake and Ben complained and pushed at each other all day, then argued with me when I said it was time to unroll their blankets. I'm tired of being their sister.

Two days later

Two days north of the soda springs the sky turned black and the air cold. In an instant a wind picked up so fierce I had to hold my bonnet on with both hands even though it was tied under my chin. My skirt blew back so tight it looked like I was wearing men's trousers.

When the hail hit we stopped the wagons and ran for cover. The poor animals moaned and cried, but there was no way we could protect them. It felt like someone was pelting us with rocks. In an instant my arms and neck were bruised.

The hailstones bounced like popping corn and soon the ground was white. Many of the wagon tops, ours included, ended up with holes. The storm passed as quick as it started, and flooded the road so that mud sucked at the wheels as we pulled out.

It was our turn to be in the lead. Because of the storm we thought nothing of the abandoned wagon we came upon. Its cover also had holes.

But when Tall Joe came back from inspecting it, his face told a different story.

"Folks, those holes ain't from hailstones," Tall Joe said. He held up an arrow with feathers on its end.

Quick as you please the men began searching in case someone from the wagon was left behind. The Indians had stole the mules and whatever treasures possible, for there was a trail of scattered goods.

Wade and Gideon made a gruesome discovery.

About two hundred yards away, inside a thicket of sagebrush, was a pair of feet sticking out of a grave, men's we think because they were big with hairy toes. It seems that after he was buried the Indians came back and dug deep enough to steal his boots, then left him just like we found him.

I thought it could've been Pa if *we'd* taken that short-cut. My stomach felt tight thinking Indians might be watching us and that they might not be friendly.

There was some talk about digging up the poor fellow to see who he was, but Tall Joe said it wouldn't be pretty that's for sure, and we'll likely find out when we get to Fort Hall, just a few days north.

He and Pa shoveled dirt to cover the dead man's feet and we piled rocks on top to keep animals away.

It was a solemn group that pulled out. Pepper and I and Wade walked together next to the wagon Gideon was driving. We watch the horizon more and wonder what will happen if we see Indians.

This is a land of sagebrush and rock, much of it black. Tall Joe says it is from volcanoes, and that the western part of the continent is full of them, old ones that don't erupt anymore.

Our animals pull hard and slow — they're plumb wore out. Tall Joe rides back and forth among the wagons, ordering folks to lighten their loads again. Some families pile belongings neatly to the side of the trail, others heave things out, letting them land wherever.

I keep my eye on Mrs. Kenker, but she has not thrown anything away. Two of her oxen dropped dead yesterday, one today, so now there are three pulling. Tall Joe warned her again.

"We'll leave you behind, madam, you and your junk and your husband. Better start tossing."

Every day there are at least two animals to butcher, either cows, horses, or oxen. What meat we don't eat, the women cut into strips for jerky. We hang them from the hoops inside our wagons, and the dry air toughens them pretty quick. The layers of dust seem to keep the flies and yellow jackets away.

Fort Hall

Aunt June was excited to see this trading post because Narcissa Whitman had been here and wrote to her about it. I think it looks like all the others with the usual bunch of dirty mountain men, plenty of Indians and tipis camped outside the log walls.

Pepper and I wonder if they are the same Indians that ambushed the wagons in front of us. I try not to look at them all with hatred, but it's hard not to when I think they could hurt us and women and babies, and families like ours.

We set up camp on the west side of the fort, near a creek. Tall Joe brought us news after he talked with the man in charge.

Seems the other wagons made it across the desert all right, but one of the young men stepped on a rattle-snake when he wandered into some brush. The bite is above his knee and now the poison has spread so that his entire leg is black. His fever is high.

When Tall Joe told us his name I remembered him to be one of the young men that raced us across the Platte, a loud fellow, but nice. For some reason this news made me so sick at heart I just sat on the bank staring at the water.

What next? I thought.

First it was the little twins that got lost picking

berries — we still don't know if they was ever found. Then it was hemlock that killed poor Cassia, and Wade's friends . . . there was the boy who fell off his parents' wagon . . . the mother who died by Chimney Rock . . .

Suddenly my chest felt so heavy I burst out crying. Who will be next? Mama? Will Aunt June have her baby without bleeding to death? I'm tired of being brave and tired of being dirty.

I crawled in the wagon where no one could see me and took off my dress. My bare white arms are bruised from the hailstones and there are many tiny scabs from mosquito bites. My wrists and hands are dry and cracked. What boy will ever think me nice to look at?

Among the flour bags I found my satchel and the spare dress still tucked inside. I unfolded it, pulled it over my head, then tied the starched ribbon around my waist. Even though Ma said it's not to be worn until Oregon, *I do not care.* I want to feel pretty now.

Next, I undid my braid and brushed my hair one hundred strokes until at last it seemed the dust was out. For near an hour I tried to twist it on top my head like Ma does, but could not figure how, so for now will settle for a long braid.

Later

When Ma saw me wearing my clean dress she opened her mouth to say something, but instead gave me a slow smile. She opened her arms for me, then whispered, "How lovely you look, Hattie."

We stayed at Fort Hall two days. It'll be a long time before we see civilization so the men got extra parts to fix the wheels that most certainly will shrink and break in the dry air. This has been a problem since we left the Platte, many, many broken wheels. (It has been tiresome to watch so many repairs that I just have not bothered to describe them.)

The young man bitten by the rattlesnake died the evening before we pulled out. His family is devastated, but there is no time to mourn over his grave. Tall Joe says we must be going. Summer is almost over.

Next day

We are heading west along the Snake River and shall do so for about 300 miles. I have never seen such a torrent of wild water.

The river is far below us, running between black canyon walls that twist sharp here and there. Even though we're in sight of so much water, getting down to it is another matter.

Forgot to mention: Back at Fort Hall, Pa and some of the other men found enough scraps to build a cart for Mr. Bigg. The wheels are such that Mr. Bigg can roll them with his arms and get around on his own. He invited Bennie to sit on his lap for a ride and away they went, bumping through the sagebrush around the outside of the wagons, twice.

I am taking care not to scratch my arms so they won't bleed and ruin my sleeves. Aunt June gave me one of her prettiest aprons to wear over my dress. It is blue with two pockets and a ruffled hem.

Another day

Four Indians on horseback appeared out of a canyon as we were starting supper. Their dark hair was braided and their legs were bare except for moccasins. Tall Joe rode over to them with his hand raised in greeting.

The Indians, turns out, were friendly, they just wanted to warn Tall Joe about some Blackfeet who are out looking for trouble. One of the men had a bundle of fur draped over his horse's rump. He pushed it to the dirt and motioned for Tall Joe to take it. It was a buffalo skin to help our leader stay warm at night, a gift, he seemed to be saying. Tall Joe picked it up, put it around his shoulders, then walked over to his own saddlebag. He dug around in it and pulled out a small sack of tobacco which he tossed to his new friend.

I have decided Indians are like white folks in that some are honest and kind, others are liars and thieves.

After supper I almost made an awful mistake. I almost took Pa's rifle and marched over to Mrs. Kenker to give her a piece of my mind that's how mad I was.

There she was serving pie to some folks, her hair combed pretty on top her head, smiling and — of all the nerve — wearing Aunt June's other beautiful apron, the white lace one we thought we left drying on the bushes at Bear River.

The reason I did not yell at Mrs. Kenker was because Aunt June saw me thinking about it and grabbed my arm. She said, "Leave it go, Hattie."

"But it's yours . . ."

"Yes," she said, "but I think Mrs. Kenker needs it more'n I do. It's only an apron, Hattie, it ain't worth making a fuss."

But to me it ain't just an apron, it was Ma's spoon, Bennie's sweater, and all the other things.

I hate Mrs. Kenker.

She gets away with being sneaky because she's old and smiles nice and most folks is too busy to keep an eye on her, or the folks that do know her tricks keep quiet because it's easier. It's not fair. I myself am very sad that my own sisters are dead, but I don't steal from people. If I *did*, Pa would be quick to wup me and make me apologize. He don't allow dishonesty in our family.

Along the Snake River

Two days ago we passed the loudest waterfalls we've ever heard. Tall Joe says that a few years back some American trappers were in a canoe, but didn't know they was drifting toward rapids. By the time they saw how close they were it was too late to paddle backward. Over they went, drowning like bugs. That's why it's called American Falls.

Some miles later the river splits in two as it pours over a huge rock, down to a churning pool. It looks like twin waterfalls, and that's what it's called Twin Falls.

The days are hot as ever. I must keep my sleeves down so my arms won't blister. Hour after hour the mosquitoes bite through my clothes, but I do not let myself scratch.

Another thing, the sand is too hot for us to go barefoot. My shoes split apart and the only way to keep them on is with a wet leather strip. When it dries, it shrinks tight so I can walk without them falling off.

Even so, the sand gets inside and feels lumpy. Sometimes all I can think about is how miserable I am. I wish I could be cheerful as Pepper. She never complains, and like her brother Wade, finds a way to joke. For instance, today she looked down at her feet and laughed.

"Hattie," she said, "I bet I'm the only bride what wears her wedding shoes tied on like a bonnet."

I know this is selfish, but I'm glad Gideon is busy all day driving their little wagon, because that means Pepper and I can talk all we want. Wouldn't Becky be surprised to learn my new best friend is a married girl!

We nooned by a creek, in a cool grove of willows. In the distance there was a rumble, like thunder, but the noise didn't stop. Tall Joe said don't be afraid, that three miles away is a waterfall so spectacular it'll take your breath away.

The families agreed to rest here an extra couple of hours and whoever wanted to see Shoshone Falls could hike in. Ma and Mrs. Anderson stayed with the littlest children and with Aunt June who's so uncomfortable she has to sleep sitting up. I think her baby will be born any day because she's big as a horse.

Jake came with us. He had trouble keeping up so Gideon and Wade took turns carrying him on their shoulders. Pepper and I had to shout because the falls were so loud we couldn't hear each other.

And, oh, what a sight. This is where the Snake River

falls 200 feet over a cliff. Spray felt like rain on our faces. There were ferns and delicate flowers along the moist banks. After so many days on the desert, it was the most wonderful cool feeling, oh, how I did not want to leave. We stared for just a few minutes, then it was time to hike back to the wagons.

It seems crazy to walk six extra miles just to sightsee, but Aunt June had said, "Go, Hattie. You'll likely never have another chance."

When Pepper and I could hear ourselves again we agreed that if only we weren't in a hurry to beat winter, we'd like to stay in a place longer than a few hours.

She said, "I'm feeling tired, Hattie, like I just want to lay my head down and sleep forever."

August 1, 1847

This land is rough and dry. Prickly pear is all along the trail and beyond, much of it blooming with yellow flowers. It's pretty, but hard not to step on. We are forever picking thorns from our shoes and the hems of our skirts.

My ankles are scratched raw and have bled onto my petticoat, which can't be helped, I reckon. Like all the other women, my hem is ragged and stained with mud. There is no use trying so hard to look pretty anymore, I decided. The boys are dirty as us, worse in fact. I have not seen Pa comb his hair since Missoura, he just runs his fingers over his scalp, then puts on his hat.

Our oxen are slower each day.

After Pa talked to Ma, he took the big trunk full of my sisters' things and left it by the side of the trail. He also set out the porcelain wash bowl and cabinet that had been our grandparents', Ma's wedding dress, and a box of his own tools.

I waited for Ma to break down crying, but she didn't. Ever since Pa reminded her that Oregon is our last chance to follow a dream, she has stood by him without complaint. Oh, that I could be as brave as Ma.

I opened the abandoned trunk one last time, to touch the calico my sisters had wore. How I wanted their dresses for my own, to remember them by, and also to look lovely as they had. Ma came up and gently closed the lid.

"It's time to move on, Hattie."

When the wagons pulled out it looked like we left behind a general store. There was piles of books and plates, a coffee mill, clothes, tools, and a roll-top desk. A few women wept to see their treasures thrown out. Even I had a catch in my throat. What will be left when we get to Oregon? I asked Ma. How will we make a home?

Mama said, "Don't worry, Hattie. Our home is our family, not our possessions."

When Mr. Lewis read from the Bible this morning, and after we prayed, I had a new thought about Mrs. Kenker. The farther away from Missoura we go, the more she takes. Maybe she's just scared, is all. Maybe the emptier she feels, the more she fills her wagon.

Thousand Springs

Our thermometer showed 101 degrees when we nooned. We wanted to jump in the river to cool off, but it was so far below with no way to hike down. I wish I could cut off the bottom half of my skirt for it is so hot.

On the other side of the river there was something unusual: a waterfall pouring out of a hole in the canyon wall, like a spout in a teapot. Pa said it flows from underground and is called Thousand Springs, but where it starts is a mystery.

During this stop Mr. Kenker got in another argument with Tall Joe. Soon there were fists. Uncle Tim and Pa hurried over to pull the men apart.

"Gentlemen, please, please, get a hold of yourselves," Pa said. "We have a long journey ahead of us."

But before he could say anything else, Mr. Kenker did a terrible thing. He brushed the dirt off his sleeves and said to Tall Joe, "You ain't telling me what to do anymore. It's hot and whether you like it or not I'm gonna take a swim."

Then, right before our eyes, old Mr. Kenker walked to the edge of the cliff, stepped into midair, and dropped out of sight.

For a moment there was silence, then the piercing scream of Mrs. Kenker.

Still along the Snake River

Pa says Mr. Kenker must've been going mad day by day, until finally everything got to him. After he jumped we crowded the edge on our bellies to look over. The river swept him away so fast we soon lost sight of him.

Mrs. Kenker fainted from screaming so hard and was carried to her wagon by Tall Joe himself. (I confess I am too shocked to feel sad.)

Someone spread a blanket in the shade for her. Tall Joe stood on a wheel and pulled aside the curtain to look inside. He stared for a moment, then turned toward us.

"Lordy," he said.

Two by two we peeked in and soon there was a crowd. I have never seen such junk. It was piled so high it had started to rip through the canvas.

Tall Joe said, "Go ahead, clean it out," when Pa and some others wondered what to do.

Out came Mr. Bigg's cart, the wheels gone. Mrs. Anderson claimed her quilt, Pa found his hammer, and there was the milking stool someone had given Pepper for a wedding present. I found Ma's spoon and rose plate.

I watched from a distance as folks took back their possessions. Mrs. Bigg stood next to me, also watching. Rolling her sleeves up over her big arms she said, "Hattie, as hard as it is, we need to be kind to Mrs. Kenker, whether she deserves it or not. That's what mercy is, honey."

Mrs. Kenker had recovered from her faint and was sitting up. She seemed surprised to see the contents of her wagon scattered about. Then as if she suddenly remembered what her husband had done, she covered her face with her hands and began weeping.

Tall Joe seemed beside himself. He looked at Pa, then threw his hands in the air. "Campbell, I ain't an expert in these matters. What d'you reckon we should do?"

Pa shook his head. "I dunno."

It was decided we'd spend the night where we was. Five men rode ahead to search the river for Mr. Kenker's body.

Ma and Aunt June invited Mrs. Kenker to sit with us for supper, but she stayed by her wagon instead. I'm sorry for her that she's lost her husband, even though he was a nasty fellow. How horrible that she saw him jump to his death.

Later

I think everyone's confused about how to act. For a few minutes Mrs. Kenker was treated with the tender sympathies due a widow, but moments later folks discovered she's the thief who took Mr. Bigg's cart and everything else that's been missing.

The next morning we moved out at well before sunup to beat the heat. Gideon and Wade harnessed Mrs. Kenker's two oxen and asked if she needed help loading her wagon.

"No, boys, thank you," she said quietly, not looking at them.

The last I saw of Mrs. Kenker she was sitting on a trunk surrounded by her things, looking at the river.

We must cross the Snake to get to Fort Boise. Up ahead there are three islands that Tall Joe says we'll use as stepping-stones.

His face is sunburned and looks sad. I heard him tell Pa that two years ago when he crossed here, four wagons were swept away and the families drowned.

Lord. I almost forgot how scared of rivers I am.

Before bed

After I tucked in Bennie, Jake and I sat up by the fire.
He said I am his favorite sister. (He forgets I am his *only*
sister.)

Fort Boise

We're almost touching the Territory of Oregon. I have
not wrote for a week or so, but Aunt June says I must
put it all down quick, before I forget. Good and bad.

Well, they didn't find Mr. Kenker's body. We reached
Three Island Crossing mid-afternoon of the next day.
Black clouds and thunder meant rain any minute. Folks
discussed if we should cross now or wait for the storm
to pass. While Tall Joe leaned forward in his saddle to
study the river, something happened that made him
decide right quick.

There came a rumbling of hooves. Indians on horseback were galloping toward us, shrieking and waving
rifles. Before we could turn our wagons into a safe circle they were gone. Tall Joe shouted instructions and
while word spread from wagon to wagon, the Indians
made another pass. No gunfire was exchanged, but we
knew they wanted us to get off their land and get off
now.

(Maybe Pa would be mad, too, if strangers were tramping on our land.)

I wanted to panic, especially hearing the terrified cries of so many women and babies. I didn't know what scared me more, Indians or the thought of crossing another river.

Tall Joe led the first wagons into the water single file. The islands divide the river into four channels. Pa and Uncle Tim watched for three hours until it was our turn, the whole time nervous because the Indians had made camp a mile away and we could hear drums.

Why God sends babies into the world at times like this I'll never understand, but He does. Just as we were ready to ford this first channel Uncle Tim cried out to Ma.

"Augusta, hurry!"

Ma and I climbed into their wagon. Aunt June was lying in two inches of cold water, soaked to the skin and breathless with pain. The current was fast for I could feel us turning sideways, then pulling straight, then sideways again as the animals swam with Pa.

I was so concerned for Aunt June I quick forgot to worry about us drowning.

As we pulled up onto the first island Uncle Tim motioned to those behind us to keep going, that we'd catch up. When folks heard a baby was being born in a wet wagon, we found ourselves being given chairs, four of them, that we were able to make into a raised bed. Mrs. Lewis handed over a dry quilt, and a clean dress for Aunt June to change into.

So we crossed the second channel with water washing over our laps, but my aunt snug and dry. Her baby daughter was born just as we pulled onto the third island. Her name is River Ann Valentine.

The baby was only five minutes old when we began to ford the last channel. Screams drew Ma and me to look out the back. There was Mr. Bigg. He was tied to his seat, leaning hard to one side for his wagon was tipping over. When I saw that Mrs. Bigg had fallen in the water and was trying to grab her husband's hand, I started to leap out to help, but Ma held me back.

"Mrs. Bigg," I screamed. "Swim!"

Her arms were splashing. Each time she managed to grab a wheel or harness, the wagon tipped deeper toward her. Three men jumped in. They held on to keep it upright as another man tried to save Mrs. Bigg.

Everything happened so fast.

In an instant Mrs. Bigg and her rescuer disappeared under the tongue of the wagon. Their splashing arms were seen on the other side, moving with the river, then they were gone.

I screamed and screamed.

Mr. Bigg cried, "Sarah!" He tried to dive in after her, but couldn't get out from the rope that was holding him to the seat. His horses kept swimming and the men holding on were able to keep the wagon from sinking.

That's all I want to say for now.

Still Fort Boise

It was close to midnight by the time all the wagons made it to the other side, guided by torches we planted along shore. The reason we kept on through the darkness, made darker because clouds hid the moon and stars, was because it would have been impossible to protect ourselves the way we were spread out.

All night we could hear Indians on the south side of the river, we could see their campfires. Pa said maybe they were just trying to scare us, move us on, and wouldn't have done any harm.

Mr. Bigg invited the Anderson family to share his wagon and to help him drive. He is so heartbroken he barely speaks.

I am furious with God.

Why did someone as generous and loving and honest as Mrs. Bigg have to die while Mrs. Kenker gets to live?

The reason I know she lives is because the morning after we made the Three Island Crossing, we saw her way on the other side, trying to coax her oxen in. There were whispers about just leaving her to fend for herself.

Finally Tall Joe and Mr. Lewis swam their horses over and brought her back. She kept her eyes straight ahead and would not look at us.

I am too crushed over Mrs. Bigg to hate Mrs. Kenker anymore. I don't know why.

Afternoon

Well, to report happier news, my little niece, River, is healthy and about the most beautiful child I've ever set eyes on. Aunt June is back to her cheerful self, walking with Ma and Mrs. Anderson. Uncle Tim made a tiny hammock to hang from inside their wagon so the baby can sleep with a cool breeze.

It bothers me that no one talks about poor Mrs. Bigg. Everytime I remember her thrashing in the water my heart races with panic. If only I could have saved her . . .

I reckon the reason no one talks about her or the other terrible things that've happened is there's just not a thing in the world we can do about them.

I asked Wade his opinion on this matter, so he told me a joke. He said, "How does an ant eat a buffalo?"

118

"Don't know."

"One bite at a time, Hattie."

In other words, we are going to Oregon one step at a time, slowly, looking forward all the way. We must put the past behind us.

As we approached Fort Boise we found ourselves in a green valley, a welcome sight after 300 miles of black rock and desert. Woods and streams and cooler air. I tasted my first salmon, traded to us by Indians who came into camp. They were friendly and smiled easy. For once I was relaxed. It really is true, I've decided: They're as different among themselves as white folks are. I'm going to stop being afraid of them.

Just like that.

Rabbits are everywhere, so many that they're easy to hunt. We're now drying their meat like we did buffalo and ox.

Leaving Fort Boise, the Snake River turns northeast and, since we must head northwest, folks call this Farewell Bend. Tall Joe says three days from here we'll climb Flagstaff Hill. If our poor ol' wagons make it to the top we'll be able to see the Blue Mountains.

The Blue Mountains of Oregon!

Oregon.

Later

The day after Farewell Bend, Pepper's two mules died. When Gideon went looking for them in the morning, he found them lying on their sides in the grass. The sad part is there's not one spare animal left that has the strength to pull their wagon, little as it is, the rest of the way to Oregon.

Pepper and I looked inside one last time at their small collection of wedding gifts. She slipped a mirror and brush into her pocket and Gideon rolled their quilt up to carry over his shoulder.

When we reached the brow of Flagstaff Hill we were winded from the altitude and from climbing. The air was so cold my clothes felt like they wasn't on. But there in the distance, rising above a layer of clouds, were the Blue Mountains. They were covered with snow. The sight of them took my breath they were so beautiful.

I wanted to shout, "hooray," but it came out as a whisper, I was so tired.

Tall Joe slapped his hat against his leg. "We gotta move it, folks. Only 400 miles to Oregon City, but looks like winter's early. If the Blues have snow, then the Cascades surely do, too. Let's go, let's go!"

Before breakfast

My back is sore, I think from carrying Bennie yesterday. Sometimes his little legs get so tired he cries for me to pick him up.

Blue Mountains

I ain't been writing like I did when the days were hot and lazy. Guess I'm tired, guess everyone is. There've been no dances, either. We've been in the wilderness six months, but it feels like forever.

Crossing the Blues was hard on the animals. Sixteen dropped in one day, so several families were forced to abandon their wagons. Men tied ropes to the carcasses and dragged them to the side, then used planks to roll them downhill. The wagons we left as is, in case folks coming along behind us need something from them.

We butchered only five oxen as there ain't enough time to do them all. Pa hopes we'll see deer or other game.

The air has changed. It's cooler, there's moisture, I can *feel* we're in Oregon.

These mountains are thick with pine forests, with plenty of grass, water, and firewood. Pa says soil that grows trees this magnificent will grow anything. He's more and more excited, thinking about the farm we'll have. It don't bother him that we'll arrive dirty and ragged-looking.

Twins were born last night! The girl was named Sarah, after Mrs. Bigg, and the boy was named — guess! — Blue. That makes five babies on this journey, counting Eliza May.

Oh, I talked with the other bride, the one who was instantly a mother. She is cheerful and has so much help from other women I don't think she'll figure she has four children until she wakes up in Oregon City. I asked her what it's like to have a husband. She blushed so red I thought she'd faint.

I wish for once someone would just answer my questions straight out instead of blushing!

I walk with Wade every day, but he has become more like a brother to me. My dream of falling in love seems far away now.

We are camped in a valley called Grande Ronde, surrounded by mountains. There was a loud fight after breakfast, but it was between Aunt June and Uncle Tim! Seems she had her heart set on visiting her friend Narcissa Whitman, and he says there ain't enough time.

It's here that the trail branches to the Whitman Mission at Waiilatpu, about two days north. Tall Joe said no way can we detour for a social visit.

"Winter's coming and it's coming quick," he said, agreeing with Uncle Tim.

A vote was taken. Only three families were willing to make the trip. It's too risky with snow on our heels and the Cascades to cross, plus our animals are so exhausted we may all end up walking.

Tall Joe took a stick to draw in the dirt. "Lookie here. Once you get to the Whitman Mission — I been there, I know — the only way to Oregon City is to raft down the Columbia River. The Columbia, ma'am! Do you know how many boats have sunk in them rapids? It's rough and more dangerous than the Snake, and with all these new little babies, no sir, I ain't takin' a chance."

He stood up and said to Uncle Tim, "Now, here's another idea if you don't mind spending the whole winter at Whitman's. You can come back this way next spring then follow our trail into Oregon City. That way you can avoid the Columbia, take you a month mebbe."

So we took another vote.

Funny enough, it was Aunt June who decided we should all stick together. "Narcissa will understand," she said, holding her baby against her shoulder.

Evening

This afternoon Pepper and I were tending the children and babies while their mothers washed clothes in the stream. Jake and some of his friends were sloshing along a creek that ran through our meadow. They were playing war with peashooters and whips made from plants.

For some reason I felt uneasy. I called to Jake but he ignored me, so I hurried after him. When I saw the plants the boys had pulled up I immediately grabbed Jake's toy, then did the same with the other boys'.

Their cries brought several parents running, but their angry looks vanished when I pointed to the up-rooted hemlock lying in the grass.

I pulled Jake into my arms and with fear in my heart asked, "Did you eat any?"

He shook his head no. We asked the others. "No," they all said.

The hollow stems are perfect for blowing pebbles at birds, Jake explained, and also for making whistles. He pointed to three boys who'd been pretending they were smoking cigars. Their lips were numb and they felt sick to their stomachs, but they promised they hadn't eaten any.

Another search brought some girls who'd started to string necklaces with the seed pods. We threw it all into the campfire, every root, leaf, and seed. I don't know why my own brother ignored Pa's lecture from weeks ago. We showed all the kids what hemlock looks like, told them to stay away and not touch, but they didn't listen. My own brother!

Mrs. Kenker keeps to herself. One or two folks are kind, they invite her for meals, but most ignore her like she was a bug on a rock. No one has offered to drive her wagon or share a tent. It's different for Mr. Bigg. He's surrounded by people night and day, helping and comforting him. That's how much folks like him.

I miss Mrs. Bigg.

Ma says that she left behind so many kind words and memories that we'll never forget her.

"Hattie," she said when we were laying out the beds after supper, "I know two things for sure. God loves us and He has a plan for our lives. I wish I knew why He took Mrs. Bigg and Cassia and the other children, but this I don't know."

"It ain't fair," I said, crying softly.

Ma bit her lip. She was crying, too.

Next day

Jake and Ben are sneezing and shivery. I wipe their noses with the hem of my dress and rub a little bacon grease on their chapped skin, but it's small comfort. I wish I had peppermint sticks to give them.

The Dalles

It has rained for six days. Nearly every blanket and shirt is wet. Pepper and I have undone our braids so that our hair will dry at night, but we still feel chilled and wish the sun would come out. It is miserable walking with wet clothes.

I am fed up.

Mud oozes into our poor old shoes and keeps our feet cold. There is no way to stay warm except by rubbing our arms hard and fast. Oh, I wish I had Grandma's wool shawl to wrap around my neck and shoulders.

(While I'm feeling sorry for myself . . .) The pages of this journal are soft from the dampness which makes the pencil poke through when I try to write. It frustrates me so bad I want to throw this thing away, but Aunt June says, "Keep trying, Hattie, don't give up."

Our canvas top ripped from the wind, leaving the front hoops bare. Finally we had to throw out our other trunks and boxes, most of our cooking pots and the sacks of flour. Even the souvenir chips folks got from Chimney Rock were thrown out.

Everyone shares everything. Ma put it this way: "Why do eight women need eight dutch ovens?" She didn't blink one tear.

Such a roaring river, the Columbia. Tall Joe gave us the good news that last year a man named Samuel K. Barlow finished a road that goes around the shoulder of Mount Hood, over the Cascades, then right down into Oregon City.

"This is the first year we don't have to ride the lower end of the Columbia thank you, Jesus, Amen," said Tall Joe.

It is supper. A light rain is making the fire hiss so I'll write quick, as long as my paper don't rip.

We made it up Barlow Pass, but our last two oxen that came with us all the way from Independence gave out just as we were ready to go down the western slope. The men rolled their carcasses off the trail like they did the others and we left our poor wagon under a ledge. Maybe it will be useful to next year's travelers.

Somehow now that we are on foot, I'm not so scared about things. My brothers are marching along just fine, like strong little goats. If Indians come maybe we can make friends instead of run. And with no wagon we don't have to fret about getting it across rivers. Maybe like Ma I'm becoming brave.

There was snow on the ground, but not deep. Our footprints pressed down to mud. Wind made it unbearably cold as most of us had tossed out extra clothes like leggings and warm sweaters, and what we were wearing was damp.

I feel chilled all day and my throat is sore. My ears ache. (It is hard to write this on account of my numb fingers!)

All I can think of is how the Donner party froze and starved last winter. If we wasn't so close to our journey's end I would give up, just give up and let a bear eat me, I'm that wore out.

Two of the wagons left are driven by Mr. Bigg and Gideon, to carry the babies and littlest children and the seedlings. The rest of us walk. Pepper says she feels sick, but she keeps going anyhow, with long slow steps. When I told Ma about Pepper's illness she just smiled and told me not to worry.

Pa encourages every tired one of us. He is in such high spirits that Ma is cheerful, too. They tell my brothers and me that we are almost there.

Willamette Valley

And we are almost there! Now that we're out of the mountains we could rest a few days, but everyone's so anxious to see trail's end that we are up each dawn and moving out quicker than usual. Noon is just long enough to eat cold biscuits and drink from the stream.

It is so green everywhere, with lush pine trees. A mist makes my face feel soft again and the ends of my braids are curly. I can't see the ocean. Tall Joe said it's a few days west of Oregon City, so it's too far away to even hear the waves. He pointed north and said just across the Columbia River is Fort Vancouver, a British fur trading post owned by Hudson's Bay Company. Soon, after we get settled, he'll take Pa there for supplies.

If only the sun would come out, even for a few minutes, we could warm up. My arms are chafed from where my wet sleeves rub, rub, rub, and there are new blisters on my feet from dampness.

Mid-October
Oregon City here we are!

I don't know how to describe our new home. Green. Wet. Muddy.

When we finally got here it was raining. There is one broad road running through town and there are fir stumps near everywhere, enough sometimes to leap from one to another without landing in puddles.

I figured Ma and the women would fall down weeping with relief and joy that we finally really truly made it all the way to Oregon, because that's what I felt like doing.

But no. Ma looked around, asked Pa what he thought about putting our tent there. He said fine. Aunt June did the same, Mrs. Anderson and so on. Within a few hours we had ourselves a neighborhood laid out at the edge of town.

Mr. Bigg's tent is next to the Lewis family and across the road from ours. Tall Joe is just around the bend, and the other families have spread out, too.

Tomorrow Pa will see about buying a lot. He says there must already be a few thousand folks living in Oregon City. There's two churches that we can see, four blacksmiths, a lumber mill, some saloons and stores, and many houses. There's even a school.

Pepper and Gideon are sharing our tent. Many families also are sharing until we can cut enough lumber to build homes.

I asked Ma, shouldn't we have a celebration right now, on account of finally reaching our Promised Land? But she said, no, there is too much work to be done yet. When our house is built, then we will celebrate.

October 22, 1847, Friday

I'm writing this to the sound of rain on our tent. Looks like my paper won't ever dry out so I must just get used to pressing soft with my pencil.

I still wake up in the middle of the night and wonder, are we really here? Then I drift back to sleep, waking later to the smell of coffee and bacon frying. No bugle. No lowing cattle or creaking wagons. No dust.

No reason to hurry up and go.

Pa has already planted eight fruit trees, seedlings he bought from the Iowa brothers. He lifts his chin and closes his eyes. "Hattie," he says, breathing in deeply, "can you smell the soil, can you smell how rich it is? We'll be eating from our orchard before you know it, daughter."

October 24, 1847, Sunday

Rain crept under the tent and soaked my pillow, which is where I keep this journal. But now the back pages are so soggy they tore. I am almost at the very last page.

December 23, 1847, Thursday

It's been a long time since I wrote. We now have a cabin. There's a window that looks out to the road leading into town. I'm sitting at our new little table, on a new three-legged stool, both built by Pa. Behind me is a stone fireplace with two hens roasting and a kettle boiling for tea.

Ma and Aunt June are rolling pie dough and Pepper is by the hearth rocking River to sleep. She must practice because sometime in the spring she and Gideon will have a new baby themselves. Pa and Mr. Lewis built them a cozy room in our barn, so in a way our dream of living next door to each other has come true.

Aunt June just called over to me, her hands gooey with flour. "Remember, Hattie, tell the good and the bad."

So I will.

Last week men rode into town with news that just about broke Aunt June's heart. On November 29 her friend Narcissa Whitman was murdered, along with her husband Marcus and twelve others, many of them children.

We don't know the whole story, but it seems there was a measles epidemic. When some Indian children died, the Cayuse thought Dr. Whitman was a sorcerer. So they burned down the mission.

Aunt June can't believe she'll never see her friend, the very friend who inspired her to come West in the first place. We've all talked long hours about "what if" we had gone to the mission for the winter. If we had, I wouldn't be writing this.

Ma said God's plan is bigger than us and it's impossible to guess why He lets things happen the way they do.

There's so much I don't understand.

In the two months we've been in Oregon City, the men have worked hard to put up houses. Many are still in tents, or snug under wooden lean-tos, such as Mrs. Kenker.

Somehow she managed to bring her wagon over the Blues and the Cascades. What she had in it, no one knows. Her tent is at the end of our street. Sometimes we see her walk through the mud into town, a basket on her arm. She is shunned by many of the folks from our wagon train, including me.

When Ma said she wanted to invite Mrs. Kenker to our celebration dinner I said no, absolutely no . . . not until she says she's sorry.

Ma smiled. She and Aunt June were setting the table for tea with our new cups from Fort Vancouver.

"Hattie," she said. "In order to move on we must forgive the past. Sometimes that means forgiving someone who hasn't apologized and probably never will. We don't have to forget what happened."

Ma poured boiling water into our new teapot. Squares of ginger cake sprinkled with powdered sugar were stacked on our new tin platter. Almost nothing survived our trip, just a small amount of money that Pa said is hardly worth counting, the worn-out shoes on our feet, our clothes, some blankets, my journal . . . and Ma's spoon and her little plate that I carried over the mountains in my pocket.

We've all written letters to friends in Booneville, telling them to come to Oregon. Pa rode our mail to the fort. From there the letters will go out on the next clipper ship bound for the East Coast. It'll take at least six months for them to sail south around Cape Horn, then back up to Boston, then by wagon and riverboat to Missoura.

Becky may not read my letter for another year!

Christmas, 1847

It is late and everyone's in bed. I'm writing by our new lamp — the wick is floating in whale oil that Pa got in trade from Fort Vancouver.

At noon Christmas day, our guests began arriving. Wade came with his parents, and Mr. Bigg wheeled himself over with the Andersons. He's living with them in a special room they built him. He brought a gift for each child: a small canvas sack that he cut and sewed from his old tent, each with a whistle inside that he carved from Oregon pine.

Tall Joe came with a sea captain who's staying in Portland and some neighbors who moved here a year ago. The family with the twins, Sarah and Blue, brought cranberry pies.

The last person to show up was Mrs. Kenker. She stood off by herself as if she wanted to join in, but didn't know how.

I had hoped she would arrive with gifts for all of us, by way of saying she's sorry. But she was empty-handed.

Dinner lasted four hours because we took turns with our few chairs and plates and cups — whoever wasn't eating was talking or holding a baby. During this confusion I kept my eye on Mrs. Kenker. Several times she reached down to comfort a crying child, but stopped herself, not sure if she should, I reckon. Several times she went to the kitchen to help, but seemed timid, like she didn't want to bother any of the women busy there.

She seemed so lonely, my heart began to soften. I hurried behind the curtain that hides my bed. Under my pillow is where I keep these treasures: this journal, Ma's silver spoon, and the small china plate with roses on it. I took off the sash to my apron. It is blue and about four inches wide, so I wrapped this around the spoon until it looked like a real present.

I tied it up with a piece of string and lay a fresh pine bough on top. I found Mrs. Kenker at the door just putting on her shawl. As she stepped out in the damp air I called, "Merry Christmas," then handed her my gift.

Light from the window made a patch of yellow on the ground. Gently she undid the wrapping. When she saw what it was, her eyes grew moist.

"Thank you, Hattie," she whispered. We stood there a moment in the cold. She touched my cheek, then walked to the road.

I felt good. For the first time in months I wanted to be kind to Mrs. Kenker. Maybe what Ma said yesterday is true. She said, if you "give forth" you are beginning to "for give." (But I'm not ready to part with my grandmother's plate.)

Well, I have much to think about. But before I blow out the lamp . . .

When I turned around to go back in the house, Wade was waiting for me in the doorway. He is taller than when we first met back in Missoura and tonight he wore a new cloth coat with a string tie. He was smiling when he stepped out and took my arm.

"Come on, Hattie."

We could hear music coming from the barn: There were fiddlers, and the sea captain was playing a banjo.

When I saw Mama out on the dance floor with Pa, her arm looped through his, and her head thrown back in laughter, I knew we were really truly finally in Oregon.

Just like that.

Epilogue

The families who arrived in Oregon City prospered. On May 15, 1848, Pepper and Gideon had a baby boy named Michael who was to be the oldest of seven brothers. On Christmas Eve of that year, Wade and Hattie were married. They were unable to have children of their own, but adopted the six-year-old twins, Sarah and Blue, when their parents died in a buggy crash.

For the rest of their lives Hattie and Pepper shared a fence and a vegetable garden.

The Anderson family started an inn on their fruit ranch. Mr. Bigg lived with them and became well-known as a tailor and a favorite "uncle" to the many children who visited.

Mrs. Kenker lived alone in a cottage at the edge of town. One summer afternoon in 1849 Hattie went to visit, but found her dead on the kitchen floor. The constable said Mrs. Kenker had died from a heart attack at least two weeks prior.

Aunt June and Uncle Tim had three sons: Henry, Tom, and Adam who all struck out for California mining camps in search of gold. Their sister, River Ann, married Paddy O'Reilly, a famous tenor with the San Francisco Opera.

In 1906 Aunt June's granddaughter, Daisy Valentine, would be one of the survivors of San Francisco's great earthquake and fire.

Life in America
in 1847

Historical Note

Americans have always had a tradition of wanting to explore new territories and search for wide-open spaces. Today, we venture forth into the frontiers of space, and the European-American pioneers of the 1800's were no different in their spirit of adventure as they bravely set out to explore the relatively unknown parts of the North American continent.

Following a nationwide depression in 1837, there was a strong movement toward westward expansion. James Polk ran for President in 1844 as an expansionist candidate. The United States had recently gained Texas as an annexed territory (and after the Mexican War ended in 1848, California and New Mexico would become part of the country, too). The United States and Great Britain had both claimed the Oregon Territory, and Polk's campaign used the slogan, "Fifty-four-forty or fight!" This rallying cry referred to the latitude of the Oregon Territory, which America wanted to claim as its own. Ultimately, a treaty was signed with Great Britain, and the territory south of the 49th parallel — what is now Oregon and Washington — became part of America. As a result, the country nearly doubled in size during Polk's presidency.

In 1845, a newspaperman named John L. O'Sullivan used the phrase "manifest destiny" in an article he wrote about westward expansion. His theory was that since American democracy was so successful, Americans had a divine — or God-given — right to take over any land they desired, and even a duty to do so. Many citizens agreed with this philosophy, and were eager to establish homesteads on the newly acquired territories. The Indians who lived there were primarily semi-nomadic and believed that the land belonged to everyone. But because the pioneers had a very different cultural concept of private ownership, they claimed the land as their own, despite the fact that the Indian peoples had lived there for over ten thousand years.

The entire Oregon Trail was first used during the early part of the nineteenth century by fur trappers; missionaries; various explorers such as Jim Bridger, John C. Frémont, and Lansford W. Hastings; as well as other adventurers. The Indians had already been using parts of the trail for thousands of years. Along with the California and Sante Fe trails, the Oregon Trail served as the main route to the Pacific Ocean from the 1830's until the completion of the Transcontinental Railroad in 1869.

The two-thousand-mile-long Oregon Trail originated in Independence, Missouri, although there were several other "jumping-off points" nearby. The journey took an average of six months to complete. The first organized wagon train of fourteen wagons left from Independence in 1836. The party was led by Protestant missionaries Marcus and Narcissa Whitman and included approximately seventy men, women, and children. Narcissa Whitman kept a detailed diary of the journey, as did many pioneer women. By 1843, the "Oregon fever" had spread, and one thousand settlers — also known as emigrants — set out on the trail. During the next few years, at least five thousand more brave pioneers followed in their tracks to settle in the rich farmland of the Oregon countryside. The Mormans, led by Brigham Young, would find their homeland around the Great Salt Lake in Utah in 1847. Countless others would head to California after gold was discovered there at Sutter's Mill in 1849.

The most famous group to travel on the Oregon Trial was the Donner Party in 1846. Eighty-nine unfortunate emigrants were stranded in the Sierra Nevada mountain range when winter arrived, preventing them from being able to complete their journey. They had left late and taken a "cutoff" — or shortcut — in order to try to save time. The decision was deadly. Many of them froze or starved to death, and the forty-seven who survived were forced to resort to cannibalism when their provisions ran out. As a result, the Donner Party became a notorious symbol of the worst that could happen during the long, dangerous journey to the Pacific Ocean. One survivor's letter to a friend back East warned, "Never take no cut ofs and hury along as fast as you can."

There were countless natural hazards to be found along the Oregon Trail. Still, more than anything else, the emigrants feared contact with Indians. But Indian attacks were actually rare. The emigrants were far more likely to die from accidents; diseases, such as cholera and typhoid; starvation; drowning while attempting a river crossing; or the perils of an unexpected blizzard. The wagon trains often encountered grass fires, hailstorms, floods, and other powerful forces of nature.

At least twenty-seven different Indian tribes lived in the areas surrounding the Oregon Trail. Some of the tribes included the Lakota Sioux, the Kiowa, the Apaches, the Pawnees, the Shoshone, the Kansa, the Arapaho, the Crow, the Cheyenne, the Bannock, and the Flatheads. On rare occasions, Indians stole livestock or provisions from the wagon trains, but most of them were more interested in bartering with the settlers. Generally, they would provide fresh buffalo meat or salmon, in exchange for cash, metal fishing hooks, calico, and other clothing items. Because the emigrants were ignorant about Indian cultures, they often behaved in an unnecessarily hostile manner toward the Indians.

Any family preparing to take the Oregon Trail needed to gather enough supplies to last for the entire journey. They would purchase or build a sturdy wagon, and buy either oxen or mules to pull it. Mules were able to travel faster, but they usually weren't strong enough to make the entire trip. Oxen could generally go only five to ten miles a day, but they were much sturdier animals. The emigrants frequently had to detour from the trail, in order to locate fresh water and plenty of grass for their animals.

Each family would stock up on lots of provisions like flour, bacon, salt-pork, sugar, dried beans and fruit, saleratus (baking soda), tobacco, cornmeal, vinegar, rice, and chipped (smoked) beef. For the most part, they lived on beans and coffee, and any wild berries or root vegetables they could gather. The average breakfast consisted of bread or pancakes, fried meat, beans, and tea or coffee. There was rarely any medical care available on the trail, so they would pack primitive medicinals and remedies like laudanum (an opium medicinal) and camphor for general ailments, quinine, castor oil, and hartshorn for snakebites. The cost of the entire trip, to outfit and transport each family, was about five hundred dollars.

Most emigrants walked next to their covered wagons, rather than riding, so that the livestock would have less weight to pull, and because there was very little room to sit inside. Firewood was always scarce, and during the day, women and children collected weeds and buffalo chips (dung) to use to heat their evening meal. Though there was very little formal schooling, children learned a great deal — from how to care for animals to the names of flowers.

Women and teenage girls worked extremely hard. In addition to cooking and caring for the younger children, they also pitched tents, built fires, drove oxen, and assumed other traditionally male duties. Some of them were pregnant during the journey, which made life even more difficult. There was never a good time to go into labor on the Oregon Trail! Women were almost always the first ones to get up in the morning to make fires and prepare breakfast, and the last people to go to sleep at night.

When the California Gold Rush hit in 1849, traffic along the first half of the Oregon Trail increased dramatically, with hundreds of thousands of people going west to seek their fortunes. By the mid-1850's, the Oregon Trail had become much safer. Ferries and bridges were common, and many trading posts were established along the way. Telegraph poles dotted the road, and some people even traveled in the relative luxury of stagecoaches and bought lodging in small inns at night. Over the years, the grueling six-month ordeal became a much safer, three-month trip along smooth, well-populated roads.

Almost five hundred thousand people used the Oregon Trail between 1836 and 1870, heading to Oregon, California, and Utah. With the completion of the Transcontinental Railroad in 1869, the use of the trail was reduced to a trickle. But for many years, it was the main gateway to the West, and helped form the United States as it exists today.

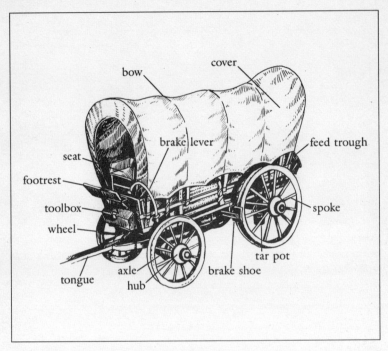

bow

cover

brake lever

seat

footrest

toolbox

wheel

feed trough

spoke

tongue

axle

hub

brake shoe

tar pot

Covered wagons were also called Prairie Schooners. The canvas tops were rubbed with oil to make them waterproof. Smaller front wheels helped maneuver around sharp turns, and axle grease made the wheels turn more smoothly. It took three to six yoke of oxen or four to six mules to pull each wagon.

The wagons could be as small as ten feet long and four feet wide and had to hold an entire family's food, clothing, medicines, and furniture. There were hooks inside for hanging bonnets, spoons, dolls, guns, jackets, and milkcans.

Wagons camped in circles for security, with the front of one wagon facing the back of another. Children often played inside the circle before bedtime.

A pioneer family after a long, exhausting day of travel. Women and girls wore skirts or dresses made from gingham and calico, sturdy shoes, and bonnets to protect them from the hot sun. Men and boys wore cotton shirts, pants made from cotton or buckskin, and wide-brimmed hats.

Women and teenage girls worked hard and became very strong physically. Here a woman gathers dried "buffalo chips," or droppings, in order to build a fire on the treeless plains. Without any of the conveniences of home, the travelers learned to be resourceful and self-sufficient.

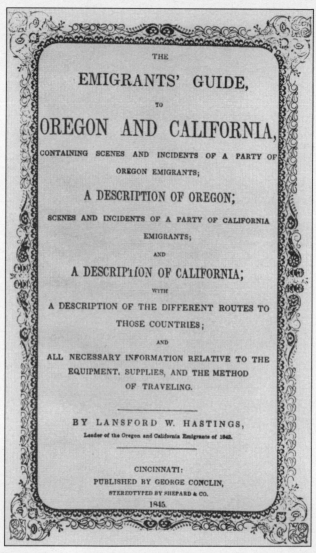

THE

EMIGRANTS' GUIDE,

TO

OREGON AND CALIFORNIA,

CONTAINING SCENES AND INCIDENTS OF A PARTY OF
OREGON EMIGRANTS;

A DESCRIPTION OF OREGON;

SCENES AND INCIDENTS OF A PARTY OF CALIFORNIA
EMIGRANTS;

AND

A DESCRIPTION OF CALIFORNIA;

WITH

A DESCRIPTION OF THE DIFFERENT ROUTES TO
THOSE COUNTRIES;

AND

ALL NECESSARY INFORMATION RELATIVE TO THE
EQUIPMENT, SUPPLIES, AND THE METHOD
OF TRAVELING.

BY LANSFORD W. HASTINGS,

Leader of the Oregon and California Emigrants of 1842.

CINCINNATI:
PUBLISHED BY GEORGE CONCLIN,
STEREOTYPED BY SHEPARD & CO.
1845.

The title page from Lansford W. Hastings' famous booklet, The Emigrants' Guide to Oregon and California. *The Donner Party followed a shortcut known as the "Hastings cut-off," described in the book.*

The pioneers were rewarded with breathtaking scenery. But it was often so difficult to travel over the steep mountain passes that people had to discard heavier belongings, or cut their wagons down to a cart with just two wheels.

River crossings were often frightening and dangerous.

This wagon had to be abandoned when it got stuck in quicksand. Its canvas has been stripped away by strong winds.

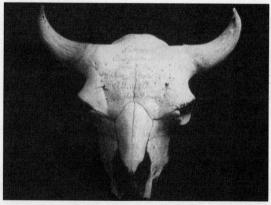

Pioneers left messages for travelers who followed behind. Sometimes they would tell them where fresh water could be found or alert them to certain dangers. This buffalo skull has a message cut into it by Brigham Young, the leader of the Mormon expedition. It says, "Pioneers camped here June 3 1847 making 15 miles today All well Brigham Young."

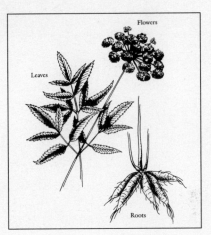

Water Hemlock roots are so poisonous, a person could die from eating just one bite. Pioneers had to familiarize themselves with inedible plants or risk death.

Many travelers died from cholera and typhoid epidemics, as well as from accidents and natural disasters. Trailside graveyards were not uncommon sights along the way west.

157

A Lakota Sioux woman. Despite the emigrants' fears about Indians, the various tribes they met were mainly interested in trading. The real wars with the Indians did not begin until the 1850s and 1860s when the emigrants began to settle permanently on Indian land.

In the 1840s, thousands of buffalo roamed the plains. The pioneers relied on buffalo meat. They learned from the Indians how to jerk (dry) the meat so it would keep for long periods of time. They attached strips to their wagons and let them dry in the hot prairie sun.

JOHNY CAKE or HOE CAKE

1 pint milk
3 pints corn meal
1/2 pint flour

Scald milk and put to corn meal and flour.
Bake before the fire.

This recipe is adapted from The First American Cookbook.

Skip to My Lou

Flies in the buttermilk, shoo shoo shoo
Flies in the buttermilk, shoo shoo shoo
Flies in the buttermilk, shoo shoo shoo
Skip to my lou, my darling

I got me another one, skip, skip, skip
I got me another one, skip, skip, skip
I got me another one, skip, skip, skip
Skip to my lou, my darling

Words and music to "Skip to My Lou." This celebrated folk song was a favorite among pioneer teenagers. The word "Lou" meant "sweetheart."

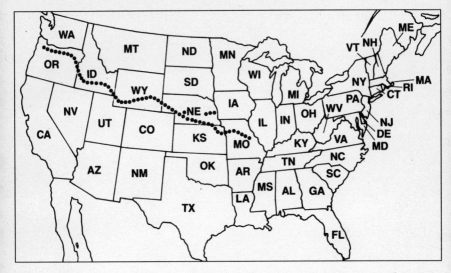

Modern map of the continental United States, showing the Oregon Trail route.

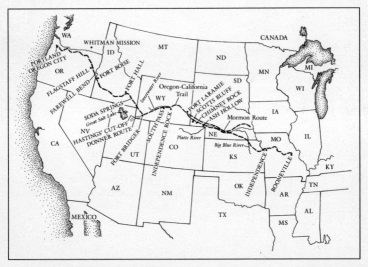

This detail of the Oregon Trail indicates important landmarks and stopping points mentioned in the diary.

About the Author

KRISTIANA GREGORY wrote *Across the Wide and Lonesome Prairie* a few months after she and her husband and their two young sons moved from California to Colorado. "The journey itself wasn't as dangerous as Hattie Campbell's," she says. "And it took just two days instead of eight months. But like Hattie, we left behind family and lifelong friends to settle in a town we'd only seen on a map, a town where we didn't know a soul.

"I identified with the pioneers' excitement and hopes, with their dream of starting a new life in a new land. I understand the despair they must have felt to leave behind loved ones, and even though there are now telephones, fax machines, and airplanes, it is still lonely when your friends are far away. But Hattie was able to quickly begin new friendships, as we have."

Kristiana Gregory is also the author of a previous book in the *Dear America* series, *The Winter of Red Snow: The Revolutionary War Diary of Abigail Jane Stewart*, which was named an *American Bookseller* "Pick of the Lists." She is widely praised for her accurate and compelling works of historical fiction, including, *Jimmy*

Spoon and the Pony Express and *The Stowaway*, both published by Scholastic Press, as well as *Jenny of the Tetons*, winner of the SCBWI Golden Kite Award; *The Legend of Jimmy Spoon;* and *Earthquake at Dawn*, all for Harcourt Brace. She lives in Colorado with her family.

This book about a journey is dedicated, with deep appreciation, to the outstanding editors who have guided and encouraged me along my own journey as a writer: Jeff Fairbanks, Charlie Ferrell, Scott Gray, Regina Griffin, Karen Grove, Tracy Mack, Ann Reit, Art Seidenbaum, and Elinor Williams; most especially to my literary agent and friend, Barbara Markowitz.

Acknowledgments

The author would like to thank Karla J. Demby, M.D., F.A.C.P., for sharing case studies on hemlock poisoning; and Anita Tanner for historical material on Brigham Young's westward journey of 1847.

Grateful acknowledgment is made for permission to reprint the following:

Cover portrait: A detail from *The Broken Pitcher* by Adolphe-William Bouguereau, 1891. Oil on canvas. Gift of M. H. de Young. Collection of The Fine Arts Museums of San Francisco.
Cover background: A detail from William Henry Jackson's *Kanesville — Missouri River Crossing*, 1856. Courtesy of Scotts Bluff Monument, Scotts Bluff, Nebraska.

Page 151: Wagon with parts labeled, drawing by Heather Saunders
Page 152 (top): Interior of covered wagon, National Archives
Page 152 (bottom): Wagons in circle at Independence Rock, The Denver Public Library, Western History Department, Denver, Colorado
Page 153 (top): Pioneer family, ibid.
Page 153 (bottom): Frontier woman gathering buffalo chips with her daughter, Bettmann Archives, New York, New York
Page 154: Title page from *The Emigrants' Guide to Oregon and California*, Library of Congress
Page 155 (top): Wagons traveling through the Rocky Mountains, Library of Congress
Page 155 (bottom): Crossing the Platte River, Library of Congress

Page 156 (top): Abandoned wagon, National Archives
Page 156 (bottom): Buffalo skull, The Church of Jesus Christ of Latter–day Saints, Courtesy of Museum of Church History and Art, Salt Lake City, Utah
Page 157 (top): Hemlock, drawing by Heather Saunders
Page 157 (bottom): Graveyard, Library of Congress
Page 158: *She Comes Out First* by Eldridge Ayer Burbank, Butler Institute of American Art, Youngstown, Ohio
Page 159 (top): Buffalo, Library of Congress
Page 159 (bottom): Recipe, adapted from *The First American Cook book, A Facsimile of "American Cookery," 1796* by Amelia Simmons, Dover Publications, Inc., New York, New York
Page 160: Words and music to "Skip to My Lou," from *The American Song Treasury* by Theodore Raph, ibid.
Page 161: Maps by Heather Saunders

Other books in the *Dear America* series

A Journey to the New World
The Diary of Remember Patience Whipple
by Kathryn Lasky

The Winter of Red Snow
The Revolutionary War Diary of Abigail Jane Stewart
by Kristiana Gregory

When Will This Cruel War Be Over?
The Civil War Diary of Emma Simpson
by Barry Denenberg

A Picture of Freedom
The Diary of Clotee, a Slave Girl
by Patricia C. McKissack

Copyright © 1997 by Kristiana Gregory.

All rights reserved. Published by Scholastic Inc.
557 Broadway, New York, New York 10012.
DEAR AMERICA®, SCHOLASTIC, and associated logos
are trademarks and/or registered trademarks of Scholastic Inc.

Library of Congress Cataloging-in-Publication Data available.

ISBN 0-590-22651-7;
ISBN 0-439-44568-X (pbk.)

10 9 8 7 6 5 4 3 2 1   02 03 04 05 06

Printed in the U.S.A. 23
First paperback printing, October 2002

MY NAME IS AMERICA

The Journal of Douglas Allen Deeds

The Donner Party
Expedition

BY RODMAN PHILBRICK

Scholastic Inc. New York

Independence, Missouri
1846

I
THE WAY WEST

May 12
Independence, Missouri

"Today I embark on a great journey."

That's what Mr. George Donner told me to write down when I bought me a vellum-bound journal from the stationery store but I didn't know what to say.

"The first sentence is always the hardest," Mr. Donner said. "The rest is up to you."

Thank you, Mr. Donner, for thinking up that first sentence, and for letting me tag along on your wagon train even tho I ain't got no kin and no wagon, but only poor old Barny, who don't want to leave Missouri if he can help it.

Barny is my horse, which I got when my paw passed. The horse and one hundred dollars in gold from selling the farm, that's all I have in the world, but it's enough to get me there, if I'm careful.

Last thing I did before leaving Independence was pay my respects to Maw and Paw. I went to the little churchyard with all the pretty white markers and prayed over 'em and explained how before long my prayers would be coming from California. Maw didn't know about California, she's been gone so long, but Paw did. Before he died, he talked about how there were valleys where it never snowed and crops that grow all year long. California is where a man can eat a fresh peach in December and never be cold, Paw said. Which is probably what gave me the idea to join up.

May 13

Our expedition is big and getting bigger. Two hundred wagons and more every day! When folks hear where we're headed, they sell their land for ten cents on a dollar and buy a wagon and follow along. George Donner and his brother Jacob organized the train in Springfield along with Mr. James Reed and Colonel Russell. Mr. Donner says he don't mind all the extra folks. He says there's safety in numbers and plenty of food along the way. All the game we can hunt and good water for the horses.

Ho! For California!

May 14

We are already two long, hard days from Independence, but have made less than ten miles progress. Mr. Reed says a few more days and we'll be clear of these dense, dark timberlands and out in the open plains where the going will be easier. I asked him how many times he's led settlers through to California, and he gave me a funny look, like I was trying to be insulting, which I wasn't. I have the greatest respect for Mr. Reed and the Donner brothers, even if none of them has never actually been west before. Paw always said there's a first time for everything!

I made a new friend today. His name is Edward Breen. His family has three wagons and twelve good horses. The way Edward's mother dotes on him reminds me how much I still miss my own maw, even tho I was but five years old when she passed. I am fifteen now, so I pulled my hat brim down so nobody'd see me cryin' like a girl. I felt considerable better afterwards when Mrs. Breen insisted I hitch up with them, and eat with them and so on. She's a real nice lady, and I like the soft way she talks, which I suppose is how everybody from Ireland talks.

There's a number of other young single men in the party, and mostly they stick together. Some of the bachelors drink hard liquor, which I made a vow never to touch, so I'm glad of the kind invitation to accompany the Breens.

While we were walking along, guiding the teams of oxen that pull the wagons, I entertained my new friend, Edward, by recounting all the Missouri whoppers I could recall (they work better if you give them a honey-mouth drawl). He laughed so hard he spit water through his nose! He especially liked the one about the catfish that swallowed the bear.

Edward says when we get to California maybe me and him can partner-up and be surveyors. He says with all the free land being cut out by new settlers there'll be a shortage of surveyors, marking out the property lines and so on, and we'll prosper. He was so excited about the idea I didn't tell him I've got my heart set on farming dairy cows, which is what my paw tried to do until he had his run of bad luck.

Nobody has ever seen anything like the Donner expedition. It is two miles from the first wagon to the last, and the ground shakes as we go by. We make such a racket it sounds like every pot and pan in the world is falling downstairs at the same time. All us men helped cutting trail today, and at first the track was firm and the wheels didn't sink. But by the time the last wagon passed, the trail weren't nothing but soggy mud, and we had to set down straw and pry the wheels clear. It is hard work, but I don't mind. Everybody is so friendly and grateful for our common purpose.

Mrs. Tamsen Donner saw me scribbling in this journal and said to be sure to put in some stuff about rations, so here goes. We got a ration of a hundred and fifty pounds of flour and seventy-five pounds of salted meat per person. You got to buy that much, or you can't join up. Seventy-five pounds of meat won't last for such a long journey, but we expect to hunt game on the way. We got rice and beans and lard for frying. Every wagon has at least one spare wheel and the fixings to make more. Each family has a tent and gear for cooking, and many have spare horses. Most every man has a rifle, and mostly they're pretty handy, even if they never shot anything but rabbit and squirrel.

That won't matter, as we expect to find buffalo near the Platte River, and they say buffalo are a mighty big target and hard to miss. I never ate buffalo steak and am looking forward to it.

May 15

We are free of the forests! This morning, three hours after dawn, we came at last to the end of the timberlands, and saw the sun rising clear over the great prairie. In Missouri I never seen anything so wide open to the sky. Just fields of tall grass as far as a man can see. No, I lie, much farther than a man can see. More like what an angel might see, looking down from Heaven.

Mr. George Donner says if all goes well it will take no more than two months to traverse the prairie lands, and that come August we'll cross over the Sierra Nevada Mountains and find ourselves in California.

Right off, things have improved considerable. Colonel Russell, who is helping to lead the party, rode ahead to spot for Indians. He didn't find any, but he did locate a fine hard trail that is in such splendid condition it can almost be called a proper road. No more wheels bogging down in the mud! By Mr. Donner's reckoning we made better than ten miles in a single day and should expect to do even better tomorrow.

I shot a pheasant and Mrs. Breen praised me so, I'm sure it made my face as pink as bunting. She says the Breens will never go hungry so long as I'm there to help provide, and she hopes I'll teach Edward to shoot as good as me. I didn't have the courage to tell her the pheasant just happened to light on a tree stump so close by nobody could have missed. Anyhow, Mrs. Breen made up a batch of fine biscuits and gravy, and that pheasant sure tasted good!

Later Mr. Patrick Breen (Edward's paw) made a fuss over putting a pheasant feather in the brim of my hat. He don't say much but when he does, it means something. I count my lucky stars to have such friends.

No buffalo yet, but birds and small game are plentiful.

May 16

Mr. James Reed kindly invited me to admire his Palace today. I never seen anything like it. The Pioneer Palace Car ain't no ordinary wagon. It's so big it takes four yoke of oxen to pull it. The Palace has got a real door and steps to get up, and inside it's all fitted out like a little house on wheels, with a wood stove to keep it warm, and a stove pipe that goes up through the canvas top. They got built-in beds below, and a loft where the children sleep, and a special feather bed for their grandma, who is ailing. She don't complain, but just lies in her bed and sighs a little. They even got a library in there, with a bunch of books!

Their daughter's name is Virginia. She's twelve years old and has a pony called Billy. When she saw me scribbling in my journal, she told me she was keeping one, too. Hers will be better, I guess, 'cause she's had more learning than me, and books to read and stuff.

The way they talk, I get the impression the Reeds don't think much of the Donner family. The Donners got three wagons, but none of them compare to the Pioneer Palace Car, that's for sure.

Just before sundown I tried for a deer, but missed, and it ran off.

May 17

After two hours on the trail we came to the Kaw River, and got ourselves across it, and on into the frontier territory, leaving Missouri behind.

Turns out the Kaw Indians own this patch of river, and if you want to cross over, you got to pay them. That's the deal, and Mr. James Reed said it was pretty fair, considering. We got 247 wagons in our party, and it cost a dollar each wagon, so the Kaw made a pile today. Mr. Breen joked how the Indians were getting even for selling Manhattan so cheap. I asked what Manhattan was, and he said it meant the same as New York, which is somewhere back east.

Anyhow, them Kaw Indians worked mighty hard for their money. What happens when you want to cross their river is this: First you pull the wagon as close to the landing as you can get it, then you unhitch the teams of oxen, which will be unyoked and then swum over. Then the Indians take charge. Each wagon gets shoved onto the landing, and from there gets manhandled onto their rickety little barge, which is a tricky business. The barge barely has room for two wagons. Once they get the wagons on board, the Indians pole the barge to the landing on the opposite shore, and then do it all over again, only backward, unloading the wagons onto the landing and then shoving them up to the shore.

They had to make a special trip for Mr. Reed's Pioneer Palace Car because it's so much bigger than a regular wagon, but they still only charged him a dollar.

Meantime, we're all busy swimming the oxen across the river. They don't like it much, but if you push hard enough, they go. And once an ox gets going forward he won't back up. Horses mostly go better. We didn't lose one animal, which Mr. Reed says is a triumph.

Naturally I got soaked to the skin, but you know what? It felt good. I ain't been so clean of dust since we left Independence!

We were all proud of ourselves about the crossing, and slapped each other on the back and said we were sturdy pioneers and how nothing could stop us now. Then Mr. Donner came by, real somber and serious-like, and said that at the next river we cross there wouldn't be Indians to help us, and no barge to float the wagons. Mr. Reed didn't say anything, but he wasn't pleased.

We got a mile clear of the landing, and then made camp. Patrick Breen has a fiddle and played it very lively after supper. Everybody sung along, even if we didn't know the words, and we all felt mighty fine about deciding to go west.

Later, when it came time to bed down, Mrs. Breen said I should sleep under their wagon, in case it rained. Edward elected to sleep outside, too, so's I could tell him some more Missouri whoppers. He's holding the lantern while I write in my journal and says "Hello."

May 19

For the last two days we been following the Kaw River. The land is flat and easy, tho it bogs down some here and there. Me and Edward take charge of encouraging the oxen while his father and the others push and shove the wagon from behind, rocking it free of the mud.

The work is hard, but nobody complains much. Mr. Breen jokes a lot and says how all of Ireland is nothing but a bog. You can tell he misses Ireland, even if he won't admit it, because he's an American now, bound for California. It don't matter where you came from because you can't go back. You can only keep going. We got that in common with the oxen!

May 20

Rain. Bad rain. Terrible thunder and wicked lightning, too. It started about noon, but we kept going for three hours, trying to make a few more miles. At last it was too much. The lightning scared the horses, so we all stopped and made camp, which today means we huddle inside the wagons, feeling scared and miserable. When the lightning goes off, you can see it flashing right through the canvas top, bright as the sun. The lightning casts a shadow, too, tho it don't last long.

Mrs. Breen weeps a little, because she's afraid we'll be struck, and her husband comforts her as best he can. They talk real soft to each other, which reminds me of my dear maw and paw, God rest their souls.

The Breens are very kind to have me in their wagon, as by rights I should be outside with the other bachelors. The wagons are up on a plateau, some distance from the river, and pretty exposed to the wretched weather. Our whole wagon shakes whenever a gust hits us. The canvas top had some waterproofing, supposedly, but it ain't holding, and we're all wet and miserable as dogs.

Edward jokes that I look like a muskrat with a pen, and I guess he ain't far wrong.

May 29

Virginia Reed's grandmother died today.

I mentioned before how she mostly just lay on her feather bed and didn't say much, on account of the sickness in her lungs. Mr. Reed says it was the stopping that did her in. As long as the wagons were moving west, her condition improved, but we been stopped the last few days, and that's what failed her.

We been waiting for the Big Blue River to go down enough to cross over. It's flooded high from all the rain, and if it don't drop, we'll have to fell trees and make rafts to get the wagons across. Meantime, we had a proper funeral for the poor old woman. I asked why she came along if she was feeling poorly, and they told me she couldn't bear to be apart from her family, because of fear she'd never see them again. I guess the old woman didn't want to die alone, and she didn't.

Anyhow, the funeral was a fine thing. Naturally, we don't have any coffins along, so we chopped down a cotton-wood tree, and some of the men hewed it into planks and made a coffin. The whole party followed the coffin to a big oak tree, and a hole was dug in a shady spot, and the coffin laid inside. The Reverend Cornwall read from the Bible, and it gave the family some comfort to know that their blessed grandmother was now in Heaven, and would help the Lord watch over us, and keep us safe until we reached our destination. Then another one of the men found a suitable stone and carved her name in, and the day she was born, and the day she died. We all dragged the stone to the grave, and then little Virginia planted wildflowers around it.

"She was the best grandma in the whole world," says Virginia, kind of fierce. "She told me stories and gave me all the hugs I wanted. I'll surely miss her."

Then she dried her tears. I think she's very brave for a girl.

May 30

All day we been felling trees and building rafts for the wagons. The stronger men handled the big felling axes while me and Edward and a bunch of the others chopped off the branches, once the trees were down. Then we yoked up teams of oxen and drug the logs near the river. The Big Blue River is still flooded with rainwater and looks like it'll never fall, which is why we got to raft across it if ever we're to get where we're going.

To make the rafts, we roll the logs together and rope them up tight, but the wagons being too heavy, they'll have to be emptied before they can be floated across. Once we get them across, each wagon will have to be reloaded and packed. Mr. Reed expects it'll take us two more days, just ferrying wagons and goods to the other side.

It sure is a lot of hard work, trekking to California!

Mr. Donner and his whole family work hard, without complaint, and do their best to ignore the sharp comments Mr. James Reed makes about how things will go faster and more efficient if someone is elected leader of the expedition, meaning him. He always seems to know what to do and isn't afraid to say so.

This evening, after a late supper, and with folks too tired for singing, Virginia invited me and Edward to see The Book.

"This is what got Father started," she told us. "Once he read The Book, we had to sell everything, and have the wagons built, and raise an expedition. He knew he could do it, you see, because of what The Book said."

She opened The Book and showed us the title page. It looked very grand. *The Emigrants' Guide to Oregon and California*, by Lansford W. Hastings. She wouldn't let us touch it, in case our hands was dirty (they were, a bit) but we studied that title page, and a few others throughout, and were mighty impressed.

Virginia told us Mr. Hastings has thought of everything. He tells all about the wonders of California and exactly how to get there: the best routes across the prairie and through the mountain passes, and what equipment and supplies we need, and how to travel and deal with wild Indians, and so on. She said he thought of everything, and then he put it in his book.

Edward and I allowed that we were grateful to Mr. Hastings for writing such a marvelous book, and to Virginia for letting us see it.

Then her father came in. One thing you can say about Mr. James Reed, he fills up whatever space he's in. At first he seemed sort of mad we were studying his book, but when he saw we had the proper respect for the thing, he give us a fine lecture, probably as good as anything in The Book.

"You began this great journey as boys, but by the time we arrive at our destination in the rich valleys of California, you will both be men. We must expect a certain amount of hardship along the way, and many difficulties, but with Mr. Hastings as our guide, we'll make it. We must cleave to his knowledge and his inspiration. He has discovered a new shortcut, and if we follow his directions, and the trails he has marked, we'll save ourselves 350 miles, and be settled in our new homes before the snow flies."

Then Mr. Reed told how he intended to have himself appointed overseer of all the Indian nations west of the Rocky Mountains, on account of his connections to a certain politician in Illinois by the name of Abe Lincoln. He puts a lot of stock in this Lincoln, almost as much as he does in Lansford Hastings, even tho Lincoln never wrote no book about pioneering.

"Say good night to your friends, Virginia. Tomorrow will be a long day."

Me and Edward then left, and I wrote all this stuff down before I forgot it, especially the part about The Book.

June 3

The Reed family tied a black flag on the Pioneer Palace Car, to mark the passing of their grandma. I notice Virginia don't sit in the big wagon much, but prefers to ride her pony. It is a splendid little pony, and very lively. Me and Edward, mostly we walk alongside the oxen, making them go. You might say we're walking all the way to California. Twelve miles a day ain't much, tho. Back in Missouri, many's the time I walked twenty miles or more, going to town and back.

We're passing through mighty rough country, and most of our time is spent freeing up wagons and such. This one time an ox that belongs to Mr. Jacob Donner got stuck in a ditch and couldn't back out. Me and Edward joined with the others to heave it out. The poor ox rolled its eyes and bawled, but it was fine and dandy once we got it free. Folks always say "dumb as an ox," and that animal might be dumb, but Mr. Donner says mostly it was scared because it didn't know what would happen next — like us human folk when the thunder starts booming.

Later in the day there was a bad accident. The German wagon tipped over and broke. We call it the German wagon because the owner, Mr. Keseberg, is always shouting and swearing in that language. Most times he's in foul temper, and today he had good reason.

A wheel came loose from the axle, and the whole wagon tipped over sudden.

Mrs. Keseberg got shot right out of her seat and ended up in a deep puddle. She had her baby in her arms, and both of them got soaked to the skin. Mr. Keseberg then set out cursing his wife like it was her fault the wagon tipped over, and he might have hit her if Mr. Reed didn't threaten to beat him within an inch of his life.

Mr. Reed balled his hands into fists and shouted that if Keseberg dared strike any woman on this wagon train — any woman, especially his poor wife — he vowed to lay his fists upon him and pummel him.

"Do you understand me, sir?" Mr. Reed roared.

Mr. Keseberg stared at him real sullen, but backed off and let his wife get to her feet.

Mr. Reed then told him if he wanted to strike something, he should strike that wheel back on the axle, and stop acting like a d—mn fool.

Mr. Keseberg then said there weren't no cause for swearing, which is pretty funny, considering. Anyhow, it did make him leave off cursing at his poor wife for a time, tho after supper I heard her crying inside their busted wagon.

Mr. Reed heard it, too, and gave that wagon such a look I'm surprised it didn't burst into flames.

June 5

We are camped on the Little Blue River. I am plumb weary, as we made twenty miles today, and twenty miles of driving oxen feels like walking fifty miles. Yes, I am tired, but it sure feels good. If we keep up like this, we'll make California in no time.

Yesterday I shot me an antelope. And I was the only one in the whole party to do so!

What happened is me and Edward elected to ride out ahead when the wagons stopped at noon, taking our bacon 'n biscuits with us. My old horse, Barny, seemed glad to get away from the dust and chew on some fresh grass.

We weren't gone but a mile before we spotted the critters.

"Look there," said Edward, real low. "Deer."

But I knew immediate they weren't deer. They were colored different and had sharp curvy horns, not antlers. Also they didn't move like deer, but leaped and bounced like they had springs on their hooves.

I told him they must be what they call antelope, and that I intended to get us one for supper.

I got down from Barny, slipped the rifle out of the saddle holster, and made signs to Edward that we'd have to advance without the horses. We crept up through the long prairie grass, blind as beetles, figuring if we couldn't see them, they couldn't see us. Every now and then I'd glimpse the top of a horn as they bounded along.

Luckily we were downwind when we spotted them, so they didn't sniff us out right away. I figured the critters didn't have much experience with people, or being hunted, and I was right. Because when I popped up out of the tall grass, the herd sort of froze for just a heartbeat, and that gave me time to get off a shot and drop the biggest antelope. It was dead before it hit the ground, with my bullet through its heart.

They are such pretty critters it makes you feel sad to have killed one. But I didn't feel sad for too long, the way they fussed over me back at the wagon train. We had that antelope for supper, shared out with the whole party, and it tasted good and warmed our bellies. Everybody remarked that antelope tastes like venison, only better. Mr. Breen has kept the horns and hung them on his wagon in my honor.

Mr. George Donner said it was a lucky day when I joined up, and even Mr. Reed said what a good shot I was, even tho he don't much like to give credit.

I must stop here, before I fall asleep. Yesterday, an antelope. Today, twenty miles! I'm mighty glad I decided to join up, and only wish my maw and paw were with me.

Maybe they are watching over me. I pray so.

June 8

At last we have reached the Platte River. The valley is ten miles wide, with great bluffs on either side, and the peaceful river right in the middle. The land on either side is firm, with no trees, and forms a natural highway for our wagons.

When we came up over the last bluff and first saw the beautiful valley before us, Mr. George Donner raised his hand. "Behold," he said. "Yonder is our earthly Paradise. Follow the valley road and we shall come to Heaven."

By Heaven he means California. He said the Platte is famous among the west-bound emigrants, for it will take us all the way to Chimney Rock, deep in the Indian Territories. Most everybody going this way passes along the Platte, and there's already a trail worn down by the wagons that come before. All we have to do is follow it, and we can't go wrong.

The river is near a mile wide but shallow enough to wade across. Looked for fish but didn't see any. Mrs. Tamsen Donner is busy writing down the names of all the wildflowers that grow along the river. Some are bluer than the sky, and others so yellow it makes your eyes hurt, and some as red as drops of blood. Everywhere there is sage that smells like lavender.

We are in Pawnee country, but so far we haven't seen

any Indians. All day we trekked along the river, which has many low islands, big and small. If we weren't so occupied with keeping the oxen going, I'd have me a swim in that river and maybe build a raft to float out to the islands, to explore and so on. But there ain't time for nothing but going forward and making up for all the days we lost bogged down. No matter. It feels good to be moving, and everybody is cheerful.

We are passing a great long island that splits the Platte River into two forks. Colonel Russell, who was scouting ahead, says the island is fifty miles long! Sometimes the Pawnee make camp on the island, but there was no sign of them today. We did come across considerable buffalo bones. They are bleached white by the sun and stick up out of the soil. There were so many we could have filled every wagon full of those bones if we wanted. Seems like this place must have been a hunting ground once upon a time.

The other thing there's plenty of is buffalo chips, which burn even better than dried cow chips. Which kind of makes sense, since buffalo don't eat nothing but grass and sage. Anyhow, there ain't much dried wood around, so once you get a fire going you just pile on a few buffalo chips and the fire will glow hot and steady. Don't smell that bad neither, considering. Mr. Breen says it's like burning peat back in Ireland, only cheaper.

I asked if they have buffalo in Ireland, and he laughed and said no. We ain't actually seen any live buffalo yet, but expect to any day now.

Meantime, we have found messages left for us written on buffalo skulls and stuck up on poles beside the road. The messages are from settlers who have gone on ahead, letting us know what to expect. Some had trouble with Indians, others got bogged down in the mud. We are most fortunate and don't have trouble from neither Pawnee nor rain. I got me one of them buffalo skulls and wrote on it: *smooth sailing* and signed my name, *Douglas A. Deeds.* I figure that will cheer up whoever finds it, to know the Donner Party has passed through with no trouble.

Later

Tonight me and Edward sat up late, after the fires had smoldered down to glowing ash. We looked up at the stars and out across the river, where the islands blended into the mist.

Edward said it was such beautiful country that maybe we should all stop and settle. Him and me could build us a fort out on the big island.

I agreed it was pretty, but reminded him it was summer, and that the winters were harder here than back in

Missouri. We must keep on to California, I said, for that is our true destination.

Edward asked if I thought we'd make it.

I had no doubt, I told him, and neither should he.

Then I told him a pretty good whopper about the Missouri bullfrog that bought himself a suit of clothes and ran for office, and got elected, too.

Edward soon fell asleep, but I sat up until late, looking at the stars and writing in this journal by the last glow of the fire.

June 13

Today is a rest day. We have made such good progress along the Platte Valley, and it has been so dry that many of the wheel rims have come loose. Part of resetting a wheel means holding it over a fire to heat the iron rims, so the whole camp smells of fire and smoke. I don't mind. It gives me a chance to catch up on my journal, which has been neglected these last five days.

Much has happened. An eight-year-old boy died, and Mr. Reed shot an elk. The boy I didn't know. He got run over by a wagon a few weeks back and died of infection. We all mourned him, of course, like we mourned Virginia Reed's grandmother. They say at the end the boy didn't even complain, but just drifted off to Heaven. Probably they're saying that to make us all feel better, but I don't mind. On the day the boy got buried, a woman from another wagon gave birth to a baby that lived, and we all took that as a good sign.

Before the elk got shot or the boy passed, we came upon some trappers. They were a scurvy bunch, with long filthy beards and black teeth. They had fur and skins to trade for flour and coffee and whiskey, and some did so. The trappers acted friendly, but I didn't trust them none. I seen hard men like that in Missouri and they'll lie to cheat you, just for the sport of it. Once they got what they wanted, they went on their way and was seen no more.

Edward Breen and me were out for elk, too, having seen them in the distance, but Mr. James Reed got there first and brought one down. He was mighty pleased with himself, but shared the elk out with the whole party. It was a sizeable animal, near as big as a horse and fed many — more than my poor little antelope!

June 15

Buffalo!

The word came back from a scout that a vast herd was sighted. Me and Edward saddled our horses and went out. Three miles from the wagon train we came to a high bluff, and once we gained the top, we saw them down below us. At first I thought it was a forest of dark brown bushes, there were so many, and then I could see them moving real slow. Buffalo grazing the prairie, all the way to the horizon.

Edward said he had never seen so many of one thing, and that there must be thousands.

All I knew was, there were too many to count. We were still so far away they looked small and delicate, but when you get closer, buffalo are bigger than cattle, with great furry coats and thick curved horns.

I told Edward we mustn't scare them. Scare them and they'd stampede, and we didn't want no part of a buffalo stampede. I advised as how we should sneak up until we got in range. Then once they sensed us, we'd ride full speed straight at them and pick out our targets.

Edward looked at me as if I'd lost my wits. "Have you lost your head?" he asked. "You just said we mustn't let them stampede!"

He had me there. I tried to explain it was different if the stampede was running away from you, but Edward kept shaking his head and wanted to know how I knew they'd run away from us instead of at us. He thought maybe we should leave the whole operation to more experienced hunters.

That riled me. I told him there weren't no experienced buffalo hunters in our party, and the only way to get "experience" was to go ahead and do the thing and see what happened.

Edward said we could get killed. I told him we could get struck by lightning, too. Or run over by a wagon like that poor boy. You worry on things like that, I said, you're in the wrong business.

I meant the dangerous business of being an emigrant to California, and Edward understood. He sighed and patted his horse and agreed to my plan.

We walked the horses a mile or so, stopping to let them graze, so the buffalo might think we was part of the herd. I'm no expert, but I know this much: Buffalo ain't scared of horses, because horses are smaller than buffalo. Buffalo are like any other wild animal. They get scared by what they don't know, and a man on a horse riding at them full speed, firing a rifle, that'd scare anybody. So the idea was to get as close as we could by moving natural, and not giving them a reason to fear us.

We got to within 100 yards before the big bulls started sniffing and snorting and wondering what was wrong about us.

"Get yourself ready," I whispered, slowly putting my hand on the horn of my saddle. "Now!"

I leaped on my horse and charged straight at the buffalo herd. Edward was right behind me. The big bull buffalo tried to get the herd running, but we was too quick. We got so close you couldn't miss. I picked out a sizeable buffalo and fired. The poor critter didn't know what hit it. Edward got one, too, and he ain't much of a shot.

By then the whole herd was running hard, heading for the far horizon. It sounded like a thunderstorm rumbling under the earth. The dust from their hooves got so thick we could barely see. After it settled down, I told Edward to ride back and get a wagon while I stood guard over our two buffalo.

Later in the day, five or six other men were also successful, and we all returned in triumph to the camp, and were welcomed like heroes.

We'll be eating steak all the way to California!

June 23

Today we reached Chimney Rock. Mr. Donner says it is the Eighth Wonder of the World. It could be, because I ain't never seen nothing like it before. We could see it for miles and miles, how it stood like a beacon to guide us, and it lifted our spirits to know we had made some progress.

We finally arrived about noon, and each of the families set up to prepare its midday meal. Some made fires, and others ate what was cold — there are those who like cold beans, but I ain't one of them.

Edward stayed with his family, and I went off to explore. The base of the Wonder is a hard, sloping rock, and on top of the rock is the famous Chimney, which is only about fifty feet wide but soars 500 feet straight up. Stand under it and look up at the sky, and it'll make you dizzy, guaranteed. Nobody knows how it got there, whether it was carved by wind or water, or by the hand of God.

I studied the Chimney for a good long while, then come back to the wagon and ate. We are still feasting on buffalo. There were biscuits, too, but the flour is getting short.

June 25

Much has happened in the last few days. We crossed over the South Platte River, and right away the country changed. Now it is more like desert, with tumbleweeds and a few cactus trees and not much fodder for the oxen and cattle. We are deep in the Indian Territories that some folks call Nebraska, though we still ain't come upon the Indians that live here.

Our group has shrunk considerable, too. We had 250 wagons once, but are now down to less than fifty wagons, because so many have quit or gone off on their own, or hitched up with other parties.

I heard Mr. Breen tell his wife he is worried about our progress. He says we are at least 200 miles behind schedule, if we hope to make California by September. Then his wife shushed him and said not to speak so in front of the children, and that all would be well once we reached Fort Laramie.

June 26

Indians!

Today we came upon several bands of Sioux. They have pitched their tepee tents nearby a trading post. Many more lodges of Sioux are expected, for they are getting ready for a war with the Crow. The Sioux warriors are finely dressed in buckskin and wear many handsome ornaments made of shells and bones. They are friendly to emigrants passing through, tho Mr. Reed says they would not be so polite if we tried to settle within their territory.

One of the younger braves kindly let me see his scalps, which he had taken in a previous battle with his Crow enemies. The scalps don't look like much, but I praised them, and he was mighty pleased. We didn't have no words in common but understood each other just fine. I suppose he is not much older than me, but already a warrior that has proved himself, and very proud.

A lot of the folks left letters at the trading post, to be taken back East. I wrote instead in my journal, which is sort of like a letter posted to myself, to read when I am older.

June 27

Today we met a real mountain man. He was dressed all in buckskin the color of dirt, and his long beard was dusty and gray. He said he had been traveling with Mr. Lansford Hastings, the man who wrote the *The Emigrants' Guide* that Mr. Reed and Mr. Donner value so highly. Except the old mountain man wasn't so impressed as they were.

The mountain man said Hastings was a fool, and didn't know any more about taking a wagon train of emigrants through the mountains than he does about riding a moonbeam.

Mr. Reed give him a look and asked if he was jesting. The mountain man said crossing the Sierra Nevada range was a hard go. He said it was one thing for a man on horseback to cross over, but an ox-drawn wagon presented another problem entire. He said Mr. Hastings didn't know his way around and had no experience. He said all Hastings has got is a load of untested, unproven, high-flown ideas that he's passed on to innocent folks like us.

"Sir, I think it is you who are the fool," said Mr. Reed, his eyes flashing.

"Think what you like," said the mountain man, "but I know the mountains and Hastings don't, and that's a fact. I have come to warn you not to trust either his maps or his advice. You would do better to follow the rest of the parties who are already well ahead of you. Follow in the ruts their wagons make, and don't deviate from their path, and you might just make it."

I could tell from the set of his jaw that Mr. Reed wasn't listening to the mountain man. He had already made up his mind that Mr. Hastings was right, and he didn't want to hear different.

The mountain man said that winter comes fast, and if we got stuck and run out of food, maybe we could eat Mr. Hastings' book. And with that, the ornery fellow turned on his heel and showed us his back.

"Pay that fool no heed," said Mr. Reed sternly. He then lectured us all on the superior wisdom of following Mr. Hastings' directions, and told us the mountain man didn't want us crossing the lands where he trapped, because he was afraid we'd hunt his game and steal his furs.

Mr. Reed said it was nothing but raw greed that

motivated the mountain man. That is why he tried to frighten us off. As to Mr. Hastings' qualifications, consider this: He has published a guidebook and the mountain man has not. Who should we believe, an ignorant trapper or a man of letters?

I expect Mr. Reed is right. The mountain man looked honest enough, but his type are crafty people and very jealous of their hunting grounds.

We continue on our way, with Mr. Hastings' book as our guide.

July 4

Today is Independence Day, and we all celebrated in grand style.

This morning we were roused at dawn by a bugle and rose to see a newly sewn flag flying from a pole on Mr. Reed's wagon. The flag has twenty-eight stars, and Mr. Reed predicted that someday soon a twenty-ninth star would be added, and that would be California. We all cheered, and many rifles were fired into the air, startling the horses.

We are encamped with several other wagon trains that are resting for the holiday. Some are heading to California by various routes, others to the Oregon Territories, but we all have one thing in common. High hopes. High hopes that we get where we're going in one piece, and then strike it rich!

That's what old Colonel Russell said when he stood up on a stump and made a speech. "Friends! Countrymen! Lend me your ears! That means listen up, cause I got a few words to say on this joyous occasion! It has been seventy years since the United States of America was born and it ain't stopped growing yet, and there is room enough for everybody, and free land for the taking!"

Colonel Russell had to shout to make himself heard, but then again, he's a man who likes to shout. He did go on and on, remarking on just about every single thing that had happened in the last seventy years, and telling us what he thought about it, and why we should all agree with him.

Edward's father finally shook his head and said, "Give a man a stump to stand on, and a crowd to shout at, and he will flap his jaw."

Me and Edward then crept behind the stump and lit some firecrackers that he had saved special for the occasion. When the firecrackers went off, everybody applauded because they thought it meant Colonel Russell's speech was finally over. It wasn't. Finally they stopped him by offering him a glass of whiskey, which he said was better than lemonade.

After supper everybody from all the wagon trains

gathered together and sang and danced. Edward's father took a turn at the fiddle and then danced a jig with Edward's mother, who laughed so hard she got a pain in her ribs and had to stop dancing.

Later, when the children were sleeping, some of the men told jokes so raw I don't dare write them down, or the page will burn.

Tomorrow we will make necessary repairs and rest the oxen one more day.

July 6

This morning I saw a most marvelous thing. Hundreds of Sioux warriors stood at attention by the side of the trail as our wagons passed. It was an awesome sight. Each had a flower in his mouth, which is a sign that they wish us a safe journey. Later the younger braves got into high spirits, galloping their ponies through the wagon train, whooping and hollering.

"They're excited about the coming war with the Crow," Mr. George Donner told us. "No doubt many of them will die in battle. Right now they are trying to fill themselves with courage, to overcome their fears."

Mr. James Reed overheard him, and muttered something about Donner not knowing his rear end from his elbow, and how would he know what the Indians were thinking? But in my opinion, Mr. Donner got it right. A man don't march to war where he might get killed without first working himself up to it.

Anyhow, we almost had a bad incident that might have turned ugly except for the Sioux chief. It happened like this: Some of the younger braves took a shine to little Virginia Reed's pony and wanted to trade for it. Her father refused, in no uncertain terms, but they wouldn't take no for an answer, and tried to take the pony. Mr. Reed got angry and rode back a mile to speak to their chief, who had promised us safe passage.

The chief, who was dressed most splendidly, came riding up at full gallop on his war horse and drove the braves away from the pony. He was so mad he fired arrows at his own men! They gave up on the pony and ran away, and the rest of the braves left us alone.

"We're most fortunate they're busy fighting the Crow, or they might be fighting us." Edward's father pointed out. "They outnumber us ten to one. If they were of a mind to, they could defeat us in less than in an hour."

For days after we left Laramie, the Indians rode among us, always peaceful, and then one morning they were gone, and we ain't seen them since.

July 8

The passage of our wagons has been slow, more like a snail than a train, and a lot of the folks have been complaining. Some of the bachelors, the men who ain't got families to care for, have left their wagons behind and gone ahead on mule or horseback. They can make thirty to fifty miles a day that way. Meantime we keep slogging along, getting no more than fifteen miles on our best day. That's barely more than a mile's progress each hour. Why a baby can walk faster! For that matter a full-grown man can *crawl* faster. But what are we to do? We could travel much faster without the wagons, but the families need all the belongings they carry in the wagons, if they are to start a new life once we reach our destination.

Yesterday we unloaded a piano and left it by the side of the trail. The man who owned it was intending to teach music, but he said the coyotes were welcome to play that d—mn piano now, as his oxen were too tired to pull it any farther. We could hear the wind in the strings for miles after we left it behind.

July 9

It has been powerful hot. Near 100 degrees at noon, even though we are slowly coming to the higher elevations.

That means the livestock must be watered frequent, and that makes us even slower. Then as soon as the sun goes down, it gets so cold we have to wrap ourselves in our new buffalo skin blankets and shiver until dawn.

I keep hoping that once we finally cross the Divide, it will be downhill all the way to California. I said as much to Edward's father, but he only smiled and shook his head. "Don't work that way. But at least we have plenty of food," he said.

That's true. There are still buffalo to shoot, but we must eat the meat right away, as we have no means to preserve it.

July 12

At present we are in the valley of the Sweet Water River. We are passing through a stark landscape such as few people have ever seen, with high bluffs and rocks that rise like islands from the bare ground. The strange scenery is a welcome change from the endless prairie of weeds and sage, but the going is even more difficult.

Yesterday at noon we passed through the Devil's Gate, which is a gap through the high mountains. It is barely wide enough for two wagons abreast, but the dark granite rises 400 feet or more on either side, and blocks out the sun. You can see the light ahead, but while you're in the shadow it's cold enough to chill the blood. Nobody said much. All you could hear was the creaking of the wheels and the grunting of the oxen echoing off the giant slabs of rock.

When we finally got through, I made a joke to Mr. Breen about "leaving the Devil behind," but instead of joking back at me, he got real serious.

"I fear we have not done so," he said, staring straight ahead. "The Devil rides among us."

I asked what he meant, but he wouldn't say no more.

July 14

This may be our lucky day. That's what James Reed said, when we came upon a man on horseback, traveling east. The man was carrying a letter from Mr. Lansford Hastings himself, addressed to any emigrants he might meet along the trail.

In the letter, Hastings says he has discovered a new route to California! If we follow his instructions, we save 350 miles. Think of it, 350 miles! It has taken us nearly a month to travel that distance! Follow Hastings and we shall save ourselves four long, hard weeks on the trail. Follow Hastings and he promises to guide us himself, once we have reached Fort Bridger!

I was so excited by that letter I couldn't help but

believe Mr. Hastings, even tho the old mountain man said Hastings was a fool who didn't know anything about guiding wagon trains, even tho he did write a book on the subject.

The only one that spoke up in opposition was Mrs. Tamsen Donner, who reminded us that the old trail was well known, and that many hundreds have gone before us, and been successful. We know nothing of this new trail, she said, or what awaits us there.

Mr. Reed took a deep breath. You could tell he was fighting to control his temper. "I fear we must, madame, for we are far behind schedule. If we do not take Hastings' advice and save ourselves a month of hard travel, that month will come to haunt us."

"What if it is Hastings' advice that comes to haunt us?" Mrs. Donner asked.

Mr. Reed had no answer, except to say that the final decision would not come for another week, when we would come to a fork in the trail, and have to make up our minds which route to take.

July 18

Poisoned water. That's but one of the troubles we've been having on our way west. All day long we fought through the sand, having to drag the wagons out time and again, until we were all so exhausted and thirsty we could hardly move.

Finally we came upon a stagnant pool of water and stopped to let the cattle drink. Right away several got sick, and two of Mr. Donner's oxen died. They lay down on their bellies and moaned and rolled their eyes, and then never got up.

We don't dare drink the water, but must rely on what little we carried, until we clear these badlands. It has put us all in a grim mood and worried about the future. Good water don't seem so important when it's plentiful, but when it's hard to come by, there ain't nothing more valuable.

July 19

Don't matter whether we feel high or low, today was the day we had to make our choices. First choice was who should lead the wagon train. Mr. James Reed made it plain that he believed he should be chosen. He has every confidence in his own ability to lead us, with help from *The Emigrants' Guide*, which he values like the Bible. But Mr. Reed is such a high and mighty man that many in the party do not like him, and so instead we chose Mr. George Donner. He does not have Mr. Reed's experience, but he is solid and friendly.

From now on we are to be called the Donner Party.

On the second choice, Mr. Donner and Mr. Reed are in agreement. We have reached the fork in the trail and must go left to Fort Bridger and to Mr. Hastings, who will guide us through the "cut-off" that will save us weeks of time, and get us to our destination sooner. We are all of us in agreement on this choice, except for our new leader's wife, Tamsen Donner, who has been fretting on the decision for a week.

Once again, Mrs. Donner asked if there was no way she could persuade us that now is not the time for experiments. What do we really know of Lansford Hastings? she asked. How do we know he is not some vain adventurer who will lead us into peril, if he leads us anywhere? Hundreds of wagons have taken the right fork, and made their way to safety, she said. Why must we be the ones to try a new way?

It was her husband who spoke first, seeking to comfort her. "My dear wife, I more than anyone am aware how this choice has troubled you. I can only say that any wagon train of emigrants must face hard choices as they travel west through lands unknown to them. This is but one more choice, and the majority are in agreement. Give us your trust, my dear, and we will not lead you astray. Every member of this party will arrive safely, that is my pledge."

Mrs. Donner nodded mournfully, and said no more.

July 20

For the whole day we broke new trail, and it was hard going. Mr. Donner estimates that Fort Bridger is but a week away, and there we shall find new provisions. There Mr. Hastings will be waiting to guide us over the "cut-off" he mentioned in his letter and deliver us to California at last.

Tonight we are camped near the Little Sandy River. There are mosquitoes here as big as hummingbirds, and we sit wrapped in our blankets, swatting these giant, bloodthirsty insects and staring at the fire, hoping we all made the right decision.

I am confident we did. Mr. Hastings wouldn't write to us about a new route over the mountains if he didn't know about it, would he?

July 26

At last we have reached Fort Bridger. I told Edward it would be a proper fort with high walls and guard towers, but I am wrong. "Fort Bridger" is nothing but a couple of rough log cabins and a corral for the horses and cattle they are selling. The cabins are owned by trader Jim Bridger, who named it a "fort" after himself.

Edward says if Fort Bridger is a fort, then he can build a lean-to this afternoon and call it Fort Edward, but he is just pulling my leg. Still, he's got a point. You can't judge anything out West by the name. Chimney Rock ain't no chimney, and Fort Bridger ain't no fort.

"I expect you boys are disappointed," Mr. George Donner said to us, "but Mr. Bridger seems to be a good man, and he has what supplies we need — tho his prices seem a trifle high."

A *trifle* high? I heard him charge a man ten dollars in gold for a pint of whiskey. Ten dollars in gold would buy a small saloon in the backwoods of Missouri! And it ain't only the whiskey that costs more. Everything does. Barrels of flour, clothing, patent medicines, oxen — everything costs ten times what it should. Old Jim Bridger is getting rich off the poor emigrants, that's for certain.

Tamsen Donner suspects Bridger is in cahoots with Lansford Hastings, because the shortcut Hastings is promoting goes right by Fort Bridger. The more emigrants come this way, the more money he squeezes out of them.

Me, I don't know what to believe. Just because Bridger charges too much don't mean the shortcut is no good. Edward's paw says you have to expect supplies to cost a lot more when they've been carried out to the middle of nowhere. He says supplies will be expensive in California when we get there, too. The only cheap thing is land itself, and mostly that's given away for nothing if you stake a claim.

It does stick in my craw, tho, Mr. Bridger taking advantage like that.

We expect to camp here for four or five days, resting the oxen and making repairs. Mr. Lansford Hastings, who has promised to meet us here and guide us over his short-cut, left before we arrived, and has gone out exploring, gathering material for his next book.

He is a very busy man and promises to make contact with our party at some future date. I ain't holding my breath.

July 28

More Indians passing through. These are not the Sioux braves in war paint, but another tribe they call Snake Indians. Mostly they are women and children walking and dragging litters behind them. They are friendly and like to shout "gee haw!" at the oxen, to show they can speak a few words of our language. Mr. Bridger says they are on the move because they want to avoid the Sioux and Crow war parties. He says the Snake People won't fight unless they have to. The way he said it meant he didn't have no respect for the Snake Indians, but why should they fight if they don't have to?

I like the Snake People, they are very polite and

respectful and never tried to cheat us. Unlike Mr. Bridger, who looks sly and always has his hand out.

August 2

Poor Edward! We were but a few days from Fort Bridger, traveling alongside the Bear River, when the accident happened. Me and Edward and Virginia Reed were riding out ahead of the wagon train. So far the land is good, with plenty of grass for the cattle, and clean water from the river. There are fish in the river, too, and some of the men have caught them.

Anyhow, me and Edward and Virginia were out riding, and Virginia, being the youngest and a girl, got to showing off. She said her pony was faster than Edward's horse, and he said it weren't, and to prove it they raced. It turned out Virginia was right — her pony was the fastest — but before the race was over, Edward's horse tripped and fell, throwing Edward to the ground.

I heard him cry out, and went running. Poor Edward was lying on the ground clutching at his knee. His leg was broke bad. Read bad. So bad the bone was sticking out of his shin.

"I done it now," he sobbed. "Paw will kill me, he sees what I done."

I told him to hang on and I would go for help.

Before I left, Virginia came up. The grin on her face sort of froze when she saw what happened. She was real sorry, and said she would stay with Edward while I went for help.

I rode back to the wagon train and shouted out what had happened, and Edward's paw came with a small wagon. Turned out Edward was wrong about his paw being mad. Mr. Breen took one look at the leg and said, "You are a brave boy for not crying. I hope you will not think less of me if the tears come to my eyes."

With that, Edward let out the tears he'd been holding back, and his father cried, too. When we lifted him into the wagon, he fainted from the pain, which his father said was just as well, as there is only so much pain a body can handle.

At every bump of the wagon poor Edward moaned. He asked would I tell no one about him or his father crying, and I made a solemn promise not to speak of it. I was worried his broken leg was bleeding so much, but there was nothing we could do.

Later

When we got back to the wagon train, folks gathered around and said they'd never seen a leg broke so bad, not since the boy got crushed by the wagon and died. Edward's maw told them to hush up, that this was a different sort of injury and her son would survive, thank you very much.

All the commotion attracted the attention of a mountain man who was heading for Fort Bridger, loaded up with furs. Soon as he heard someone had broke a leg, he made it known he was an expert in fixing busted bones.

"I broke both of my legs and set them myself," he bragged, showing off his skinny, bowed legs.

He was a bit scrawny for a mountain man, but made up for it by being hairy as a bear. I swear, even his ears sprouted hairs thick enough to braid.

Anyhow, once the mountain man heard about poor Edward's misfortune, he wouldn't take "no" for an answer. "I fixed more fractures than any doctor. Show me to the boy!"

Folk brought him along to the Breen wagon. Edward had already fainted dead away when his paw clicked the bone back in place, and bound it with a splint. The mountain man looked down at Edward, and the blood-soaked bandages, and he said, "If that leg don't come off, it will kill him."

Edward's maw moaned and cried out to the Lord.

"The flesh will putrefy, that's a certainty, ma'am."

Mr. Breen asked was he sure, and the mountain man

said he had seen legs that weren't broke half that bad that killed their owners. It must come off, and the sooner the better, or it would be the death of him.

Just then Edward's eyelids fluttered. "Maw!" he cried out. "I dreamt they took my leg! Is my leg still there?"

The mountain man went off to get his knife and saw that he kept in a pack on his mule.

Edward then begged that his leg not be cut off. He said it was better already, since his father had set the bone. He offered to swear on a Bible that he wouldn't die, if only they'd let him keep his leg.

The mountain man came back with a piece of folded leather. He unwrapped a small, wicked-looking meat saw and held it up to the light. "Three strokes and it's off. Quick is best, ma'am. Better tie the boy down, so he don't squirm."

Edward then kicked up such a fuss, begging and a-pleading, that his maw and paw finally agreed to put off taking his leg, to see how it might heal.

Finally Mr. Breen had to pay the mountain man five dollars to make him go away, which he did, muttering that Edward's flesh would putrefy, and that he would surely die.

We are all praying that the mountain man is wrong, and that Edward's leg will heal.

August 6

Yesterday we crossed a most perilous river. The water was white with foam. We had to unhitch the oxen and take them across, bellowing and fighting us every step of the way. I can't blame the poor critters, as the river frightened all of us. One wrong step and we would be swept into the savage currents and smashed against the boulders.

Mr. Breen shouted that we must keep their heads above water. I promised to try, and did my best. We managed to get most of the oxen over safe (one disappeared into the water and didn't come back up) but then had to work the wagons over by hand, pushing and pulling with all of our strength. I weren't strong enough to make a wagon move, so I stood on the wheel spokes to add my weight and help make them turn.

Edward and his maw were in the wagon, hanging on for their lives. Poor Edward is still hurting bad, tho he says the pain ain't as bad as it was. I could tell he wished he was out with me and the other men, and not having to lay abed at the mercy of others.

He moaned only once, when the wagon struck a boulder sideways. Little damage resulted, and we soon had them safely ashore, and the oxen hitched up again.

"That was fine work you done," Mr. Breen said, thanking me. "We were lucky the day you come along and shared this journey with us."

I had to cough and pretend to fuss with the oxen, so's they wouldn't see my eyes were wet. Because I'm thinking it was me who got lucky when the Breens took me in and treated me like one of their own.

Maw and Paw must be watching over me.

August 7

Stay where you be, and send for me.

That's from the note we found upon entering the canyon. It was left on the limb of a tree for us by Mr. Lansford Hastings, who is out ahead exploring his short-cut, and has promised to lead us. No one knows what to make of it, exactly, and many of the women are angry at the men for following Hastings in the first place.

Tamsen Donner pointed out that we never even laid eyes on the man, and yet we are trusting him with our lives as the rumor of him leads us farther and farther into the wilderness.

Her husband has sent Mr. James Reed and two other men ahead to find Hastings and to see why he wants us to wait. Meantime the hours and days are passing, and we ain't getting any closer to California.

August 10

James Reed returned this day. The news is all bad.

Mr. Reed told us how he rode deep into the canyon and soon understood why Hastings had requested that we wait.

We gathered around the fire to hear the news. Mr. Reed didn't mince words. He said it was a nightmare ahead. The way it is strewn with boulders and pits that would swallow a wagon whole. There are more dead ends than you'd find in a maze, and stretches so thick with bushes and cottonwood that we'd be hacking at them until the world ends.

Tamsen Donner stood up and asked the question we were all thinking. Why then did Mr. Hastings send us here? What of his shortcut?

He said on the third day he finally got clear of the canyon and caught up to Mr. Hastings and his party, just south of the Great Salt Lake.

What did he say, we all wanted to know? What did Mr. Hastings have to say about his guidebook to California, and his shortcut?

Mr. Reed at first mumbled, and then had to repeat himself. He said Mr. Hastings sent his regrets.

Edward's paw jumped up from where he'd crouched

by the campfire and demanded to know if Hastings would lead us, as he had promised.

You could tell James Reed didn't want to look Patrick Breen in the eye. He didn't want to look anybody in the eye. He said it wasn't likely Lansford Hastings could spare the time to lead our party. It seems that Hastings had bad intelligence about this particular canyon. He had been told it would be clear enough and easy for wagons. Obviously whoever told Mr. Hastings that was mistaken.

Tamsen Donner looked ready to jump up and down, she was so steamed. "What you mean to say is that Mr. Hastings was mistaken, and that we were mistaken to follow his so-called shortcut! A shortcut that obviously does not exist!"

Mr. Reed took that very stiff. He said we should not blame Mr. Hastings. An explorer must rely on intelligence from various sources. Guides and trappers and Indians and so on. They were at fault, not Mr. Hastings.

Another one of the men stood up and said it was obvious that Hastings, the great author and explorer, wasn't man enough to face us. The Hastings' shortcut was a bust.

Mr. Reed was silent for a time and then said whoever was at fault, it was done, and we must find our own way.

The last thing Tamsen Donner did before she went to bed was carry out their copy of *The Emigrants' Guide to Oregon and California* and throw it into the fire. Her husband looked like he had a mind to stop her and then changed his mind. Mrs. Donner didn't say nothing, she just turned away and stormed back to their wagon, while her husband looked most sorrowful and watched the book shrivel up and burn to ash.

I have writ this all down late at night, by the light of a candle, long after the campfires burned down. I have never seen the party so discouraged. The blackness of this canyon has seeped into our hearts and stolen away our hope.

August 11

The canyon is so dark, and the walls so high that only a small strip of stars is visible overhead. It is as if we've fallen to the bottom of the world and can't see our way out.

If we are lost, then how shall we get to California? Somebody suggested to go back on our tracks and return to Fort Bridger. But if we return to Fort Bridger and take the old path, it will be too late. There will not be time enough to cross the mountains before the snow comes. Nor do we know if Mr. Bridger would let all of us abide with him for the winter, as we do not have enough supplies to see us through, and it is unlikely that he would undertake to feed us for all those months.

So there's no point going back. We are doomed if we do and doomed if we don't. That is what the men say, and Mr. Reed did not disagree.

The bad news has hit Mr. Reed very hard, for he feels responsible for promoting the idea of the shortcut. I do not like Mr. Reed much, because of his arrogance, but even I can see that the fault is not his alone. Mr. Donner pushed for the shortcut, too. The whole party voted to take the shortcut, and now we must suffer the consequences.

Never has the hour been so dark, or my heart so cold. I can only pray that dawn will bring us new hope, or at least a way out of this terrible canyon.

August 13

Our progress has slowed so it ain't hardly progress at all.

What happened is Mr. Reed took it upon himself to find a way through the canyons, since Mr. Donner didn't have no ideas on the subject. His wife, Tamsen, is still mad enough to spit about the fix we're in.

Anyhow, Mr. Reed went exploring and found us another canyon that didn't look quite so bad as the first one. Only it turned out worse. We made less than five miles, most of it in the wrong direction, and then discovered we'd have to cut and chop our way through miles of cottonwood that grow so thick a man can't walk through it sideways.

August 14

The women and children stayed in camp today while we cut a narrow road through the canyon. Tomorrow we shall get free and be on our way.

August 15

Today we discovered another blocked-up canyon less than a mile beyond where we cut a narrow path. So we are back to cutting and chopping. The men are trying not to act discouraged in front of the women, as everybody is very frustrated. No one talks much about it, but we're all afraid we'll be trapped in these canyons until winter comes.

August 17

At last we cut our way out of the canyons and came to a gap in the mountains, but we had to cut through that, too. Mr. Reed named it "Reed's Gap" after himself. He can have it. We had to hack our way through a thicket of green willows, and every time I swung my ax I thought how mad I was at Mr. James Reed for acting so high and mighty, and for causing all this trouble just because he was too bullheaded to admit a mistake.

Had we taken the old and proven path that a thousand wagons have taken before us, we'd have made 100 miles by now. Instead we're fighting willow thickets and cottonwood tangles and giant mosquitoes and flies that bite like rabid dogs. We're working from dawn till dusk, until we drop from exhaustion. So hard we can't see straight, and can barely talk.

I don't mind the sweating or the bug bites or how tired it all makes me, what scares me — what scares us all — is the time we're losing. I never thought much about time or what it means, but time is everything when you got to get over the high mountains before winter.

Already the nights are very cold, and some folks claim they can smell snow coming. I said there ain't no way snow can stick in August, and they reminded me that we're almost halfway done with August, and that winter comes very early in the high elevations. They say there ain't no autumn season in the Sierra Nevadas, it goes from summer to winter overnight.

August 18

Finally we got done with the cutting and started the hard work of getting the wagons through the gap and over the mountain. It ain't a real road we cut, but only a clearing through the trees. We still got to work the wagon wheel over the stumps with the oxen straining and everybody shouting.

A few stragglers joined us lately, having made the mistake of following our path, and we are now eighty-eight people divided among twenty-two wagons.

Finally we got the last of the wagons through the gap, and come down the mountain a little ways. There are more mountains ahead of us, but the slopes are gentle and the way looks clear from here.

Next stop, the Great Salt Lake.

August 20

"If it wasn't for bad luck, we'd have no luck at all," said Edward's paw.

Edward is on the mend. What his paw meant was, the way down the mountains we thought would be clear and easy turned out to be neither. When we got over the last ridge, we came upon another canyon, this one so dense and thick with timber we ain't got the heart or the strength to chop our way through.

We are more discouraged than when we heard that Hastings intended to abandon us. Some talked of abandoning their wagons and continuing on foot, but that is foolishness. Others talked of going by horseback and riding light, but that is equally foolish, as George Donner pointed out.

Even on horseback a man can't carry enough to keep him alive for 700 miles. We know nothing of game or whether hunting might be fruitful.

No, we must stay with our wagons and our supplies, and find a way out of these mountains.

August 22

Finally we came to a decision. Rather than try and cut our way through yet another canyon, we decided to drag the wagons up over the last mountain between here and the Great Salt Lake.

Mr. Donner suggested that we team all the oxen together and pull each wagon up the side of the mountain, one at a time. He thought it would take a few days. We all agreed and got to work.

It's hard enough for a team of oxen to drag a heavy wagon over level ground. Going steep uphill is much worse. Even with the oxen all teamed up together, they struggled. Sometimes the oxen refused to pull, and then we'd have to get behind them and push, or shame them into pulling, shouting "Haw! Haw! Move you stubborn, stupid ox, move! Haw! Haw!"

August 25

Luke Halloran died this day of consumption. We paused to bury him and then got back to work.

August 26

In the end it took much, much longer to pull the wagons over the mountain one by one than it would have to cut our way through the canyon. Seems like every decision we make is the wrong one and costs us time.

Tonight Virginia Reed asked why did I look so glum. Her daddy says we have but a short way to the Great Salt Lake, and the grass is good for the cattle.

I mumbled something about being tired, but it isn't getting to the lake I'm worried about. It's getting to California. It seems like the more we go forward, the farther away it gets. Like we're chasing a bright cloud that keeps slipping over the horizon.

It has taken us eighteen days to go forty miles. A man

on horseback can do that in a day. I have a horse of my own, and could leave the party and make my way alone, as others have. I'm a good hunter and could trust to finding game. But even thinking such thoughts makes me blush with guilt, because the Breens have been so kind to me. How could I abandon them now? Leave my friend, Edward, with his broken leg? Leave his maw and paw to fend with the others?

Only a coward would act so, and I am no coward. Even if I am afraid.

August 27

We came at last to the Great Salt Lake with little difficulty, having finally crossed the Wasatch Mountains that gave us so much trouble, with all the dead-end canyons.

The Great Salt Lake is shallow and so salty it can't be drunk. No one lives there, not even Indians, but near the southern part there are springs not yet contaminated with salt, and we were able to water the cattle, and ourselves.

"We have but one long day's drive across the salt desert, and then we shall be in good shape," said Mr. Reed, standing high upon his wagon so he could be heard by all. "I expect we shall be in California within a month, surely by the end of September. Indeed, I feel confident that I may promise safe arrival by then, if not sooner."

Nobody said nothing when Mr. Reed finished his speech. We've heard him talk that way so many times it don't mean nothing.

August 28

Today we found a ragged note from the cursed Mr. Hastings, tacked on a board set in the crook of a tree. The note had been torn to bits by birds. Some of us thought being torn to pieces was the right fate for anything connected with the so-called explorer, but Tamsen Donner took it upon herself to piece the note together, in case it might contain some crucial information.

It took a while but when she finally got the note put back together it was more bad news.

"Two days, two nights. Hard driving. Cross desert. Reach water," she read, with her voice shaking, and then whispered, "Lord help us."

"Two days and two nights hard driving." We all know what that means. The way across the salt marsh is much longer than we anticipated. Cattle can't go more than one day without water, so what are we to do?

Can we carry enough to get us there? Nobody knows,

not even Mr. Reed, who says he knows everything. All we can do is go forward, and trust to Providence. But so far, Providence ain't been good to us. We fear the oxen may die before we get to water, and us with them.

In a few minutes I will lay me down to sleep. Maybe things will look better in the daylight.

August 30

At last, night has come, and the cursed sun is finally gone from the burning sky.

So far we been two days and nights crossing the salt desert and can't see the end of it yet. No water anywhere. Not even dew drops. The salt sucks up every drop. If a man is foolish enough to waste water by spitting, the spit disappears the instant it hits the ground. No water but what we brought along, and there ain't near enough of that.

We must keep moving. If we stop, we die, that is the law of nature.

August 31

Another hard day.

The salt flats are hard and white and dead flat, and go out as far as a man can see. They might go on forever, for all I know. Seems like it, most times. Nothing grows here, not even a cactus, because the earth is poisoned with salt. You can smell the salt in the dust, and it makes you thirsty. You can feel the salt parching your mouth, your nose, your lungs. My skin is so dry it feels like the paper I'm writing on.

The poor oxen, with their noses in the white dust, cry out for water most piteously, but the water must be rationed. All we can do is soak rags in a bit of water and lay the rags against the oxen's tongues. It seems to give them some comfort.

At the height of noon the sun sits on top of your head and burns through your skull, into your brain. A sun so bright it's hard to see. I keep my kerchief partway over my eyes, and the brim of my hat down, and still it shines so hard it hurts, and makes your eyes dry and itchy.

The light plays tricks, too. The heat comes off the salt flat so thick it makes the air woozy, and everything blurs. The wagons are strung out, with the lighter wagons miles ahead, and sometimes the distant oxen look like giant creatures — like elephants, or something even bigger and older than elephants.

Far over the horizon you'll see a magical mountain kingdom floating above the world. Then you blink and the magical mountains are gone, and there's nothing but the palest blue sky and the blinding sun, and the white, white nothing of the salt flats.

Some folks think they've seen the Pacific Ocean floating in the sky. They say they seen the waves breaking, white with foam, and that California beckons us, that we shall cleanse ourselves in the sea, and drink from the springs of Eden.

Thirst is making them crazy. Thirst is making them see things that only exist inside their sunburned heads. Although, truth be told, today I saw another wagon train, identical to ours, some miles away across the salt flats. The heat tricked my eyes into thinking the wagons looked much larger than ours, and the people were ten feet tall or more, a race of giants! But when I raised my hand to wave, one of the giants waved back, exactly as I did. I raised my hat and he raised his hat, exactly as I did.

It was a kind of strange, mirrorlike mirage. There was no other wagon train, only us, and we saw ourselves reflected in the heat.

September 2

It is night. We are still crossing the salt desert. We been rationing ourselves to just a swallow of water every two hours, and at night the swallow stays with you for a while. The cattle complain less, too. They are all 'round better natured than most of the people.

This evening, just before sunset, one of the men came to the Breen wagon, believing that the Breens have water to spare and are hoarding it for themselves. He had his kerchief up over his face, but we recognized him from one of the straggling wagons, some miles behind. He had come up on foot and would not be turned away.

"I must have water," he gasped. "Gimme a gallon or two, I know you got plenty!"

Mr. Breen looked around like it was a cruel joke. Where would he keep plenty of water? "You are mistaken, sir," he said, and suggested the man return to his own wagon.

With that the fella pulled out a pistol and waved it in Mr. Breen's face and said he must give him some water or he'd put a bullet in Breen's head. So Mr. Breen gave the man a jug of water, and he vanished into the night.

My guess is he drunk the stolen water himself, long before he got back to his wagon or his family. Out here in the desert, when thirst drives a man crazy, water is like whiskey. It makes you do things you'd never think of doing, if you wasn't so mad for it.

One thing is for sure. We're no longer a party of emigrants, helping one another along the way. It is every family for itself. Mr. James Reed may have the biggest wagon and the most cattle, but he and his wagons and his family are falling farther and farther behind, and no one is much inclined to help, even if they could.

September 4

We saw James Reed come riding by on his best horse some hours ago. Said his oxen had been unhitched from the wagons, and were being driven ahead to find water. Meantime he bragged how he'd ride to the end of the desert and bring water back to his family. That is his plan.

Once he'd gone riding off like a man leading a cavalry charge, Mr. Breen turned to Mrs. Breen and said, "How'd you like it if I left you stranded in the desert to go off on an adventure? Would you like that much?"

Mrs. Breen shook her head and said she felt sorry for poor little Virginia because she believes her father can do no wrong. And so far he has done nothing right.

Mrs. Breen is right to say "poor Virginia." It's not her fault her father is bullheaded, and took us so far from the regular path, and lost us in the canyons.

At the same time I'm not so sure James Reed is doing the wrong thing, riding ahead to find water. What else can a man do, if his family is dying of thirst? Do nothing and you die, same as what happens when you stop moving. Maybe he'll find water and maybe he won't, but at least he's trying.

I will stop here. I am too thirsty to write more.

September 5

We are resting at Pilot Springs, having at long last made it across the blasted salt flats with most of our cattle surviving. That is, most of the Breen cattle surviving. Many others had cattle and oxen that perished, or stampeded away as thirst drove them mad, and have been lost in the desert.

All but a few of the wagons had to be abandoned in the desert, too. Whole families walked the last twenty or thirty miles on foot, at night, with nary a drop to drink.

Mr. Donner said we must rest here at the springs for several more days, and go back at night to recover the abandoned wagons, one by one. All of us will help, whether the wagons belong to us or not. I think we are all ashamed of how so many of us acted when death stalked us on the cruel salt flats, and want to make up for it by acting neighborly.

Edward is now nearly able to walk, and talks of nothing but joining me again on our adventures. His maw and paw are content and grateful for having survived the ordeal of the salty desert.

The Reeds have not fared nearly so well. All of their wagons were finally abandoned, including their greatest pride, the grand Pioneer Palace Car. It seems that James Reed finally made it back to his family, but with only just enough water for them, and not for his cattle or oxen. So he and his wife and children had to walk the last thirty miles on foot, at night, in a howling windstorm. Meantime all his cattle got loose or stampeded, and are gone. He blames the men he hired to drive the cattle, for giving up and thinking of themselves, but no one else blames them.

Let him rant and rave about lazy fools and cowards. It will do him no good, for overnight the Reed family went from rich to poor, as most of their fortune was tied up in cattle and wagons. He has no one to blame but himself, and yet he blames everybody but himself. He vows he will return to the salt flats and recover his wagons.

September 6

You got to hand it to James Reed. The man don't give up. He went out onto the flats with one ox, hoping to find his missing cattle. All but one of the cattle were gone, but he somehow managed to get the Pioneer Palace Car back to the camp. His other two wagons he had to leave in the desert. His daughter, Virginia, was overjoyed to see their main wagon again, as most of her belongings were in it.

"Oh, Father!" she cried out. "You have done it! You have done it!"

Mr. Breen heard her, and muttered, "Oh, he done it all right. He has taken us halfway to Hell. Most likely he'll take us all the way, if he gets a chance."

Then Mrs. Breen told him to hush up, and he did.

September 10

Finally we left Pilot Springs and continued on our long journey, but not before trouble found us yet again.

When I first got up this morning, shaking and shivering with the cold, Edward cried out, "Look! Snow!" And sure enough, the hilltops were dusted white, tho none of it touched us down here. It looked fresh and clean, but it sent a chill through my bones.

Many of the smaller children laughed to see snow so early. The children don't know enough to be afraid. The rest of us took a mournful aspect because we know that snow means winter, and winter comes early in the high mountains. We got to get through the high mountains or perish. Snow is our enemy.

Time is our enemy, too. Mr. Donner figures we got three weeks to make up for lost time, and if we don't, we will be lost, too.

Before we left the springs, the men took inventory of our supplies. No surprise, we ain't got near enough provisions. So we took a vote to send a couple of men ahead to Captain Sutter's Fort, in California, as fast as they can. Charles Stanton and William McCutchen were chosen. They will go on muleback — much faster than by wagon — and if they make it, will explain to Captain Sutter that our party is in a bad way and needs help.

George Donner asked me if I wanted to go with them, and take my chances, but I will not leave so easy. I have cast my lot with the party, for good or bad.

"I thought you'd say that," said Mr. Donner. "Good. The Breens need you, and the party needs you, too. You are a fine shot and a hard worker. I must hope that your loyalty will be repaid with kindness and with good fortune."

I told him I was sure it would, but that was a lie. I ain't sure of anything, except I never felt so lonesome in the midst of so many people. They say we are closer to California than to Missouri, but it seems like our destination keeps getting farther away. The harder things get, the more I dream of my old home, and the less I dream of California. I suspect there are others who feel the same

way, but no one speaks of it. Talk of home is forbidden —
we must only think of our destination.

Anyhow, I watched the two men ride off until they
disappeared over the horizon. We don't know if they'll be
able to get supplies at Sutter's Fort, or if we'll ever see
them again.

Mr. Donner says they are good men, but what does
being good have to do with it? About now I'd rather be
lucky than good.

We covered more than twenty miles today. That's
good. The bad part is, we have hundreds more to cover.

More oxen died. So we ate them.

September 13

Much fighting today. It ain't the Indians we are fighting,
but one another. It started with the women. Some of
them got together over the morning campfire and started
complaining about the men, and all the stupid things we
done, like taking Mr. Hastings' short-cut.

"Hastings Short-cut!" one of the women crowed. "Two
words and both of them a lie! Hastings is a liar, and there
ain't no short-cut! We should be over the mountains by
now and instead we are still on the plains, with hundreds
of miles yet to go! All because the men believed a liar!"

Mr. Reed took exception and defended himself. He

said he understood they were all disappointed in our progress thus far. "But we all voted to take the short-cut," he said, "and must live with the consequences."

"Voted!" the woman shrieked. "It was only the men who voted! But it won't only be the men who die! No, sir, women and children will die, too, if something isn't done! It was you got us into this! You and the other men! All so you could have an adventure and pretend to be explorers. You forgot our purpose!"

James Reed had his hands on his hips, and he wouldn't back down. His eyes looked like chips in a cold fire. He asked what they thought their purpose was.

The women said it was to get their families to California the best and safest way possible. And that he had failed, and that we should already be there but we were not.

Mr. Reed didn't have a reply. He grunted and strode away, and later I heard him complaining to his wife about the ungrateful people, and how if he'd been elected leader of the expedition instead of George Donner, things would be different.

The fighting didn't stop when Mr. Reed backed down. Soon the women were fighting among themselves, and insulting one another's husbands. Many of them were so angry they cried tears of rage.

I kept to myself. I am a man but can't argue with the

women, for they are right. It was pure folly to follow Mr. Hastings' suggestions. But the mistake happened weeks ago, so what good does it do to chew it over now?

Mr. Breen whispered to his wife that there must be bad air from the sulfur springs that makes people so angry. Maybe so. But the women didn't say anything that wasn't true. We are in a bad way. We have barely enough oxen left to haul the wagons. There is some bacon left, and barrels of flour, but not near enough to last all the way to our destination.

We know our situation is grim, but we keep moving. We keep going. What else can we do?

September 20

We are camped this night in the Ruby Valley. It is cold enough that my breath comes out like fog and my fingertips tingle with the cold. I ain't bothered writing in this journal lately because each day brings more discouragement, and writing about it makes me weary.

Shoshone Indians have sneaked into the camp at night and stolen two of Mr. Reed's horses. He says he will kill the horse thieves if he catches them, but Mr. Patrick Breen said he wouldn't know a horse thief from the wrong end of a horse, and Mr. Reed took offense and retired to his wagon.

There has been much unpleasantness between the people. Nobody shares the campfires no more. Each family sticks to itself, and fends for itself. We ain't no longer a party together, but only a cluster of wagons traveling in the same direction. Bust an axle and you are on your own, or dependent on a few friends.

I asked Mr. Donner if there was something could be done, but he sighed and shook his head. "We are in a bad patch," he said. "Maybe things will improve, once we get over these mountains."

He means the Ruby Mountains, which surround us on all sides. Seems like we been among these mountains forever, and have made little progress west. We been following a wagon trail, the mark of emigrants that have gone before us. Emigrants that are far ahead of us, likely because they never took no short-cut.

One good thing, there are many fresh springs, and plenty of water, and enough grass to keep the cattle alive. Edward says the worst is over, and from here on it'll all be downhill. I didn't have the heart to tell him we got many more mountains to cross, and higher ones, too. He's in a fine mood because his leg has stopped hurting. Seems like a million years ago he broke it and the mountain man wanted to cut it off, but it was only six weeks ago. Six of the longest weeks that ever a man has lived.

Another good thing happened. I laid out in the bush

for two hours, tracking paw prints, and shot three rabbits. So me and Edward and his family had a good hot meal for supper. Rabbit stew, seasoned with a little salt and pepper.

We didn't share with nobody else, as there wasn't enough to go round.

October 6

A terrible thing has happened. A thing so awful I can hardly bring myself to write it down.

Yesterday, after lunch, James Reed killed a man.

It happened like this. The wagons were having a hard time of it getting up a hill, and tempers were short. There were three wagons ahead of Mr. Reed's wagon, and he got impatient and tried to pass one of the other wagons, as his oxen were stronger.

When he came alongside the other wagon, Mr. John Snyder, who was driving, cursed at him and said he was there first and must take his turn.

Mr. Reed took exception to Snyder's language, and Snyder said if Reed didn't get back in line he'd whip him like a dog.

Snyder then showed Reed his whip, which he'd been cracking over the head of his poor oxen.

Reed said only a coward whips dumb animals.

"I'll show you who is a coward!" Snyder roared, and he leaped out of his wagon.

Snyder then scampered up to where Reed was driving his own team of oxen, and struck Reed a blow with the butt end of the whip.

Reed was stunned by the blow, but soon recovered. He shoved Snyder away from the wagon and snatched a hunting knife from his belt. "Keep away from me!" he screamed. "Keep away, or I swear I'll kill you!"

I had never heard Mr. Reed scream. It made him sound young and different, like he wasn't in charge of himself no more. He waved the knife at Snyder, who laughed in his face. Reed started after him, but Mrs. Reed leaped out of the wagon and pulled him away.

Then, as Mrs. Reed tried to lead her husband away, Snyder unfurled his whip and cracked it over their heads, and this time the lash struck Mrs. Reed, who cried out in pain.

I saw the color drain from James Reed's long face. His eyes got big and round, and he ran straight at Snyder with his knife. Twice more Snyder's whip struck him, once on the arm and then again on the head, but it was like Reed couldn't feel nothing but his anger.

Snyder tried to whip him a third time, but by then Reed was upon him and stabbed the knife into Snyder's chest.

Snyder fell down, looking surprised.

Reed threw his knife away and made a high, wailing sound. "What have I done?" he cried. "What have I done?"

Snyder got to his feet and staggered a few paces. He come toward our wagon, holding his hand to his chest. Mr. Breen jumped down to help him, but he couldn't be saved.

After Snyder died, Mr. Reed acted regretful and offered to help bury the man he had killed. He wasn't allowed. The sentiment among the party was that Reed had committed murder.

Lewis Keseberg, who hated Reed ever since Reed admonished him for beating his wife, saw his chance for revenge. He said it wasn't fair for a knife to go up against a whip, and that Mr. Reed had committed murder.

Many others agreed. James Reed had made many enemies with his arrogant ways. Even George Donner did not rush to defend him, but said the matter should be settled in a court of law, once we reached California.

While Snyder was being buried, Virginia Reed helped bind up her parents' wounds. Her mother was bleeding from where Snyder's whip had struck her neck, and her father from the blows upon his head. They both looked very downcast, as if they knew the incident would not end with Snyder's burial.

We banged up a plain coffin for the dead man and set

him into a shallow grave. Nobody had much to say on his behalf, as Snyder wasn't no more popular among the party than Reed, on account of his quick temper and his foul mouth.

Edward's paw said a few words over the grave. That was all. There wasn't time for a lot of Bible reading, because the party still had to decide what to do about Reed.

Keseberg made it plain he believed Reed should hang for his crime, the sooner the better.

Mr. Donner said that Reed had gone too far and killed a man out of anger. Then he proposed a vote that instead of hanging, Reed be banished from the wagon train. He asked for a show of hands.

And so we voted to banish James Reed. I blushed when Virginia saw me raise my hand, but I didn't see no other way. If her father stayed with us, the next thing he'd be in a fight with Keseberg, or with somebody else. Some folks were already talking about burning his wagon if he stayed. There weren't no choice about it — he had to go away.

"Run him off!" somebody shouted after the vote was taken, and many of the folks thought he should leave with nothing but the shirt on his back and the boots on his feet.

Mrs. Reed then begged us to let her husband take his horse, his guns, and such supplies as he might need.

In the end, George Donner agreed that Reed should take a horse, but denied him any supplies, as all supplies were needed for the members of the expedition, and for that matter, Reed's own family.

When he left, James Reed sat tall in his saddle and promised his wife and daughter that he would go ahead to California and bring supplies back to the wagon train.

Little Virginia wept most piteously as her father rode off, until her mother shushed her and put her in the wagon.

Later

Tonight after the party had camped and eaten what little we had for supper, I snuck into the Reed wagon and found Virginia still crying.

"Go away, Douglas Deeds," she blubbered, hiding her face in her pillow. "How could you vote against my poor father?"

I explained, the best way I could, that being banished was better than hanging, or having their wagon burned. My heart ached for the heartbroken girl, and I agreed to help her in any way I could.

Before I quite knew what was happening, Virginia

took me by the hand and led me out of the back of the wagon, into the darkness. She had bundled up her father's rifle with some powder and shot, and three day's ration of food, and intended to carry it to him.

I didn't really want to help James Reed, but couldn't say no to his daughter. And so we snuck away from the camp and hunted about until I found the marks of his horse. There was just enough moonlight to see the faint trail in the sandy soil.

As we walked along following the hoofprints, Virginia said her father was not a murderer, but only defending her mother.

I did not argue.

We found Mr. Reed no more than a mile from the camp. He was hiding behind a hill, holding the reins of his horse, and waiting for us in the darkness. I understood then that he had arranged to have Virginia bring out his rifle and the supplies, and had been waiting for us as near to the camp as he dared.

He asked if I would go with him to California and I said no thank you. I didn't say that riding into the night with a known killer wasn't my notion of a good idea.

Just before he left, Reed kissed his daughter on the forehead and made a solemn vow that he would find Virginia and her mother wherever they might be, and save them, and that someday soon they would all live happily together again.

Then he rode off.

Virginia wept quietly all the way back to camp.

I slept that night under the Breen wagon, and hoped they'd never find out what I had done. Not even Edward, who is my best friend in the world.

II
STARVATION LAKE

October 20

It has been two weeks — two very long weeks — since last I wrote in this journal. At times I've been so discouraged it felt like what is the point of writing when all is lost?

I mean, who cares what happened to Douglas Allen Deeds of Independence, Missouri? If he was dumb enough to join up with a wagon train of greenhorns and head out into the wilderness, who wants to read his stupid journal? Probably nobody. But still I feel like I should write things down when I get the chance, if I ain't too exhausted to hold the pen and make my marks.

I say we are "greenhorns" cause that's what they call beginners who don't know nothing, and we didn't know nothing about exploring or crossing the country by wagon, and that's a fact. We didn't have no business going west without an experienced guide. We know it now — even Mr. Donner admits it — but there is nothing to be done except keep moving as long as we can, and hope supplies reach us from Sutter's Fort.

If they don't, I may have to eat this journal, page by page.

October 21

We've been having a load of trouble from the Payhoot Indians. The Shoshone tribe pretty much kept to themselves, but the Payhoot delight in making us miserable. Payhoots are always ready for war, and if they can't find a war to fight, they raid. Mostly they prey upon our cattle. Those they can't steal, they kill. So far they killed or stole more than forty head, which leaves us barely enough to pull the wagons we got left. There are less wagons, too, as we have had to abandon quite a few along the way, when they got broke or stuck, or didn't have no oxen.

Tamsen Donner says the Payhoots are dogging us because we look weak. She says they think we are stragglers who don't know how to find our way, or to fight, and mostly she's right. Expect we do know how to fight, only it's with one another.

For instance, one day Edward's paw, Patrick Breen, got his horse stuck in some bad mud. At the time we was far back from the others. I ran up as fast as I could and begged a man to come back and help us pull the horse out.

The man refused. He said Patrick Breen had hoarded his water when we crossed the salt desert and wasn't deserving of help.

By the time I got back, the horse had died, and I didn't want to tell Mr. Breen what the man said, as it would only cause more trouble.

October 22

Tonight only a few of the wagons camped together, and the Payhoots got bold and came up so close we could hear them breathing in the dark. They hooted like owls, just to provoke us, and then laughed when one of us fired off a gun and didn't hit nothing.

All of a sudden we heard this strange whistling noise — you couldn't tell where it came from — and then arrows whizzed out of the dark and stuck in the wagons. Nobody got killed, but I figure if them Indians had wanted to kill us, we'd all be dead by now.

October 23

Some of our trouble is just plain blockheaded stupidity! The men who were supposed to guard the cattle from the Payhoots decided to come back into camp and have breakfast, leaving the cattle and oxen unguarded. That's exactly what the Indians were waiting for, and they swooped in and stole or killed about another two dozen head.

All this trouble with the Payhoots makes me wish Mr. Reed was still with the party. Maybe he'd know what to do. Certainly he wouldn't allow the horses to be left unguarded.

Of course we don't know if he's alive or dead. But I think he's alive. Say what you like about him, he's a tough buzzard, and if any ignorant tenderfoot can fight his way to Sutter's Fort, all on his own, he can.

Not quite everything was bad today. Before sunset we got our first sight of the Sierra Mountains, away off in the distance. They looked cold and sort of faded blue, and about as far away as the moon.

Then the clouds came down and we couldn't see them no more. I can feel them, though. I can feel those high Sierra Mountains, just a-waiting on us. On the other side is our destination. Cross the Sierras and we have but sixty miles to go!

I am hopeful once more, if we can only get to the mountains before the snow falls.

—◦◦◦—

October 24

My old horse, Barny, died this day. He was a good horse, and I will miss him terrible.

October 25

Today is a great day! Help has finally arrived! Charles Stanton has found us, and he carries food and supplies for our bedraggled party. Stanton was sent off on a mule six weeks ago, with instructions to find his way to Sutter's Fort. By the grace of God he did so, and Captain Sutter in his great generosity gave him fresh packmules and supplies to bring back to us. Flour, jerked beef, beans, and such. Glorious, most glorious!

At first we thought he was a mirage made by our desperate situation. We had just begun our assault on the Sierras, and were faint of heart, for the peaks are higher than the clouds themselves. It seemed impossible that any man might find his way across such an imposing mountain range, let alone a party that included women and children.

Then Edward, who had been alongside the oxen, caught sight of something. He jumped up on the wagon and shaded his eyes, looking off in the distance.

"Men," he said. "Three men and seven mules!"

That was enough to make us hurry forward, driving the mules up the slope, to make our rendezvous with the miraculous mirage.

But it weren't no mirage, it was Mr. Stanton and two Miwok Indians who were hired to guide him. At first we was all so stunned we could scarcely speak. And then everybody started talking all at once, and it took a while to sort things out. Stanton told us he'd had many hardships, and would have perished were it not for his Indian friends, who are called Luis and Salvador.

Then Stanton dropped a stunner. He told us that James Reed sent his regards. He said Reed had also reached Fort Sutter and was now mounting a proper rescue party, with more supplies than Stanton could carry.

Except by his family, James Reed hadn't been missed. Now, however, in light of our situation, we were all prepared to accept him as a hero again, if he should manage to rescue us.

Virginia and her mother wept to hear the news. The rest of us were too busy making up biscuits from the flour, and frying them in the bacon grease that Stanton gave us. He only carried enough food for six days or so, but it is enough to give us hope, and to admire his courage for risking his life to find us.

The real miracle is that he has been over the Sierras to California and back. If he has done it, maybe we can, too.

Mr. Donner pointed out that we have come near two thousand miles since we started this trek. Sixty more miles will get us there.

That's all, just sixty miles. Surely we can make sixty miles in six days? That is only ten miles a day. Walk a mile an hour for ten hours, and we shall easily make ten miles a day!

Can we take this as a sign from Heaven that our prayers have been answered? Can we?

November 4

This day has broke my heart.

Yesterday, after a brave and ceaseless struggle up the steep and perilous trail into the high mountains, with Stanton and his Indians to guide us, we came at last to the final pass. The trail was so narrow we had to leave the wagons behind and carry our things on our backs. Set a foot wrong and you'd slide all the way back, or worse, slip over the edge of a cliff and fall to the bottom of the world.

It was late in the day, and everyone was very discouraged. There was a foot or more of snow on the ground, and some drifts much higher, which made for hard going. To make it worse we could barely see. The wind blew from the west, fierce and cold and wet with freezing rain.

Then one of the packhorses slid into a gully and was nearly killed, so we stopped and couldn't seem to get going again.

I have never in my life been so cold and miserable and tired.

When Stanton saw the state we were in, he advised that we rest until dawn and then work our way through that gap. He tried to sound lighthearted, for our sakes, but there weren't nothing lighthearted about the cold and the dark and the howling wind.

Luis and Salvador, the Indian guides, didn't complain about the miserable weather. They just wrapped themselves up in their blankets and stood under a tree, as if they'd been planted there. Pretty soon the snow dusted their blankets so that they almost looked like trees themselves. Once in a while they'd shake off the snow, but other than that, they never moved.

The rest of us gathered around a small fire of pinewood and tried to keep warm the best we could. Nothing worked. It was like you could sit right in the fire and the wind would steal the hot away.

Nobody said much. We all knew this was our last chance, and that we must seize it and trust to Providence. Already Stanton's supplies have run out, and we are dependent on what little we've hoarded. Our wagons are left behind, or taken apart, and we have only what we can carry on our backs. Our prospects could not be more dire, if we do not get over the mountain soon.

Stanton remained calm. He puffed on his pipe and said, "Pray for deliverance, my friends. Pray for the sun to shine, and the snow to melt."

November 5

Our prayers, alas, were not answered.

All night the wind shrieked, and the rain turned to icy pellets of snow. The flames of the fire soon faded and died. No one could manage to strike a spark and relight the fire, the wind was that mean. Ice formed on the dead white logs, and the cold settled into our bones, as if our own fires had gone out, too. The night lasted forever, it seemed like, we did not even know for sure when dawn came.

Later, with a little light in the sky, Stanton and the two Indians went forward to see what the night had left us. I followed behind them, slogging through knee-deep snow. My feet were so cold I couldn't feel nothing from the knees down. We come around a stone outcropping, the pass or gap that led down to the other side of the mountain, and that's when the full force of the storm hit.

In an instant, the air was white and thick with the storm. Snow pellets smacked into us like a hail of frozen bullets. Stanton tied a rope to his Indian guides, and they went down into the gap, to see if it was passable.

They didn't get far. The snow was ten feet deep, and they sunk up to their necks, and had to dig their way back out. I helped as best I could, and me and the Indians managed to drag Stanton back behind the rock, where the wind wasn't quite so bad.

It took Mr. Stanton some time to get his breath back. His throat was partly froze by the snow he'd swallowed, and it was hard to hear what he said.

"Retreat," he croaked. "Must retreat."

And so we have retreated a few miles, and found shelter near a frozen lake. Shelter from the wind, but not from the snow, that continues to pile up, covering everything in a thick, frozen blanket until it looks like the mountains were carved of ice, instead of stone.

Mr. Stanton, who is usually cheerful and confident, was crushed by the turn of events. He said had we got here two days sooner the pass would have been clear, and all would be well.

But two days are gone, and we cannot have them back. Winter has come and will not let us go. We are trapped in the Sierra Nevadas, only sixty miles from civilization, but it might as well be ten thousand.

November 6

The Breens and I were lucky. We've found refuge in a deserted cabin that may have been built some years ago by a fur trapper. The cabin is very crude — felled logs with no windows, and roofed with pine branches. There are holes in the roof. The stove is broke, but it is a great improvement on being outside. Outside where the storm rages, and the wind screams through the mountaintops and over the lake. Outside where the last few cattle are dying almost without complaint, as if grateful the end is near.

Soon we will eat the frozen cattle, and scrape what little meat we can from their skinny bones. And then, when that is gone, what shall we eat?

Shall we eat the snow? Shall we eat the ice? Shall we eat the bark on the frozen trees?

What shall we eat?

November 10

We are still alive, but prospects are grim and getting worse.

After the pass got snowed in, we had two more storms, and the wall of snow that blocks our way is now twice a man's height, with drifts even higher. We are no longer a party, but the survivors of a failed expedition.

We've split up, more or less, and must live on our own. Or die on our own, if it comes to that.

November 11

There are twelve people abiding in the Breen cabin, including me. The dirt floor got slick and muddy once we got a fire going, and warmed up considerable. Since we moved in, Keseberg and his family have built a lean-to against the side of our cabin. The Murphys, the Graves, and the Reeds have all built themselves shacks not far from us, and shelter inside them the best they can. Nobody visits that much. All the families keep to themselves, and eat what they have managed to hoard or hunt.

It has snowed most of five days steady. The snow gets deeper every hour that passes.

The Breens are better off than most. Patrick Breen had six head of cattle, and we soon slaughtered them. The meat and bones were then stacked and hidden in the snow, where they have froze up hard and won't go bad.

Mr. Breen thinks he may have enough meat to keep his family alive for the whole winter, if need be — and if he don't have to share it out with others less fortunate. Share with them and his own family would likely starve.

He didn't say so, but I knew he meant a time may come when I am not welcome at his table. Were he forced to choose between his family and me, the family must be chosen.

I'm not angry, as it is only natural to protect your own, and I am grateful for any kindness they may give me. For the time being, Mrs. Breen sees I get a little beef to chew upon, and I have kept up my strength.

November 14

Edward looks at me with sorrowful eyes, as if he suspects that one day I will be banished from the family cabin and will be his friend no more.

I told him not to worry, that soon an expedition would arrive to rescue us.

I wished I believed it was true, but how can anyone think to rescue us with all this snow? You can't walk through snow so deep. It's like trying to swim in thick water.

We got word the Donners have made camp a few miles away, nearby the creek. They are in bad shape, as the Indians killed most of their cattle, and they have very little to eat.

Mr. Stanton came by in a rage, as Indians slipped into the camp last night and stole three of his mules, that he was hoping to take down the mountain when the weather cleared. He is very vexed because the mules was loaned out by Captain Sutter, and Stanton feels he must return them.

I asked why the Indians who stole the mules didn't help us, as they must be aware we are slowly starving. Stanton pulled a little on his pipe and said it was because other settlers and trappers have shot and killed some of their people. White men treat them like animals. So they take their revenge by stealing.

Poor Mr. Stanton, who was brave enough to set out trying to rescue folks he didn't even know, is trapped like the rest!

Something must be done, he said, and we must do it, because no one can mount a rescue party under these conditions. I asked what could we do, and he said he didn't know yet, but he was thinking on it.

Charles Stanton has very little food of his own, but must rely on portions from those who do. So far folks have been generous, as they can't forget it was Stanton who risked his life to bring us supplies, and they are still grateful to him.

That may change as supplies dwindle. Hungry folk ain't likely to share when all they can think about is their own hunger and staying alive.

November 22

Yesterday I joined Charles Stanton and some others, as we attempted to get through the pass and down the mountain on our own, with some help from Stanton's remaining packmules.

The attempt began with high hopes, on a fine, sunny day. It had not snowed for most of a week, and enough of the snow had melted for us to get through the pass without too much difficulty. Partly this was the crust of ice on top of the snow, that lets us walk above it. The poor mules, being heavier, were not so fortunate, and had to struggle through six feet of thick, heavy snow.

Our little expedition was lead by Stanton's Indian guides, Luis and Salvador. They ain't from a mountain people, but know more than white men do about trekking through deep snow. I think they are fine fellows, but some of the others grumbled that we shouldn't put our lives at risk on the word of no Indians.

Wasn't it Indians who killed or stole so many of our cattle and horses?

Mr. Stanton said he trusted Luis and Salvador as much as he trusted any white man and made it clear he didn't want to hear no more complaints about our guides, and from then on it was only whispers. You can't stop a whisper. It always finds a way to fly from ear to ear.

Our progress west was good, once we got through the pass, and by nightfall we were several miles down the mountain. We'd have made it even farther than we did except for the mules. We had to keep stopping and waiting for the mules to catch up, and by the end of the day the poor critters were exhausted with their efforts.

November 23

Last night, as we sat warming our hands and feet around our little campfire, Mr. William Eddy allowed as how we should abandon the mules. He said dragging them along slows us down, and suggested we leave them behind and race to the bottom of the mountain while the weather was still fair. He said this crust of ice was a blessing. A man can almost run across it, and that with conditions like this we can make Sutter's Fort in two or three days.

Stanton heard him out and then shook his head and said he could not leave the mules, as they were not his to abandon.

Mr. Eddy insisted and said surely Captain Sutter would understand that a man's life was worth more than a few mules.

But Stanton refused and said he gave Sutter his oath he would return his property. We could do as we liked, but he must return to the lake and wait for a better chance.

Many of the men argued with Stanton for hours. Finally they threatened to go ahead without him, using his Indian guides. But Luis and Salvador were loyal to Stanton, and would not leave without him saying so, which he would not.

In the end, Stanton won the argument by being as stubborn as the mules. The mules wouldn't budge, and Stanton wouldn't budge.

Finally we gave up. Took us all of one day and most of one night to get Stanton and the mules back to the camp on the other side of the pass. By then we was all spittin' mad, and terrible disappointed that our expedition had been a failure.

November 25

Too late.

Some of us younger men was about to mount another expedition through the pass when a storm hit us bad. The icy crust that made walking easy has been buried under another foot of snow, and more of it piles up every hour.

Stanton has seven mules left but they are in poor health, with their ribs showing.

I did a terrible thing today. I prayed the mules would die soon, so that Stanton and the Indian guides would feel free to lead us down the mountain to Sutter's Fort.

December 1

The great storm is over.

The steady snowfall worked itself up into a blizzard that blew most fearsome for two days and two nights. The shrieking of the wind was so loud we couldn't hear ourselves talk. The wind sounded like the mountains screaming. Finally we quit trying to talk and huddled closer and closer. The stove in the Breen cabin only gave out a little heat because the wood was almost gone, and no more could be found with the storm raging.

I tried going out for wood but didn't get five feet. The wind wanted to tear me apart and bury me. I gave up and barely made it back to the cabin. They said I was a fool to try, and that I could have been lost in the storm, and they were right on both counts.

Patrick Breen said we must wait it out, that no storm lasts forever. Maybe not, but it sure seemed like forever. Then when the wind finally stopped screaming, we went out to find we had been blanketed with six feet of fresh snow.

Worse, the remaining cattle and Stanton's mules are nowhere to be seen. Either they were driven off the mountain by the wind, or the Indians used the storm as cover and come by to steal them away. Either way it don't matter: The critters are gone, which makes it all the more useless that Mr. Stanton wouldn't leave them behind when we had the chance.

He came by the Breen cabin after the storm and all but apologized. He said he regretted that he could not foresee the future, and that had he known the mules were doomed, his decision would have been otherwise.

For some reason that made me laugh. "Heck, if I could see the future, I wouldn't be here at all," I said. "I'da never left Missouri in the first place."

Stanton nodded. He didn't seem quite so low as I expected, considering, and soon enough I found out why. He said he had a new plan, and that some of the people were going to make "snowshoes" and walk out. Was I interested in coming along?

I asked what were snowshoes, and he said they were an Indian invention. With snowshoes it seems you can walk on top of the snow, according to Luis and Salvador.

It sounded like a crazy idea, but what have we got to lose? I told Stanton I was his man, and would help make snowshoes if somebody showed me how.

I figure if Jesus could walk upon the water, then maybe we could walk upon the snow, if we prayed hard enough.

I'm praying hard.

—⟊⟋⟊—

December 8

Clear weather today, but the snowshoes still ain't ready. Charles Stanton and William Eddy are making the shoes out of oxbows. First they have to split the oxbows into thin frames, then bind 'em together and weave rawhide across the frame.

They are making twenty pairs and it seems like it's taking forever. Partly this is because both Stanton and Eddy are weak from hunger. Stanton has to leave off working on the snowshoes to beg for food, but he don't get much.

Even Patrick Breen, who is normally a kind man, won't let me share with Mr. Stanton. What little they give me is out of my friendship with their son, Edward, Mr. Breen reminded me. He said Stanton is a good man, but must fend for himself.

December 9

There is nothing to eat but frozen pieces of lean and stringy beef that Mr. Breen thaws out on the stove. No flour, no bread, no salt, no vegetables. I keep dreaming of turnips swimming in salty butter, and potatoes, and green peas, and sweet corn, but all I get is a few ounces of gray beef that tastes like soggy bits of leather. It's enough to keep you alive, but you still feel weak all the time, and your stomach is always begging for more, and making sure you never forget how hungry you are.

It must be much worse for Mr. Stanton, tho he makes no complaint. Neither do the Indian guides, Luis and Salvador, who are just as starved as he is. All of them are getting so thin the wind blows through them.

It ain't fair, but I can't seem to make it right. I went out today looking for game to give to Stanton and the Indians, but didn't find none. I had hoped to find a squirrel out of his nest, or a bird lighting on a branch, but there ain't much game this high up the mountain, and what there was of it got shot in the first few days. Going was hard, as the snow came up to my chest. It is like swimming against the current in a frozen river.

I am eager to try the new shoes that promise to float on top of the snow, and would do it while the weather is still good.

December 10

Word came up from the Donners, who are still camped with a few other stragglers down by the creek. They say the Donner family is in much worse shape than the rest of us. They lost most of their cattle in the first storm, and have taken to eating mice, and chewing on buffalo hides.

I feel bad for Tamsen Donner, who was right to worry

about taking the shortcut. She knew the thing to do was stick to the trail, but couldn't make the men agree with her. Now she must nurse her poor husband, who is very ill, and take care of her young children as best she can.

When I told Edward how unfair it was, that good people should starve because they made a mistake, he said we were in God's hands, and if God wanted us to live, he would provide food. I said I hoped he was right, but just in case God left us to fend for ourselves, I aimed to leave with Mr. Stanton's expedition, whenever the snowshoes were ready.

Edward thought it a bad idea to leave the warmth of the cabin and take my chance in the open air. He urged me to remain with the family and said he would see his paw gave me enough to live.

Edward is my friend and thinks of me as a brother. But his paw don't think like that. I can tell by the looks he gives me that he'd as soon have me leave and save that much more meat to keep his own family alive.

I try not to take it personal, but sometimes it feels like no one can see me but Edward, and maybe his maw. The others tend to look right through me like I wasn't even there. It don't matter that I could have left them months ago, but stayed to help. All that matters is what happens right now.

It seems that hunger makes a man forget his thankfulness.

December 11

Snow and rain. Firewood is getting very hard to find, and we must huddle around a cold stove. Miserable weather!

December 13

More snow. Everyone short-tempered and quick to take offense. I fear it will never end, and that we will be trapped until hunger kills us, or we kill one another.

Mrs. Reed gave Stanton a little dried meat for our journey. She is the only one who remembered his previous kindness.

December 14

More snow and freezing rain. Snowshoes ready when the weather improves. It must improve, it must!

December 15

We are ready at last.

III
THE FORLORN HOPE

December 17

The sun finally came out this morning as we made our escape from Starvation Lake. There are seventeen of us using the snowshoes. They really do make it possible to walk on top of the snow, once you get used to it.

Charles Stanton and the Indians will guide us. He says there is an outpost forty miles to the west, and believes we can get that far in four or five days, if the weather holds.

We carry very little with us. A small portion of tobacco and some dried meat and coffee, enough to last four days if we're careful, and don't give in to our hunger. It is important to travel light and move fast, and besides, that's all the food that could be spared for us.

We call ourselves the Forlorn Hope. Our little party includes ten men, two boys, and five women.

When we came up to the pass and saw the mountain peaks marching higher than the clouds, and how far away the valley looked below, Mr. Stanton raised his walking stick and said, "Look about you! We are as close to Heaven as we can get!"

Then the wind came up and took the words from his mouth. Like the mountains were laughing at us for trying to escape.

It was hard going, but we got through the pass okay.

Then, like they say, it was all downhill — only downhill is a lot harder than you might think, unless you done it on snowshoes. We knew about the cold and the wind and the snow, but the sun was a surprise. Here we been praying for clear weather, and now that we got it, the sun wants to burn us blind. It comes off the snow something fierce, like a cold flame that burns through your eyeballs and fries the back of your brain.

I got a scrap of cloth over my eyes that helps a little. It's much worse than the blinding glare in the salt desert, because everything is covered with snow, and snow is brighter than salt. Somebody said it was like lying in a white mirror at high noon and freezing, all at the same time.

We ain't traveling together, exactly. We're stretched out, with the fastest in front and the slowest bringing up the rear. Following along in one another's snowshoe tracks. I expected the women to be the slowest, but they are not, not by a long shot.

The slowest, big surprise, is Mr. Stanton, who was supposed to lead us.

The thing about snowshoes, you got to run sort of bowlegged, and it wears you out. Plus we're already weak from not eating right. Poor Mr. Stanton had trouble keeping up and kept falling behind.

The first time it happened, I went back to help him. He was slumped against a tree, catching his breath, and waved me off.

He told us to go on, that we mustn't slow down for one man. He said our purpose was to reach civilization and send a rescue expedition back to save the others. If we wait for him, we would put all of them in peril.

It still don't seem right, but I did like he told and went on my way. I got so far ahead I couldn't see him when I looked back, and that fretted me constant, almost as much as being so hungry all the time.

We made about six miles downhill before night fell.

Stanton finally caught up about an hour after we'd already stopped and built a fire. And when he did come straggling in, he just sat down and didn't have nothing much to say, like the words would cost him too much energy. Turned out that even when the sky got dark he was still mostly blinded from the glare off the snow all day, and the campfire hurt to look at.

"See to yourselves," he muttered, and would say no more.

"We did good today," said William Eddy, nodding to each of us. "Tomorrow we will do better."

We will sleep crouched by the fire, as close as we dare, and hope the sky stays clear, even if that means suffering from snow blindness. Better snow blindness than snow blizzards!

I am dog tired and can't write no more.

December 18

Two of our party gave up this morning and returned to Starvation Lake, as they are too weak and hungry to continue.

We bid them luck, and farewell, and promised to send a rescue team back for them, when we have reached civilization. Then we picked up our packs and tightened our snowshoes, and moved on, traveling west. Always traveling west, with the cruel sun to guide us.

I'm much worried about Mr. Stanton. He can't keep up with the rest, but lags far behind. None of us dare slow down for stragglers. We are running for our lives, and must make the outpost before a blizzard buries us or the wind turns us to ice.

Flurries came up in the afternoon, and the sky turned

a mean shade of gray. Nobody will talk about it, but we all feel a big storm coming.

December 20

This night we stopped and made a fire, but Mr. Stanton never did catch up.

Earlier this morning, as we gathered our packs to leave the campfire behind and hurry on our way, Stanton remained by the smoldering fire, puffing calmly upon his pipe.

When Mary Graves, who is one of the strongest of the Forlorn Hope, told him we must leave, Stanton said he would be along soon. But he didn't move from his log by the fire.

I noticed his eyes never went to Mary when she spoke to him. So I shuffled over, careful to keep my snowshoes out of the fire, and crouched beside him, and asked was he blind.

He did not look at me, but told me again not to worry. He said I had miles to travel and mustn't fall behind.

I told him he had been a great inspiration to us all and then took hold of his arm and tried to raise him up. Gently he removed my helping hand. "Thank you, Douglas. Go on. I'll follow soon. I promise. Let me rest a little more, and then I'll be on my way."

Some of the others shouted at me to get moving, or be forever left behind.

I knew they were right, and that I must keep moving or die, but I never felt so wretched as when I left Charles Stanton sitting by the fire, smoking on his pipe like he didn't have a care in the world. Like he was finally at peace and didn't want to be disturbed.

The going was very hard this day. Not only because poor Stanton made my heart so heavy, but because the wind began to howl through the trees. We walk upon ten or twelve feet of snow, and at any moment the wind can lift a foot of it and fling it in your face.

And the cold. I've come to hate the cold like I'd hate my worst enemy. The cold goes through your bones and makes you weep, and then the tears freeze and you're still so hungry it hurts inside, and crying don't help, it only makes you weaker.

The Forlorn Hope didn't make but four miles today, struggling for every inch. By now we should be well below the snow line, on solid ground, but we ain't. The snow is so deep we walk among the tops of trees. Maybe the snow goes on forever, no matter how low you get. It sure looks that way.

Nobody said much as we built our fire, and sat close with our blankets joined, holding in the heat. But we was all thinking about Mr. Stanton, and hoping he would come stumbling into camp like he did before.

We sat together for two hours, our stomachs rumbling something awful, before William Eddy suggested we share out our last ration of dried beef.

"What about Mr. Stanton?" I asked. "We'll put aside his ration, right? For when he catches up?"

Mary Graves sighed and said she saw no point in saving out his portion. She said the poor man was gone and would need no more of our precious food.

I then went over to Luis and Salvador, the Indian guides who had traveled so far with Mr. Stanton, and at such risk to themselves. "Does he live?" I asked them. "Is there hope?"

Luis looked at Salvador, real sorrowful. Then they both looked at me and shook their heads. So we divided up the rations without accounting for Mr. Stanton, and nobody spoke no more about it.

I must write this here, in case I die, and won't be alive to tell the world: Charles Stanton is a hero. It don't matter that he was stubborn about the mules, or if he couldn't keep up because he's been hungry for so long, longer than the rest that wouldn't share with him. He is the only hero among us.

December 21

Bad storm, can't write.

December 22

Yesterday, in the midst of a terrible blizzard, we got a small surprise that pleased us.

Fourteen survivors of the Forlorn Hope gathered in a tight circle around a small fire. The fire kept going out because the snow was coming down so heavy. Each time it went out a pang of cold would shiver up our bones, and make our bodies cry out for food. But there was nothing to eat, as we had consumed all our rations.

Patrick Dolan said he felt more dead than alive, and wasn't sure he could tell the difference no more.

Jay Fosdick agreed, and said we had nothing to fear, because it couldn't get any worse than what we had already endured.

Many of the group then confessed they felt on the verge of death, and that if we weren't delivered of our suffering, they would just as soon join Mr. Stanton in eternity.

Then William Eddy spoke up. He was a good friend of Mr. Stanton and as close to being a chosen leader as we've got. He said Charles would be greatly disappointed to hear such mournful talk and then begged me to try some of my driest tinder and see could I find another spark for the fire.

I did as he asked, and sure enough, the tinder caught and soon we had another fire going, and our spirits raised some. That's when a small miracle happened. William Eddy went into his pack, to read the loving note his wife had left him, and found behind it a small package wrapped in oil skin.

Inside the package was a small chunk of dried bear meat his wife had saved out for him, for a time when he would need it, and think how much she loved him.

Eddy wept like a child, he missed his wife so, and then he shared out the meat with all of us. He could have hoarded it for himself, but he is a good man, and he gave us each an equal portion, exactly the same as he kept for himself.

Cold, dried bear meat. Back in Missouri I wouldn't touch bear meat. Turned up my nose at it. Said I'd rather eat dirt. But out here in the miserable wilderness, with the blizzard screaming through the trees, I chewed it down most heartily. Like it was the juiciest steak in the world, with potatoes and gravy and pie for dessert.

God bless Mr. Eddy for his kindness, and his generosity. He saves us this night, and staved off the Grim Reaper for another day.

December 23

More snow, can't move. Hungry again.

December 24

Tonight, in the icy rain, we miserable few are huddled together and cannot move.

This morning the sky broke clear for a few hours and we were able to make three miles west, with the greatest of difficulty, because the snow drifts were so high and light that even our snowshoes sunk deep with every step.

A little while before noon the weather changed. We are far enough down the mountain so it came in the form of rain. Hard cold rain. Rain that don't have the look of stopping anytime soon. Rain so hard and steady no fire can be lit. The rain soaked into us worse than the snow, sucking away our strength, and left us stumbling around so weak and pitiful it was hard to talk.

It was Mr. Eddy that saved us. He had a plan. He said he'd heard of a thing the trappers do when they get caught in a storm with no fire. It is called the Warming Circle, and we must try it or die of exposure.

At first nobody would listen to him. It's like we was so numbed with the cold and wet he couldn't make us see the sense of his plan. Warming Circle? Blankets? Snow? It didn't mean nothing.

Finally Mr. Eddy grabbed me by the collar and forced me to listen. The rain was running down his beard and freezing on the end, so he looked like a talking icicle. I thought that was funny and started to laugh until he slapped me.

"Douglas Deeds! Listen to me, please! Help me get the others together!"

That slap in the face brought me back to where I was. Outdoors in the freezing rain, hungry and cold to the bone, and about ten minutes from being frozen to death.

Following Mr. Eddy's instructions, I helped him get us all in a circle. He said he would be the last man in the circle, as things had to be done outside of it first. He made us sit in a tight circle and hold our blankets up to the rain, with our feet all together in the middle. Then he piled snow up around the back of us, to hold the outside edge of the blankets down, and keep the wind from getting under.

The last thing Mr. Eddy did was jump into the middle of the circle and close up the top with his own blanket.

The rain froze on the top of the blankets, freezing them all together. Then snow fell, and sealed up the blankets even more. Like making a tent when you ain't got no tent.

After a while, no more than an hour, we began to get a little warmth inside, from our own breath. Soon it was warm enough that many of us began to shiver, where before we'd been so close to frozen we couldn't even shiver, and shivering helped warm us up some more.

Thus we passed the night.

December 25

Raining hard again. We ain't moved in twenty-four hours but remained huddled and frozen together, half buried in the snow. Can it really be Christmas? I think so but am not sure.

All I want for Christmas is not to die.

December 26

I got my wish and am still alive.

Three of the Forlorn Hope were not so fortunate, but went to the Lord yesterday, in the middle of the night, as we huddled together under our blankets, alone in our misery.

Patrick Dolan was the first to go. He had been babbling words that made no sense, as if speaking to invisible people. Laughing and giggling to himself like he was a child again. Suddenly he lurched to his feet, sang a few words from a song, cried out "Mother, I see you!" and collapsed. He didn't move for a long time, and then after a while we realized he would never move again.

Mr. Eddy said the poor man had been driven mad by starvation, and it killed him. Nobody spoke no more about his madness, because we were half dead ourselves, and nearly as crazed with hunger as Patrick Dolan.

I asked should we bury him.

William Foster said the ground was frozen. He sounded angry, as if he wanted to strike someone but didn't have the strength.

I said we could bury him in the snow.

Mr. Foster said, "Leave him be! He might yet prove useful."

Foster then looked around at the others. Several of them nodded, as if in agreement about something that couldn't be discussed. I asked what he meant. How could a dead man be useful? He told me to shut up and mind my own business.

Mr. Eddy made peace by leading us in prayer, and we prayed for the salvation of Patrick Dolan's soul.

Soon after we finished praying, two more died. They just stopped breathing and froze up, and it was some time before we realized they were gone.

Foster looked around at the survivors and said that soon all of us would perish, unless we took advantage of what had been provided.

I was so tired that my poor brain could not attach a meaning to his words. What did he mean, *take advantage of what has been provided*? I meant to ask him, but did not have the strength to speak.

December 27

Last night I dreamt I was lost in a strange country and did not know how to get back home. I heard voices but could not understand. Then I smelled the sweet scent of baking bread and followed the smell, but never could I find where the bread was made, and the not knowing and the not eating made me so dizzy I fell into a blinding white light.

When I woke up, my stomach hurt so from being empty that I had to cover my mouth to keep from screaming.

It was daylight, and the rain had stopped. The other survivors were awake and had thrown off their blankets and were moving around, shivering and talking among themselves in low voices.

I asked what was happening, and what they were talking about, but they all ignored me.

Foster's eyes were glowing strangely. He said we must build a fire, and then we would eat.

I cried out and got shakily to my feet, and asked what there was to eat.

Foster stared at me so hard it felt like a punch from his fist. Then, speaking very slowly, as if to a child, he said, "We will eat what has been provided."

I asked again what he meant, but he would not answer.

Then I watched as Harriet Pike began screaming about our salvation and then tore apart her coat. At first I thought she had gone mad like poor Patrick Dolan, but she had a purpose. Her coat was stuffed with cotton, and in the deepest layer she found a handful that was dry enough to take a spark.

When she held up the dry bit of cotton, the others shouted as if she had discovered gold. In a way, the dry cotton was as good as gold, because it meant a fire could be lit. There was no dry wood, so someone suggested a pine tree be set afire, right where it stood rooted in the ground.

It seemed an act of madness to me, that a whole tree be burned where it stood. We had an ax, why not chop it down? But the Forlorn Hope would not wait, and soon the tree was ablaze.

It was a wild thing, to see a group of ragged, half-frozen men and women gathered around a blazing tree, rubbing their hands in the warmth of the flames, their eyes shining with the mad light of starvation.

My whole body screamed for food, but the horror of what they were about to do made me run away from the burning tree, and from the people there. I ran into the woods, atop the snow, with tears freezing in my eyes.

I ran away out of fear that if I stayed, I, too, would become an eater of the dead.

Later

Mr. Eddy found me in the woods, sobbing and crying out that the Lord should deliver me. Like me, he had refused to eat. Luis and Salvador had refused, also, and had gone off by themselves so they would not have to watch the others fill their bellies.

He said we must keep our strength for as long as we could, and he gave me a small strip of rawhide from his snowshoe. He said I should chew upon it to dull the hunger pangs.

I asked him how the Forlorn Hope could do such a terrible thing. He said they could not help themselves. Hunger makes us animals, and animals do what they can to stay alive.

I moaned that I would rather die than participate.

Mr. Eddy looked at me with sorrowful eyes and said I might feel differently after starving for a few more days.

I pray he is wrong, and that I will not do as the others have done.

December 28

Hid in the woods most of this day, but finally returned when I saw the survivors had built another fire. Could not feel my feet or hands. Huddled by the fire with steam rising from my blanket, but couldn't get warm, no matter how close I got to the flames.

The others looked at me with contempt, as if it is me who had done wrong, and not them. I had not the strength to argue with them. I don't feel angry about what they did. I don't feel nothing much at all. Like my insides were as froze up as my hands and feet.

My hand moves across this page, but I can't feel the words. I am numb to everything, even the prospect of dying.

The strange thing is, I'm no longer hungry. It's like my stomach give up telling me to eat. All I feel is cold inside my bones, and so tired I can't stand to be awake.

I will sleep now and dream of hot bread, fresh from the oven.

December 29

Too weak to write.

December 30

For three days we remained in the same place, close to the burned pine tree, while the others built another fire and fed on forbidden meat and gathered their strength for the long journey ahead.

I did not eat, but saw their hungry eyes upon me. I decided I must use the last of my strength to walk as far into the woods as I could, so they would not find me when I died.

There was a terrible silence in the woods. The ice on the trees made it look like the forest was made of white bones. I wasn't much better than a skeleton myself.

Finally I came to a tree that had been blown down by the storm. It was a huge tree, and the upturned roots gave me shelter from the wind.

I crouched there and looked up at the sky and thought how beautiful the world was and how sorry I was to leave it.

Strangely enough, I was not afraid. It does not hurt to perish so. Just sit still and the cold will make you warm. You will never have to move again, or feel hungry.

I thought of my maw and paw and hoped they would be pleased to see me.

That's when I saw the rabbit. It had come out of a burrow under the tree roots. It was a big, plump rabbit, fattened up for winter. It looked right at me but was not afraid. Probably I did not look alive enough to frighten it.

I knew then the rabbit was a miracle, and that I must seize my chance or die.

Mr. Eddy said starvation makes a man into an animal, and he was right. Like an animal I grabbed the rabbit and killed it. Like an animal I ate it.

And like an animal I did not think to share with the others.

December 31

I returned to the Forlorn Hope with my strength renewed. No one asked where I had been or what I had been doing.

I did not ask them, either.

We all have our secrets. Mine is the rabbit. I have hidden the leftover meat in my pack, and eat when the others can't see.

———◦◦◦———

January 3, 1847

Luis had been guiding us these last few days, through canyons so deep they block out the sky, but today admitted he was lost, and had no landmarks to go by, as the snow was too deep, and had buried all the places he knew.

Foster cursed him, and asked what was an Indian good for, if he couldn't find his way out of the woods?

That made poor Luis afraid for his life. He and Salvador quietly limped away from the Forlorn Hope. They soon blended into the trees and were gone.

I asked Foster how he could be so cruel, but he would not answer. Then I asked Mr. Eddy what he thought and he said it was better not to think. Just walk, he said. We must keep walking, as salvation may be over that hill.

But there is nothing over that hill, or the next. Or the next. We wander in a world of snow, circling back upon our own tracks, as if trapped in a nightmare that keeps repeating.

I have forgotten what it is to be dry and warm, or to have a roof over my head. I have forgotten what it is to see a person smile, or to smile back, and feel the spirit of human kindness.

What have we become? I cannot see myself — and for

this I am grateful — but the other survivors look more like cadavers than human beings.

We are sacks of bones, and the wind blows through us. We are skulls, marching in circles in the wilderness. We try to keep walking, because salvation may be over the next hill. We try not to think, because if we think too much we'll scream, and keep on screaming.

Later

This is the last of my ink, so these shall be the last few lines I write.

I don't know if I will survive this terrible ordeal. Salvation may be over the next hill, or it may not. But one thing I know. Some folks will do terrible things to stay alive.

Epilogue

———⌘———

Bear Valley, California

On the seventeenth day of January, in the year 1847, a young woman named Harriet Ritchie heard a knock upon the door of her small cabin, situated on the edge of the wilderness, within sight of the Sierra Nevada Mountains.

The knock was so feeble she thought at first she'd imagined it and went about her business. After a few minutes there was another knock, fainter than the first. Curiosity aroused, Miss Ritchie unlatched the door and swung it wide.

What she saw startled her so badly that at first she could not speak, and then was moved to tears. Standing in snow up to its bony knees was the skeletal ghost of a young man.

It was only when he moaned that Harriet realized the human skeleton was actually still alive.

"Bread," the ghost whispered. "Bread."

Douglas A. Deeds, a fifteen-year-old from Independence, Missouri, was one of eight survivors of the Forlorn Hope. Weeping at his pitiful state, Miss Ritchie fed the boy a hot buttered biscuit and then put him to bed.

Young Mr. Deeds recovered his health and briefly took up dairy farming, as his father had done before him. However, less than a year later he formed a partnership with his friend, Edward Breen, to survey land in the vicinity of Sutter's Fort.

It was to be a lucrative arrangement. By sheer luck, Douglas Deeds and Edward Breen were among the first to discover gold in the most famous gold rush in American history. Both men prospered, settled down, had large families, and rarely talked of the ordeal at Starvation Lake, or among the Forlorn Hope.

Deeds has numerous descendents who still live in the lush and beautiful Sacramento Valley.

Life in America
in 1846

Historical Note

Go west, young man — John Soule

All hope abandon, ye who enter here!
 — Dante Alighieri

In the year 1846 an invention called the sewing machine had just been patented. Ether was first used to dull the pain of surgery. Edgar Allan Poe, the famous author of "The Raven," was publishing horrific stories about being buried alive. Telegraph lines were being strung as the first means of "instant" communication.

The idea of America itself was about to undergo a great transformation. Although its area was already vast, the new nation had a rapidly growing population of twenty million, almost four million of them slaves or indentured servants. Many forces, including the rapid industrialization of the cities and offers of free land, would soon uproot thousands of citizens and send them westward, looking for a new life, and a chance at prosperity.

Just the year before, a new idea had taken root in the American consciousness. As eager American settlers poured into the Mexican territory of Texas, editor John L. O'Sullivan wrote that "it is our manifest destiny to overspread the continent allotted by Providence for the free development of our yearly multiplying millions." The populace was soon persuaded that it was America's "manifest destiny" not only to inhabit Texas, but to fill up the entire continent, from the Pacific Ocean to the Atlantic shore.

Mexico had claims on Texas, New Mexico, and California, but had failed to establish any large settlements there. In the months prior to the departure of the Donner Party, President James K. Polk annexed Texas and declared war on Mexico, with the intention of gaining new territory. Promoters like Lansford Hastings were confident that all of North America would soon be in friendly hands, and sure enough, by July 1846, the fertile new territory of California came under American control.

The controversial military triumph over Mexico notwithstanding, America needed to populate California if it wanted to keep it. Potential emigrants were told they would have access to tracts of free acreage, and that the land itself was more fertile and much richer than any previously settled. Books and newspaper accounts made

California sound like a veritable Garden of Eden — as indeed it would prove for the luckiest of the settlers. The idea of "going west to get ahead" took on a religious intensity, and even those who were very well established were tempted by the dream of starting a new life in a new land.

And all of this was before anyone even suspected that the hills and riverbeds of California were strewn with nuggets of gold!

When the survivors of the Forlorn Hope finally stumbled out of the mountains looking more dead than alive, that nation was stunned by the tragedy. Within days, rescue expeditions were dispatched, intent on reaching the marooned Donner Party with the greatest haste. Salvation would not come easily. The weather was so bad that winter — the worst in memory — that the first rescuers very nearly died of starvation themselves. It was not until almost a month later, on the nineteenth day of February, that a rescue party finally reached the encampment.

The scene of horror there was almost beyond comprehension. Human bones littered the landscape. Like the Forlorn Hope, those who stayed behind finally resorted to cannibalism. Of the eighty or so emigrants trapped at what would come to be known as Donner Lake, nearly thirty perished. Most were consumed by the survivors.

It took three rescue attempts to save the wretched survivors. James Reed led one of the rescue missions, fulfilling his promise to return. William Foster led another, although he arrived too late to save some of his family members. Conditions were extremely bad and many of the early attempts failed. With only mules and horses for transportation, and winter storms that continued to rage, it was not until April that the last of the doomed Donner Party were finally brought out.

Among the survivors were all the members of both the Breen and Reed families. The Donners themselves fared much worse. Years later Lewis Keseberg, notorious throughout the West as "Keseberg the Cannibal," never denied consuming the frozen body of Tamsen Donner, the noble lady who had foreseen the horror, and been unable to prevent it. It was reported that he often rocked upon his porch, muttering about those he had eaten.

No one in the Donner Party was ever prosecuted for cannibalism, but the horror of what they had done was never forgotten.

The unfortunate members of the Donner Party were not the only eager emigrants who departed from the major jumping-off point of Independence, Missouri, that year. Nor were they any less well-equipped or more badly led than many of the other wagon trains, almost all of which arrived safely.

In the end it was a combination of bad directions, bad timing, and bad weather that doomed the Donner Party to an ordeal of starvation that served as a ghoulish warning to the thousands of settlers who followed in their path — including a little known religious sect that would settle and thrive in the forbidding region of the Great Salt Desert, and become known as the Mormons.

Written by Lansford Warren Hastings (below), The Emigrants' Guide to Oregon and California *provided many people with the incentive they needed to head West in search of a gentler climate and lucrative business ventures. However, the inexperience that informed Hastings' guide would prove disastrous to the people in the Donner Party Expedition, who made the mistake of trusting their fate to that little book.*

THE

EMIGRANTS' GUIDE,

TO

OREGON AND CALIFORNIA,

CONTAINING SCENES AND INCIDENTS OF A PARTY OF
OREGON EMIGRANTS;

A DESCRIPTION OF OREGON;

SCENES AND INCIDENTS OF A PARTY OF CALIFORNIA
EMIGRANTS;

AND

A DESCRIPTION OF CALIFORNIA;

WITH

A DESCRIPTION OF THE DIFFERENT ROUTES TO
THOSE COUNTRIES;

AND

ALL NECESSARY INFORMATION RELATIVE TO THE
EQUIPMENT, SUPPLIES, AND THE METHOD
OF TRAVELING.

BY LANSFORD W. HASTINGS,
Leader of the Oregon and California Emigrants of 1842.

CINCINNATI:
PUBLISHED BY GEORGE CONCLIN,
STEREOTYPED BY SHEPARD & CO.
1845.

Inspired by the promise of fortune and fame in the West, Lansford Hastings wrote his infamous guide in the hopes that hordes of people would follow him and his shortcut to California. While Hastings was indeed a visionary, an experienced traveler he was not. He had never traveled his route with a wagon train, so he could never know the challenges those parties would face.

145

While each family had at least one wagon, some families, like the wealthy Reeds, had several. And few were as luxurious as the Reeds' Pioneer Palace Car, which housed them along the journey. It had built-in beds and bench seats, and it even had a second-story loft where the children slept.

The Donners and the Reeds employed young men to do the work of driving the oxen on their wagon train. But every person had chores to do each day. Women cooked, cleaned, sewed, and tended to the children while the men cared for the animals, maintained the wagons, and hunted for food.

The Breens were an excellent addition to the expedition as they were farmers, and could also read and write. Patrick Breen added music to the bonfire gatherings each night as he played his violin. Pictured here is the entire Breen family. In the center (top) is Isabella, who was the last living survivor of the Donner Party.

Although Patrick Breen's diary contains mostly notes about weather conditions and accounts of the days, it is evident here that the situation of the party was worsening. He writes "… it snowed faster last night & today than it has done this winter & still Continues without an intermission … Murphys folks and Keysburgs say they cant eat hides. I wish we had enough of them …"

There came a moment on this expedition that would haunt its members until the end. When they had the choice to follow the path they had planned or to head for the alleged shortcut otherwise know as the Hastings Cutoff, they took a vote and unfortunately chose the latter.

Although Charles Stanton became a hero when he returned, as promised, to the expedition with bread, fruit, and meat, he died peacefully by the fire along the trail of the Forlorn Hope.

149

Although Hastings had promised the Donner Party that he would meet them at Fort Bridger to guide them personally, he never did arrive. And, while supplies at Fort Bridger were excessively expensive, they had no choice but to purchase them there—the next supplier was more than 600 miles away.

The conditions for the expedition were difficult at best. Getting across the Platte River was risky and trying. When the water was too deep, the oxen had to be pulled through and the wagons had to be floated across on rafts.

The treacherous Sierra Pass proved to be a defining moment in a string of terrible luck for the Donner Party. When they couldn't get over it before the first snow, they knew their defeat was inevitable.

It took four separate rescue teams to save the Donner Party. The rescuers employed the use of snowshoes to get them to their destination. Once they got across the frozen, snow-covered lake, they were stunned by the appearance of the survivors, who were desperate and delirious from starvation.

The Reeds finally settled in San Jose, California, where they recovered from their ordeal and became as successful as they'd always dreamed. Here they stand at their lavish home along with Mary and Frances Donner, whom they adopted.

About the Author

Rodman Philbrick says, "One of the books that made a big impression on me as a young reader was *Boone Island* by Kenneth Roberts. It tells the true tale of several men shipwrecked on an island within sight of the coast of Maine. The winter weather was bitter cold, they had little hope of being rescued, and at the point of death the survivors finally resorted to cannibalism. Partly the story fascinated me because on a clear day I could just make out the Boone Island lighthouse from the house where I grew up. I could imagine what it must have been like, to be starving and freezing, all within sight of home. "The story of what happened to the people of the Donner Party is, I think, similarly horrifying and yet fascinating. To me it symbolized all the excitement and danger of the Western Migration. I'm sure I'm not the only reader who wonders what I might do, faced with a similar dilemma in an extreme situation.

"Of course, I'd rather starve than eat liver, or soft-boiled eggs!"

Rodman Philbrick is the author of a number of books for young readers. His first novel *Freak the Mighty* won the California Young Reader's Medal as well as several other state awards. It was made into the feature film *The Mighty* starring Sharon Stone. Philbrick's sequel, *Max the Mighty* received starred reviews and his novel *The Fire Pony* received the 1996 Capital Choice Award. His most recent books are *REM World* and *The Last Book in the Universe*, both published in 2000.

Mr. Philbrick is married to the author Lynn Harnett. They collaborated on the celebrated *House on Cherry Street* horror trilogy, and divide their time between homes in Maine and the Florida Keys.

Acknowledgments

The author would like to thank Jean Feiwel, Amy Griffin, and Beth Levine for encouraging him to write this book, and for their thoughtful editorial guidance about a difficult subject.

Grateful acknowledgment is made by the author for permission to reprint the following:

Cover Portrait: Detail from *Albert's Son*, 1959, tempera on panel. Copyright Andrew Wyeth. Courtesy of the National Museum of Contemporary Art, Oslo. Photograph by Jacques Lathion, Nasjonalgalleriat.

Cover background: *Chamonix and Martigny* by John Robert Cozens. Private Collection/Bridgeman Art Library, New York.

Page 145 (top): *The Emigrants' Guide to Oregon and California*. Reproduced from the Collection of the Library of Congress.

Page 145 (bottom): Lansford Warren Hastings. Reproduced from the Collection of the Library of Congress.

Page 146 (top): A Pioneer Palace Car. Courtesy of North Wind Picture Archives.

Page 146 (bottom): Wagon train. Painting by William Henry Jackson. Courtesy of Scotts Bluff National Monument.

Page 147: The Breen family. Courtesy of the Bancroft Library, University of California, Berkeley, California.

Page 148: Patrick Breen's Diary. Courtesy of the Bancroft Library.

Page 149 (top): The parting of the ways. Courtesy of the Wyoming Division of Cultural Resources.

Page 149 (bottom): Charles Stanton. Courtesy of the Bancroft Library.

Other books about the Journey Westward from
Dear America and My Name Is America

Across the Wide and Lonesome Prairie
The Oregon Trail Diary of Hattie Campbell
by Kristiana Gregory

West to a Land of Plenty
The Diary of Teresa Angelino Viscardi
by Jim Murphy

The Great Railroad Race
The Diary of Libby West
by Kristiana Gregory

Seeds of Hope
The Gold Rush Diary of Susanna Fairchild
by Kristiana Gregory

The Journal of Sean Sullivan
A Transcontinental Railroad Worker
by William Durbin

The Journal of Augustus Pelletier
The Lewis & Clark Expedition
by Kathryn Lasky

For Lynn Harnett, my Constant Reader

Library of Congress Cataloging-in-Publication Data available.

ISBN 0-439-21600-1;
ISBN 0-439-44569-8 (pbk.)

10 9 8 7 6 5 4 3 2 1   02 03 04 05 06

The display type was set in Nicholas Cochin.
The text type was set in Berling Roman.
Book design by Elizabeth B. Parisi
Photo research by Zoe Moffitt

Printed in the U.S.A. 23
First paperback printing, October 2002

———∿∿∿———